SWEET WATER

SWEET WATER

CARA REINARD

THOMAS & MERCER

Text copyright © 2021 by Cara Reinard.
All rights reserved.

No part of this book may be reproduced, or stored in a retrieval system, or transmitted in any form or by any means, electronic, mechanical, photocopying, recording, or otherwise, without express written permission of the publisher.

Published by Thomas & Mercer, Seattle

www.apub.com

Amazon, the Amazon logo, and Thomas & Mercer are trademarks of Amazon.com, Inc., or its affiliates.

ISBN-13: 9781542024938
ISBN-10: 1542024935

Cover design by Shasti O'Leary Soudant

Printed in the United States of America

For Justin, Jackson, and Charlotte,
the water is sweeter wherever you are.

CHAPTER 1

I reach for my phone inside my purse slung around my neck. It's dangling behind my back because I had nowhere else to put it while examining the body.

"Sarah, is she breathing?" Martin asks. I turn my head to find him, but it's too dark.

I stumble, disoriented under the canopy of trees. We're somewhere off Fern Hollow Road, the closest turnoff to Finn's pinned iPhone location.

"I d-don't know," I sputter, still shocked we found her and not Finn when we parked the car and hiked the rest of the way into Sewickley Heights Park.

"Check her—now. I need to find Finn." Martin's voice fades into the forest, and all I want to do is follow him, but I just spoke to my son on the phone. His speech was slurred, and his girlfriend is . . .

"Oh God." I open my mouth and let out a strangled breath, so sick that I sway to the side.

My eyes water as I kneel beside Yazmin Veltri, a girl I've known for only the briefest period. The wetness soaks through the holes in my jeans, settling into my bare kneecaps, ice on bone.

"Yazmin?" I shine my phone's light in her direction, but I'm stopped by the certain hint of marijuana.

Shit. All these years working with at-risk young women, and I couldn't see that Finn was dating one.

"Please," I beg the starlit sky peeking through the trees. "Let her be breathing."

I sniffle and inhale the truth through the rotting leaves. Something terrible has happened here, and I'm too late. The autumn mist snakes in through my nose, out through my mouth, emitting tiny white puffs of air. The forest ground is slippery, a feathered blanket beneath my knees, slathering the tops of my shoes.

I hear more hurried footsteps. Martin sounds like a mouse lost in a maze. Has he found Finn? I need to go to him, but my husband told me to stay here.

The branches scratch the tops of my feet as I move closer to her, the fallen leaves collecting between my knees. Yazmin could still be alive. A bitter taste rises in my mouth as I bite my tongue, and I'm close enough to touch her now.

My arm trembles as I place two fingers on the cold flesh of her neck. Not only cold—wet. I can't see what I'm touching, but I can feel her absence. Right below her jawline, in the space beside her trachea where I know a steady drumbeat should exist, there's nothing.

No pulse. My heartbeat quickens and plummets. *Oh God.*

My blood is rushing. Pounding. I'm sweating despite the near-thirty-degree temperature. I dip my head closer to Yazmin's chest, careful not to tangle my hair with hers. I've checked on my kids enough times in the middle of the night to know this girl's not breathing. I shut my eyes and listen anyway.

Sure enough, the steady whoosh of Yazmin's breath is absent along with her pulse.

"She's dead. We have to call the police," I announce, loud enough for Martin to hear, but not nearly as loud as the screaming in my head.

Call somebody! Help!

I hear Martin crunch closer, and I turn my back on the girl.

I scoot up on my legs and use my hands to push myself into a crouching position. My breath is heavy, and everything on my body—my hands, my knees—rattles with fear. I hear a cry in the distance.

My son's cry. And then Martin's rustling footsteps. Beside me again.

"Where is he?" I ask.

"He's okay, but . . ." Martin nods to the right. "He's injured. We need to get him out of here, Sarah."

"Okay," I say, but I close my eyes because my head is a ringing bell of stress even though this wooded area is one of the things that drew me to this town. The park is near the country club where we're members, where Martin's family have been members for years, and things like this just don't happen here.

"Let's go, Sarah!" Martin urges.

My eyes snap open, and I hold up my phone. "Wait. I'm calling 911. For her."

"No." Martin swats my hand away with the flick of his strong knuckles. The blood on my palms makes everything slick, and my cell phone goes flying across the forest like a bar of soap in the shower. I slip sideways into a bramble of branches and land on my left hip, staring at my husband's garish face in the moonlight. He looks unfamiliar, that expression one reserved for when he loses business at work, a rare occurrence. Martin is an innovator, his causes noble. Sometimes I don't approve of how he does things, but I usually approve of why.

"Damn it." Martin scrambles to find my phone. Right now, I don't approve at all.

"Why did you do that?" I ask, but I'm more surprised that he's hit me than I am by the fact that he doesn't agree with my decision to call the police.

"It will get reported tomorrow. We need to leave with Finn. *Now.*"

"What? That makes no sense."

Martin retrieves my phone, and I'm trying to get his attention, but he's looking right past me at the gas pipeline in the distance, a clear-cut, inclined path free of foliage about a thousand yards long in the mountainous terrain. Martin and I messed around with sleds one winter on a protected slope of land just like it, and I think maybe Finn and Yazmin planned their own adventure out here tonight and something went terribly wrong.

"Martin." I try to get up, but my foot slips on a mossy rock.

He grabs my arm. Then drops it. "Watch yourself," he says, but he doesn't help me rise. He's too busy texting.

It's then that I hear water rushing nearby. The river rocks are indigenous to this area, like everything else woodsy and serene in Sewickley.

Sewickley, the Shawnee word for *sweet water*, derived from the tribe's belief that the borough's shores were a little sweeter on that stretch of the Ohio River, the maple trees that grow at its shores only part of the saccharine story.

"Who're you texting?" I'm crying and my hands are still wet, but I can't wipe them. There's blood all over my palms, and I can't remember how it got there; head wounds bleed the worst.

"Hold on!" Martin is standing with his back to me now, holding his phone in the air like he's trying to decide what to do with it, a six-foot silhouette of trepidation. He scratches his dark hair and rubs his cell phone on his sweater-vest, but he doesn't use it to call anyone, only texts.

"I'm getting legal advice from my father," Martin says.

His father?

I picture William Sr. texting back from the comfort of one of his high-back chairs inside his home, one of the few estates that make up Sewickley Heights like a richly woven patchwork quilt—the expensive kind sewn together with colonials surrounded by alabaster columns and mile-long driveways.

"Martin?"

4

William's house is a fat-thatched Tudor hiding behind manicured bushes, a peek of white here, a slip of brown there, but there's no hiding from this.

"Of course you have to report it!" I look again—at her—and the blood is already congealing around her open head wound, her neck bent at an awkward angle, a matchstick snapped in half. The rushing water streams just behind her.

Martin's tugging on my coat. "Get up, Sarah. We have to go."

"We can't leave her." Yazmin's long black hair is covering the expression on her face, although the one I imagine is stuck there will haunt me more than the one I cannot see. She rests on her back, and it would be an odd way to fall, backward instead of forward, her hands crossed over her chest as if she were thwarting an attack. It reminds me of a tae kwon do block from when Finn used to take classes. We'd enrolled him when he was a child because he was painfully shy, whereas Spencer, his older brother, was frequently mentioned by his teachers as *boisterous* or *exuberant*, adjectives used in private schools to describe disruptive overachievers. I might expect Spencer to get into trouble with a girl like this, but not my poor Finny.

I turn toward Martin. He's speaking, but I've stopped listening.

His eyes are pleading. "She's dead. We can't help her. Finn was the last person with her."

"But—"

"He's on something, Sarah. Drugs." Martin shakes his head furiously. "This looks bad."

I can hear what he's saying, but I've retreated into my own body, and I don't even know who we are right now.

We used to be Martin and Sarah Ellsworth of Blackburn Road.

We were the couple sitting at a corner table at a fancy restaurant, splitting a bottle of wine. Laughing at each other's jokes.

"We have to do something for her." My voice is swallowed by the humming sounds of the forest and the flapping of the leaves on the trees, the river. She's already dead, but we need to make sure she's at least taken to the hospital so her parents can identify her. Bile rises in my mouth. My heart is beating so fast, drowning out everything else, but I faintly hear Finn's voice again nearby.

"I'm sorry." Martin extends his arm to help me up, but I waggle my finger in the air at him, pointing to my hands, reminding my brainy husband that I'm bloodied and pulling me up isn't a good idea. I must've made the mistake of touching Yazmin in the wrong place.

"Right." He draws his palms back.

My legs won't work. I gaze up, silently praying. The large enveloping trees of Sewickley Heights tower above us like old wealthy gatekeepers winking in the night.

"I need your help. I can't move him on my own, Sarah," Martin reveals.

I close my eyes, wishing it all away. *It's all a bad dream.*

"Can we just make an anonymous call from a pay phone or something? For her parents' sake, at least?"

"You can't. They'll try to interview Finn, see the drug use, and assume the worst. He'll go to jail." His voice is thick with desperation. "Sarah, this will ruin Finn's life. This isn't his fault!" Martin kicks a stone with his worn loafer, a product from one of the posh boutiques that line downtown Sewickley, a mishmash of overpriced things people don't really need displayed in windowed storefronts on cobblestone streets. There's a place to reupholster old furniture with patterns better left to die with their original owners, a claw-foot-tub specialist, an herbal spa with enough fresh fruit remedies to double as a bakery, the imported-leather-shoe store.

I bought Martin the shoes he has on now, and he's worn them down to the soles. He's practical, a computer engineer and CEO of a robotics start-up in the Strip District. He does things that make sense. But right now, he's not making any.

"Maybe she slipped." My voice is shallow like the night air sneaking away from my lips, but the idea of an accident fills my heart with hope. "We'll leave an anonymous tip." If I had my phone, I'd call myself.

I'd explain this is exactly how we found her. She wasn't even near our son when we discovered her body. Unless . . . we've messed with the scene of the crime so much that we've hurt Finn more than helped him. I look down at my bloody hands and cringe. As far as we know, Finn is the last one who saw Yazmin alive. This could be very bad for him. *"Shit."*

Martin grabs me by the arm. "We have to *go*, Sarah. Get up." I can't see much of Martin's face but the stringy blue vein in his forehead that only comes out when he's upset.

It's been only minutes, but we need to move—faster.

"We need to go to him," I say.

"Yes." Martin nods.

I'm in shock. That's what's wrong with me. I blindly follow Martin, adrenaline fueling my limbs. Finn is off the beaten path, and I feel as though I've already failed him for taking so long. He's huddled over a pile of leaves, his knees tucked into his chest like he used to do when he was a little kid. He looks so small right now.

So young.

A little boy who fell off his scooter and skinned his knee. I wish this problem were as easy to fix.

I wipe my hands on my jeans and throw my arms around him.

"I'm here. Mom's here." Finn's crying and I don't know how to make it better for him. He obviously didn't mean for the girl to get hurt, but this was no accident either. He's made a terrible mistake, gotten himself into a horrible predicament. So Finn did what we always told him to do if he was ever in trouble—he called us.

7

CHAPTER 2

Before—2000

Martin is spinning me so fast, I think I might be sick. "Stop. You must!" I'm laughing and my bladder is full, not to mention I get motion sickness.

"We're not quite ready," Martin says.

He's giggling in a way my gruff father refers to as *"effeminate,"* but I love everything about my new husband, including his laugh. However, the spinning could stop any moment and I'd be okay with that.

"Who is *we?*" I ask.

Martin hugs me this time and twirls us both around. "I can't tell you that or it will ruin the surprise."

"At least stop spinning me if you can't take off the blindfold." It's not so much the spinning that's got me in a tizzy as it is the combination of the circular motion with the darkness. If he lets me go, I will surely fall on my ass.

"Fine." Martin stops and points me in one direction.

I wobble. "Whoa!" He steadies me at the waist. I'm wearing a spring dress even though it's early March, because Martin told me we might be taking photos today and to wear something nice. Although I've come to understand that his idea of *nice* is not the same as mine. I laid out two options before him, a comfy Banana Republic knit dress that I preferred and a J.Crew, A-line dotted number with tiny blue flowers on it that I thought was kind of ugly, but it cinched my waist so nicely, I purchased it anyway. Martin chose the floral one, and I can barely breathe.

"Come on, I have to pee."

"Of course you do," he says. I laugh harder, which doesn't help my situation any. "Does that mean you're almost done?" I inhale Martin's cologne, and he's not wearing his everyday Polo but the Calvin Klein fragrance he reserves for special occasions.

"I'll have a wonderful bathroom for you to use soon," he says in a singsongy voice.

"What?" I giggle again and nearly grab myself so I don't spring a leak, so unladylike. Dresses aren't my thing. I was raised by a single father, and pants-less clothing still feels foreign to me.

"I can't take this, Martin. I'm starting to sweat under here." I'm blind, but my other senses are starting to take over—the feeling of the sun burning into my shoulders, the crinkling of the leaves whirling around me, the tickle of the wind pulling my hair from its headband, the babble of a nearby brook. So much unseen beauty. I try to tug on the handkerchief tied around my head, but he won't let me. My college-sweetheart-turned-husband has always been a pleaser, but I wish someone would tell him he didn't need to try so hard anymore. He already has me.

"Don't you dare," he warns, subtly taking a piece of my earlobe in his mouth and drawing my offending hand behind my back.

I'm a little turned on by the ear nip coupled with the blindfold. I'm wondering if this is some sort of crazy sex-capade, because things in the bedroom have only gotten more interesting since the honeymoon, but I rule it out. I hear other people milling around, and as adventurous as Martin is, he's not *that* adventurous.

The only endeavor Martin has invested in more than keeping our marriage interesting is the odd hours he's been working at his side gig with the hopes of striking it rich. I'm wondering now if this surprise has anything to do with it.

I'd lucked out with a college internship in the public relations department at St. Jude Children's Hospital, sure to score a full-time position upon graduation. Martin says he'll support both of us so I can help save the world, because even though his job may be more lucrative, mine will always be more important.

It doesn't matter to me if Martin hits it big, but I know he's bound and determined, sure to be a family failure if he settles for middle class. He also has something else besides a big brain and an entrepreneurial spirit to keep him motivated—a trust fund that would make the Kennedys weep. Those with financial safety nets have more power to dream.

I was fortunate enough just to attend Carnegie Mellon University, my father's position as maintenance supervisor my free ride, although everything I've taken away from that place still feels like it's on loan— my borrowed life.

There's whispering and commotion all around me, and I've been blindfolded for way too long.

"Okay, we're ready!" Martin announces.

"Thank God!"

Martin takes off the blindfold, and my eyes are deceiving me after too much time in the dark. I blink twice, then reopen them and watch as Martin's whole family appears before me—on the porch of a house that is not their own but one I know very well. It's all wrong, and I wonder if the owners are here and if they'll recognize me after all this time, outed as the girl who's only been kept in the shadows of this fine estate, never good enough to hang out on the front porch, in the daylight, like we're doing now. It doesn't make sense.

Has Martin found me out? Is this some kind of weird Ellsworth intervention?

Martin looks far too happy for that, and so does everyone else, but if they knew about what happened with the boy who used to live here, they wouldn't be smiling at all.

The women in Martin's family are wearing dresses with far more obnoxious floral patterns than my own. My sister-in-law's dress trails to her ankles, mere toothpicks set off by gold stilettos. The whole scene feels dainty and overdone, like an ad plucked out of a 1950s issue of *Good Housekeeping*.

As if the scene isn't surreal enough, Martin's family releases balloons into the sky, tiny translucent offerings to the gods, and William Sr. uncorks a bottle of champagne—Dom Pérignon—with a big old "Surprise!" just for me.

"Wow," I say, but not before I'm blinded by the sudden flash of light.

A photographer, who I assume has been hired for the occasion, snaps my picture, which I'm sure is awful, because my mouth has fallen wide-open and won't go back into place.

I don't say anything because I'm not sure what this party is or why we're here. All I can determine is that Martin's family is gathered on the porch of the house I'd named Stonehenge when I was a little girl, my absolute most-loved home on my father's Sunday drive-by route. We usually drove it after church, something to do on afternoons between the morning rush and lunchtime, but I never tired of it. Every season, the houses were decorated differently. Then later, it was the place that I fell in love with for an entirely different reason. This house held a piece of my heart, but not one I necessarily wanted to share with Martin. It belonged to someone else, and I can feel him like concrete in my bones when I stand here, sweat prickling my forehead. There was a boy who lived here, Joshua, and this place was his.

Well, it was ours, but Martin doesn't know that.

This house was supposed to be passed down to Joshua someday. He would've never given it up. What happened to the Loudens? And why are the Ellsworths on their porch?

I glance up at Joshua's bedroom window dormered in copper.

Stonehenge isn't huge and it isn't prodigal, but to my childhood eyes and even now, it is lovely, built entirely of chalky, craggy blocks with a large, castle-like wooden front door and leaded stained-glass windows at its sides. It has a backyard fit to serve a few fountains and a pergola closer to the road on the side yard that always seemed to have its own hemisphere. The pergola's formation of long stone columns and open slatted roof reminded me of something out of my Greek mythology class and then later, after watching a TV special, of the great wonder of the world—Stonehenge.

So that's what we called it, my father and me. We named many of the houses on our drive-by route—the Castle, the White House, Gargoyle Manor—but Stonehenge was my favorite. Mother, a florist, would've loved our drives. She liked pretty things, nature and plants especially magnetizing to her. Sometimes on our drives, Dad would pick out a flower or tree with her in mind and comment on how much she'd love it, and those were the moments between us that were truly special. It made it feel like she was still alive.

As I grew older, we didn't go on our Sunday route as much, but sometimes on summer nights, I'd borrow my dad's truck and cruise by this very house because I loved it so much. I'd told Martin all about it, but I didn't think he was paying attention.

The part I didn't mention was that if it were dark outside and the lights were on in the house, sometimes I'd see him—Joshua—the boy around my age who lived there. Such a large place for a single child and his two parents. I imagined he was probably lonely, and sometimes I fantasized that he'd see me passing by in my pickup truck and hail me to stop, invite me inside, play his guitar for me. But if I were really lucky, he'd be sitting outside strumming away, and I'd roll down my window and hear his sweet, sad melody. It sounded like the inside of my broken heart, the one that still longed for my mother and all the mysteries of the world I didn't understand in her absence.

"Why are we *here*?" Now that my eyes are fully focused, I turn to Martin, and he seems very pleased with himself, standing there with a half-cocked smile.

"Sweetheart, don't you see?" Martin dangles keys in my face. They aren't a standard bump key set, as my handyman father would say, but a collection of skeleton keys on a large brass ring, the kind found in fairy-tale books. Right now, I feel like I'm in the middle of one, but the story is tainted. This house can't be mine. There are things about the boy who used to live here that Martin doesn't know. Even though the snow is melted now, I can still see the place from the porch where we last kissed.

Where are the Loudens?

This place was all decorated for Christmas just a few months ago.

I was here with him—Joshua. But Martin doesn't know that, and I certainly can't tell him now. Martin must've bought it, but I don't remember a FOR SALE sign in the yard. Joshua didn't mention they'd be moving, and surely he would've told me. What happened to them? I have a sickening feeling that they've vanished along with the red-bowed wreaths, never to reappear next season.

My dress feels tighter from my burning bladder, and I rub my abdomen, thinking of Joshua and all the pain he's caused.

Tears crowd the corners of my eyes. The Ellsworths aren't emotional people, and I need to maintain my poise. "Is it ours?" I take the keys, and they're heavy in my hands. Laughter fills my ears, but I can't properly feel the joy.

"It is now." Martin's smile is wide and devilish, and out of all the things he's done, I already know he'll never be able to top this.

"Was it even for sale?" The photographer's oversize camera flashes again, capturing my agony, and there is a gentle cooing sound coming from the porch, because Martin's family must certainly think these are tears of joy, but they're not, because this place was never supposed to be mine. It belongs to the first boy I ever loved.

Martin winks. "Of course it wasn't. But everything's for sale for the right price." He wipes a tear from my face. "Go to the restroom before you soil the lawn, dear."

I look down and realize I'm holding my belly, my bladder groaning with dissatisfaction, just like the first time I walked through these doors. I walk past him, stunned, and try to smile at my guests as I open *my* front door. I know just where the first-floor bathroom is located. I memorized every detail of this house years ago.

I hide in the bathroom, taking in the familiar wallpaper, the navy-and-pink-flowered pattern with the metallic stripes—striking, not gaudy, like something I imagined I might find at a quaint bed-and-breakfast in upstate New York or a ski chalet in Vermont.

The white porcelain pedestal sink greets me as I wash my hands, the subtle smell of rose oil lifting to my nose as if it's naturally embedded in the coffee-colored woodwork. The bath rugs have been swapped out from mauve to beige, which I prefer, but everything else in the room is the same as I remember it. It's like taking a piece of my childhood and slapping it in my face. Joshua and I talked about living here together someday, and even though Martin bought it fair and square, nothing about it feels right.

Although most of what Joshua said to me here was in hushed whispers.

"Sarah, why don't we go on the back porch? It's quieter there."

We snuck around a lot on this big estate, searching for alcoves where no one would hear our labored breaths or see our teenage bodies pressed together. We met up only at night. In the day, it was almost as if he'd never existed, or the sins we'd committed. And now that he's gone for real, no trace of him or his family, it's playing a wretched game on my mind . . . *Were you ever real?*

I can't catch my breath.

It's not just Joshua I think about in Stonehenge's presence. If I close my eyes, I can almost hear my father's voice, deep and gravelly, echoing in my head from the first time we were here.

He had many tall tales about the owners of the houses just like these, the executives who liked to block their fine abodes with leafy veils and climbing green vines, situating their homes down in the private cuts of the hillsides, proud of their wealth but not proud enough to share it with the rest of us. *"It's like the old houses back right into their paintings and disappear!"*

"Like a secret," I replied in a whisper.

"That's right! They keep the best kind."

Sometimes he'd even pretend to know what the homeowners were doing inside: watering their rare African orchids, balancing their checkbooks with king-size registers, combing their curly mustaches with special brushes.

Dad's a hoot.

The afternoon we saw the inside of Stonehenge for the first time, Dad and I were cruising through Sewickley Heights on our normal Sunday drive. All our years scouting Sewickley real estate, and we'd never seen an open-house sign before. In some ways, I thought Dad was searching for the perfect house in these parts for Mom, even though she wasn't here anymore. We both looked for ways to hold on to her. I still remember how Dad's eyes had lit up at the Realtor arrow and the way my belly flopped when he asked the question, "Want to check out one of these bad boys from the inside?"

My skin tingles with the memory, the way I bounced up and down in the cab of his truck like a ten-year-old girl who'd just been told she was going to Disney World for the very first time.

We couldn't afford Disney, but this was the next best thing.

"Do you think they'll believe us?" I asked nervously, my ponytail bouncing along with me. I'd never lied before, and I was absolutely terrified to pretend we were legitimately looking to buy one of these houses when I knew we couldn't afford it.

"People will believe whatever you tell them, Sarah Bear. We're not hurting anyone; we're just looking at a house, for Pete's sake. Come on—let's have some fun!"

Dad's truck was already winding up the hill, following the arrows of the open-house signs before I could give my final vote.

"What do you want your name to be?" he asked me.

"What do you mean?"

"Well, we can't sign in under our real names; they might try to contact us. So how about I'll be Arthur and you be Janie? Those sound like rich-person names," he decided, laughing at himself.

"Um . . . okay," I said, but I was always taught not to lie, and I didn't know if I could go through with it.

"You have to answer me when I call your name." Dad made his voice deeper. *"Janie."* He laughed again, and so did I.

"My name is Janie." It sounded weird coming off my lips. I pretended I was rehearsing for my first play. "My name is Janie," I said again, more confidently.

Dad cackled so hard, he started coughing, his eyes crinkling at the corners, getting a little wet as they did.

We turned on Camp Meeting Road. It had a natural stone wall up one side that reminded me of one of my favorite movies set in Ireland. When I saw the arrow for the Realtor sign to turn on Blackburn Road, I could barely hold in my squeal.

"Oh boy!" Dad said.

"You don't think *it's* for sale, do you?" I asked, squeezing my eyes closed.

"Janie, now, you have to put on your game face. It might be our lucky day."

Dad sped down the road, half-gravel, half-paved, because it was way, way back in the woods.

"Okay, Arthur," I joked.

"No, no!" he hollered, but even his yell had a smile hidden in it. "Now, why in the world would you ever call your father by his first name?" he asked.

I put my chewing gum in between my top and bottom lip and bit down hard. "Oh, darn it. I'm no good at this! I'm going to mess it up."

Dad eyed me sternly. "No, you won't! Just call me 'Dad,' nod, and smile at the nice salesman. Let me do the rest."

"Yes, sir," I said, because my father was a good talker. He'd talked hotels into giving us a free night's stay because he was a single father, and while he'd never swindle anyone out of something they'd earned, he wasn't afraid to take it if they hadn't. When we saw the sign pointing straight down the long driveway for Stonehenge, potted plants lining the way, I crossed my legs and screamed.

"What's wrong?" Dad asked.

"I don't know if I can do it, and I have to pee." My weak bladder always showed up at the most inopportune times.

Scary movies.

Softball games, right before my turn up at bat.

The minute after I jumped into a swimming pool.

"Well, I'm sure they have a few bathrooms in there." He pointed at the house, pecking at the air with his finger, as if he was finding all the bathrooms with each stab. "You can't chicken out, Sarah Bear. We'll never get a chance to look inside again." His stone-blue eyes were glittery in the afternoon sunlight.

"I can't pee on Stonehenge." I placed my hand over my face, hiding my eyes, which were the same shade as his. It seemed disrespectful somehow, like peeing on someone's gravestone. Stonehenge had a magnificent rose trellis over the pergola that could clearly be seen from the road, like an archway to Heaven. Mother loved roses, and I know that's why Dad thought this house was special too.

"Sure, you can. Hell, drop number two if you have to. Do your thing on that throne, baby girl; we're paying customers!"

"Dad!" I screamed. The heat in my face spread like hot pokers. My father's crass humor was something I'd always secretly found entertaining.

My dad chuckled as he dismounted from his truck. He was wearing a pair of faded blue jeans and a flannel shirt with a Rolling Stones T-shirt underneath. The open buttons of his shirt exposed the long, iconic tongue symbol of the band, and I wanted to tell him to button up, but I was too focused on not peeing my pants.

I waddled behind him.

"You're walking like you've got a stick up there, Janie. Come on."

"Dad," I whispered. Not only did it feel like the pee might trickle down my leg at any moment, but I was so nervous, my knees were starting to shake.

My heart thumped as we strode up the limestone walk. A fashionably dressed woman in a black suit and red ascot opened the front door before we'd even knocked. It made me nervous that she'd been watching us, imposters that we were. Her gold hoop earrings were large and shiny, and I could barely make out her face in the September sunlight.

I could hear my father speak, but I couldn't concentrate on anything but the reflection from the earrings on the blonde lady's face and my bladder, ready to explode. There were introductions made, but I remained silent.

"So nice to meet you, Vanessa; we're the Bowmans. This is Janie, and I'm Arthur Bowman of Bowman Construction." He exhaled one of his infectious laughs that always came out flirtatious in front of women. Vanessa giggled in response.

And we were *in like Flynn*. One of Dad's favorite sayings.

Dad's pretend occupation explained our truck and clothing. A man in the construction business could be rough on the outside and drive utility vehicles but still have bucketloads in the bank. I was starting to feel okay, but I had to pee so badly, the pain had formed a hardened bowling ball in my abdomen.

"Please come in," Vanessa said, waving her hand out in front of us. She might as well have been the queen of England escorting me into Buckingham Palace.

Once inside, I could make out Vanessa's perfect face, the shading of her makeup like that of the actresses on the daytime soap operas Dad shouldn't have let me watch in the summertime but did, because we couldn't afford summer camp. Vanessa's wispy hair fell in tailored pieces around her sharp smile, which looked as though it could twist into a scowl at any moment.

"Do you mind if Janie uses the restroom before we take a closer look? I think she's been holding it since the parkway."

"Oh my, certainly. Let me walk you through the parlor to the powder room."

The parlor and the powder room? It sounded like a game of Clue.

Dad raised his dark eyebrows at me with a funny grin, making his fingers dance as if telling me, *"Go on, pee on Stonehenge."*

Vanessa ushered me through the wide hallway dressed in dark wainscoting; the inside did not disappoint. "Wow," I said in a hushed whisper. It reminded me more of a museum than a house.

"Here we are." Vanessa pointed to a closed door that matched the dark wood of the rest of the home. Without hesitation, I went in and quickly shut the door. I almost cried as I relieved myself.

And now, somehow, I've found myself back in the same place, the same room, a nervous wreck, misplaced but in wonder, uncomfortable but in complete awe of my brand-new borrowed life.

Martin knocks on the door. "Sarah? Are you ever coming out of there?"

"Just a minute," I manage. The party has moved inside, and I'm still hanging out in the bathroom, trying to pull myself together. What Martin did was so amazing and so wrong at the same time. He didn't even invite my dad to the party, but he probably figured the gesture would be too grand for him, and he's probably right.

I close the door to the powder room, but my mind is still stuck in 1988.

Martin grabs my hand and pulls me into a gentle hug. "Hi," he whispers into my hair.

"Hi," I whisper back.

It's the one-word phrase he said to me the morning after we'd spent the night together for the very first time, bedsheets tangled around frantic limbs, the day when we knew our relationship was the start of something real. It was hard moving on after Joshua split town, his transition out of my life phantomlike, much like how we came together. I hadn't told anyone about him, my little secret, and I was angry with myself for letting a few hot summer nights destroy me. My broken heart craved security and a level head, and Martin Ellsworth reeked of those things from the minute I'd met him. Martin was proud to have me by his side, like I was some kind of trophy.

This house is the place where we'll start our new lives, which feels strange yet appropriate. I've always dreamed I might end up here, just not with Martin. I try to make myself feel better because only the outskirts of the house are contaminated with memories of Joshua and me; he was so intent on keeping me hidden. The contrast of the moment isn't lost on me: that I'm here now with Martin, center stage.

Martin wants to show off me and our house to the world. It's more confirmation that he's the man I should be with. Maybe we *can* make this place ours.

He nods in the direction of the great room, where the others are standing, and I follow him and remember how Dad and I both allowed Vanessa to lead us into this very same room, our eyes traveling up nearly thirty-five feet to the apex of the ornately carved ceiling. The much-lighter maple wood makes it appear even grander in contrast, the focal point of the home.

"That used to be a pulpit for an organ." I'm pointing to a raised wooden platform on the right side of the room. It's closed off now with no access point to reach it.

"I told my parents this house was sometimes used for religious celebrations." Martin smiles, and I can tell he's expecting brownie points for remembering what I've told him about the history of the house, but it's hard for me to grant them. I should be over-the-moon thankful, gushing like a bashful new bride, but this gift is too much, and he doesn't know everything there is to know about this house. And I certainly can't tell him now.

"It's so lovely, Sarah." Greta, my sister-in-law, turns around slowly, agape at the biblical stained-glass windows on either side of the walls. One of them has a beautiful angel on it, beaming in whites and hues of sparkly golds and oranges, and I imagine it's my mother gracing me with her presence for the special occasion.

"Thank you," I say, but all I can think is that Joshua's parents bought this house for him because he liked to play the guitar, the maple ceilings made specially for great acoustics.

"There's an indoor Olympic-size swimming pool on the bottom floor with a dome over it and changing rooms to the right and left, our own Club Med right here on the lower level," Martin says.

I exhale and fake smile, my mind flashing to the time I skinny-dipped in that same pool with Joshua. Is this how it will always be? Am

I doomed to live in a place where I wake up every morning, reminded of my teenage mistakes?

Mr. and Mrs. Ellsworth nod, very pleased, and I hope they haven't paid for all of this. Martin was blasé about the fact that his parents had paid for his tuition, as if it were something owed to him by birthright. He knew how different my situation was, but he didn't understand the pain I'd experienced in my early years, so fearful that one misstep would cost me everything my father had worked so hard for.

As if sensing my thoughts, Martin says, "I have backers for my automation software, Sarah. They paid a mint for it, and I had enough for the whole down payment. I wanted to keep the news under wraps until I closed on the house. I thought the combination of the two would make for a bigger surprise."

Oh, I'm surprised all right. *"Closed on the house"* sounds so final, and as excited as I am, I don't love that Martin didn't at least ask my opinion on purchasing the property. I guess after all I'd blubbered about this place, he thought he didn't have to.

After all, it's my dream home. It just isn't *our* dream home.

"That's fantastic. Congratulations!" I hug my husband because it feels like the right thing to do, and maybe my dad will be okay that Martin bought this place for us if he used his own hard-earned money to do so and not his parents'. Dad always loved the way Stonehenge made me smile.

He was wrong about one thing regarding this house, though. He said there was no harm in stopping in and checking out Stonehenge and pretending we were the Bowmans, because we'd never get the chance again. But we should've driven on by. Because instead of just fantasizing about Stonehenge from the outside, I fell in love with the inside too, my want for it visceral, skin-deep, a part of everything I lacked and everything I wanted to become.

CHAPTER 3

Present

When we get home, the orders continue—strip my clothes, place them in a plastic bag, shower. I'm freezing and filthy, so I quickly do as I'm told, and when I come out, Finn is still shaking like he can't hold heat, despite the blankets we've placed on top of him.

"Martin, hospital," I plead.

He hasn't put that damn phone down, and I'm about to take it from him and break it into a million pieces. He hasn't given me mine back yet either.

"Bath!" he commands.

"What?" I ask.

"Upstairs now, run the bath," Martin says urgently. "We need to warm Finn up. Mom says *now*."

"Okay." Mary Alice, Martin's mother, is a nurse, and the only reason I comply is because the closest thing I have to a hospital right now is her. And because Finn is violently shaking.

I can feel the night's terror pull down the bags beneath my eyes. Emotionally and physically exhausted, I concentrate on filling the garden tub with hot, sudsy water.

Being useful helps when you're running on adrenaline. *This will help Finn.*

I hear Martin struggle up the stairs with him. "Help me," he huffs.

I kneel beside him, and we both remove Finn's soiled clothes as he yelps.

"It's okay, baby," I tell him, but it's not okay. It's wrecking me.

Martin carefully lowers Finn's half-conscious body into the water. "Wash off the dirt. Keep him warm and above the water."

"Okay," I say, but I'm just going through the motions, my nerve endings numb, in shock. Martin dashes out of Finn's bathroom, and I hear him walk quickly into ours. The water turns on, and it's Martin's turn to get the dirt off, but can we ever? He lets me do the washing, because I'm the mother, and it's the natural order of things.

Mother bathes the children.

But Finn isn't a child—he's a grown boy.

An injured grown boy.

I cry as I run the terrycloth washrag over his stomach and shoulders. There're signs of bruising, already purpling in places, and I don't know if it's from sports or from what happened tonight.

"What're these, babe?" I ask, but he doesn't answer me. He *can't* answer me. And what is wrong with him?

I feel helpless not knowing, responsible somehow. If Finn was in trouble, I always thought I'd have a better sense for it because of my work, but here I am—shocked and disappointed, like every other parent who's ever had tragedy befall their teenager.

I've failed you, Finn.

I wash his hair as quickly as I can, but that's when I see the worst of it.

"No," I whisper. There're nail marks—indentations, really, like half-moons—etched into Finn's neck.

"Finn, who did this?" I ask him. "Please tell me."

No response, and he's settled into the bathwater now, which is good—no more shaking. But his neck. It's like someone has taken ahold of him but not hard enough to form a scratch. Just looking at the marks makes my own hands shake, because only females leave marks like that.

It's a sign of a struggle. *What did you do to that girl?*

Martin comes back in, freshly showered, and lifts Finn out of the tub without asking me if I'm finished. "We need to get him to my parents'. Dress him." Martin towels him off and throws clothes he's grabbed from Finn's room on the floor.

"No. He needs to go to a doctor, Martin!"

"Yes. At my parents'!"

"There will be a doctor there?" I ask, and it's not totally out of the realm of possibility. The Ellsworths once paid a child therapist to fly from Nepal to counsel Livvy, William's much younger sister, when she refused to eat for a solid month.

"Yes," I hear him echo down the hall.

I can hardly pull on Finn's clothes. It's as if he's a sleeping 160-pound toddler. "Come on, honey."

I get them on, and he lets me because he isn't capable of doing it himself, and it takes everything I have.

Finn hasn't needed me to do these things for him in so long, and the fact that he needs me to do them again is eviscerating to my soul, like he's been reduced to a pitiful child by this event. I fear somehow I'll never get him back.

Martin lays Finn down on my in-laws' office couch with a wool afghan pulled up to my son's neck, his face splotchy and red from the cold, or maybe the wool, but most likely the drugs.

The drugs. I shiver.

It still hasn't sunk in.

A formal council is set up in my father-in-law's den, complete with local politician (Martin's brother), town sheriff (Martin's cousin), and retired nurse (my mother-in-law) all seated in a stiff semicircle of wing-back chairs. My father-in-law is perched at the center at his antique attorney's desk, presiding over us. Tiffany lamps provide the only light in the room.

I can't clearly see their faces to gauge their reactions. How much has Martin told them, and why didn't he consult me first before calling in the dogs? I was angry enough about his texting his father in the woods, but this feels like an ambush. No one is speaking, and I'm so upset about this family affront, I can't turn back around to face them. I also don't want to leave Finn on the couch. He isn't well, and I'm worried, because this isn't the first time we've had a meeting like this one.

Years ago, we met to discuss an indiscretion with Livvy, who'd been involved in a car accident. The driver had threatened to sue because he said she'd distracted him, causing him to crash and break his femur. He wanted compensation for loss of work at his construction site.

"Some lowlife from Carnegie trying to take us for every dime," William had said. "Fat chance."

It was early in our marriage, and I was still trying to please the Ellsworths. Livvy didn't seem to have a voice in the matter, even though I found out later that she'd been drunk and the man had just been trying to give her a ride home from the bar, and she had in fact distracted him when she'd vomited all over his lap. The circumstances that led to her face being so close to his crotch were still in question.

"They'll have evidence of distraction. From her sick," Mary Alice had said in embarrassment.

"No," William had said with sternness. "They won't."

A meeting was called back then to discuss our course of action. If the media approached us, we all had fine-tuned answers to give. I didn't like any of it, but I went along with it because William made it sound like our family was being taken advantage of, and he explained—*"this is what happens when you are wealthy."*

Rich people problems, I thought, and then remembered I was one of them. It was the hardest transition of my life, fully acknowledging which side of the economic fence I was on, often being reminded of where I came from with comments like William's about the rules of the wealthy and feeling inadequate because of it. I was pregnant with Spencer at the time of Livvy's accident, and Martin swore we didn't know about the baby at the time, but that was only because I hadn't told him. There was no way I could leave the family circle after I found out.

"Sarah?" Martin says.

I finally turn to face the music, and everyone is staring at me like they've been waiting too long for a server to bring them a drink.

I look past William to the books lining rows of shelves behind him, law treatises and hardcover classics. I see a Charles Dickens novel that looks old enough to be an original, but I know for certain he hasn't read it. When I marveled at his collection at our first meet and greet, he scoffed at me and said he didn't really care for fiction and those books I'd been admiring were *"just for decoration."* I should've known right then and there that I didn't belong with these people, but I assumed the privileged didn't have much of a need for imagination because they were already living their wildest dreams.

"Have you called a doctor?" I ask no one in particular.

William gives his wife a commanding nod, but no one answers my question.

"Martin said there would be a doctor here." I panic.

Mary Alice rises from her chair and walks to Finn's side. Beside him is an old-school black doctor's bag I've never seen before. Mary Alice regards the bag with the curiosity of a child sifting through her first Fisher-Price medical kit. I watch as she turns on the otoscope for the ear canal and waves it around like she's performing a laser-light show on the back of her veiny hand.

"Martin, where is the doctor?" He doesn't answer me. *Liar.* There was never going to be a doctor.

I watch as Mary Alice sets down the otoscope and picks up the blood-pressure cuff, then slips Finn's arm out from beneath the blanket, the skin there blotchy as well. After a quick pressure check and a flash of Martin's penlight to Finn's pupils, she proclaims, "All vital signs are good."

"He should be in a hospital being looked over, not here." My voice is disruptive, an annoying echo in a circle of people who've come here to conduct business. I don't understand why we're here, but at the same time, I do. This is the place we go to discuss family problems. Problems we want to make go away.

"Finn's going to be fine. He's just fighting whatever it is he took," Alton says curtly. Alton Pembroke is Livvy's only child, Martin's first cousin, and the town sheriff, a man I gather was nearly cast out of the family for not going to college and then fully embraced once they learned how he could better serve them.

"How do you know it's not something more dire? He may need medical attention." My voice is pleading.

"Because Mary Alice checked him out." Alton likes to keep everything high and tight beneath his cap, family dirt included.

Mary Alice returns to her seat and nods at William as if to say *proceed*, but I'm not ready yet. "And what if his condition worsens?" I ask.

"Cross that bridge then," Alton says.

This is bullshit. Finn probably needs that new spray everyone's been stocking up on in schools because of all the overdoses, but when I mention it, Mary Alice rolls her eyes and tells me he's not that bad.

I'm not at all convinced of her nursing abilities and especially the ones needed to deal with an overdose patient. When I asked her years ago why she'd chosen nursing as a vocation, she simply said that back in her day, you either became a nurse or a teacher, and patients talked back less than children.

"Thank you for getting everyone together so quickly," Martin says as he sits down in a chair, leaving me hanging behind the family circle. It always irks me how Martin thanks his parents for everything, so formal.

I don't want to sit in this damn circle of chairs, because if I do, it feels like I'm agreeing to something insidious, like when I covered up for Livvy even though I knew the Ellsworths should've settled their case and helped the man with the broken leg.

It made me think of my father and how much it would've crushed us if he lost a few months' pay when I was growing up, but this is nothing like Livvy's situation. This is about much more than lost wages. This is the loss of a young girl's life.

"Are you going to join us?" Mary Alice asks in her flat tone. She softened to me in the beginning, when Livvy was really going through it, admitting she'd always wanted a daughter of her own. She made me feel special, the daughter she wished she'd had. I didn't love how she bad-mouthed Livvy. She was so much younger than William and had made mistakes, but I tolerated it because I'd craved a mother-daughter relationship so badly. I wanted to be the *good* daughter. But I soon learned our relationship flourished only if I did what she said; Mary Alice made our boundaries clear after the boys arrived, that things be done a certain way where her grandkids were concerned.

I sit down, even though they never wanted me in their circle anyway.

If I am going to remain in their circle, I need to play by their rules.

William gawks at me with his cheeks sucked in like he's just made nice with an especially tart lemon. It unnerves me how they couldn't let Finn come down from his high, grieve for his dead girlfriend, before they called this ridiculous impromptu meeting. But I'm more upset that no one has called in a doctor for Finn, placing their needs before his well-being.

William and Mary Alice were good to my boys in the way grand-parents are, spoiling them with presents. But what they overcompensated for in material things they shorted in affection. Spencer and Finn often returned bristly after spending the day there.

"Sarah?" Martin beckons. "Are you listening?"

"Yes," I say, although I've missed everything. I know Martin tried to tell the council what occurred tonight, but this cannot be just another roundtable meeting about how to make someone's mistake go away.

A girl died.

And I died a thousand deaths after bathing my teenage son, as the Ellsworths recommended (ordered), while they were preparing their little meeting.

With rising horror, I see it wasn't to warm Finn; it was to wash off evidence—for the Ellsworths. Martin manipulated me to get Finn here.

I didn't fully realize it until I got to that room with the Tiffany lamps and the circle of people, specifically Alton. A member of law enforcement, he'd obviously been called in to help circumvent the fact that we'd left the scene of the crime—and the crime itself, whatever that may be. No one is intent on seeing this boy behind bars, especially me, but if I had my choice, I'd still be at a police station right now.

I hear Martin say rumblings of things like "she was already dead," "there was nothing more we could do."

"Drugs." "They weren't Finn's."

We don't know that for sure, though, Martin. They could've been Finn's.

I don't like to assume. But the Ellsworths will make it their truth and then my truth.

I let it become my truth that my children would attend the Barclay Classes at the Edgeworth Club from third grade to eighth grade, where they would learn proper manners, how to shake hands, and of course, ballroom dancing. Little boys in full suits and little girls in cotillion dresses twirled across polished country-club floors in a giggly mess of lace and bow ties. I let Mary Alice dictate my actions not because I was completely subservient but because I never had a proper mother and thought she knew best.

For primary school, the boys attended the Academy, which Martin and Bill had attended and which William and his brother, Edward, had attended before them, and then Livvy. The Ellsworths were legacy, William still served on the board for the school scholarship he funded, and none of these decisions was optional.

I never had a say in many things as my boys grew up, and I clearly didn't have one now, but my silence in this case shouldn't be mistaken for tacit agreement. I'm not sure if my son was drugged or if he took them of his own accord, but my primary concern is finding out if he had anything to do with Yazmin's death, not sitting around talking about it. This isn't like other decisions made in this family. I need to have a say here—where my son's welfare is concerned.

"I have my men on the scene now, but we need to work out a few details," Alton informs us. And I want to think that *"men on the scene"* means other officers doing right by Yazmin, but this circle makes me think otherwise.

"Absolutely. Just tell us what we need to do," I hear Martin say.

"I don't think—" I begin, but I'm cut off by a quick rap on the office door.

I jump. My heart races in my chest and chokes my speech. *It must be the police!* I clench the cushions of the chair and turn my head in Martin's direction, but he remains faced forward, stoic.

"Martin?" I whisper. He holds his finger up—*wait*—and won't make eye contact with me. This isn't like Martin. He always acknowledges me, eager to please, but then again, we haven't been faced with a situation like this before.

Alton gets up and strides quickly to the door, then opens it. A man dressed in all black hands him bundles of plastic. "Thanks," Alton says. The man takes off, and I'm not sure who he is or how he got into my in-laws' home, but they don't seem the least bit surprised at his intrusion.

31

I'm shocked. *Who is this guy?* I thought our part in what happened tonight was confined to this little room, and now that it's reached outside these walls, I want to crawl out of here and cry for help.

"Aunt Mary Alice," Alton says, and there seems to be an unspoken system going on here.

My mother-in-law rises again and takes the parcels from Alton and then kneels beside Finn.

I stand up. "What're you doing?"

Mary Alice doesn't answer me.

"Sit down, Sarah. She's examining him again," Martin says.

She doesn't look like she's examining him. Mary Alice removes syringes and surgical tubes from the bag and takes Finn's arm, the same one she used to check his blood pressure. She then plunges a syringe attached to a test tube into the underside of it.

I gasp, horrified. "*No.* I didn't agree to this." But Mary Alice only shakes her head, and everyone else remains quiet. "Martin?" I try to summon my husband, but he won't look at me. "Martin!" I try again, but he holds up his hand, quieting me, and I want to scream and grab my son and run.

It's all so disturbing—the random midnight courier, the on-site phlebotomy session, the fact that Finn hasn't flinched a bit from the brief examination or the sudden needle prick.

Martin grabs my hand. "We need to know what he's taken, Sarah. Sit down."

I sit in the chair, stunned, and turn to my husband, who doesn't seem like my husband at all, his normally gentle face a mask of urgency. "Martin, we need to get him to a hospital if we're concerned about what he's taken."

"We'll have the results back quicker this way," he reassures me.

I give him a bewildered look, and he turns back to face William, the side of the gargantuan chair blocking his face. I suddenly wonder what they'll do to me if I completely lose it and call the police. I've never acted out before, but then again, I've never had reason to. Then I realize Alton is the police, and this scares me even more, because it means there's no one I can turn to with the law sitting right here.

Mary Alice glances at me as she bags the blood, her thin lower lip twitching with disgust.

When the boys were younger, I tried so hard to be the type of mother I knew she expected me to be. I didn't know what normal was, so I did what I could to appease her, treated her grandchildren in ways I thought she'd find pleasing. Even when I had a minor case of the baby blues, I didn't let her see, afraid of the judgment and the feeling of failure that I knew would follow my admission. Bill Jr. and Martin were her pride and joy, and there was no way she'd excuse my depression after having two perfect little boys like Spencer and Finn.

But I couldn't care less what she thinks of me now.

Because real mothers cry for their children.

I'm here asking the Ellsworths for help tonight only because Martin has assured me they'd *"figure it out."* That's why I followed Martin out of the woods and into the car, holding Finn up beside me, his body a limber mess. Martin always figured things out for us, and I desperately wanted to do what was right for Finn, so I followed Martin like always. But it all feels terribly wrong now.

After Mary Alice is finished extracting blood from my son, she hands Alton the specimens in a plastic bag. Then Alton walks to the office door and taps on it once. It opens, and I'm shocked to discover the man in black is still waiting behind the door. I see the long black arm of his jacket reach in and grab the bagged tubes of blood, and then he's off. To where, I don't know. The secret lab, perhaps.

Are they taking my son's blood to be quickly analyzed for drugs so they can find the chemical in his system and help him? Who would even do that this time of night? Or are they using his blood for something else, to plant it somewhere? I swallow hard. "Martin, who is that man?"

He just pats my hand. "Don't worry—he's one of the good guys."

"Who does that make us, then?" I ask, pulling my hand away from him.

Martin shoots me a look of disapproval, eyes wide behind his glasses. William clears his throat. I've clearly offended the other people in the circle, but someone needs to tell me what the hell is going on here.

I peer at the people in the dim room, the ones I've called family for two decades. They're fully composed, basking in the light of the reflective lamps, seemingly unaffected by the events of the evening. Mary Alice's long face is offset by a turtleneck, a mint color that's so pale it's almost white, except for the sleeve dotted with the tiniest speck of red—Finn's blood.

And then I finally understand how exactly the Ellsworths are going to *"figure this out"* for us. This party of individuals carefully positioned around the room is meeting to cover up whatever happened in those woods tonight.

We are staging an accident.

That's what we're doing here.

There are only five seats in the semicircle, but no one speaks loudly enough for me to hear anything over the clatter in my chest. When we finally make eye contact again, Mary Alice's flat-faced features are nearly translucent in the lighting, a true fright. When Martin and I were dating, I asked if she ever smiled, and he said not really. If she did, I imagined her skin might crack.

It's then that I think of Yazmin's beautiful olive skin, probably beginning to decompose now. A roll of nausea falls over me, sweat dripping down my back in a chilled stream.

This is wrong. We should call the police. We should call Yazmin's parents.

"How much did he tell you before he went lights out?" Alton points to Finn, asking for his point of view for the first time all night.

"Only that he and his girlfriend had gone for a walk in the woods, smoked pot, and got into a fight. He remembers nothing else," Martin says. I wince when he says this, remembering the car ride home, how agitated I became when I asked Martin, *"What happened? What did he say?"*

And Martin simply replied, *"He doesn't remember."*

I'd feel so much better if I knew what the fight was about. This is the first I've heard of it, but all I can think about now are the fingernail marks on Finn's neck.

Alton stands to address the room. "Okay. There're a few things we'll need to do, but we have to be careful about what we say from here on out."

Martin grabs my hand again, and this time I don't let go. He forces me to look at him. The throbbing blue vein in his forehead has subsided, and his eyes mimic an exasperated sigh, because he knows I'm not on board here, and he desperately wants me to be.

"This is for Finn," he whispers.

No, it isn't. This is for them.

I look away and stare at the far corner of the wall, the thick binding of a John Grisham book catching my eye—*The Innocent Man.* The only fictional work I can find other than the classics is the one in the field in which William works. Ironic that it includes the word *innocent* in the title. He shouldn't own a single thing with that word on it, and I've known it since the first time I'd sat in that semicircle, shackled to it with what I had brewing in my belly.

Even if they can stage Yazmin's death to look like an accident, create a scenario to clear Finn, what does that teach our son about accountability? He won't always have a rock-star team of lawyers and law-enforcement officers at his side. If he hurt the girl, he should be taught to pay for his crime.

Or he might keep on hurting girls. I think back to the nail marks, feeling sick again.

My head jumbles with horrible news headlines, cases of privileged, wealthy boys who were found not guilty after an incident with a less fortunate female victim.

That cannot be my son. That will not be my son. He's not the boy who would force a girl to do something she didn't want to. He isn't the kid who uses drugs and tricks girls to slip away into the woods with him, their only way of escape physical attack.

A cry escapes my lips, and I suck it in, but the tears are already falling, these thoughts of what Finn could've done making me crumple.

"I'll make some tea." Mary Alice stands from her chair and runs off to the kitchen. I seem to have made her uncomfortable with my weeping.

Martin tries to put his arm around me, but he can't fully circle my body because of the sheer girth of the bulky chairs. For maybe the first time ever, I shift away from him. I want Finn to own up to his actions, whatever they may be, but I know in my heart of hearts that this wasn't his doing. Yazmin was his first real girlfriend, and they barely held hands in my presence. Finn is my shy kid, my straight-A, straitlaced, soccer-playing sweetheart. What the hell happened tonight?

Finn never came home from school, but he did text me that he was going for a walk with Yazmin and that they might circle back to our house. I was working late at the shelter, trying to find housing for an unwed mother and her child fleeing an abusive relationship. I was having trouble securing a place but didn't want to leave until I did. Martin was home; I didn't need to worry about Finn, but Martin never let me know that Finn hadn't shown up—until he called me to rush home because something was wrong with him.

Is this my fault? Should I have had him check in at home first before I let him take off with Yazmin Veltri?

The guilt is so widespread. What could I have done differently to prevent this?

Martin doesn't feel the same way, I can tell. I glance at him and see the determined shimmer in his eye, the same one he had when discussing the difficult zoning issue he'd been having for opening the new location for his business on the riverfront. Martin is concentrating only on how to fix the problem as quickly as possible.

The engineer, always the fixer.

I can't stand that about him right now. This is not a quick fix.

This is a young girl's life.

A young girl who's never liked me.

CHAPTER 4

Before

When I meet Yazmin for the first time, my only thought is—*those eyes.*

They're large and dark, her black eye makeup drawn around the lids with swooping lines at the corners. *Cat eyes,* they call them, the kind that could shock a drunk person sober. Her sheet of black-brown hair is so shiny, it's nearly aqueous.

Finn's first girlfriend, and she's a knockout.

"Mom, this is Yazmin. The one I've been . . . um . . . telling you about." My younger son has always been on the immature side, and I giggle a little when he tries to introduce her as his own.

"Why, hello. The famous Yaz." I drape the tea towel I've been holding over my shoulder and lean in for a hug, but she leans away. "Oh," I say, obviously overstepping my boundary. It happens sometimes. I don't always know what's appropriate contact, the unfortunate consequence of growing up without other women in my house.

Finn makes an awkward sound in his throat.

"Hello," Yazmin says. I settle for an awkward handshake, but she doesn't seem to like that either. Her hand quickly slips away, and her fingernails lightly graze my hand. I notice her nails are very long. Too long, with little jewels glued to the tips and tiny specks of paint outside the cuticle lines.

I pedal backward over the Persian runner in our foyer and take in the sight of her from the top of her pretty head to the—bottom of her white stockings?

"Oh my, where're your shoes?" I ask.

Finn looks down, confused, and then kicks his own shoes onto the doormat.

"I took them off before I came in," she says in a low voice, but I catch her Pittsburgh accent sneaking through—*"took 'em off."* Yazmin shakes a large chunk of her hair in her face, and I wonder why she's trying to hide from me.

"Well, now, that's silly. You could have at least waited until you got inside."

She stares at me, seeming uncertain of what to say next, and I think she'd better brush up on her communication skills if she's ever going to really run for office. Yazmin is newer to the Academy, but she's gained quite a reputation for being a strong female presence, running first term for student body treasurer and winning the seat. "Well, okay . . . please come in, make yourself at home." I make a welcoming gesture with my hand, hoping she'll loosen up.

She steps into the foyer slowly, almost tiptoeing.

Finn said that Yazmin, an ace at math, wanted to go into finance. She thought a treasurer seat would help with college admittance.

Smart girl.

Finn went to her house to help make campaign signs, but this is the first time she's come to ours, and only after I threatened Finn with a mandatory family dinner if she didn't. Finn let me know that Yazmin was passionate about the immigration situation in our country. Her grandfather had immigrated, and she thought everyone else should have that right too. It's probably one of the reasons she gelled with Finn, a boy after my own heart. Our house is divided that way.

Martin and Spencer—right wing, like the rest of the Ellsworths. Finn and myself—left.

"Congrats on your first elected seat." I try to make conversation and want to mention my thoughts, that I'm on her side, but the air in the room has gone stiff and sour since I attempted an embrace.

"Thank you." Yazmin gives me a small, crooked smile. Her body language isn't exactly the kind that speaks of trying to impress the parents, and I immediately gather Yazmin isn't here to impress anyone— least of all me.

Her gaze drifts to the inside of my house instead. Stonehenge has been described by guests as an altar to Jesus himself, a sacred space, but when Yaz's large eyes gravitate to the high ceiling held up with thick, lovely wooden beams, she looks displeased, like I've sprinkled salt on her tongue.

She walks farther into the great room for inspection, leaving Finn trailing behind her. She grabs her long black hair and shakes it uneasily down the back of her white blouse. The kids are both still in their uniforms from the Academy. Finn casually mentioned that Yazmin is there on scholarship. I intended to tell her I went to school on scholarship too, common ground, but something tells me she wouldn't be interested.

"Finn said this room was used for baptisms," she says.

"That's right. Celebrations of all sorts." I watch her carefully.

"Is that incense?" she asks.

"I have a candle warmer. The scent is called Damascus Rose," I reply.

"I'm having a hard time breathing." Yazmin's eyes are watering.

"If I could turn it off, I would, but the high ceilings lock in smells in this house," I explain, but I feel she's being dramatic. It's just a candle.

She whispers something in Finn's ear, avoiding my eyes.

"Mom, we're going to grab a bite somewhere else."

The look of relief that washes over Yazmin's face flattens me.

"The kitchen doesn't look so cathedral. Maybe you can hang out in there? I just whipped up some strawberry-pretzel Jell-O salad, your favorite, Finny. And there aren't any candles burning in that room. Do you like iced tea, Yazmin? I have hot tea and coffee too."

I spent last summer helping the contractor upgrade the kitchen into a sleek masterpiece, lime-green subway tile, white-washed cabinets, a far cry from the Gothic revival look I had going on in the great room. But none of my offerings seems to appease Yazmin, an immobile chess piece frozen in place.

"Jell-O?" She looks like she might laugh but bites her lip instead. "No thank you."

"There're lemon bars too," I try. "We also have a large outdoor area where you might be more comfortable." This place is magic, and I won't let her ruin it.

"No thank you." Yazmin turns and cuts me open with her deep, dark eyes, shaking her head, and I wonder if I've now offended her somehow. Most of all, I worry she'll shred my son with those eyes. He isn't equipped to handle them.

"The candle smell is bothering Yazmin, Mom," Finn defends his girlfriend.

"What about outside, though?" I ask. He has to know this is killing me, and even though I want to protest, I'm not about to get into a fight over it, with a teenager, no less.

Yazmin whispers in Finn's ear, and I look at him to register his reaction, but he's staring at his feet, his uncomfortable stance ever since he was a little kid. Spencer would charge upstairs and slam doors, but Finn was much less demonstrative.

The years wind back in that moment.

I can see Finn in his bare baby feet, just learning to pad around the house, and then in his extra-wide baby sneakers. Because his feet were so fat, we had to buy him special shoes. And then in his yellow rain boots, squishing worms in between the flagstones on the front walk.

He shot up and thinned out like Martin and had eventually advanced to his first pair of hiking boots.

All in a minute.

I can see it happening. A time-lapse video.

And the only thing I can think is that this girl with the killer eyes shouldn't be the one standing beside him. A ray of sunshine pierces the room, and Yazmin's eyes gravitate to the windows, so lovely when the sun hits them just right.

But Yazmin stares straight at one of the stained-glass windows as if it's a pentagram painted in blood. Her olive skin fades to gray, and she looks as if she's going to be sick. "I didn't expect this. Those windows are . . . too much."

She looks away, blinking back tears.

"I'm sorry?" I ask. And I'm sure by the way she pronounces *"too much"* she doesn't mean extraordinary. There isn't a single person who has walked through these doors who hasn't immediately fallen in love with my windows, but she looks as though she's just seen a ghost. "What do you mean?"

"They're . . ." Yazmin looks at Finn to rescue her.

"Very unique to the house," Finn answers.

"Even those?" she asks, pointing to the side windows, the newer ones featuring an English coat of arms with curly banners draped around the letter *E*.

"Martin added those. Family crest." I try not to sound like a braggart, but the surprise Martin gave me for our one-year anniversary still holds up. He knew how much I loved the other stained-glass windows in the house, so he added two more with the crest to make Stonehenge our own. Variations of the crest made it onto a lot of things the Ellsworths owned, and no one else pointed out that the newer windows didn't complement the biblical ones, but I think Yazmin just did, and it bothers me.

I take another look at them, upset that she's making me second-guess something I've always loved.

"Right." Yazmin rocks on her heels and then makes a waving gesture with her hands. "I think I need to leave." She coughs and grabs her throat.

Finn moves to her side, placing a hand on her back. "Are you all right?" he asks.

I walk up beside them.

Finn nudges her shoulder toward the door. "We can just go to the French Café," he suggests, talking about the local diner.

"Okay," Yazmin says, relieved.

This is ridiculous. Finn loves strawberry-pretzel salad; that's why I made it.

I clench my dish towel. "Please stay. I have all kinds of food here. Why don't you see if you like it better outside, on the patio? Maybe you won't feel so closed in. Fresh air," I say.

Finn is leading Yazmin to the door, and neither one of them turns back in my direction to acknowledge me. If she apologized first, it would've gone a long way. *"I'm sorry, but the smell in your home is bothering me."*

But she doesn't. So I'm left disliking her despite the fact that she's distressed in my home and possibly ill.

Finn makes contact with Yazmin's hand, grabbing it.

She whispers something in his ear again, and I don't have to hear it to know she's telling him what to do. I find their interaction oddly forced, and nothing about their courtship reminds me of when Spencer dated his first real girlfriend, Allegra, a bashful girl with a tinkling laugh. Away at college now, premed, Spencer can't be bothered with a girlfriend, but this young lady seems to really have her hooks in Finn.

"Bye, Mom," Finn says.

She says nothing.

Do not order my son around. And do not disrespect me in my home.

I want to protest, but they're already gone, door slammed, the hammering echo of a boy lost to the wrong girl beating off the rafters.

My heart jumps around in my chest after they're gone, a feeling I haven't experienced since Martin told me his company might be opening an office in London. My panic came from fear of leaving my father and the careful group of neighborhood friends I've built here over the years. I tentatively chose my connections, because I wasn't very good at making them, a problem that most likely stemmed from my mother's death when I was in grade school.

It wasn't just her death but how she died—terminal cancer, a form of non-Hodgkin's lymphoma that'd infiltrated her bone marrow and every lymph node in her body by the time they found it. I remember feeling like she'd just been taken from me. I watched as she faded away in a hospital room, in a wing with one other patient with the same rare disease.

That woman had disappeared from the hospital before Mom did, and I'd assumed the worst. Only she'd been flown to Switzerland for an experimental treatment that was still in clinical trials. The doctor had talked to my father about it, but we didn't have the money for that kind of travel, and the hospital couldn't provide it. Not that the doctors promised a better prognosis even if we had, because the therapy's efficacy was unknown.

When my mother died, there were so many gorgeous flowers thrown on top of her coffin, I agonized over the fact that she'd never have the opportunity to see them. It was so unfair. Mother was special in that she always enjoyed the magic in the present, not worrying too much about tomorrow. She could treasure the beauty of a flower even though it would die in a week. People said these things at her service and how lovely she was in the brief time she was here, her life like that of a flower, too short. I loved the metaphor, but I was also saddened at seeing the mountain of plants she'd never grow in her own flower shop she'd wanted so badly, in a house up the hill with better landscaping.

But nothing had upset me more than the fact that the woman, the other patient who'd flown to Switzerland, had attended my mother's funeral. I almost didn't recognize her until she introduced herself to me and hugged me, because she had all her hair back, and it was actually down to her chin by then. And she wasn't bony like I remembered; her embrace was firm and healthy.

I was shocked. She'd survived. The treatment had worked. And she was in remission.

It was only then that I truly understood what money could buy. My father was happy to see her and whispered to me, "She got lucky. And God bless."

I wanted to be one of the lucky ones too.

Years later, I researched the price of an airline ticket to Switzerland and determined that I could've possibly saved my mother's life for $800, and I cried. And no one would ever understand that pain, so I chose my friends carefully, because if they couldn't understand what I'd been through, I didn't think they could really know me.

One kindhearted soul here who gained my trust was Camille Sugarman, a fellow member of the PTA, and I'd hated the thought of leaving her when Martin got a bid for opening a London office.

But if I'm being honest with myself, my true angst about moving came from leaving my house. When the deal fell through and Martin wasn't charged with opening the new satellite location, he was disappointed, but I was so happy that the next afternoon, I opened a bottle of wine and drank the whole thing by myself as I quietly cried tears of joy beneath my pergola.

Just another Sewickley SAHM (stay-at-home mom) day-drinking under her trellis, I thought to myself, snickered, and cried some more, patting the cement bench and letting it know I'd be around for another summer.

All the parties we'd had right there in that same outside entertaining space. B. F. Jones, the steel tycoon, had built this Gatsby-era English Gothic residence as his summer home, an offshoot to his mansion, a present to his wife for their anniversary. I could feel the energy in the walls. It was special. I forgot the moments with Joshua when I was younger. I tried to, anyway, but we were happy here, Martin and me and the boys. Who would ever want to leave?

Why does Yazmin despise my house? It makes me instantly despise her.

The front door opens and shuts, and I know it's Martin, but I can't focus on his arrival, my eyes seared to the stained-glass windows. The old ones complement the newer ones fine, and she was just being terrible.

"Honey?"

Martin stands before me with his suit jacket draped over his arm like he always does when he comes home from work.

"Hi," I peep.

"What's wrong?" he asks.

I shake my head, signaling nothing, but I don't make a habit of staring blankly at the walls, so I know I'm not fooling my husband, a man who practically came out of the womb cum laude.

"Oh, Sarah, did you lose your glass slipper again?" Martin asks.

I crack a smile.

In any other household, his comment might sound derogatory, but it isn't. It's a phrase Martin uses often when I complain about something trite or nothing at all and he doesn't have any other way to console me. He wraps his arms around me and kisses me gently, my prince. He'd find my glass slipper and return it even if I didn't know it was missing. The only problem is he'd also take someone else's slipper to make me happy, and that's where our lines sometimes got crossed.

"No, that's not it." I can't collect my thoughts to describe what has just transpired in my home. I'm probably overreacting, but something deep in my soul feels fractured, and I'm not sure why. "How was your day?" I ask, trying to deflect.

"Oh . . ." He sighs. "Still trying to work out the zoning on the riverfront property. There're some people who think that area is designated specifically for Pittsburgh sports arenas and their corporate companions."

"Hmm . . . maybe you should dip your pen in black and gold, then." Even though Martin's attempt to branch out overseas hasn't been successful, he's opened a few other regional locations. His latest venture is some property on the Allegheny Riverfront in downtown Pittsburgh, but zoning has been a bear.

Martin's glasses are bumping the top of my head, and he's rocking me back and forth in a silent dance. "Perhaps. Donations not go as expected?" he asks, breathing into my scalp, still fishing for answers.

"It was a productive morning, actually," I say of my meeting in the city to discuss my newly appointed position as chief fundraiser for the new Impact Program to assist inner-city single mothers. "I suggested they include single fathers in the mix for funding too."

Martin looks down into my eyes with his half smile. The laugh line on the left side of his face remains long after his smile has gone. It's one of the things I'll never tire of because I'm pretty sure I've provided most of the laughs to form it.

"And?" he asks.

"And they said they don't really have the population or the need for that."

"Oh . . ." Martin stares up into his lenses, lips pressed firmly together, as if he's trying to carefully word his response. "Well, I'm sure it's because of city demographics, not because you're all alone on the I-was-raised-by-a-single-father island," Martin concludes.

"Sure," I say, and sometimes I think I come up with these initiatives just to find the few kids who are struggling the same way I did, but I know that's not fair. Then again, it's not fair that Martin gets to sign off on any self-serving thing he wants. London would've been a done deal if the acquisition went through, whether I wanted to move or not.

"So you're bummed they didn't put out the funding for the dads? You want the money to go to the people who really need it, don't you?" Martin asks, always the voice of reason.

I sigh, because that isn't what's wrong at all. I didn't get into non-profit work because I'm looking for something to do. I grew up on the lower side of middle class, and I love helping others in the same situation. My mother was a volunteer at church, and she often took me with her, and it was *"in my heart to do that type of work,"* as my father always said following our first food drive.

I've been allotted an undeserved fortune for someone of my status, and I know it's partially due to luck, but suddenly, after meeting Yazmin, it feels as though my luck has run out.

It's a fear that crept up during our early days of marriage, when I was just assimilating to this new lifestyle, and then more recently as we approached the empty-nester stage—when is the fairy tale going to end? It didn't start out honestly, first with the circumstances surrounding the engagement and then with the purchase of the house. I have a horrible feeling that it's all a ruse.

"Do you want me to make a call to Bill?" Martin asks of his older brother, who also happens to be city commissioner. Martin's brow twists in a way that always makes it look like he's about to tell a joke, but he knows how much I despise using politics to push my own agenda.

"No, no, it's not the project, actually. I met Finn's new girlfriend today." My voice has gone dry. I inhale Martin's cologne, still Polo, still casual comfort.

"And?" he asks, holding me at arm's length so he can read my expression.

"And she was awful," I say honestly.

"*Sarah!*" Martin laughs at me, and it echoes all the way to the ceiling like it always does in this room. And usually when laughter travels in our home, I love it, but not today, because this isn't funny.

"Well, she was. She wasn't friendly, and she . . . was controlling Finn, whispering in his ear, and she . . ." I sigh, embarrassed that the last fact is more bothersome to me than the rest.

"She what?" he asks, as if this is all so amusing.

"She insulted our house," I say.

"Oh no," Martin says, and then he stops chuckling, staring down at me with a rare grace of seriousness. He knows there's no way I can accept her now. "Well, hopefully their relationship will be short-lived."

CHAPTER 5

Present

Blackburn Road creeps up on me like a snake through the trees, the popping of the gravel onto the turnoff where the road ends and our driveway begins shaking me out of my shocked stupor. I wipe my nose with my wet sleeve, the buttons of my shirt scraping the skin of my chapped cheek. "How can you just drive home as if nothing's happened?" *As if we didn't leave a dead teenage girl in the woods?*

"Something has happened. To our son. You need to start putting him first in this situation," Martin says.

"But . . . what about the girl? And what if someone hurt her?" *Like our son.* This doesn't make sense to me, the way Martin and his family rationalize our part in this atrocity.

"We do what we have to do to protect our family, Sarah. You know Finn isn't the one who hurt that girl. I'm sure of it. It's time for you to stop doubting your son." His voice is icy and punishing. I don't know this side of Martin.

"I don't doubt him." I hug the shoulders of my puffy vest, feeling more alone than I ever have in my entire life, because I doubt my own husband far more than I do my son. This is an ugly side of his human prism I've never seen before.

"Everything will look clearer in the morning." Martin's reassurance is empty, and I don't believe him one bit. The morning is where light lives, and it will most certainly shine a beacon on what we've done and the monsters we truly are. Yazmin was seventeen years old. Her beautiful eyes were rolled in the back of her head—lifeless. I gasp.

The temperature is dropping. Her parents are probably worried sick.

"Martin, has someone at least taken her by now?" I whisper, thinking of Alton's men at the scene. "To the hospital, so her parents can . . ." I cover my mouth and stifle a cry, trying not to imagine my own son on one of those awful pullout metal slabs in the morgue, a paper tag attached to his toe.

"It's being taken care of," Martin says.

"What does that mean?" *What does any of this mean?*

"Do you remember what you're supposed to say in case there's company waiting for us at home?"

As much as we practiced our alibi with Alton before we left, for the life of me, I can remember only bits and pieces. The fact that we've done something like this before somehow softened our scripted dialogues this time, but it shouldn't have, because it isn't the same thing. No one died in Livvy's accident.

Martin grabs my hand. "Look at me."

I do, and my supportive, warm husband is back in a flash. The mercurial way he does this frightens me. It reminds me how he lied about the doctor to get me to do what he wanted. "You can do this. For Finn." He keeps hammering this fact, that it's for our son. That I need to do this for him, but it's hard to justify.

I try to remember what we practiced.

Finn and Yazmin got into a fight (true). But, according to Alton, Finn walked home upset afterward, went straight up to his bedroom, and fell asleep (lie). I was at the women's shelter, but Martin was home to confirm Finn's return. This works for everyone involved, because

I was neither home nor comfortable fabricating the truth, whereas Martin was home and apparently fine with it.

I swallow the thoughts burning on my tongue. *What else is Martin comfortable lying about?* It's not an entirely new thought but one that hasn't reared its ugly head in some time.

I remember what Martin said to me with such exuberance the day he surprised me with Stonehenge, about paying for the house himself with the windfall from his new backers.

That was a complete and utter lie. Turned out he'd only had enough for half and pulled the rest from his trust. The only reason I'd found out is because I was cleaning his office a year into our marriage and found the paperwork. I confronted Martin, and he tried to use the excuse that the money in the trust was his, so what was the difference? But to me it made all the difference in the world. Especially since I'd told my dad that Martin bought Stonehenge the old-fashioned way, with his own hard-earned money.

One lie runs into the next.

I've made peace with it, because he was just trying to make me happy, but I've come to understand that a lie is a lie and should not be discounted. Accepting the old lies makes the new ones seem less significant. William stood right there and heard Martin say he'd paid for the house himself and didn't correct him. They are a family of liars. And I'm tethered to them because of the secrets we share—and no better than they are in this case.

Martin pulls the car up close to the driveway and then stops short of pulling in. I can see our house illuminated by brilliant outdoor spotlights, our welcome-home halo. Martin loved the large lot, the property itself a treasure because of the privacy. But now I'm wondering if he purchased it because he thought it might make a good place to hide. Before I can fully postulate the disturbing thought, I realize Martin has stopped the car because there's something moving in our driveway.

Brake lights. A black sedan, long enough to be a limousine, is pulling out at rapid speed. "Who is that, Martin?" My voice is scratchy with stress, but I'm worried the car is the real police (not Alton) or the FBI.

"They're okay," Martin explains, a totally unsatisfactory answer, much like his comment about the man who went around collecting bags of blood in the middle of the night. *He's one of the good guys.*

I look at Martin for more information, but he won't acknowledge me. It's like I've been invisible all night, a completely foreign feeling in my husband's presence. My doting husband is treating me like I'm not even here, and I'm waiting for him to flip that switch and turn back on. Who is the real Martin?

Maybe the police have found her. That would be a blessing, actually. Once Yazmin's body is discovered, Alton said it will be determined that she went for a walk in the woods to experiment with drugs and somehow fell and hit her head. Alton explained that when deaths of teenagers are associated with drugs, there tends to be a lot fewer questions and less sympathy from the community and much quicker closure.

It could be what really happened.

But what if it isn't? The nail marks suggest otherwise. I feel my body involuntarily shudder.

Hopefully Finn will wake up soon and tell us what happened to his girlfriend.

I can't remember the tiny things Alton said that I know are important, like if the kids did alcohol or drugs in the past or what Finn's friends thought of Yazmin. It's either that they liked her or they didn't, and these details are important, but they're escaping me right now.

"Martin?" I ask, but I've lost him. It's as if we're still beneath the canopy of trees in the woods and I can't find him. We might as well be—we're so far apart in the front of this car right now. "Tell me who those people are."

I'm impressed by the driving skills of the man in the black car, because we have a very long, winding driveway and he's navigating it entirely in reverse. Martin waves as they back out around the stone pillars that mark our lot. The two men in the driver and passenger seat wave back quickly, as if they know Martin, but not well enough to roll down the window and chat.

"*Shit*. I forgot to double-check with you. Did you place Finn's bloodied school clothing and shoes in a plastic bag and the clothing and shoes you wore tonight in a separate bag?" he asks, and I can't believe how calculating he sounds when speaking of things like bloody clothing. Who is this ruthless maniac and what has he done with my husband?

"Yes," I answer woodenly.

"Oh, good. Those are the cleaners," he says plainly. Quietly.

I look at him sideways, and he doesn't flinch, and if I could picture myself right now, it would be a reflection of the most haggard woman on the planet, bags under my eyes hanging to my jawbone, greasy blonde-brown hair matted in a knot on my head. The lies early on were clues that this could happen, that he had it in him to say one thing and act a completely different way, but this is a whole new level. This is terrifying. "Our cleaning people come on Thursdays, and they drive a van."

"Not those cleaners." Martin clears his throat as if I should just be okay with this answer.

It takes me a moment with my eyes shut to figure out exactly what he means.

Cleaners? As in the Ellsworths not only have hired servants to clean up the dirt on their floors, but they also have cleaners to mop up the spilled blood of the dead bodies they leave behind?

I grip the door handle of Martin's Lexus and contemplate jumping out and running, but my son is in the back seat. "What are they going to do with our clothes?" I ask. And what will the Ellsworths do to me if I run and tell?

Darkness settles in around us, the kind that cloaks desolate back roads under starless skies. I wonder if Martin is in shock, too, and if that's why he's acting so calm in the middle of this horror story. Perhaps his pragmatic engineer brain is running on autopilot, and he's operating in a strictly process-driven fashion.

Dead body—dispose.

Bloody clothing—dispose.

Frazzled wife—keep calm.

It's much like he behaved when I had a minor case of postpartum depression. He fluttered around doing task-y things like making sure baby bottles were washed and organized and picking up the cooking and cleaning when all I really needed was a hug.

"They're going to burn them," he says in the same even tone.

"Oh," I reply back, but my chin begins to wobble with fear. I think of my favorite pair of jeans with the tiny holes at the knees and my favorite Tory Burch flats all going up in flames in a rancid burning barrel in a back alley somewhere. Those articles can all be replaced, but the real loss lies in the fact that any evidence linking me to the crime will burn with them. It's just what the Ellsworths want—to make it all disappear.

I was the last one to touch Yazmin's lifeless body. I should be held responsible for leaving her there. It isn't fair to Yazmin and it isn't fair to her parents.

Martin pulls up to the garage, and I open the door and fall onto the driveway. My stomach is knotted, and I place my hands on the damp concrete. I try to retch on the sidewalk, but nothing comes out.

Martin walks over and puts his hand on my shoulder. "Everything is going to be all right, Sarah. It'll feel better in the morning."

"How can you say that?" I'm weeping, and terrible sounds are leaving my mouth, all the terror I suppressed at my in-laws' house coming out in bits of saliva and sick.

Fuck the morning. I'm going to have to turn us in in the morning.

I can't see Martin's face, but his hand retreats from my shoulder, his warmth leaving my body like a blanket slipping off my feet in the middle of the night. "I have to take care of our son now," he says.

The driveway is wet and cold. It bites into the bruises left on my knees from kneeling on the river rocks.

"This isn't about you and all you've been through tonight, Sarah. It's about protecting Finn. Someday you'll see it that way too."

"This isn't about putting my needs before Finn's; it's about doing the right thing."

Martin is hovering above me but doesn't offer to help me up. "Finn didn't hurt that girl, and they will demonize him for her death. He's eighteen. They'll try him as an adult. Finn won't survive prison. It. Will. Kill. Him." Martin drives home every last word as he walks away.

He's probably right.

We held Finn back a year in school because he was a late birthday, born in August, of all the dreadful months. Painful decision, but he was emotionally unfit to go to kindergarten, still clinging to my leg when I dropped him off at preschool, crying when he was pushed or teased—hence tae kwon do classes. So he is eighteen, whereas many of the other seniors are still seventeen. Adult prison could be a possibility for him.

He'd get eaten alive.

Martin is right. Martin is always right. Maybe things will look better in the morning.

He's opening Finn's car door now. I hear Martin huff as he picks up our son. He wrestles with his limp body as he carries him to the front door—our baby boy. I remember when we brought him home from the hospital. He slept the whole way, hardly made a peep, a gentle kid from birth.

No, he didn't hurt that girl. But something or someone did.

I think about the marks on Finn's neck. What else could've caused them? Perhaps they were an opponent's soccer cleats that had gotten him good when he'd fallen down during a game. A cat that hadn't played fairly was a possibility too.

But soccer cleats wouldn't make five distinct marks, and we don't own a cat or know anyone who does.

Then I think of the first time I met Yazmin and her long, bejeweled fingernails. They weren't fake, I could tell, because the tips were uneven and the paint job was imperfect. They were real nails, the kind that could leave marks—like the ones on Finn's neck.

I realize my fears have all been about those marks since the minute I saw them.

Deep breaths.

I get off the ground and follow Martin to the porch, but I know nothing will ever be the same once we step through those doors. This is where our divide continues. It started in the woods when I wanted to call the police and Martin didn't, and it will continue as we enter our home and close the door on the decisions we've made tonight. Martin is maneuvering our long son in his arms, shimmying from side to side to balance the weight, mechanically, the machine that he is.

Still, I open the front door for Martin so he can get our son inside. The doors groan in dissatisfaction, and I want to apologize for bringing the turmoil inside. *I'm sorry,* I silently tell Stonehenge, because this house is my protector. It's protected me from other secrets and kept the ones from when Joshua lived here too. I'm just not sure its old stone walls are strong enough to withstand the burden of this one.

Martin unloads Finn onto the hulking yellow leather couch in our living room, an overpriced statement piece that now looks ridiculous beneath Finn's sleeping, ragged body. I imagine the leather is very cold and immediately rush over to cover him with a cashmere throw, prop a pillow under his neck, place a bucket below his head in case he has to vomit in the middle of the night.

Not that I'll be sleeping. I'll be checking on him every few minutes to make sure he's still breathing.

We really do want what's best for Finn, Martin and I. We just have very different ideas of what *best* is. I'm not sure what my son's involvement is here, but I'm positive the better course of action would've been to report the incident and let the chips fall where they may.

But then I think—*prison*.

Martin gave me my phone back only after we left the Ellsworths', and it's buzzing in my pocket with unanswered messages. The last time I checked it, there were just texts from Camille Sugarman on which dress to wear to the Children's Heart-to-Heart Gala this weekend. I glance again. The last two messages aren't from my friend Camille. They're from Alisha Veltri, Yazmin's mother. My heart sinks to the ground along with my body.

Of course she's calling and texting me. She wants to know where her daughter is.

Alisha: Hi, Mrs. Ellsworth, this is Yazmin's mom. I asked Finn for your number last time he was here, just in case. Yazmin isn't home yet. Do you know where she is? Is she with Finn?

As soon as Martin sees the text, he sits down beside me, eyes wide. He looks startled, as if he didn't expect the text, whereas I've been expecting it all night. It makes me think he's missing the mark on parenthood if he didn't think she'd at least contact us.

"You must do exactly as I say," Martin says.

My insides scream *no*, because I know he doesn't want me to tell her anything is wrong, but she at least needs a clue that there's reason to be alarmed. But that's not what Martin wants, because Alton's men are still likely in the woods cleaning up our mess. This was manageable when it was just us, but I can't lie to Yazmin's mother.

The phone bobbles in my unstable hand. *"I can't,"* I cry.

Martin's fingers dig into either side of my shoulders, too rough. I look up at him, and it's as if the vein in his head has its own pulse. He's kneeling and facing me. "You can and you will. You have to for Finn.

You need to be strong for your son right now." It takes my breath away that Martin's definition of being strong for Finn is lying through my teeth to his dead girlfriend's mother.

"Put yourself in her shoes, Martin. This is horrible." I cry some more, because this isn't just a dead girl in the woods anymore; this is someone's daughter.

"You made a decision to leave those woods to protect Finn, and you have to stick by it. Now, type what I tell you." His voice doesn't leave room for debate.

And honestly, I don't want it to, because I don't see any way out of this but to continue down the dark path we've started on. Martin is right. We made a decision to leave those woods, and if I tell Alisha what we did, we'll all be arrested—the whole lot of us—Martin and Finn and the Ellsworths and me. What good would it do? Especially if Finn didn't do anything to cause Yazmin's death.

"We can't bring her back," Martin whispers, and those are the right words, because I was just thinking them.

We can't bring her back, but we can do our best to move forward.

I nod through my tears, and he wipes one away now that he knows he has me on board. Martin dictates every syllable as I type.

"Explain that Finn said they had a fight after school, and he hasn't spoken to her since. When she asks what the fight was about, tell her he wouldn't tell you the specifics, only that it was something to do with an Instagram post she didn't approve of that he's already taken down."

I type it. All of it. "Why didn't you tell me about the fight?" I feel left out that Martin knew about it. He must've gathered as much from Finn before he passed out. Martin doesn't answer me.

Alisha: Can I speak to Finn please?

Shit. "She wants to talk to Finn."

"I'm sitting right here," Martin says.

"You don't have to get a crappy attitude with me." I sniffle.

He's staring me down as if I've said the wrong thing, and he's the mercurial Martin again—the bad one. I shiver. Then he rips my phone out of my hand.

"*Martin.*"

"Let me."

He pulls it farther away, and I feel violated, like the last time he took it away. "What're you saying? At least let me agree to what you're sending, since it's my phone."

"Yes, it's your phone. It can be tracked."

He pushes characters into the text window and flashes the screen at me.

Sarah: Finn is sleeping. He has been for hours. Please let me know if you still can't find Yazmin in the morning.

I nod, approving even though I never would've had the strength to write that message myself, and he knows it. That's why he stole my phone. Sadly, I feel a little relief that he asked my permission before sending it.

Yazmin's mother doesn't text back.

We both stare at the phone, waiting for her to reply, but she doesn't. She's probably angry, and I don't blame her.

I try to think about what I would do in this case, and I'd probably ask the parent to wake up their child and question them, but not everyone feels comfortable crossing those kinds of boundaries. My father would've gotten in his truck and driven to the parents' house and shaken the answer out of the kid. His actions wouldn't have surprised me one bit when I was Yazmin's age. That first year I'd gone to college was the hardest on him, separating from me indefinitely.

And now Alisha will be separated from her daughter forever, and she doesn't even know it yet.

CHAPTER 6

Carnegie Mellon Campus—Fall 1996

There's a sweet buzz of excitement in the quad as upperclassmen help freshmen carry cardboard boxes into their rooms. From my small dormitory window, it looks like a Costco has exploded on the pristine lawn. So many rolls of unopened toilet paper and paper towels are scattered around, I wonder if the parents know those supplies come included with tuition.

Dad said this would happen on move-in day, overly prepared parents storming the buildings with too many paper products— *"emotional supplements for sending off their firstborn."*

"We won't be victim to these first-timer crimes," he declared.

The pretty brick buildings crouched among the other historical sites in and around downtown Oakland are nothing new to me. However, today one of them will be my new home. Dad used his university connections to have me placed in one of the newer dorms with a mix of upperclassmen and a few lucky freshmen.

I feel privileged for the first time in my entire life. Other students will ask which dorm is mine, and I will proudly announce "Resnik" with the kind of coolness reserved for the kids at my old high school who rented out the riverboats on the North Shore along the Allegheny for their sixteenth birthday parties. Resnik doesn't have an upper deck fit to host a dance floor or a big red paddle wheel like the riverboats, but it's the best I could've asked for on campus.

While everyone else schleps in their overflowing boxes and laundry baskets, I'm already spreading my tie-dyed bedspread over my single mattress in anticipation of meeting my mystery roommate, Hanna.

Dad is absent from helping me fix up my room, rigging free television cable to my dorm, because after all his years of service to the university, he decided I should have it. I don't think that's the real reason he isn't helping me settle in, though. The other parents may have padded their empty nests with extra Charmin, but Dad is dealing with my leaving the only way he knows how—by fixing something, using his hands.

I realize sending me off is probably the hardest thing he's had to do since burying my mother, so I've tried my hardest to go along with all his shenanigans. It seems as though Dad has spent his whole life trying to make up for everything my mother never had the chance to do for me. *"Free cable, who wouldn't want that?"*

I asked him if he wanted me to commute instead of living on campus, and if he'd be okay on his own, but he insisted that I have the full college experience with all the benefits of my family-affiliated free tuition, which includes campus housing. Dad always wanted what was best for me, and giving me the gift of a free education at a premier institution is, to him, the best offering he has.

I couldn't say no, not to the school and certainly not to the coolest dorm on campus.

Although we both know my absence isn't what's best for him.

As my elbow jabs a package of ramen noodles and a box of hot cocoa on the windowsill, I'm reminded of the fact that Dad can't cook all that well. He still mixes up his whites with his reds when he does laundry, and God knows what will become of the indoor plants without me around to water them.

We could still spend our weekends together, but will we? Dad said Sundays would be our day, and this makes me sad, because every day was *our* day prior to the start of college.

"Wow, either you're the quickest unpacker in the history of mankind or you somehow got an early pass." I jump slightly. One of the movers has poked his head into my room.

I look up to find a boy with overgrown dark-brown hair and a wry grin nosing into my dormitory. "I've got connections," I say for probably the first time in my entire life.

It's a little unsettling having a boy appear in my bedroom, just like that. Then I realize I'm living in a coed dormitory and I should probably get used to it.

"That's so money; I like your style." The boy's wearing a tie-dyed shirt with Greek letters on the front. He points to my bed, as if we aren't the only two people in the room, and I can't figure out the correlation.

"Right. Thanks," I say, but seeing his body, long and lean, pointed toward my bedsheets sends warm shock waves down my stretched bare arms.

The little buzz quickly defuses when a much smaller kid decides to invite himself into my room as well, and suddenly I feel bombarded.

"There you are. I'm here to serve, Marty." The boy makes a dorky salute sign at Marty—that's his name. The smaller one has the kind of smile that could light up a billboard, a real this-is-a-nice-kid kind of grin, and I decide he's okay.

"I've got this, Tushy," Marty says.

"Tushy?" I giggle. What an awful name.

The smaller guy rolls his gorgeous umber eyes. "It's Tushar Patel." He reaches out his arm and shakes my hand firmly.

So polite.

Marty says, "Tush is a sophomore like me, but he's just deciding to join us, so he's trying to kiss up because I'm in charge of the pledges."

"Ah, Mr. Important," I joke.

"Sure." Marty winks, and he's kind of dorky too. A very cute dorky. "She's all set, Tush. Find someone else to harass."

"Oh . . . I see how it is." Tushar makes an awkward but sweet bow, then leaves.

"Is that a lava lamp?" Marty's eyes dart to my bedside table. I guess he's not planning on going with Tush. His body is fully in my room now.

"Uh-huh. A Spencer's store special. Thought it tied the room together," I say.

"Come on, Marty!" I hear someone scream from the hallway. "At least wait until we get to the fence to harass the freshmen!"

Marty flushes from his cheeks to his lamb-chop sideburns, which I don't particularly like or hate; they're just different. He's not like the guys I'm used to at home. Even though Josh's hair was on the longer side, there's a polish well hidden by Marty's ratty T-shirt. But I don't want to think of Joshua. He's not here—and Marty is.

"Don't pay attention to him. That's Meat, the president of the fraternity," he says. "He just likes to order people around," he whispers.

"Meat?" I ask. "What's up with the names in your fraternity? And why do they call him that?" I'm leaning on my metal bed frame, and I'm never quick to judge people, but I instantly like Marty. There's an energy about him that makes my insides flutter, anxious but in a good way.

Marty shrugs. "You don't want to know."

"Marty!" Meat yells again. "There're other people who need help. Just tell her to meet you at the fence tonight."

"You'd better go. Duty calls," I say.

"Right. You should come tonight, though. To the fence," he says as he backpedals the two steps to my door, bumping his head on the entrance as he does, blowing his cool act.

"Which fence?" I ask.

"You have to find it on your own. I can't be the one to tell you." Marty is out the door before I can say another word. I haven't even told him my name.

Hanna Flaherty, my new roommate, shows up a few minutes later with her parents. Her mother and father are dressed in nearly matching plaid shirts. Their moving boxes are neatly taped from one side to the other.

Mrs. Flaherty holds a brightly colored tote bag. "Hello, I'm Ramona and this is Gregory."

"Hi, I'm Sarah," I say with a quick wave. I'm not used to adults introducing themselves by their first names, and I don't like the way these two eye my dormitory decor like something ugly might crawl out from beneath the sheets.

"Hi!" Hanna rolls her large bright-blue eyes lined in charcoal. They're so vibrant, I wonder if she has colored contacts. I smile back. I'm not great at female relationships, but I heard that dormitory roommates are supposed to be like insta best friends. Sorta like my hot cocoa—just add water and stir. I had high hopes, but I clearly don't belong with the offspring of these two.

"Are your parents here?" Ramona asks. She pulls out a container of cookies from the tote bag and places them on a nightstand. The cookie carrier is in one of those specially designed Tupperware deals with the formidable red lid. We've never covered our cookies with anything but aluminum foil, which immediately confirms that Hanna and I will not be a good match.

"My dad's hooking up our cable," I say.

"Oh, I didn't know cable was an option." Gregory grabs a tabbed university brochure from Ramona's tote bag and begins to browse it for confirmation.

"Cable is all set!"

Ramona and Gregory jump when my dad charges through the door. He wipes his sweaty hands on his jeans, and his flannel shirt is flapping open to reveal yet another concert tee, this one Van Halen. Ramona's eyes run over his shirt the same way they did my bedding.

"I'm sorry, Victor Denning, head of campus maintenance." Dad sticks out his hand, and Gregory sets down the brochure on Hanna's bed to shake it.

"Gregory Flaherty, Hanna's father. Head procurement officer at Lockheed Martin," he adds for good measure.

"Oh, well, I guess someone had to pull the short straw and take the boring job." Dad laughs with his deep rasp, and so do I. Even when Dad is picking on people, it still sounds like he's cracking a joke. The Flahertys look puzzled, crinkling their brows in unison, although Mrs. Flaherty's forehead doesn't move an inch.

"Right. Well, I didn't see cable included in the brochure," Gregory says.

"That's because it's not!" Dad smiles because it's hard for him not to. He's so alive, unlike these two stick-in-the-muds. Their willowy bodies sway for a minute as they process the information.

"So you mean . . ."

"I know the back wires of these buildings better than the men who built them, that's what it means." Dad slaps Mr. Flaherty on the back, and he lurches forward.

"Right, well, Hanna, we'd best be off for our dinner reservation. Nice to meet you, Sarah, Victor."

"The pleasure was all mine. And please call me Vic. Everyone else does," Dad says.

"Right. Okay, then, Vic," Mr. Flaherty says. "Bye now." They nod and exit the room in a hurry.

Dad gives me his seal of approval with two thumbs-up and says he has a few more things to take care of, and then we'll be off for dogs and root beer floats at The O. No fancy dinner for us—we'll save that for when I make dean's list.

When I return to my dorm, Hanna is unpacking her stuff. I thought I was in for a year with Little Miss Goody Two-shoes, but the minute I open my mouth to say hello, she pulls out a rolled cigarette.

"Thank God they finally left. Wanna find somewhere to smoke this? I need to chill out."

Betty Crocker's daughter packed a joint. I'm speechless and just stare at it. I've smoked only a few times, and only because Joshua said I couldn't vibe to him playing Pink Floyd without it. And I loved to listen to him play. I've already convinced myself that what happened in that house, with Josh, was only my fantasy manifesting itself into the briefest of realities. I'd half convinced myself none of it had even happened at all. Especially after how it ended.

I shake my head at Hanna.

"Oh, you don't smoke?" she asks.

"Nope," I say. Better to set the ground rules now so I don't get into trouble later.

My worst offense before Joshua was a stolen beer here, a bottle of Boone's Farm there, but no drugs. I was too focused on getting straight As so I could maintain the grades needed to get into CMU and use my father's free ticket. In a way, everything led me right up to this point. I couldn't just smoke it all away.

Hanna shrugs and sets her joint down on *my* end table, since her side of the room is still mostly in boxes. She proceeds to yank a black pencil out of her purse and color her top and bottom eyelids with an insane amount of eyeliner. I guess light charcoal just won't do. "My parents don't like it when I wear too much, so I have to sneak it in my purse. Just like high school, right?"

"Right," I say, even though I don't wear makeup.

"So glad I won't have to do that anymore." She sighs.

"Totally," I say, although I can't relate at all. I don't even know how to put that stuff on. Being raised by my father didn't outright make me a tomboy, but it sure didn't help make me a girlie girl.

"Hear of any parties tonight?" she asks. It's then that I notice Hanna has also changed her clothes from jeans and a polo shirt to a jean skirt, a white tank, and black combat boots. With her blonde hair pulled up in a long ponytail and all the makeup, she reminds me of a Spice Girl.

"No . . . but one of the frat boys said I should come to the fence tonight."

Hanna stops lining her eye, blinks, and then glares at me like I've been holding out on her. "The fence? Who invited you?" she asks.

"Some kid named Marty. He's a sophomore."

The memory of Marty floats over me like a midday tease—*"You have to find it on your own. I can't be the one to tell you."*

"We have to go. Didn't you attend orientation? Didn't you see the big painted fence in the middle of campus? It's legendary."

I wince inside, as if Hanna has just kicked me in the ribs. She isn't allowed to know things about this college that I don't. This is my stomping ground. I was practically born on the doorstep of the student union.

"What's so legendary about it?" I ask, because now I can picture the ugly fence, layered with years of paint, the eyesore on campus painted different colors with random words and symbols plastered on it like bad graffiti. Carnegie Mellon has a rad art program, and I somehow always connected it to that. Dad gave me the ins and outs of everything at the college to make me a better student but left out all the fun parts.

"I guess it's been there forever. If you want your painted message to stay, you have to camp out and guard it. There's even an electrical outlet for people to plug in space heaters outside."

I laugh at the ridiculousness. "Isn't that vandalism?"

"As long as you use a paintbrush, I guess it's not. We have to go! There's only one thing." Hanna pauses and dusts her face with some powder.

"What's that?" I ask.

"I guess if you get invited your first night on campus, they call it a 'paint streak.'"

"What does that mean?" I ask. Hanna is from out of town. She's supposed to be asking me questions about CMU, not the other way around.

I know which cafeteria items are gross and which are not. I know about the shortcut beside Carnegie Library that cuts the wind in half on frigid Pittsburgh days and that Tuesday is new inventory day at the campus bookstore. But now I realize these are all lame facts, and none that will help me at all in making new friends or fitting in.

"It means you have to run to the fence in your underwear!" Hanna screams. "Find your prettiest bra and panties set; we're streaking in the quad at midnight!"

And he certainly didn't teach me about the fence.

We stay up until midnight drinking beer and playing the alphabet game—pop stars (Paula Abdul, Beck, the Cranberries), movies (*A Few Good Men*, *Backdraft*, *Coming to America*), animals (alligator, beagle, caterpillar). We never make it to *D* before switching categories, and Hanna names only selections with hot men in them. Animals are boring.

It's a good roommate icebreaker, and I somehow rationalize that if I balance my drinking with a childish, nerdy exercise like the alphabet game, it somehow makes it okay.

And if I'm going to run half-naked, I'm going to need some reinforcement. Hanna doesn't seem fazed, and I can't believe she even owns the black Victoria's Secret getup she's planning on wearing, let alone is willing to run in it.

I've consented to a sports bra and matching underwear—sporty yet sexy, I think. It basically looks like it could be a swimsuit, which, after a few drinks, I'm convinced is a totally decent thing to wear in public. And I want to see Marty again. That's the real motivation. It's not like

I can get into trouble for it. Not real trouble anyway, like I could for the pot.

Hanna drags me out the door, the sound of my sneakers skidding on the linoleum hallway almost as loud as our laughter.

"No!" I beg. "Can't we just say we couldn't find it?" I ask.

"No way! It will be fun!" Hanna insists.

A few students stick their heads out of their dorm rooms, regarding us with curiosity, but not too much—just two drunk freshmen trotting the halls in their undies.

"Nothing to see here, people!" Hanna yells. A bunch of doors slam, and we skitter down the stairwell.

When the midnight air hits us outside, we start running, and I'm okay with that because the exercise warms me up.

When we get to the fence, there's already a handful of kids painting.

"Shit, we forgot the supplies," Hanna says.

I look at her cross-eyed and bust out laughing. We got so banged up, we forgot the paint and brushes we'd scored at the bookstore.

Another girl in pigtails and a nightgown carts over a red Radio Flyer wagon full of art supplies. "Here ya go."

"What's this?" I ask.

"I'm the fraternity's little sister," she says, as if that explains everything. Then she resumes her solo project of the SAE Greek letters and an advertisement for a party at their house tomorrow night.

"Thanks!" Hanna says and takes a brush out of the wagon and dips it in paint. I do the same. Hanna cups her hand over my ear. "She obviously got a mixed memo on proper paint-and-streak attire."

My giggles transform into frantic gulps as I wonder if Hanna is the one who got it wrong. Maybe it was a nightie and not underwear we were supposed to wear, but then I look around to see two young guys in boxer shorts running for their life to the fence.

This makes me think I'm going to be okay until Hanna paints: *The best things in life make you sweat.*

"I am not staying up all night to guard that message."

"You're no fun." She dots all her *i*'s with hearts.

We paint for a while, and it drips everywhere, and I'm too drunk to even form letters that are readable. Hanna's right, though—this is fun. She's a bit wild, but I decide she's good for me, because I would never have had this adventure on my own. I'm drawn to her the same way I was drawn to Joshua. She pulls me out of my comfort zone, makes me realize the spontaneous part of myself I've buried for fear of messing up.

"Hey, you made it!" My breath catches in my throat just hearing Marty's voice.

I whirl around, holding the paintbrush in front of my breasts, terrified. "I did."

But Marty's not looking at my exposed, paint-splattered body. He grabs a piece of my hair and picks the paint out of it. "Try to get some on the fence next time."

He starts walking away. *No.* "Where're you going?"

"I can't stay long. This was a preliminary hazing event. Rush isn't for a couple more weeks, but those who haven't figured out the simple riddle of where the fence is may not be worthy of a bid." There's a spark of something mischievous in his eyes, that energy buzz I caught earlier in my dorm room. Aside from my summer romance, I haven't had much excitement in my life, and Marty's energy consumes me. I want more of it. He's so sure of himself, confident—everything I lack. His aura isn't assuming, though, and I like how dedicated he is to his frat brothers. He's loyal to the people he cares about. Unlike Joshua.

"You're tough," I say.

"Only as tough as I have to be." He winks, and I feel my face creep with a blush. Hopefully the paint is covering the parts he's making color hot and pink. "You should come by the SAE house for the party, Sarah."

"How do you know my name?" I ask.

He looks right at me. "I would be remiss if I didn't find out the name of the prettiest girl on campus."

It's so cheesy, the pickup line, the formal use of the word—*remiss*—but he says it so confidently, it makes my whole face break into a reluctant smile.

"Oh yeah?" I slap the paintbrush I'm holding back onto the fence, because I'm a nervous wreck. More paint splats on my face.

Marty laughs, jogs back, and picks it back out of my hair.

"Thanks." I laugh.

I look over and notice Tushar Patel, the first of his potential new recruits to make it to the fence, in his red boxer shorts littered with tiny saxophones on them. Tush waves at me with that gorgeous smile, and I wave back, embarrassed that I'm in my underwear, hoping the paint acts as a good concealer from that far away. There are other would-be pledges still running, but Tush is the smallest and the fastest, apparently.

"My best potential pledge," Marty says, as if he's going into battle and these are his troops. He says it in this completely silly manner, though, and I love a guy who doesn't take himself too seriously.

"Why the saxophones?" I ask of his best pledge.

"Well, in addition to his brilliant mind and stunning body, Tush can also play the fucking saxophone. How remarkable is that?"

I'm laughing hard now, and I want to give Marty an answer, but before I can respond, he's rounding up his boys and telling them to hightail it back to the house. "See you later, Sarah. Hopefully tomorrow." He points at the advertisement for the party on the fence and then darts away.

I wave and can't help but notice his perfect ass in his boxer briefs as he shouts obscenities at the other boys. "First one back to the lion statues gets first bid!"

"He's showing off for you," Hanna says.

As they all take off in a dead sprint in the middle of the night, all I can think is—*God, I hope so.*

CHAPTER 7

Present

Everything is not clearer in the morning.

I fill the K-Cup coffee machine with water, but my hands shake fiercely. I can still see remnants of wet leaves stuck beneath my fingernails.

I'll never wash her away.

She'll always be with me.

Recurring images of river rocks matted with dark hair flash before my eyes, along with reimagined episodes of my son submerged and half-conscious in bathwater.

The hiccupping spasms came in waves last night, moments of temporary peace followed by a shaking sensation that gripped me at the chest and percolated out through my mouth in ragged breaths. I never slept, but while ruminating under the sheets waiting for morning to come, I did doze off a couple of times, only to wake with a start. Strangely, my first reaction was to run to the bathroom to make sure Finn hadn't drowned, only to find him sound asleep downstairs on the couch. I checked his breathing each time to make sure it hadn't stopped, a fatal side effect of certain narcotics, I know. But each time I checked on him, his breath was steady.

Sometime during the night, I opened the window to take in the fresh air, only to be disturbed by the melody of a guitar from under the pergola. I was inanely sure it was Joshua, but when I looked out over the lawn, it was just the wind.

Madness is what has become of me now. All the while, Martin slept soundly in bed next to me, which made me hate him in a way I never thought possible. How dare he sleep when Yazmin will never wake again? I thought last night he was at his absolute worst. But watching his breath slow, how his callous heart could fall into a soundless sleep after all we'd done, was so much worse.

To be able to rest while another mother stayed up all night waiting for her little girl to come home—how could he?

His soul was poisoned by the Ellsworths. Maybe he tried to be good, but when it came down to it, he was just like them—evil.

I should leave him and take my boys with me.

These were the spiraling thoughts that hit me from every angle as I lay next to the man I'd called my husband for two decades, and it was devastating.

Martin runs into the kitchen, freshly showered with tailored jeans on and a button-down shirt suitable for work, even though he announced earlier this morning that none of us was to leave the house. He throws his iPad across the quartz countertop, and it slides too fast.

I drop the plastic container of water for the coffee maker—*"shit"*—and catch the iPad before it skids off the end of the counter. "What're you doing?"

The headline on the screen stops me cold. Yazmin's body has been found by a man walking his dog through the park about an hour ago. The discovery of a young girl and the closing of the park make the breaking news, although they haven't identified the body yet. The breath drains out of me. Yazmin's mother must've seen today's news report too.

She is likely praying all the way to the morgue that maybe it could be someone else but knowing deep down after hearing the description that it is her daughter. I can't imagine the agony of that car ride.

These are the true injustices of what we've done—the pain we caused others and are still causing.

I strap my arms over my chest in a crisscrossed pattern. "It's happening."

This is the end.

Martin was in denial yesterday. If we'd called in Yazmin's body when we found her, the two of us, Martin and I, could at least have worked tirelessly on helping Finn. We could've hired the best attorney money could buy, sorted things out with Yazmin's family properly.

Now we're all doomed. They're going to think we're guilty because we didn't report the crime. I'm pretty sure the fact that we didn't report the crime is a crime. It should be if it's not. I've heard the phrase *leaving the scene of an accident* on more than one crime show, but what sentence does it carry with it? What if the person was already dead when you arrived? We definitely tampered with evidence.

I resume the labored breathing I started yesterday. My chest is so sore with stress from the night before. It's like someone has tightened a vise around my rib cage.

"Get it together, Sarah!"

I bristle, because I'm still not used to Martin yelling at me. One of the things that drew me to him was his take-charge stance, his ability to remain cool when things heated up on the home front and at work. I knew I'd always be safe with him, my steady arrow. I'd gone along with everything he'd asked of me so far—Livvy, the lie about the house—but I don't think I can go any further.

"We need to at least tell them we know who the girl is. An anonymous tip." I rake my hands through my freshly blow-dried hair. Martin made me wash it this morning. *"At least make an effort to look like you've slept."* He's never talked to me like that before, and I can't remember a single time when he's said a negative thing about my appearance, at least when he wasn't joking.

"I'm sure the parents have already been alerted. They probably reported her missing." Martin starts pacing, his reasoning barbaric.

Most of the young women I've worked with at the shelter are victims who've suffered at the hands of someone who thought he had the right, the power, the justification to make them hurt, and here I am, no better.

I pause and grip the counter, feeling my body weaken at the core. *What have we done?*

How would I feel if it were Finn?

Left out in the cold all night, all alone.

"No," I whisper and close my eyes, pushing the thoughts away before they bury me.

According to Finn, Alisha Veltri is a single mother who works nights as a dealer at Three Rivers Casino. Martin claimed that it wouldn't be hard to convince her of Finn's alibi, and I hate that he assumed she is unintelligent just because she doesn't hold a white-collar job.

Does he have any idea what kind of effect his comment had on me? I don't know if he even cares at this point. It's like watching him turn into the worst version of himself, the darkest side of his human prism.

I press my hands to my cheeks and start breathing rapidly. "I can't do this, Martin!" I made coffee but left it steaming on the countertop, wanting to climb inside my cup and disappear. Martin ignores me, picking up his phone.

I won't be able to keep this up. It's not in my genetic makeup. I'm not one of *them*. I'm not a true Ellsworth. I wear the fancy clothes, attend the glam galas, groom my kids with the right social circles and schooling, but it's all a ruse. It always has been.

"You will do it for Finn," Martin says, but his ear is pressed to his phone. He covers the receiver only briefly to admonish me, to tell me what I will do.

Who's he calling anyway? Another connection? Another cleaner?
My father was right.

He told me when I married into a family like the Ellsworths, I wasn't just marrying their son. I didn't understand what he meant at the time and laughed it off. *"Come on, Dad, they're not so bad."*

I thought he just didn't like them because the Ellsworths have gobs of money. He doesn't despise Martin like he does some of the other family members, namely, Martin's father, William.

Dad was still hung up on an incident that had occurred at Martin's fraternity my freshman year. One of Martin's fraternity brothers drank too much, and there was a fatal accident because of it. William was legacy at the fraternity and went down to help smooth over the mess, going to bat for the fraternity's charter when it was in jeopardy. Dad was upset because he didn't think the fraternity had been properly reprimanded. He thought there should've been criminal charges pressed against the boys. As he always said—*"money talks."*

That was part of it, but I know he harbored some ill will toward people like the Ellsworths because of what happened to my mother. I always wondered why he didn't want me to be one of the lucky ones who would receive the best of everything—including medical treatment. I think I understand now, though. Wealth comes at a steep price. You have to pay in pieces of your soul to protect your fortune.

Martin points upstairs, too deep in conversation on the phone to verbally communicate with me. We took turns trying to rouse Finn in between Martin's morning calls, but we need to ramp it up. Finn was okay, sober, but he kept dozing back off. We aren't sending him to school today, and it'll only be a matter of time before the police are at our doorstep.

It's understandable that Finn is having trouble waking up. The blood sample Mary Alice drew last night showed that Finn had Rohypnol, marijuana, and methamphetamine in his system. Alton called it a "smoofie," when kids mix marijuana and Rohypnol—the date-rape drug—together. One more thing I couldn't process.

The drugs.

I explained to Alton after we returned home last night that there was no way Finn was into that stuff, and I knew I sounded like every other parent in denial, but Alton knew it too. He's been around Finn since he was a baby. Finn is so cautious, he didn't jump into the swimming pool until he was in middle school. Spencer would cannonball like it was nobody's business, even at the country club where splashing wasn't allowed, but not Finn. He always used the ladder.

"Sometimes kids experiment, and they don't know what they're getting themselves into," Alton said. "The pot could've been laced, and he could've thought it was just pot. That's why he was so knocked out. Roofies can sometimes cause complete blackouts too, so when he says he can't remember, don't think he's lying to you."

I'm certain Finn wouldn't lie to me. It's someone else in this house who's not being forthright. He's done it before. I know he's capable. But not in my wildest dreams did I think he could participate in something as malevolent as this.

I shake Finn's pillow hard this time. In between phone calls, Martin tells me my one job is to get Finn up and dressed and sitting at the kitchen table with a hot cup of coffee—*"presentable."*

They found Yazmin, your girlfriend, dead this morning, Finn. Please get up and brush your teeth and look presentable for the cops so they believe your lies.

What the fuck, Martin? How does he just expect me to snap to attention?

I'm trying to steady my breath again when Finn finally speaks. "Mom?"

His eyes are hazy, but he's there.

Thank God!

I couldn't find him yesterday in the pit of his intoxication, and all night I wondered if I lost him to it, the combination of Yazmin's untimely death and whatever illegal substances he'd consumed killing his spirit, if not his actual body.

His body. I kept putting my ear to his chest last night to make sure he was still breathing. And I placed my fingers to his neck to make sure his pulse was still beating, unable to get the feeling out of my gut when I did the same to his girlfriend and came up empty.

I know it was the head wound that likely killed Yazmin, but a small part of me fears it might've been the drugs.

And that they might take Finn too.

"Finn, thank God."

It was only because of Mary Alice's lame examination that I didn't drive him to the hospital myself. I rationalized there was no way Mary Alice would let harm come to her own grandson. As awful as the Ellsworths are, they love their grandchildren, and if Finn was in real danger, she would've gotten him proper medical care.

His face twists horribly, and he sits up slowly, grabbing his head. "Ahh." His eyes cross. "Yazmin . . . is she . . . ?" He's there. It's really him. He's not ruined by the drugs, but he might be by what I'm about to say.

"Oh, Finn. She cracked her head open hiking. They don't know how. I'm so sorry, honey." The words rattle out of my mouth as if they're trying to escape. I can't slow them down, and I don't know if they're true. But much like when I used the words Martin scripted for me when I texted Alisha, I use the ones he scripted for me to speak to Finn, because it's easier than having to create my own. I don't know how to tell Finn his girlfriend is dead.

"In the hospital?" he asks. His sentences are fragments. He must've hit his head good too, but it's most likely still the effects of the drugs.

"No, sweetie, she didn't survive the wounds," I say.

Finn pulls in his shoulders. "No, no," he says. He places his hands on his head, which is likely pounding. I wrap my arms around him and try to console him, but the only thing I can feel is the awful heat of deceit creeping up my skin as the minutes tick by.

We're running out of time.

"I'm so, so sorry, Finny." *I'm so sorry, but I'm so glad it wasn't you.*

I need to get him up, showered, and presentable. He's shaking in my arms, and I hate that I'm starting to think like Martin—tactical.

"I just can't believe she's gone."

"Do you remember anything about what happened last night?" I ask. *Please, God, don't give me an answer I can't unhear.* I shudder.

"No, not really. I just remember . . ." His voice is muffled into my chest.

"What, Finn?"

"I remember Yazmin saying, *'No, don't.'* Yelling. But I can't remember why."

Fuck. That sounds bad. I look down at the little half-moons on his neck and can't imagine a scenario where these two facts are not related. *Did you try to do something to the girl, and she resisted?* I taste salt in my mouth from biting my tongue. I don't realize it's bleeding until I do. I can't handle the truth if that's what happened.

"I know this is a lot for you to take in right now. Finn, we didn't call the cops because Dad thought they'd haul you in right away, and we didn't think you hurt Yazmin."

"Didn't think I hurt her?" Finn hasn't looked at me with eyes that torn up since his pet terrier got run over by a delivery truck, but what he's told me does not paint this situation in a good light. It's impossible for me to imagine him hurting another kid, especially a girl. He was the kid on the playground who didn't squish the bugs on the pavement like the other boys because he didn't want to hurt them.

Finn is our sensitive kid. He made it all the way to second-degree black belt in tae kwon do. He can spar like an MMA fighter, but I've never once seen him show aggression outside of the dojo.

I remember the positioning of Yazmin's body again on that river rock, her arms up like a block, and wonder if it means anything. My first thought was that she'd been attacked. And now I'm fairly certain she was, after what he's told me, but I can't believe it unless he tells me himself.

"Well, honey"—my voice shakes—"we didn't know what happened, if maybe there was an accident. We wanted to talk to you first, but you were so out of it."

His face drains of all color, and he leans forward and places his hand over his mouth. I grab the utility bucket beside the couch and place it in front of him. He yacks up something brown and foul, food and drugs, most likely. I turn my head but hold the bucket steady.

"I'm so sorry . . . ," he groans in between heaves.

I give him a tissue, and he wipes his face. "About the drugs, she said it was just a joint. But it wasn't." He's shaking. "It definitely wasn't." He's in withdrawal, but I only feel sorry for him right now, not angry.

"We're not mad about the drugs."

He looks at me strangely, one eye shut because he can't open them both the whole way.

"I mean, we're not happy, but that's the least of our worries."

Finn is chugging the bottle of water I'd set overnight on the end table, nodding at me for believing his story, his skinny arms shaking on his six-foot frame.

"Finn, what happened last night?" Now I'm desperate to know, because the not knowing or talking about it will kill us both.

He stops mid-drink and places the cap back on the water. "I don't know. Yaz got the drugs from some guy in town, just some pot. I told her I didn't do that stuff, but she teased me, said it's practically legal."

"And then?"

He sighs. "We hiked, then fought about a stupid Instagram post. The next thing I remember, I was waking up in the woods, Dad was there, and I knew something bad had happened, but I couldn't remember what."

The air is sucked from my chest. Finn's words are so lucid, too raw to be those of a liar.

And Martin is right. The drugs were Yazmin's idea. Of course they were. They'd been laced with methamphetamine and roofies, and she'd sold Finn on a tale that the weed was as safe as medicinal CBD oil. Whether she knew it was doctored or she didn't really doesn't matter.

Yazmin's smart—the school treasurer; she should've known better. Every other week, kids were dying in the area from laced drugs, usually heroin cut with fentanyl, but none of it was safe. And now it got her killed. Not Finn. Not my son.

They would've blamed Finn whether he'd fled the scene or not.

Martin is right. I hate that his side of the story is starting to hold up.

I shake my head, though, because it still doesn't make it right.

"You need to shower. The cops will be here. You need to tell them that you smoked the joint with Yazmin, you two got into a fight, and then you came home. Your dad is going to cover for you that you were home all night and that you went straight to bed before nine o'clock, slept all night. I was at the shelter."

"So you want me to lie?"

I inhale, the stench of vomit and sweat and teenage mistakes meeting my nostrils with regret. I made mistakes in this very house. I was just lucky none of them came back to bite me. It's my job to protect Finn from his mistakes. We need to make him promise to do better in the future. Now that I have most of the facts, I decide this is a learning opportunity, but not one that he should go to jail for. I wasn't sure until I talked to him, but Finn has been misled, and I will help get him back on the right track, no matter what I have to do.

Too late to change our course now.

"Only about going into the woods. Please get in the shower." I pat down a piece of Finn's slick hair. He's far from Martin's version of presentable.

If Finn was at the scene of the crime and on drugs but couldn't remember what happened, it could be cause for them to charge him with involuntary manslaughter. There is a whole Netflix series based on people wrongly accused of crimes and not proven innocent until years later. This quiet community won't settle until Yazmin's life is accounted for, and Finn is the easiest person to point their finger at. They'll nail him to the wall if they can. I still don't know exactly what happened, but I know enough to deem Finn innocent.

Finn shakes his head. "But—"

"Finn, they'll stick you in jail. Dad says they can't arrest you if they can't place you at the scene of the crime. If Dad says you were here, you were here. All night. And they can't take you away in handcuffs." I stress *"Dad,"* but I realize I'm just as complicit in all this and the one giving him the exact instructions on how to lie. It's the distorted reality that we're trapped in. *Why am I including Finn in it?*

Finn blanches. Reality has set in.

This is why. Because he won't survive if we don't. He can't even stomach the word—*jail*. Finn covers his mouth again, and I raise the bucket, but instead, he looks at me angrily and throws off the blankets. His limbs involuntarily shake, and I think he might fall off the couch, but he successfully makes it upstairs and into the bathroom because I hear the water running.

I've just told my son to lie. About a teenage death. I'm the worst mother ever. I'm teaching him bad moral lessons. How to abandon a body and get away with it.

But he's left us with no other choice. This is a rough patch, a bad page in our family history book, I tell myself, and we'll get through it—I hope.

I go upstairs and lay out clothing for him. A pair of boot-cut jeans, sans holes, and a casual blue-collared shirt. I even lay out his boxers and socks so he doesn't have to think about it.

As I descend the stairs, Martin gives me a thumbs-up from his office, and I assume it's for getting Finn in the shower. He's pressed to the front window like a Labrador waiting for the mail truck to arrive. I presume he's waiting for the real police (not Alton).

After a short shower, Finn uses the handrail to thud down the steps, half squinting. I want to be upset with him for being grossly hungover, but the poor kid was drugged last night.

"Here, honey." I have a hot cup of coffee waiting for him in my spotless kitchen, and as soon as his ass hits the chair, I exhale. I've completed my first assignment. My next job will be holding it together while they question him.

As soon as Martin sees us in the kitchen, he ends his call and strides hurriedly into the room. I thought it was to embrace his son, but instead, he grabs Finn's arm so viciously, he almost spills his coffee.

"*Martin.*"

"Ow, Dad."

He twists Finn's arm around so he can see the underside of it, then rips off the damp cotton ball and tape Mary Alice fastened to his skin after the blood withdrawal last night. "*Fuck,*" Martin swears. "This could've screwed up everything."

I'm shocked by his reaction. That's what he was doing on the phone. Retracing our steps to make sure we've covered up the right ones.

Finn looks scared. "Did I shoot up last night?" His voice is pitchy like he hasn't hit puberty yet.

"No, son. We did a blood draw to see what was in your system. The joint was laced, but you can't know that right now when the police question you. You remember nothing. Just say the drugs made you sick and that's why you came home."

"Okay." He looks confused, understandably so.

"Your grandma took your blood last night and Alton screened it," I explain. I'm trying like hell to be strong, but I want to knock Martin out. He isn't helping here.

"Did you go over everything with him?" Martin asks. He's smoothing down Finn's collar.

"I think so."

"You think so?" he asks. Martin looks like a molded replica of William from the night before, when he asked us to sit before him in his sick little circle of liars. The corners of his mouth are sliced with deep lines where a gentle smile used to exist, panicked eyes behind thick frames.

"Yes. I did. All truth except for the woods."

"You left the woods early last night, Finn. You never called us to come get you." Martin slams down stapled documents in front of his face. "If they pull phone records, you were calling Mom at the shelter to see if she was coming home for dinner, because I asked you to. Our house is close enough to the park that it will track from the same tower." I can't help but feel startled that my husband is aware of this fact.

Finn jumps and jostles his coffee. "Okay," he says.

My hands shake as I grab a tea towel and wipe up the dribble quickly. Everything in its place. *Presentable.*

"See these college brochures—Brown, Harvard, Penn? You might as well burn them if you say you stayed in those fucking woods for more than two minutes—do you understand me?" The vein on Martin's head is like a pulsing snake, and I have a sudden urge to tap it with my finger and puncture it.

"Yes, sir," Finn whispers, and he is scared. His eyes are filling with tears.

"You're upsetting him, Martin. He's been through enough."

"Tears are good. He needs to grasp the gravity of this situation."

Finn shoots a look in my direction, but I can't meet it, because I'm too ashamed to be a part of this. Martin may have turned into a monster—but so have I.

"I'm glad tears work for your story," I mouth off, and now I'm fighting my own.

"This is for Finn. He messed up and did drugs and things ended badly for him, but it shouldn't destroy him. It's one mistake. He won't make it again. Right, Finn?" Martin asks.

"No, I definitely will not," he says. And for the first time, I don't know if I believe my son.

I stare at my husband with loathing, not because he so desperately wants to help Finn but because he's so methodical about it. Yazmin Veltri's life means nothing to him. She was a mistake and nothing more.

"We just need to get through this. These next few weeks will be really tough and the months to follow might not be great, but once the year is over and Finn is off to school, this will be nothing but a bad memory we don't care to recall. Think long game here," Martin says, as if we're betting at the tables.

The doorbell rings, and Martin springs to his feet.

"Get it together—the cops are here," he says over his shoulder.

I sit down beside Finn and squeeze his hand. "I'll love you no matter what you tell them," I say for only Finn to hear, secretly hoping he'll have the strength to tell them what I couldn't.

"Thanks, Mom. I love you too."

My heart breaks, because I realize I hope more than anything in the world that Finn decides to lie. I don't want to see him ruin his brilliant life because of a bad decision.

Lord knows I've made my fair share.

CHAPTER 8

1996—Freshman Year

"Well, honey, I expected you to let your hair down a little when you got here, but I didn't think you'd strip down to your skivvies on the very first day." Dad is in my dorm room delivering the hot plate that I forgot at home, but my face is what's warm. Hanna explodes into a fit of giggles.

"Ugh . . ." He's got to be talking about Monday night's visit to the fence, and I can't tell if he's upset with me or not.

"I thought you'd at least make it past syllabus day before you ran around campus naked. That usually doesn't happen until second semester."

"I. Um. Am . . ." Speechless.

Hanna was tucked under her bedspread reading, but she's laughing so hard now that she's kicked off her sheets and is almost crying.

"Listen here, Hanna Banana, I'm sure Ramona and Gregory wouldn't exactly be over the moon about you riding shotgun on this little adventure either." Hanna stops giggling and draws in an enormous breath.

"Riding shotgun? She was driving," I say and then feel immediately guilty for throwing Hanna under the bus.

"Where do you think streaking through the quad fits into Gregory's procurement checklist for the best college experience?" Dad's rubbing the stubble of his beard in a thoughtful way.

Hanna pulls her comforter back on and shrinks beneath it. "Please don't tell them. I'll be grounded my entire fall break."

Dad shoots her a Cheshire Cat grin. "Don't worry, Hanna. I won't tell."

She lets out an audible sigh and releases a handful of bedding.

"Just remember, I work here. When you ladies prance around campus with no clothes on, I'm going to find out about it."

"Are you mad?" I ask. I'm sitting at my desk, covering half my face with my hand because—*how embarrassing*.

"No, hell, I'm not mad. The fence is as legendary as this university. Just wanted to let you know, for full disclosure, I have eyes everywhere. And I mean *everywhere*."

"Oh crap," Hanna says.

"That's right. You don't have me fooled either, sweetheart. Tight-ass parents make the most rebellious children, and your mother's sphincter is tighter than the Tupperware container she—"

"*Dad!* She doesn't know you. You're scaring her." I palm my whole face now, because how can he not know he's being inappropriate? I've tried to teach him over the years. It's the reason I didn't ask for playdates when I was in elementary school. The kids never came back.

"I'm just kidding around." He lets out one of his deep, raspy laughs that would make someone certain he's a smoker even though he hasn't touched a cancer stick since Mom passed away. Hanna forces a smile, but the damage is already done. I'm not sure how Dad planned to end his sentence about Hanna's mother, but any version I imagine can't be a good one.

"No worries—just be safe out there, ladies. Greek rush is coming up. Stay away from those frat boys; they're nothing but trouble. Promise me." He looks right at me.

"Okay," I manage, then hold my breath. My ears are burning, because it's the first time I've ever lied to my father right to his face.

I feel Hanna shoot me a worried look. I know what she's thinking. Is the maintenance man going to know about every guy she sleeps with? Does he know about my date tonight?

Dad gives me a huge hug, which strangely isn't awkward given his little speech. I've lived with his blatant honesty my whole life.

Dad whistles playfully before saying, "That's all, folks."

Hanna waves goodbye, then dives under her covers again, practically hemorrhaging the words, *"Oh my God, oh my God."*

Shit. I hope she won't put in for a room transfer. Hanna watches out for me. Not to mention, I suck at making new friends, and I need someone to go to frat parties with. Although there's only one frat boy I'm interested in seeing again, and he's picking me up in exactly one hour.

The night after our streak to the fence, Hanna insisted we go to the SAE party. Marty was surprised to see me and wasted no time telling me about a new place he had to show me that'd just opened up on Liberty Avenue. He used words like *incredible architecture* and *a building with an old soul*—descriptions that really spoke to me, like the museums Dad used to take me to as a kid. My mother loved museums too—*"an opportunity to take in the world's beauty,"* she used to say.

I couldn't say no when Marty asked me if I wanted to check out the place.

Hanna squeals. "Is your dad going to lose his shit when he finds out about your date? Because you know he will!"

"He made that rule after I already had the date," I argue.

"So then, it doesn't count?" Hanna throws a pillow at me.

I catch it and shake my head. "Right. Besides, it would be rude if I canceled now. Less than fifty minutes . . . I need to get ready!" I toss the pillow back.

Hanna punches it with her fist. "Yes, you do. Go, girl, go! I'm totally on board with your rationalization for lying to your dad, by the way. I was just teasing. It sounds like something I would do."

I bite my cheek, both at her saying the words—*"lying to your dad"*—and at the realization that Hanna is rubbing off on me. But if things don't go well tonight, I swear I'll at least try to keep my promise to him—no more frat boys.

"Will you do my makeup?" I ask Hanna.

"Sure." She leaps out of bed, grabs her Caboodle, and positions herself in front of my desk. I try to brush my hair while she messes with my face. My hair has always been stick straight, so I just run a brush through it and give it a little spritz for shine.

"Look up." Hanna adds the last stripe to my eyelid, and then there's a knock on the door.

We both glare at the clock. "Your boy's ten minutes early. Damn, you already have him trained," Hanna whispers.

"Shh." I run to the door, a nervous wreck. I haven't even checked the smoky eye Hanna insisted I needed, part of the grunge-rock revolution, which all seems contradictory to the Backstreet Boys humming from the radio in the background. I open the door.

Marty leans in. "Hey, Sarah."

My breath catches, and I can't respond.

"Hi, Marty." Hanna saves me.

"Hey, Hanna." He waves. "My car's outside. Are you ready?" Marty is a doorway leaner. He did it the last time he was in my room, and he's doing it again now, balancing his narrow body between the cream-colored walls, his brown leather jacket hanging at his side with his arms outstretched like he owns the place.

I stare down at my jeans and the nicest sweater I own, an emerald-green number from American Eagle with a braided-rope pattern down the front in a vertical line. It was my Christmas sweater from the year before, and I purchased it because I knew I'd be able to get a lot of wear out of it. Everything I buy is thought of in terms of utility. "Is this okay?" I point to my outfit. "For tonight?" I ask, because I'm still not sure where we're going.

Marty's eyes zip up and down my body, and his little half grin appears. "You look perfect."

Perfect. My cheeks lift into an involuntary smile.

Hanna pulls off her headphones. "You look hot, Sarah."

"Thanks." I giggle. Hanna cracks her gum and places her headphones back on, giving me a thumbs-up while pretending to read this month's issue of *Glamour*.

"You really do. Let's go," Marty says.

"Okay."

Now that Marty has agreed with my indisputable hotness, my body is tingly and on edge like the first time we were together. They call it butterflies, but these are more like pterodactyls.

I have such little experience with boys, I'm not sure what to expect on a real first date. My crash course on sex ed occurred just this past summer with Joshua, my guitar-playing crush. It was never supposed to be anything serious, a summer fling, but he was my first, and I got caught in his tailspin when he skipped town without saying goodbye. Joshua left a giant hole where my heart used to be, and I promised myself the next one would be different.

The next one would be reliable, educated, steady, not some reckless artist with a score to settle with the world.

The few real dates I went on in high school were mostly doubles, a friend of a friend who was going out with me as the obligatory fourth wheel. The boy usually got off easy with a tub of popcorn at the theater and an extra soda for me. So this version of dating, where couples went out like proper adults, dined with silverware, and were expected to make small talk for the better part of an hour, was something I'd seen only in the movies. Joshua and I mostly stayed at his house, out of the view of his parents. We spent more time with our lips pressed together than apart, but the talks we'd had were intense, mostly big-picture topics—drugs, abortion, war. It wasn't normal teenage chatter, I realize, but somehow I don't think anyone else could stack up.

"How're your classes?" Marty asks.

"Fine," I say, but I'm worried that he's already asking this question. It's one I planned on asking over dinner when I'd obsessed about this date for the better part of the last forty-eight hours. "I'm surprisingly underwhelmed. I expected them to be much harder, actually." The fall air tickles the hairs on my head, and I would've worn a jacket, but I didn't have one that went with this sweater.

"Well, aren't you an overachiever," he jokes.

"I wouldn't say that." *Oh, damn.* I don't want to sound full of myself, but I'm surprised by how manageable my classes are. My father made CMU sound like the military. *The students are early to rise and keep a strict schedule to make their grades.*

Marty's car is parked on the street, a black Saab convertible, old but in mint condition.

"Nice ride," I say.

"Thanks. It was my mom's," he says, and I love that he admits this. Most guys wouldn't. Marty has scored a few more small points with me in the humility category that are starting to add up.

He didn't peek at my bare flesh at the fence.

He had blatant candor about things that would embarrass most guys his age.

And the background info on his car tells me that Marty is wealthy enough for his parents to own a Saab but not wealthy enough to buy him a brand-new one. I'm okay with this, although hanging with even the semiwealthy is outside my comfort zone.

Marty opens the door for me, then hops in the convertible driver's side without opening his door. I laugh at him, and I like the way the leather seats feel worn and loved.

"What is the name of this place?" I ask. We turn on Bigelow Boulevard, heading out of Oakland.

"It's a surprise." His voice has a teasing quality to it that I like, similar to when he told me I'd have to find the fence on my own.

"Oh, okay," I say, trying to hide the excitement in my voice. All the classic novels I grew up reading spoiled me with debonair men who met their love interest wit for wit, like Mr. Darcy in *Pride and Prejudice*.

Of course, this left me disappointed in real life. The only boy I've met with any wit was Joshua, although it might've only seemed like he had wit because he was high most of the time we talked, which always made him sound more philosophical.

Marty is the first person I've met of interest since Joshua, and I'm not sure if all these little details I'm picking out are remarkable qualities or if he's just so opposite Joshua that I'm using them to validate my attraction to him.

Marty parallel parks on Liberty Avenue like a practiced race-car driver, and I want to sleep with him based on his spatial ability alone. There's something sexy about a guy who can handle a wheel.

He hops out and opens my passenger door. "Come on."

"Thank you." I exit the vehicle, but all I see along the busy street are old row homes, businesses, and one gigantic church with a line of people in front of it.

"I thought we were going to dinner," I say, confused.

Oh no, I hope he's not one of those religious nuts taking me to his New Age church that operates more like a cult.

They've been springing up everywhere, and since Mom lost her battle with cancer, I've had mixed feelings on religion.

"We are," he says with a laugh, and his voice immediately relaxes me. "They just converted this place from a church to a restaurant over the summer. It's brand-new. Thought we could check it out."

I take a closer look at the banner hanging from the church—THE CHURCH BREW WORKS.

"Oh, cool." I'm relieved. A brew pub sounds low-key, just my style. And I like that Marty is into trying out the new place in town.

Hanna went out with a guy over the summer who took her to the mall food court on their first date, where they ate greasy Chinese food and then had sex in his bedroom while his little brother was asleep on the opposite side of the room. I told her that sounded awful, and she said that it was, and that neither the food nor the sex was satisfying.

I smile at the memory, happy that I've made a real female friend. Hanna seems to understand my social ineptness and accepts me, in all my awkward forms. She helps break me out of my shell, does all the talking when we're trying to get into parties, and taught me how to put on eyeliner. Hanna's taking care of me in her own way—a *"good egg,"* as Dad would say.

As we stand in line, I shiver at the slight chill in the air. Marty doesn't ask; he just takes off his coat and drapes it around my shoulders. The sexy whiff of Polo cologne touches my senses, and I close my eyes for a moment, because I can almost imagine the fragrance pressed against my body sometime later. "Thank you."

"You're welcome." I open my eyes, and he shoots me a wide smile, and his teeth are perfectly straight. "I didn't expect a line on a Thursday," he says.

"It's Friday Eve, as my dad would say."

"Ha. I like that."

I smile, thinking—*I like you.*

When we finally make it inside, I'm mesmerized by the wooden pews converted into hardtop booths, ornate carvings on the sides that resemble symbols on playing cards, and beautiful stained-glass windows lining the walls. The white ceilings peak and trough with wooden beams accented like a meringue whipped topping.

There's something intrinsically beautiful about a fragile and forgotten object that's been repurposed. Like me, being here in college, sitting across from this boy who probably never would've known I existed if we'd passed on the street last week. But in this space, this place, I matter. Josh made me feel like I mattered, but only in the confines of the hidden corners of his house. In truth, he kept me a secret. Here I am now in this beautiful place with this gorgeous boy, and he's not trying to hide me from anyone. And it's the sexiest thing in the whole world. Marty's playing on an inner soft spot he doesn't know exists by taking me to an old building, something else my mother loved.

There's a chain of abandoned steel-mill warehouses the city bought up and renovated into industrial-style lofts, and the online pictures made me drool in awe. But that's not what this place reminds me of.

The waiter comes by to take our drink orders, and I ask for a soda, because I'm not old enough to drink beer *here*. Not that I need alcohol to entertain myself tonight.

"What do you think?" Marty asks.

"Very cool. Reminds me of this house I love in Sewickley." I shrug, as if to say, *Who could ever afford that?* "It has old woodworking and biblical windows too."

"Oh yeah? Whereabout in Sewickley?" he asks.

"In the Heights. Off Blackburn Road." I wave my hand in the air, because there's no way he's seen it. He's probably just making conversation. I don't want Marty to know of it, because I want to leave that place in the past. It just won't leave me for some reason.

Marty nods. "I think I know the one."

"Really?" I ask, doubtful that's possible. Even if he did know the back roads of Sewickley, that house is pretty well hidden. There's no way Marty knows where Joshua's house is; that would be too ridiculously coincidental. And awful. No part of this life should ever touch any part of that one. I'm a different person here. I need to leave that Sarah behind.

"Yeah, I went to the Academy," he says.

I look down at my hands. "Oh . . ." Marty Ellsworth may drive an old Saab, but he's not semiwealthy; he's filthy rich. Especially if he's familiar with the houses in the Heights. Certainly he's not familiar with Joshua or he'd say so. There's no way for me to ask Marty if he knows Joshua without revealing how I do, so I won't. "Very impressive."

"Not really." He brushes it off. "So you're a business major. What kind of work do you want to do?" I like that Marty seems genuinely interested in my future plans. The fact that we are both here, at this university, following this natural path together makes me feel closer to him. Joshua was always one to buck the system.

"Work for a nonprofit, I think. Preferably an organization that benefits children. I did a lot of community work with my father before I came here, and I really enjoyed it."

"Nice. That's admirable."

"Thanks. How about you?"

"I'm in the robotics program, engineering. But I help out on the community front too. My uncle's a state legislator. I've worked on his campaign."

"Oh, really? Who's your uncle?" I ask.

"Edward Ellsworth," he says, and I try not to crinkle my nose. Now I know where I've heard Marty's last name before.

"I lean right but tread somewhere closer to the middle," he says, as if sensing my judgment.

I nod, because most boys I know don't even watch the news. Having someone up on current events is more important than someone who has the same exact political views as I do, although I sure wish he "leaned" the other way.

"Is it a deal breaker?" he asks, making a pained face that's so cute, I'm almost convinced to change my affiliation. *Almost.*

"No, who can trust any politicians anyway?" I ask, then immediately regret it. "I mean, except your uncle, of course."

"Of course." He shoots me a wry smile, and I'm relieved when our drinks are delivered.

We both order sandwiches and fries, and he could've let it rest. Even I know politics and religion are taboo on first dates, but Marty isn't like other guys.

"I mean, your president can't even appropriate campaign funds correctly. Hello, Whitewater. Or admit to smoking a joint, but if you like that sort of guy, I can work with that," he says.

My cheeks color. "He's disappointing, but a man's personal actions don't always bleed into their professional ones. I mean, who hasn't smoked a joint?"

"Right. So just admit it, then," he says.

"He didn't say he never tried it, just that he didn't inhale." And even as I say the words, I feel like a hypocrite.

"Right." We both laugh, and Marty makes a gesture with his straw like he's smoking a cigarette. "That doesn't speak very highly of his character, though, does it? He should own it."

I bite my straw because I agree with him, but I don't want to admit it. Couples have survived opposing political viewpoints before, haven't they? Maybe it would make for good debate. Since Marty is a leaner—a doorway leaner, a political leaner—maybe I could get him to lean my way.

"Anyway . . . ," I say. We look at each other and laugh. We sure haven't run out of things to talk about like I feared.

Our food is delivered, and it's a great time to dig in.

"How's rush recruitment going?" I ask.

"I'm glad you brought it up. I wouldn't have normally jumped the gun so quickly in asking you out, but I'm going to be tied up for the next couple of weeks. We give out eight bids, and it's a trying process, and then I'm responsible for those boys."

"Right." I think it's cute that he's making excuses for asking me out so soon. "It's hard enough to babysit Hanna; I can't imagine adding seven more girls. I had to wash vomit out of her hair Tuesday night.

She's a good girl, though," I conclude, because I don't want to talk badly of her.

Marty laughs. "She's not afraid. She went right up to Meat and asked him if he got his name honestly."

I nearly spit out the bacon from my club sandwich. "No, she didn't."

"She did. It's funny. Meat is a big guy, but he doesn't know how to accept female flirtation. He's not confident unless he's in the driver's seat. I don't think he gave her much of a response. Your girl should chill a bit."

I shrug. "Her dad's in procurement. She's led a dull life."

Marty cracks up. "Right. So anyway. Don't think I'm going MIA on you the next couple of weeks."

My heart flutters that he cares so much about what I think already. This hottie from the Heights. "I'm okay with it as long as Tush gets a bid."

Marty gives me a smirk I can't read. "He will. I don't know why the kid tries so hard. He attempted to keep up with Meat the other night at beer pong and nearly drowned in the frat house toilet. Someone physically pulled his head out of the water."

"Ugh. Gross. He's not big enough to keep up with Meat."

"He's not big enough to keep up with any of us, but God help him, he tries."

I grin. "Well, as long as you keep your promise, I'll excuse your absence."

Marty's smile stretches to the corners of his lamb-chop sideburns, and even though I don't love them, they're my favorite shade of brown and they match his warm chocolate eyes. "You've got a deal, Sarah Denning."

CHAPTER 9

Hanna and I receive an invitation to the next SAE party delivered as a cryptic flyer under our door. Marty said he'd be busy, and I smile at the paper, thinking he's trying to be coy.

When we arrive at the party, the pledges greet us at the front door. They're polishing the lions guarding the front steps, the iconic statues that have been there since the fraternity was erected. We giggle at the polishers and learn it's a hazing ritual. I can almost hear Marty's commanding voice in my head doling out the silly orders. *"Now, polish the beasts!"*

The frat house is packed to the gills, and when I finally have enough guts to ask Meat where Marty is, I'm told he's busy with the pledges. "Rush started; he likely won't be available for a while."

I'm disappointed, but he warned me of this. The live music from the living room distracts me. A Jay-Z song got muted, and a pleasant sound now fills my ears. The only music comes from a single boy standing in the middle of the room playing a saxophone.

Hey, I know that boy.

There's a group of girls fawning over Tushar Patel as he crushes it on saxophone. I've never seen a kid that small with pipes so big, but damn he can play, and I love his pick.

He's playing Dave Matthews Band, the saxophone solo from "Ants Marching." I'm practically salivating as he knocks it out of the park. I'd take DMB over Jay-Z any day of the week.

"Kid's gotta work what he's got, and he's got that good," Hanna says.

I nod, because even though Tushar has maybe twenty pounds on me, he's sexy as hell playing that saxophone. There's always been something about musicians that drives me wild. It's probably because music bleeds into my body when it resonates, and when someone can play well, it's like my soul teems with it. Tush reminds me of Josh right now, eyes closed, playing what he knows so intimately, he doesn't need an audience.

Josh never needed one either, playing on those steps of the pergola at Stonehenge. My heart aches at the memory of him and then at the awful way he left, fast and with no goodbye.

The alcohol is making me nostalgic and angsty.

Once Tush finishes his set, I'm overcome with emotion and make a point to tell him how talented he is.

"Thanks!" he says, and I let him recover because he's awfully winded.

He wipes the sweat from the skin above his bedroom eyes and places his saxophone back in its case. My heart melts, and I wonder if I'm swooning over the wrong boy. "Where's your fearless leader anyway?" I ask.

"He's MIA," Tush says, and if I'm guessing correctly, he's slightly disappointed I brought up Marty in the hopes that maybe his sexy sax playing was enough to turn me his way.

"I see that." I look around.

Tush closes his case. "I think he had a sniffle or something like that. He went to the nurse today. I'll go see if I can find him."

I can't help but crack a smile at his choice of the word *sniffle*. "Okay, great talking to you."

"You too." His smile is brilliant and white, and his slim body is easily swallowed by the mass of people as he walks away.

Hanna spills beer on me as she hands me a red Solo cup. "Sorry, they overfilled!"

I take it even though I don't need any more alcohol.

"Excuse me," one of the frat brothers says as he squeezes by, and all the guys in the house are nice and preppy, not smarmy and belligerent as I had expected from watching cult classics like *Animal House* and *Revenge of the Nerds*. By the time we leave, Hanna is disappointed she hasn't been accosted, and I'm bummed I haven't bumped into Marty.

Everything is fuzzy when we get home, and I don't know what was in that beer, but I fall into an unprecedented black hole of sleep until the next morning. Hanna is still speaking when I doze off. When I wake up, I discover I haven't even taken off my clothes first or climbed under my comforter.

My hair smells like smoke, sweaty and stuck to my face with drool. I don't want to open my eyes, but there's an awful sound outside, and I'm wondering if we're having a tornado, because there can be no other plausible reason for a whine that loud unless we are under attack.

"Wha . . . what is that?" I ask, but I realize my voice doesn't register because my throat doesn't have enough moisture to make sound.

Hanna springs out of bed first and peers through the blinds. She's wearing tiny shorts and a tank top, her clean hair pulled up in a nice ballerina's bun. She tosses me a leftover bottle of water and says, "Something's going on out there. The campus police are flying down the roads and the city cops are too."

We're close enough to the hospitals, and Oakland isn't exactly the nicest part of Pittsburgh, so the thrumming of cop cars isn't rare, but they usually blare at night, and there typically aren't quite so many of them all at one time making horrid noises.

"Oh shit. They're on campus. Like, parking right outside."

Hanna slips on some sloppy sweatpants and a GAP hoodie. "Come on, Sarah, get your ass up; someone could be hurt."

I roll my eyes and put my pillow back over my face. Hanna is full of shit. She doesn't care if anyone is hurt—she just wants to see what all the drama is about.

I hear her grab her toothbrush caddy to go to the community bathrooms. "You'll be sorry if you miss this."

Yeah, well, you said I'd be sorry if I missed the party last night, and today I feel like hell.

Slowly, I sit up in bed and decide whether motion is possible. *"Fuck,"* I groan. My head feels like it's going to split in two. I almost wish I'd hurled last night and gotten it out of the way already, because I feel like I still might.

"I can't change my clothes," I say. Motion is possible, but there are limits.

"Cool. Get up." Hanna is persuasive, and I've told her multiple times that if the engineering thing falls through, she should try sales.

I stand and place a ball cap on my head, pulling my matted hair through the other side and knotting it in a ponytail so no one can see the grease factor. Then I obediently follow Hanna to the bathrooms and brush my teeth. Hanna splashes water on my face and applies moisturizer and concealer over the dark circles under my eyes. She also smears some lip gloss on my mouth for—*color.* "Don't say I never did anything for you."

"Thanks," I say, but I feel barely human.

Hanna marches us down the stairs, and we join the crowd of students on the sidewalk walking toward the commotion. There are fire trucks, Pittsburgh police cars, ambulances, and campus security barricading the roads, all lined up on Morewood—right in front of the SAE house. I'm fighting the urge to move faster, every step a struggle, but the panic is so thick, it's like a fog making it hard to breathe. I manage to inhale and exhale, and it hurts.

The sun is so bright, it makes my stomach flip. I try to turn around so I can vomit in the comfort of my own dorm room, but Hanna grabs my arm. "Ugh." I'm too weak to resist her.

"What happened?" Hanna asks a fellow student.

He presses pause on his Walkman and slips off his headphones. "I heard one of the SAE pledges died last night. Alcohol poisoning. Hazing exercise. They're in deep," he says and then puts his headphones back on and continues walking.

"Oh no," I say.

"Someone freaking died. At a party we were at last night." Hanna almost whispers the words, and it's the quietest I've ever seen her. Her face is the color of fresh-driven snow, and if I'm to guess, it's her first brush with death. It's unfortunately not mine. "Poor Marty," I say out loud, because as awful as it feels to lose a student—possibly a friend, if it was one of the guys I knew—I'm worried about Marty, the pledge master.

Hanna's azure eyes light up like she's just hit the Powerball of gossip. "There are other frat boys, Sarah. I don't think you want that one. He sounds like trouble."

"Hanna, he made people paint a fence and polish lions. I can't imagine this is all his fault."

She pulls a face, making me feel like the most naive child on the planet. When we walk closer to the scene, more details are revealed.

Two girls in sorority jackets are hugging each other and crying. They must be upperclassmen. "Poor Tush."

I gasp for air and tug on the sleeve of the one closest to me. "It was Tush who died?" I ask.

She nods sadly, and I begin to sob. *"No."* He was such a cool kid.

"Oh shit," Hanna says and gives me a hug. "He could rock it on the sax; what a shame. I saw you talking to him last night. Must be trippy that he's gone today. Sorry, Sarah. Damn, your boy is in trou-ble."

"He must be devastated," I say, clawing at my eyes.

"Wake up, Sarah. It happened at a hazing event. Marty is in charge of the pledges."

It's a long week, and I don't hear from Marty. The school is buzzing with rumors, and none of the brothers has been formally charged. Hanna and I are in the cafeteria, but I'm not hungry. The school newspaper says the pledge master was not on campus the night in question due to illness. "I should bring Marty some soup."

Hanna takes her ponytail and twists it around her finger while she sucks soda through a straw. "Huh?"

"He was recently sick. I should get a to-go container and bring him some soup."

"You're hopeless." She sighs. "There're other boys, Sarah. Lots of other boys."

There were other boys, but all of them would've looked at my body that night at the fence, or at least taken a peek. And none of them had been wrongly accused of murder and were in dire need of soup.

Hanna excuses herself to get to class. I'm not even sure if Marty will be at the frat house, where he lives, but I can at least try. So I make the trek to Morewood. It's getting colder across campus as fall settles in, the wind tunneling through the city streets, cutting through my thin corduroy jacket.

When I make it to the front door, half-frostbitten, I ring the doorbell, and a kid with curly bedhead and squinty eyes asks me who I'm looking for.

"Marty Ellsworth."

The kid stares at me oddly. "You're not a reporter, are you?" he asks.

"No, definitely not."

The kid looks behind him. "Is Marty back to school or is he still at home?"

"Back. Upstairs," someone mutters from inside.

"Back?" I ask.

"He took a sabbatical until his dad could talk to the dean and until they could clean the house. Hold on. Marty!" the kid yells.

I'm left on the doorstep feeling like a dope, and I wonder what Marty's dad has to do with anything.

Then I see Marty walk down the stairs. When he sees me standing on the stoop, he looks dumbfounded, closing the front door so we're standing on the flat patio by the stairs with the polished lions.

"Hey, Sarah. I heard you were looking for me at the party, and I meant to call you, but I've been a little busy." He looks sheepish and tired but not the least bit sick. Hopefully he's recovered, but the gift in my hand seems ridiculous now.

"Oh yeah, the guys must've told you I stopped by. Marty, I'm so sorry about Tush. I heard him play his sax that night . . ." My throat gets caught on the memory, but I steady it. "And to be wrongly accused and go through all that . . ."

"Yeah . . . it's been a rough week." Marty's easy smile disappears as he looks out over the porch into the autumn trees, losing their leaves one by one to the cold front rolling in. "Oh, hey, and Sarah . . . call me Martin. The guys call me Marty," he says, and I feel like I've been upgraded.

"Okay," I say, taking a good look at him. Everything about Marty seems to have matured since the last time I saw him. His clothes look less shabby, he's lost the sideburns, and now the formality of his name.

Tush's death has changed him. As it should.

"Here, I brought you some soup." I hand the container to him.

"Soup?" he asks, confused.

"Because you're sick," I say.

It doesn't seem to register at first as he takes the container with a half grin.

"The school paper, it said you were sick, and that's why you weren't . . ."

His dark eyes ignite with recognition. "Oh, oh yeah. That was, uh . . . a few days ago. I'm sorry, I'm fuzzy, just getting my senses about me again after everything."

He touches my arm, and I like the warmth of it, along with the sincerity in his voice, the reflection of the autumn leaves in his earnest brown eyes. There's good there. But other people won't see it now because of this. "Thank you so much for the soup. Let me pay you back. Let me buy you dinner. Somewhere nicer than the last place."

My heart leaps out of my chest, and never did I dream I'd get a date out of cafeteria soup. But more so because this is a boy who's suffered. A boy who needs me.

"Yeah, that sounds good," I say.

"Okay, I have to go home to get caught up on classes and some legal things, but I'll give you a call before next weekend." He grabs a pen that's hanging from his shirt pocket and holds his palm out like he's waiting for a high five. We both laugh as I scribble my digits on the underside of his hand, which I notice is remarkably smooth.

That boy's never held a hammer, my father would say. Or a guitar.

And maybe that's okay. The kids who go to school here don't have to hold hammers. They're learning how to make the robots that will someday replace hammers.

"Don't grab the soup with that hand; you'll smear the ink," I joke.

"I'll protect it with my life." Marty places the scribed hand over his heart, and I'm in love. Something about Tush's passing has me even more invested in Marty than before. The campus gossipers have been on a crusade to find someone to blame, and they chose him. I want to prove them wrong.

There's good there.

Marty probably thinks everyone hates him. I want to be the one to love him. I know what it feels like to be all alone, irrelevant in a sea of people who seem to have a clear direction of where they're going. Sometimes you just need someone to believe in you.

"You're a good one, Sarah Denning. I need a good girl like you to keep me out of trouble." He winks, and I melt into pieces right on the doorstep. I feel my face break into a smile, even though I fight it.

"Well, step number one: hit the books," I demand.

"Yes, ma'am. Talk soon. Thanks for the soup, very sweet."

"You're welcome."

He closes the door, and from that moment forward, I am his.

His good girl who will keep him out of trouble.

CHAPTER 10

Present

As expected, a policeman arrives shortly after Finn is situated at the kitchen table with his hot cup of coffee—*presentable*. Detective Harvey Monroe, on the other hand, is a bit on the scruffy side.

He introduces himself at the door with a stone-cold face that hangs flat and square. Detective Monroe's head is bald and misshapen, and although he's shorter and squatter than Martin, I can see the intimidation on my husband's face. I think back to the kid who leaned in the doorway of my dorm like he owned the place and then again the way he presented himself on our first date at the new hot spot in town. He always had it together, but his confidence has seemed to drain in an instant, and we are in trouble.

Martin confirms that we heard about a girl on the news and already pieced together that it is likely Yazmin, because Finn said they were near the park last night and her mother texted us looking for her.

Maybe telling the cop this is a mistake, but in any case, Detective Monroe doesn't seem happy that we already heard the news.

"Small town, news travels fast," Martin explains.

"I'd like to speak to your son. May I come in?" he asks, but it's not really a question.

Martin looks hesitant but opens the door wider. As it creaks open, so does my heart, and I'm suddenly aware of every sound around me: the sharp squeak of the brass hinges that need oiling, the *thud* of the detective's heavy boots on my cherry-wood floors, my own breathing.

We can't shield Finn any longer. He has to face the detective on his own.

Monroe positions himself at the breakfast bar where Finn is sitting. "Finn, honey . . . ," I say.

His eyes travel slowly between Detective Monroe and me. "Oh no." He places his head in his hands. "He's here because of Yazmin," Finn says, his voice unsteady, almost theatrical. Finn manages fresh tears, and if this is part of an act, he sure is good at it.

I place my hand on his shoulder. "I'm so sorry, Finn. She's dead."

Finn lets out a heated puff of air and cradles his head further, crying harder. I'm disturbed by how genuine his hurt appears. Maybe the drugs stilted his emotions earlier and he's finally able to feel the pain.

Or he's really good at pretending, which reminds me of Martin. Strangely, I can't see Spencer doing the same thing. Finn seems more like Martin that way—his presentation more serious and structured. We were always trying to temper Spencer's flame, whereas Finn's could always use a little more ignition. Martin and Finn also excel at the same subjects. Although Spencer went full science, he hated math, and that was Martin's and Finn's favorite subject. It makes sense, I guess, all things considered. This is just the first time their similarities frighten me.

"I knew I shouldn't have left her," he says, a little cry in his voice that reminds me of the boy who wouldn't jump in the pool.

He's a ladder climber, not a killer.

"Yes, I'm very sorry about your girlfriend," Detective Monroe says, but his voice lacks empathy. It sounds more obligatory than anything. "You can just call me Monroe, by the way."

Finn takes a large breath. "Okay."

"I need some information to try to piece together what happened, Finn. Can you do that for me?"

"Yeah," he manages through tears.

"Why did you go for a walk in the woods last night?" Monroe deadpans, and Martin opens his mouth to say something, but Finn speaks first.

"It was Yazmin's idea. She liked to walk there."

"To do drugs?" Monroe asks.

"Yes. The drugs were hers. They were Yaz's." He whispers the last part, as if saying her name hurts.

Monroe nods. I notice he's come alone. "Are you the only one investigating this?" I ask, but really, I'm just trying to give Finn a break to catch his breath after the last question. I need a moment to catch mine too. I'm not cut out for this. My palms are perspiring, and I can't keep my eyes from billowing with tears. I'm afraid I'll let loose.

"There's only one homicide detective assigned to my division because this type of incident is rare in these parts. In fact, I haven't investigated an unsolved death of a minor in Sewickley in the thirty years I've worked it, due to retire in a few months." He says the fact with such disdain, I gather Yazmin's case could be the one to leave a black mark on his near-perfect career.

"Where did you do the drugs?" Monroe taps his pen on a tattered notepad. He's wearing plain clothes, which doesn't make things feel casual, only worse, like some guy in the back room of a bar browbeating my son.

"In the park. That's where she liked to smoke, but she was scared to go alone. Her brother used to walk with her, but he'd pressured her to quit. Afraid she'd mess up her scholarship."

Monroe looks down at his notepad. "Her brother, Cash?"

Finn's shoulders hike at the name. "Yes. He doesn't like me too much."

"Yeah, well, you don't want to know what I did to scare the shit out of the guys who dated my sisters." Monroe finally shoots us a gap-filled smile, the memory of torturing his sisters' beaus a complete joy.

"He was very protective." Finn nods. "I'm sure he's upset." Finn's breath hitches. I lightly touch his shoulder again.

"I'm sure," Monroe says. Finn holds his coffee, bleary-eyed but steady. He's only started drinking coffee over the summer. I should've put hot cocoa in front of him instead, something more juvenile.

"I need to know more specifics, especially since there are drugs involved, and I need your help, Finn."

The echo of the words *"drugs involved"*—fills our spacious kitchen. They bounce off the lime-green subway tiles and soak into the whitewashed cabinets, all I can feel or taste. The law will use that phrase to crucify Finn later if this thing goes south, I just know it.

"She said it was just a little pot. I don't smoke pot, but I did last night." Finn makes eye contact with the cop. Good. He probably doesn't realize his body gesture is a sign of truth-telling. Martin couldn't have had time to coach him on that trick yet. My eyes cross at the thought, and I blink them back into reality.

"Where did she get the drugs?" Monroe asks.

"I don't know."

"So you didn't go with her to buy them?" Monroe's questions are fast, unflinching.

Finn grips the handle of his coffee mug. "No."

The detective leans forward into the quartz breakfast bar. "You don't know where your girl got the drugs. Come on, kid. Sure you do."

"If he says he doesn't know, then he doesn't. He wasn't even dating her that long," Martin defends.

"Just a month or so," I confirm. It is an insignificant amount of time to be together. Although I fell in love with Joshua in much less time than that when I was Finn's age. It sure hadn't felt like we'd been together for only the last month of the summer. Human connections can't be gauged by length of time, but for Finn's sake, I'll let this **logic** ride.

The detective glares at Martin. "We can do this here, or we can do it at the station."

Finn sucks in a deep breath, and I squeeze his hand. I'm so torn with playing both sides of the fence right now, I'm stilled in the middle, taut, like the center of a tug-of-war rope.

Should we just come clean? Would it be better for all parties involved?

I look at Monroe and think that it definitely would not. Monroe will take our admission of lying about Finn's whereabouts as a confession to murder. And so will everyone else. I'm trapped. We're officially trapped in the lie that we've spun, and we must remain suspended here until everyone believes it.

"On what grounds? He was here last night. With me." Martin's speech is clear and concise, without an ounce of doubt or pretension. My husband knows his rights. He's likely received legal advice from William on one of their hushed calls. He would likely have a lawyer present if it didn't look suspicious. It would mean we knew about Yazmin's death with enough notice to retain an attorney.

"Doesn't mean he wasn't at the scene of the crime before he came home," Monroe argues.

Martin shifts in his seat. "That would be highly unlikely, considering he came home almost right after school. As soon as he took that stuff and realized it wasn't what she said it was, he left."

I don't like that Martin is victim blaming. Finn took the drugs of his own free will. They may have been Yazmin's drugs, but it wasn't as if she forced his hand. Martin's determination to win at all costs has undermined everything we've ever tried to teach Finn about truth and morality.

Finn makes a rattling noise in his throat, and a tear runs down his cheek. He wipes it with his hand, and I wish I could take his pain away. I wonder how much he really cared for Yazmin. Teenage love can be an obnoxiously powerful, volatile thing. Or it can be something much more frivolous, fodder for an Instagram post, a label on a Facebook status. Something easily changed, disposed of, like what Joshua did with me. I'm not sure what Finn's true feelings are here—if he's upset because he feels guilty, or if he's upset because he really loved her.

"Is that what happened, Finn? Did you come home after you realized your girl was doping you up with some bad stuff?" Monroe asks.

"Yes, sir," Finn answers.

"If you don't smoke pot, though, how would you know it wasn't what she said it was?"

My heart loses gravity.

Damn it, Martin. The cop doesn't know we did a blood draw, so Finn shouldn't know the drugs were laced with anything.

Monroe is trapping Finn. And he's trapping us.

My face burns with the remorse that if we'd just come clean like I knew we should've, Finn might be okay.

"I meant, I did it once or twice, and this was nothing like the other two times," he confesses, looking at us for mercy.

I exhale in relief, not because I'm happy that Martin's coaching has worked but because Finn is not incriminating himself. That's the goal, I try to remind myself, as we suffer this inquisition. To survive without cracking.

"But you said you didn't do it before. Were you lying?" Monroe asks.

Martin clears his throat. "He just clarified his answer. Is this necessary? He was here most of the night." Martin keeps driving home the piece of information that will keep Finn safe.

The false piece of information.

The lie.

And I'm sitting here letting it happen.

But. This. Is. My. Son.

"It is," Monroe says, glaring. Martin backs off. I take a sip of water from the glass I placed on the table before we started.

Finn sighs, frustrated. "I tried it a couple of times with the Coulsons. You can ask them for proof. Matty and Joel. I didn't like it and then decided I wouldn't do it again, is what I meant. This was nothing like those other two times. I felt horrible, dizzy, my mind was racing, my skin was itchy, and then I couldn't keep my eyes open."

"Sure. Got it," Monroe says. But it's clear he isn't convinced. "Any idea why your girlfriend would go for a walk in the woods alone after you left? Was she meeting someone else?"

"No. She didn't like to be alone, especially in the dark. Her father was killed in an accident at night. She was in the car and survived, but I guess she was stuck there for hours before they found the car." His voice trembles.

So does mine. "Poor girl."

Martin looks at me as if I'm a traitor.

Monroe doesn't appear moved by this information at all. "We're trying to pinpoint the timing of events. When did the two of you leave the woods again?"

Martin and I exchange a frenzied look. They weren't supposed to have left together; Finn was supposed to have left without her. Monroe is trying to ensnare Finn again, but Martin remains quiet this time, only raising his eyebrows at our son. Finn nods, apparently catching on to the nonverbal cue.

"I left first, without her. It was after school but before dinnertime. Between five and six?" Finn answers.

Martin appears satisfied. Meanwhile, I'm horrified. Not only can Finn take his dad's cues, he can lie just like him too. Just like me. Martin and I both know Yazmin's death occurred well after Finn supposedly returned home. We just need to keep Finn out of the police station until *they* believe it, and then maybe we'll be okay. I can tell Martin is looking at me to see if I've made it to his side of the pond yet, and I shoot him a small, reassuring look.

"You're sure that was the time?" Monroe asks, and Finn looks at him, confused. He's thinking the same thing we are—is he asking this question again because he knows something different? It's clear to me now that if we don't work together, Finn will go to jail for Yazmin's death whether he had anything to do with it or not.

"I'm not sure why you're second-guessing everything my son says." Martin crosses his arms and takes off his glasses, rubbing the space between his eyes before placing them back on his face. "He had to have been here, at home, when she went for a walk in the woods and hurt herself."

"Forensics hasn't come back yet with reports on when the victim died or how she died, and your son was the last person to see her alive," Monroe argues. He wants to insinuate that because they did drugs together, Finn had a part in her death, and Monroe can't make that leap. I won't let him and neither will Martin.

"What did you eat for dinner last night, Finn?" Monroe asks.

A piece of Finn's barely dry hair falls into his surprised eyes. Finn didn't eat dinner last night.

I clench my legs under the table so I don't pee my pants. It's like what they say—one lie leads to the next. We asked Finn to lie about where he was last night, and now we're asking him to lie about what he ate for dinner.

What's next, Martin? Where does it end?

"I didn't eat. I was so sick, I went to bed and passed out."

"That's funny, because marijuana usually stimulates your appetite." Monroe doesn't miss a beat.

"It made me too sleepy to eat," Finn responds, and he's almost too good, convincing. It sends a shiver down my spine. *Could he lie to us just as well? Has he really told us everything he remembers?*

I need to believe, for my own sanity, that he has told us everything.

"Are you sure you don't want any tea or coffee?" I ask Monroe, trying to give Finn a moment to breathe again in between questions. He's fragile. He could crack at any moment, bring the whole house down with him. Spencer would be left selling off our assets to finish school, the sole survivor of his corrupt family.

"No, Mrs. Ellsworth, I am not thirsty." Detective Monroe's eyes roam around the kitchen. They seem to rest on the stainless-steel pot filler protruding from the wall above the six-burner stove. Silly thing. It looks as though the wall is impaled. I've never seen it that way before, but my lens is suddenly colored with a morbid palette, everything dark and shadowed with death.

Monroe clears his throat. "I'd recommend having legal counsel with you the next time we speak." The pull in my gut is visceral. I know we all hoped there wouldn't be a *next time.*

Martin is right. The police don't care about right or wrong or due process. They do not care about the how or the why behind Yazmin Veltri's death. The only thing they want is the quickest way to resolve this, a fall guy for their quiet upscale community so everyone can feel safe again. And Finn is by far the easiest target. Monroe will not end his career with the unsolved death of a young girl on his record.

"Have you wrapped up for the day?" Martin asks, overly eager to get Monroe out the door, as am I.

"Not quite," Monroe says.

I exhale sharply. If Monroe stops the questioning right now, we have a fighting chance of pulling this off. Finn's only mistake so far was his inconsistencies of previous drug use, but most teens don't want to disclose substance abuse in front of their parents, so I think Monroe might give that one a pass.

"You argued about more than the drugs last night, didn't you, Finn?" Monroe asks.

Finn tentatively lifts his eyes from his coffee mug. "Yes."

The fight. Damn. How does the detective know?

I've been trying to gauge this whole time whether Monroe went to Yazmin's house first and then decide after this question that he did, because how else would he know about the fight? I regret texting Yazmin's mother about it last night. If it was an Instagram post, I can only guess the younger brother saw it, too, so he could've filled in the blanks for the detective if Alisha mentioned the argument to Monroe. Or perhaps Monroe already interviewed Yazmin's friends.

The fight is the one thing that I hoped wouldn't get out, because a dead girlfriend is one thing, but a girl found dead after a heated argument with her boyfriend is another.

Finn is in trouble, but Yazmin is dead.

"What was it about? The fight?" Monroe asks.

Finn sighs. "It was stupid. Yaz hated having her picture taken. Unlike any girl I've ever met." His voice sounds woeful, like he found a rare gem and lost it.

Maybe he did. Most teenage girls I've met would practically trade their real life for positive likes on their fake one—their social media page.

"I snapped a candid shot of Yaz on my phone because I had so few pictures of her. She didn't see me; she was so into the article she was reading in *Time* magazine. Yaz was always trying to keep up with current events, very focused on school and her job as student treasurer. She had her sunglasses on while she was reading that day because we were sitting outside. She wasn't even looking at the camera." He sighs, and his breath quivers, a sound of desperation.

"So what was the problem, then?" Monroe asks.

"I posted the picture on my Instagram, captioned #MyMafiosoQueen #VeltriInVersace." He shakes his head.

"And she didn't like that?" Monroe asks.

"Not at all. She said she came to this school to shake her former reputation. I think she was trying to project some kind of image, a member of student council and all, and she thought I was ruining it."

"That all?" Monroe presses.

Finn looks at Martin, not me, for guidance. Martin nods, as if to say, *"Go on."*

"No, she said it was disrespectful to her culture. That I had no right to use her heritage like that."

"Did you realize you were being derogatory?"

"Now, wait a minute. That comment was not derogatory," Martin defends.

My shoulders slump, and I cross my legs to keep from having to excuse myself. This is bad, and I can already see the headlines Monroe is trying to create.

Son of tech firm owner connected to death of girl after slanderous Instagram post is leaked—and then deleted.

I cringe. It doesn't matter if it is true or not; the public will be overly satisfied with this conclusion. I place my hand over my mouth. I think I'm going to be sick.

"Of course not to you, Mr. Ellsworth," Monroe says with salt in his voice.

"Or anybody. She was being a silly, difficult teenager." Martin sounds stuffy, like William, and I want to kick him under the table and tell him to shut up. Martin is only making it worse.

"Well, she's a silly, dead teenager now. How do you suppose that happened?" Monroe bites on his pen cap and then puts it back on the tip with his teeth.

Martin loses his scowl quickly. "I don't know."

"Did you take the post down?" Monroe asks Finn.

"Right away. But everyone at school already saw it. She got angry because her brother texted her about it. That's how she found out I'd posted it."

"Officer, that post obviously did not have ill intent," I speak up. Poor Finn. He probably thought he was being sweet, but he'd been in over his head with this girl.

"Perhaps, but it angered her. Did the drugs occur before or after the fight?" Monroe asks.

"During. It's also part of the reason I left. I wasn't feeling well, and we were fighting."

Monroe's aggressive affront is making Finn's lies okay for me. Monroe is not on our side.

The police are on no one's side, I remind myself.

Except Alton. He's on our side.

Monroe clears his throat. "Why the drugs? Yazmin doesn't seem the type. You've painted her as very studious, good morals. It doesn't seem to fit."

Finn shrugs, and he looks absolutely, bedsheet-white exhausted. "Like I said, she was still dealing with a lot from the car accident. She said the pot chilled her out. The only other thing she seemed to do to relax was play her guitar. She took lessons. Both she and her brother."

Music and reading were my emotional buffers for surviving childhood too. I remember thinking I'd heard a guitar player again last night. This time Tom Petty instead of Pink Floyd. I told Joshua that my parents had met at a Petty concert, and I wondered if it was a sign from my mother to stay the course, or maybe drive off it.

The song was "Learning to Fly."

Monroe straightens up on the breakfast-bar stool. "Tell me about Yazmin's brother."

Finn makes a face. "Cash is quiet, a year younger than Yazmin, not very friendly. He goes to a city school, so I don't know him well, but I don't think he likes me."

"Why did they go to different schools? Yazmin and Cash?" Monroe's notepad is threatening to bleed to death with ink, he's written so much.

"Yaz scored higher than he did on her entrance exams and made it into the Academy on scholarship. It was some alumni-funded academic award."

"Where was she from again?" Monroe asks.

"The Rocks," Finn says.

McKees Rocks is a lower-income area of the city, and all I can think of is Yaz introducing herself to William, mentioning where she was from, and then insulting him on his watch and his political party. No wonder Finn hasn't talked to his grandfather since then.

She met William a few days after she met me, but it was her idea, Finn said, which I found odd. William and Martin both wear Bell & Ross watches because they think they symbolize humbleness at a mere five grand. *"Wouldn't want to wear your wealth on your sleeve,"* William said. *"Then people will know how much they can take you for."*

Monroe nods. How awful for this girl to have been exposed to William and Mary Alice. They probably made her feel like trash. The stress they caused was probably the reason she needed to smoke pot in the first place.

"She had so much to live for. She's been through so much." Finn can matriculate lies out of his mouth as proficiently as his father, but he did care for Yaz—I can tell. Is he lying to protect her somehow? I could've never lied to a cop at that age. It makes me wonder what else Finn has lied about, though, and with such competency. Martin too. The slipup about the drugs makes me desperate for answers. What the hell were these kids up to?

"I think that's enough for today." Monroe closes his notepad. "I'm sorry for your loss, Finn. I'll be in touch."

Martin follows Monroe to the front door and lets him out, but Martin and I are far from done here. We made it through today, but tomorrow is uncertain. A few more days of this and one of us will falter. And it'll probably be me.

"I need to lay down," Finn says.

"Good job, son. Go rest," Martin says, but his voice is chilly.

Good job are never the words I would've chosen for successfully lying to the police. What horrible lessons are we teaching here, and at whose expense?

Does Martin really think things went well with Monroe or is he disappointed in his son? I'm so disappointed with everyone at the kitchen counter, including myself, I could scream. This is not the way I was raised. And this is not the way we raised our sons. What we did just undermined eighteen years of good parenting, and there's no way we can get it back.

Does Martin understand this?

That he's just destroyed us. That he's destroyed Finn. We can't let him go off into the world thinking what happened here today is okay, but I let Finn lumber up the steps. "Get some sleep, honey," I tell him.

"We need to talk. About everything," I tell Martin once Finn is out of earshot.

"Sarah, I don't have time to talk. I have to go to my father's and discuss options for legal representation for Finn. He has a lot for me to look over."

"This can't wait, Martin."

"It can, Sarah . . ." His voice breaks, but Martin isn't even looking at me as he says the words, and I'm so unaccustomed to him talking to me this way, I don't know what to do. It reminds me of how he treated me in the car, like I was invisible.

"I need to go stay at my father's tonight, then, and I'm taking Finn with me." I can't sort my thoughts out with Martin running in and out of the house to poison them. He should experience a night alone, because if he keeps this up, he'll have a lot more of them. It's not that he doesn't want to talk about it right now; it's the way he dismissed me, as if my opinions on the matter are no longer important. These are decisions about our son we need to make as a couple, Finn's legal representation included.

He looks at me, stunned. "I know you're upset, but we need you here tonight, Sarah. We need to be united as a family to get through this."

"Exactly, so why are you running to your father's alone? If you're going to see yours without me, I'm going to see mine. I won't tell him what happened. I could never tell him what we've done." I choke on my words.

Martin halts in the office doorway, leaning on the massive wooden paneling. My doorway leaner. He's strayed 180 degrees from that kid lingering in my dorm room, completely unrecognizable now. There's nothing cute or wily or intellectual about this cold-blooded, manipulative man.

Everything's changed, including the room he's standing beside. It used to be the parlor when the real estate agent ushered me through this place so many years ago. It's now an office where Martin spends his evenings, positioned directly across from the window he installed with his family crest and the curlicue *E* standing for a name I'm not sure I want to be associated with any longer.

"I don't know why you think your dad's so perfect; he's no better than the rest of us." Martin's angry with me for running to another person, another man, but his words feel especially vicious and unjustified.

"I think you're wrong about that." I dangle my car keys in his face. "I don't care how much money you have; you'll never be as rich as my father."

Martin laughs, and it's ugly and mocking. "You've always had your head in the clouds, and I've let you live there, my dear, because that's what made you happiest, but it's time to face the facts. Your father isn't the perfect man you make him out to be. We all make mistakes."

I grip the keys in my hand and let them rib my palm. "He would never do what you did."

Martin chuckles. "What I did? No, what *we* did, Sarah. You don't get to take yourself out of the equation just because it's convenient. Because it makes for a better story in your head." His words stop me cold, and I wonder if he's just talking about what happened in those woods. What else does he know about? I've always thought he had a

hunch about the events leading up to our engagement, but the word—
convenient—really gives me pause.

Martin was the more convenient choice for me at the time. But
I'm now coming to realize that *convenient* didn't mean better and that
I made a bad choice when I told him yes. Does he know I'm thinking
that now?

"Don't go anywhere, Sarah," he says.

I don't answer him, and when Martin leaves through the front door,
it slams shut, his version of the truth punching me in the gut. There's
no way I can go to my father's now. Martin knows I don't have it in me
to lie to him—or tell him the truth.

He said just the right thing to keep me locked here, a prisoner in
my own home. I can't go cry to my dad when I'm just as much at fault
as Martin. My father will make me own my mistakes, and I can't do that
without putting Finn at risk. I promised my father I wouldn't become
like the awful rich people who used their money to push others around,
and here I am screwing over a poor single mother, and it's a terrible
feeling. I'm the person I never wanted to become, and I can't even talk
to my father about it.

Martin is able to run to his daddy and get counsel while I'm stuck
here, alone, to face my demons. I throw my keys on the kitchen island.
My throat is sore from arguing, and I need a glass of water.

A glass of sweet water.

When my hand touches the faucet, I get a flash of Yazmin's dead
body, and the wave of guilt hits me like a truck.

My body rocks as I grip the sink. The waves come on so suddenly.

My fingertips graze the windowsill in the kitchen, the vertices
strong and encased in metal, the protective windows thatched in a
crisscross pattern with the same girding material. I reach for a heavy
crystal glass in the cabinet. Everything is so weighty in this house; it
feels unnecessary. "What now?" I ask Stonehenge.

When I talk to the house, every once in a while, I get an answer. I stare out the window to the side yard, where the leaves on the tree are depleting fast.

No matter how much sweet water the trees absorb, it's still time for their foliage to wither and die. To shed all that's grown there the year before.

Everything has its season.

Death and rebirth. This is a different season in our marriage than we've experienced in the past, cold and barren of love. Maybe there'll be a time for rebirth, but right now it doesn't feel like it. My attention is drawn to the bench under the pergola—Joshua's old stage, where he used to play his music. There's a flash of something red that catches my eye. "What have you got for me?" I ask the house, wiping away a tear.

I slink out and sit on the bench framed by pillars. I'm like a grain of sand in an hourglass, so small and insignificant, I feel like I could disappear at any moment and no one would notice.

A single rose lies on the thick cement bench, brilliant red and full like the ones that used to grow there on the wooden trellis. I wonder if my mother has heard my pleas in Heaven and sent me a gift to ease my soul, because this rose can't have grown here.

We assumed the roses would still grow after the tiny outdoor renovation we did, but the bushes died after we tore out the foundation, and I was upset that we'd somehow disrupted the rooting of the old bushes.

Joshua hadn't liked much about his life here, but he had liked the outside area of his house most. It's where he played his music. There's still a loose stone on the steps in the far-right corner that I wouldn't let Martin remove. The deep hole beneath it is where Josh used to hide his weed.

Even though his parents bought the house with the ceiling fit for acoustics in mind, they later decided they didn't want to hear the noise, which always made me sad.

I don't know where the rose came from, certainly not Martin.

A gift from the house, perhaps.

In any case, I pick it up and inhale the petals' scent and let the thorn prick my finger. "Thank you," I tell it. "But I've done a terrible thing." *And I deserve to bleed.*

I wipe the blood on my jeans and shudder, these dark thoughts a part of me now. There is no turning back.

I'm not sure how long I sit out there, but when Martin's headlights reappear, it's dark and I'm chilled, and we have so much to talk about. Finn's legal options for one. And our consequences. How we're going to handle speaking to Finn about what we've done, how it's morally wrong—he needs to understand. This is not how we handle situations.

I carry the rose with me and go back inside. Martin is in his office, doors shut. I don't knock; I just yank open the french doors and poke my head inside.

"Damn it!" Martin jerks up so hard, his knee accidentally jams a ledger in between the desk and the drawer. He yelps like an injured cat. "You scared me. Did you call your dad?"

He doesn't look at me when he asks the question. He wouldn't dare.

"No," I answer. He doesn't care about anything else—where I was when he got home, why I've been crying. Only that I didn't tell anyone about what we did.

I decide that the questions I have for him don't matter because he won't include me in the decisions surrounding them anyway. Decisions that affect our son's future. "I'll leave you to work." I close his office doors and walk to the stairs, a ghost of the woman I used to be.

At the base of the stairwell, I put out the candles on the console table that Martin lit when he got home. It's an almost nightly ritual, especially in the fall. Martin prefers his home to smell pleasant when he walks through the doors, so he lit the candles when he arrived to a stale house.

He's trying to pretend like this is any other Thursday night.

Meanwhile, Finn stays in his room all evening, a prisoner too. In an attempt to secure our freedom, we've locked ourselves up anyway.

I climb the steps, exhausted, and they make an awful creak. The house disagrees with me.

"What now?" I whisper.

This time there is no sign, no answer from Stonehenge. No rose or offering.

And I don't know why Joshua keeps invading my thoughts, but as I clutch the rose in my hand, all I can think about is the first night we met. The night he gave me a rose just like this one.

CHAPTER 11

Summer of 1996

I pull over on the back road until my tires come to a complete stop. The low branches scratch the top of Dad's truck. My heart skips a beat at the thought of getting caught, but I can't drive by tonight.

After I hit my teenage years, Dad and I didn't ride by this place as much, but then when I started driving, I found myself missing Stonehenge.

And I began cruising by on my own. Then I discovered the boy, and I kept on driving by.

The boy with the guitar is strumming his chords, and I've listened to him play through my driver's side window more times than I can count. I can see him from the road, but tonight he sounds different, more urgent, the pain in his lyrics piercing me just right.

With my headlights dimmed, head back, eyes closed, his melody floats through my window—*from his soul to my ears*—the sound of anger and beauty wrapped in a slow and steady beat.

The intro is familiar. I'd know that song anywhere.

The boy with the guitar is playing Pearl Jam.

Usually he sticks to the classics—the Doors, the Stones, Floyd—but tonight he's crushing it to "Better Man," and I think I might be in Heaven. I've never done it before, but I allow myself to sit there awhile, because this song is killer, and I'd do anything to hear him play it.

I'm hidden behind the brush, obscured by the starless night, the flurry of fireflies like tiny lighters held up for this young wannabe Eddie Vedder, and everything is right in the universe.

My body settles into the upholstered seats.

There's something about the boy's voice tonight that pulls me in. The ache is so real, I can almost reach out and grab it.

The words dance on my quiet lips in rhythm with the rustling trees. The summer breeze trips across my bare arms, daring me to follow it to the next moment, whatever that moment might hold. The music is stirring something—a longing for all the life that hasn't happened yet. I lean back into the headrest and inhale the heavy air.

But the music is rousing all my unloved wounds too, everything I've missed in my time here—parties I haven't attended, boys I haven't kissed, female friendships I haven't made. I'm not prepared for life's next adventure.

And Kurt Cobain.

I'm still sad about him too. Everything. All of it. The world.

I've been struggling ever since I received my acceptance letter from CMU. I haven't experienced enough to go off to college yet, and I fear the other kids will smell the immaturity on me like a new puppy that's just soiled the rug.

I even made a list of all my Nevers. Things I feel I should've done by now but haven't, and it's all completely depressing.

Sure, I got into CMU, but what have I lost because of it?

My dad's parental siren worked—*"Don't get pregnant. Don't do drugs. You'll screw everything up."* I was convinced the first time I had sex that I'd get knocked up, and that my first hit of any drug would turn me into an addict. It could happen. We weren't lucky people.

There's a light rap on the side-view mirror. "Oh my God!" I jump in my seat, hitting my elbow on the door handle.

"Uh. Hi," my guitar player says. *When did he stop playing? How long has he been standing here?*

"Hi," I try to whisper, but I barely make a sound.

"Sorry, didn't mean to scare you." He has the sexiest voice I've ever heard, a little on the deeper side but calming—mesmerizing—like the musician at the beginning of the show talking freely to the audience.

My eyes readjust to the darkness, and I'm so startled, I can hardly speak. My heart is in my throat and there he freaking is—the boy with the guitar. He's staring at me up close with his serious eyes, but they're not dark like I pictured; they're light—blue or green—and they're confused.

"You lost?" he asks.

"No," I manage.

Crap. I had my eyes shut for so long, I'd either been lulled to sleep or sat there way past the time he'd stopped playing, tired from my waitressing shift, lost in his song.

"Well, then, what're you doing?" he asks. He smiles at me like I'm a peculiar creature, but damn, he's fine, a delicious cross between Leonardo DiCaprio and Christian Slater, a vision reserved for *Teen Beat* magazine—not me.

"I . . . um . . ." Should I tell him the truth? Well, I can't tell him the whole truth, that I'm his drive-by stalker, so I decide for second best. "I had my window down and heard you playing. You're really good, and Pearl Jam is my favorite. I'm sorry. I'll go now." I feel my cheeks sizzle with embarrassment.

"Wait," he says. My hands freeze on the keys dangling from the ignition. "Do you want to hear some more?"

Did he really just ask that?

My heart is still pounding from being scared out of my seat, but there's something else that's got it beating wildly. The boy's T-shirt is stretched and ripped, exposing a little black rubber necklace, but up close, this kid with the dirty-blond hair is the sexiest thing I've ever seen.

He's squinting at me with one eye, the other buried under his hair. His whole body is wet with a summer sheen.

"Well?" His smile makes me take a sharp breath, and there can only be one answer to his question.

I exhale. "Sure."

"Okay . . . well, why don't you pull in the driveway this time." He gives a little laugh. "My parents aren't here."

His parents aren't here? *His parents aren't here!*

"Right," I say, picking up a hint of cigarette on his breath.

I start Dad's truck, and it sounds so loud in the middle of the quiet woods. After I park in the driveway—Stonehenge's driveway—with my dream boy, I draw in a sharp breath of surrealism and hop out.

He grins at me, and every nerve ending on my arms comes alive.

"What?" I ask, smoothing down my hideous black work pants.

Is it my snazzy red Applebee's polo or my big-ass truck that's got you looking at me sideways? Maybe this is a mistake.

He laughs. "I've just never seen such a small girl drive such a big truck before."

Five foot five is not that small, I almost say, but I can't tell if he's making fun of me or not. I decide that he is. "We're not all bequeathed with Beamers at birth." I nod to the white convertible parked in the driveway.

"That's my mom's. She's out of the country. I have a Jeep in the garage. I actually love your truck. It's rad," he says.

"Oh. Yeah, it's my dad's truck, but I dig it," I lie.

He nods and twists his lips as if he doesn't believe me a bit. "*Bequeath* is a nice word. Let's go make some more words together—come on."

He walks over to me, and the only thing I can think of when he says *"make words together"* is *make love*—and it's the most provocative thing anyone's ever said to me.

His rough hand grabs mine, and my body responds with quiet quivers. His fingers are calloused from playing, but somehow I find them strangely seductive, amatory, hands that have been worked until they were rubbed raw and then healed again.

He leads me across the lawn, and Stonehenge is a little creepy at this hour. We weave through lawn ornaments, tall statues with white heads that seem to watch us as we walk by, a fountain that doesn't run at night. Time has stopped—just for us.

We make it to the pergola on the side of the house, where he usually plays guitar beneath the stone pillars. It's illuminated with spotlights, and I wonder if he feels like he's onstage when he plays there.

He picks up his guitar and doesn't ask, just starts playing "Yellow Ledbetter," another of my favorite Pearl Jam songs. My knees go weak at the introduction. I collapse into a sitting position on the bench and listen.

His music is intoxicating, his voice unlike Vedder's, because he doesn't howl into the microphone, more a soft drone but smooth—like sad silk running down my skin on a hot August night.

We're the only two people on earth, and nothing can hurt me here.

The world reached in its dirty hand and swooped my mother away in a matter of months, and ever since I've felt exposed to more disaster.

Anything could've taken me out—not getting into CMU, Dad falling ill like Mom.

Cancer.

We weren't one of the lucky ones, but here I am.

In this kingdom of the wealthy with this boy, at Stonehenge, and I am safe.

He taps me on the shoulder, and it's only then that I realize I've closed my eyes again.

"Jeez, do I put you to sleep?" he asks.

He's sitting beside me now, and I giggle, embarrassed. "No, you're so, so good. Sometimes I close my eyes when I listen to music. I can hear it better that way." I feel like such a dope when I say it, but his eyes light up with hunger at my response. Maybe because I've just complimented him, or maybe because he likes my answer.

"My name is Joshua. Josh," he says, and I think that it's a delicious name and that it suits him. "What's yours?"

"I'm Sarah. Sorry we're just getting to introductions now," I say, but all I can concentrate on are his lips, wet with perspiration like everything else on his tall, wiry body. Joshua has to be over six feet tall, and even sitting down, he towers over me.

"That's okay. Better late than never." He brushes my hair away from my face. It's come undone from my ponytail, and I must look like a mess, but he doesn't seem to care. I lean into the brush of his hand as he pulls strands behind my ears, tipping my face up.

Those lips. He parts them, and I almost stop breathing. I lean in, hoping he'll close the gap between us.

"My mother told me I should always learn a girl's middle name before I kiss her, but I'm okay with just knowing firsts if you are."

I'm. On. Fire.

"It's Elizabeth. Sarah Elizabeth, but that's okay," I whisper.

I can feel his body sliding closer to mine.

"Joshua Michael." His lips are inches from mine.

This is so happening.

Joshua leans in again slowly; I hear his breath. My body surges, pure fireworks. His top lip sucks on my lower one just long enough to drive me completely insane. I slide closer to him on the bench, swinging my leg over one side, so I'm flush with his body.

He's so much taller than I am. I'm leaning against him, and I'd do anything to have him lay me down flat. His kisses are hungry, his tongue curious as it roams from my lips to my neck. I hear the breath fall out of me as he pushes my hair back, then breaks away to take me in with his eyes.

No one's looked at me like that before. Ever.

"Do you want to go somewhere more comfortable?" he asks. His hand flexes on the cement bench, and he's the best at talking in subliminal phrases and turning them into much bigger statements. It's like we have our own language already, and I think he's asking me if I'd be comfortable screwing on a cement bench, and maybe if I'd tried it before (screwing, that is), I'd say yes. But first times are painful, so I hear, and cement benches can't possibly make that process any better.

I'm ready to knock this Never off the list.

"Sure," I say, still a little breathless from his kisses.

He takes my hand and stands up. His jeans are baggy, and I can see the ribbing of his boxer briefs, and I don't know what to do with myself, but I hope he shows me. He leads us back to the house, our breath ragged, our footsteps eager.

We enter the basement of Stonehenge from a bottom-floor door, and the lights are dim in the pool area, an amber glow that reminds me of school halls after closing time. I let out a deep breath. I feel like I'm breaking and entering, having reimagined this place so many times in my mind. I can't tell him I know what's down here, that I was in his house on a tour on the same day his parents put in their offer, and that I know he's taking me to the downstairs pool.

"We can cool off in here." Josh takes off his shirt, and he's thin, but his shoulders are broad, his stomach perfectly muscled. I restrain myself from running my fingers over his taut belly.

"Nice pool."

"Could be bigger," he jokes.

Then I do something I've never done before. I lift my red polo over my head and chuck it to the side, revealing my little white bra with pink flowers at the center. I'm glad the pool room is poorly lit, but when his eyes roam my body in one quick swoop, I freeze and let him take me in.

"You don't have to do anything you don't want to," he says, but his voice is hungry for me to do everything. And I want to.

"Okay," I say.

He beckons me to follow him to the pool, his eyes glinting with dare and desire. *"Come in, the water's fine,"* they say. I kick off my stretchy black pants without a thought and slip into the warm water. His arms find me and wrap around my waist, pulling me into the heat of his flesh. His lips find mine, and he tastes like everything I've been waiting for.

He's the boy in my dreams I haven't kissed, but the one I imagined, the one who belongs to those chords and those words I've listened to so many times. He's the boy with the guitar whose parents ended up buying Stonehenge, the one I'd envied long before we ever met.

He's one of them, one of the lucky ones.

I want to be one of the lucky ones too.

His lips ease back just enough to murmur my name. "Do you want this?" I nod and push my mouth onto his, closing the space between us.

I don't want to talk.

Josh unhooks my bra, and I imagine it sinking to the bottom of the pool with all my inhibitions. He slides my underwear down my thighs, and I use my foot to snag them all the way down. He takes off his briefs as well, grabs all the articles, and tosses them over our heads onto the side of the pool. There's nothing between our bodies now. Just skin on skin and—need.

"I want you, Sarah." He breathes the words into my ear, and goose bumps rise all along my neck and shoulders. "Can I have you?"

"Yes," I say. "But I've never done this before."

"I'll go slow," he promises.

I nod, and he sucks on my bottom lip some more and lowers himself until he's almost entirely underwater and I'm standing up straight. He positions his body beneath me. He uses his fingers to play me like a guitar. I gasp, his touch alone almost enough to make me come undone. Joshua backs me up against the wall and grinds his hips into mine, until our bodies are so close that they can't be separated. I close my eyes and let him rock me into the greatest pleasure I've ever known.

Afterward, we lie on lawn chairs in robes left on hooks in the adjoining his-and-hers changing rooms. He holds my hand and shuts his eyes, and I do the same. It's probably getting late, and I'm sure my dad is wondering where I am, but my body is so lax, I can't leave just yet. This is too perfect. Mandy, my work friend, lost her virginity in the back of a Buick, and I always wanted mine to be different. It was. It was amazing.

"What do you want to be when you grow up?" Josh's hair is too long and matted over his closed eyes. I want to brush it off his face, but I'm exhausted and content, so I leave him alone.

"I'm going to CMU for business. I want to work in public relations. Maybe for a nonprofit," I say proudly. "How about you?"

"Very nice. Much to my mother's dismay and that of the Academy, I've decided to pursue my music and not attend college this semester."

Josh grabs his well-worn jeans and pulls a rolled-up cigarette out of the pocket. He lights up without asking if I mind and doesn't seem to care if his parents will smell it when they come home. He passes me the cigarette, which I can only guess is weed, and even though I've never smoked pot, I take it and inhale it anyway. If there's any night to cross a line, this is the one.

"I think that's a wonderful idea. You're very talented."

He smiles at me as I try to figure out how to smoke it. "Thank you."

I know right away I have too much lip on the bud and take too deep of an inhale, the skunky smell choking me. I cough and give it back, satisfied I've crossed off several Nevers without incident tonight.

"What will you do for money? Or don't you have to worry about that?" I ask.

I've never had any choice about my future. The dream that I would get into CMU and attend for free under my father's family-affiliated tuition program was the only one I was allowed to have. And here Josh is, carving his own path around the world, his parents be damned.

"I'll be okay for a little while. I try not to think about money too much. It turns people into loveless monsters. Like my parents. The world is so big and they're just concerned with their small, pathetic lives. I want to do something to help in a bigger way."

I look at him—he sounds like me. "How so?"

"I don't know. Go overseas. Help pick up the pieces our country waited way too long to help clean up."

I think I know what he's talking about and take a stab. "Bosnia?"

He pauses on his inhale and looks surprised that I've caught on. "It's a damn tragedy. It took us four years to do anything. All those poor people." He shakes his head, and I think I'm in love.

"Just because there wasn't any oil involved, they dragged their feet. Nothing in it for them," I whisper.

He looks at me, nodding vigorously, and this is my guy. We kiss again, and this time it's so slow and deep, I think I might lose myself to him again. But I picture Dad on the front porch waiting for me. I break away from him. "Speaking of parents, I'd better get back." It's starting to get light outside, and I didn't wear my watch. I have no idea what time it is.

"Okay." Josh gets up and drops his robe to the ground without a care. His ass is perfectly round, and my mouth drops at his symmetrical beauty. I can't believe that sexy boy was inside me. He jumps into his jeans, no underwear, because they're all wet. Then he slides his T-shirt over his head, his hair getting mussed and sticking up wildly in the process.

He turns, looks at me, and says, "Well, come on."

"Right." I need to quit watching him like I'm still sitting in my truck. I'm so much more of a watcher than a doer. I stand and gingerly begin unraveling my robe. It seems silly to ask him to turn around after all we've just shared. The one hit I took isn't working a damn to lighten my insecurities, so I hurriedly drop the white terry-cloth robe, too plush for personal ownership, and quickly put my wet undergarments back on.

He watches me the whole time with an amused smile. My clothes smell, and when I pick up my shirt and leave it hanging by my fingertips, Josh immediately takes his shirt off and slips it over my damp head. I love the way his giant T-shirt feels sliding over my body. "Thanks," I whisper.

"You're welcome," he whispers back.

I follow him out through the door, and it's definitely early morning, and I'm in so much trouble.

"Wait," he says.

Joshua darts for the pergola and carefully removes a rose from the impressive wooden trellis and then jogs back and hands it to me. I smile, because even though it's never been on my list of Nevers, I've never received flowers from a boy that didn't come mandatory with a school dance either. "Thank you."

"You're welcome," he says again, and we're so postcoital polite right now, I can't stand it. We walk back to my truck, one hand in his, the other holding the gorgeous red rose.

When we reach the driver's side, he asks, "Will I see you again?"

"Do you want to see me again?" I ask.

"Yes," he says simply, and there's not a hidden message in there this time.

"I work again Monday night."

"Stop after your shift," he suggests.

"Sure," I say.

And that's the way it worked for the rest of the summer. I'd leave for work excited, bringing a change of clothes, and we'd meet up afterward. That way we didn't have to figure out dates. I'd tell my dad I was going out with friends after work, and he never questioned it. I could've told Dad about Joshua, but I wanted to keep him all to myself. Joshua's parents were never home, so my work schedule turned into our schedule, and I came to love working at Applebee's more than I ever thought possible.

There were only a few weeks of summer left, but I looked forward to each and every one.

Summer came and went, and so did Josh—so abruptly that it wrecked me for a little while.

I couldn't even cry to Mandy, because I hadn't told her, so I just tried to pretend none of it had ever happened.

There is one thing he said to me back then that I still think about, especially on the day Martin surprised me with Stonehenge.

Right before I went off to college, during one of our last encounters before he disappeared, I revealed to Josh that I'd been in love with his house since I was a small child, and that when I first heard him play, it was because I was coming back to visit the house and not him.

He said, *"Well, this house is mine. Once my parents pass on, they'll leave it to me. Maybe if I come back one day, we can live here together."*

It's one of the last things he ever said to me, and I know he was being facetious, but it somehow seemed like a promise, a way to hold on to him—and Stonehenge—forever. It's one of the reasons I've never felt quite right about Stonehenge becoming mine. Especially after I found out how Martin paid for it.

This day is the first time since Martin handed me the keys that I feel like I've disappointed the house. That I've failed it somehow, tainted it with my dirty secrets. I never felt like I truly deserved it to begin with, but I thought if I played the part, treated it with the reverence it deserved, I could live here.

But no longer.

Maybe the rose is an offering of peace.

The house is telling me to turn us in before it's too late.

CHAPTER 12

Present

Alisha: We need to talk. I think you know why. Meet me today before I go to the news with this.

Night came last evening, and no one left the house. Martin slept, I did not, who knows about Finn, and we woke up to this.

Martin! The internal scream is so loud inside my head, it numbs me. My arms prick cold with sweat and fear. No sound can leave my body.

I grip my phone, my stomach churning with leftover sick from staying up all night worrying, turning my insides to rot. If this is a waiting game, as Martin suggested, I can't keep pace, one land mine after the next.

Martin, on the other hand, looks ready to take on the world already, showered, button-down shirt, glasses cleaned, pushed all the way up—in the game. "It's clearly a threat," he says. "Now she's going to sue us. See, Sarah, this is why we did what we did."

Our lines of thinking couldn't be more different. My only frenzied thought is, *She knows!*

She knows Finn was in the woods with her daughter when she died.

She knows Finn had something to do with it.

She knows we lied to cover it up.

But all Martin can think about is protecting his money.

"Martin, she obviously knows something," I whisper. I'm emotionally rocked, and I can barely speak.

"She can't know anything. Everything there is to know is gone." He's fucking smiling when he says this, and it's the most repulsive thing in the world. It's like he's proud of himself for having the crime scene swept so thoroughly.

"Well, maybe Alton missed something. Or she found something! She claims to have newsworthy information." I point at my phone in case he's missed it, and my chest hurts so badly, I feel like I'm going to have a heart attack. *How can he be smiling?*

Finn walks into the kitchen. "What's going on?" He looks terrified to ask, and I don't blame him.

"Yaz's mother wants to meet," I say.

Finn's face goes from terrified to sullen. "What does she want?" He opens the pantry for cereal and then closes it. He hasn't eaten much, and this would've been his first attempt in two days, but no such luck. We're robbing this kid of his existence.

"We don't know," I say, and I'm lying to him, because I'm so trained now, I don't even have to look at Martin for my script. And I realize in that moment that if I don't break away from him, this way of life will become my future. This is exactly how Mary Alice came to be.

I don't want to become Mary Alice.

"Are you going?" Finn asks. "To meet her?"

I hesitate for a moment deciding the best course of action.

"She is. She's going," Martin says.

There it is, the command. I knew it was coming. He's gotten used to telling me what to do, and that's not something I'll let become part of my future either.

I glare at him, and he smiles and shakes his head side to side as if to say, *"This is what you signed up for."*

My stomach turns, and I look at Finn. "Have some breakfast, honey. I need to shower so I can meet her." I kiss him on the cheek, but he pulls away. "Please don't be mad at me," I whisper in his ear.

He stares at me despondently. "Can I go to soccer practice tonight?"

I look over my shoulder at Martin for his reaction and hear Finn reopen the pantry door. He's missing school again today, and I want Finn to look alive again, but I'm not sure how he can think about soccer at a time like this. It seems insensitive, especially for Finn.

"No, but this is the only practice you have to miss. We just need the air to clear a little," Martin says. That son of a bitch thinks we're out of the woods—no pun intended—but I think our true nightmare has only begun. And I'm sure my lunch date will reveal more. How can he be so smug? He probably knows something I don't.

"Text her back, dear. Don't be rude," he says. "Just say—"

"Don't tell me what to say!" I yell.

Finn drops the cereal box on the table, fear flittering across his face, and then puts it back in the cupboard.

Damn it. Strike two. This kid is never going to eat.

Martin puts his hands up in the air. "Okay." But he watches me as I type. Probably to make sure I really do it.

Sarah: Okay. No problem. Sewickley Hotel. Noon?

Alisha: Yes. Come alone or I'll leave.

Martin can hear the ding from my text message. He approaches, and I hold my hand up this time. I don't need to be any closer to him. "I'm meeting her at noon, and she wants me to come alone."

Martin's smile falls right off his face. He can't coach me, control me in any way, if he isn't there, and he should be worried.

Finn looks worried too, and I don't want him to be. "Finny, I was thinking of having Grandpa over for dinner; what do you think?"

His look of alarm twists into a pout, and I think he might cry. "*No. I hate Grandpa!*"

Martin steps forward now, and I allow him in my space.

"Finn, you haven't seen Grandpa in months," Martin says.

Finn lifts his head to meet mine, and it's then I see the sunken half circles beneath his eyes and the slight tremor in his eyelid from no sleep. Yaz's death has robbed us all of so much, but Finn has lost the most. "Oh, I thought you meant Grandpa Bill."

"Well, what's your problem with Grandpa Bill?" Martin says of his father.

Finn's lip quivers, and he looks a little crazed. "He wasn't nice to Yazmin," he says with venom in his voice.

I hate Grandpa Bill too, but even I think Finn is acting extreme.

Martin tries to defend the old goat. "It was my understanding she'd insulted—"

"That's all bullshit!" Finn yells.

"Hey, son."

"Hey, yourself. It's all bullshit! This whole family."

Finn storms away, and Martin goes to run after him, but I grab his arm. "Let him go."

Martin stops and drops his head. "What was that about?"

"William can be a cantankerous old prick," I say flatly. "You know it didn't go well when Yazmin met him."

Martin looks at me, startled. "It didn't go well when she met you either," he says, and I wonder if he's trying to say we're one and the same, but he wouldn't dare. Then he whips a checkbook out of his shirt pocket, and I wonder if he always keeps one in there—just in case. "Bring this with you today."

"Why?" I ask him, breathless, but I think I know.

"If she has something on Finn, offer her whatever she wants."

"Martin." My blood seethes beneath my skin. "We cannot pay her off."

This was his plan all along, wasn't it?

"Offer to help with her expenses for having to take off work since Yazmin's death. If it's over five thousand, tell her you'll get the rest in cash so there's not a long paper trail. Just give her what she wants and get out. Make her aware we don't do blackmail. She saw what happened to her daughter."

"What're you suggesting?" I ask, feeling ill.

"It's in your hands, Sarah. Get in, get it done, and get out."

Martin walks away, goes in his office, and shuts the door. He expects me just to accept his marching orders, no questions asked. He's closed the topic for discussion, and of all the things I signed up for in our marriage, this isn't one of them.

CHAPTER 13

A whip of wind stirs up leaves beneath my boots, the sunlight touching everything around me. My late-model Infiniti is caked with leftover rainwater and a crust of autumn debris.

The car keys shake in my hands. This is my first day out of the house since the night we left the woods.

The light is where the truth lives. The light will shine a beacon on what we've done.

After our showdown in the kitchen, I'm a jittery mess. My husband has transformed into an unrecognizable sociopath, my son a mentally fractured young man who will no doubt have long-standing psychological issues from this incident, and none of it seems remotely worth it.

I don't think the bulk of Finn's issues will stem from his girlfriend's death but from our reaction to it. My years of dealing with trauma victims have taught me that those abuses that occur in the home are typically the ones that most profoundly affect a person later.

I turn before climbing inside my vehicle. Martin is watching me from the office window, his eyes like laser beams, flickering in and out with the sunlight, homing in on me through the blinds—*"stay the course,"* I can hear him say in my head. I'm so fortunate that I'm allowed to borrow a couple of hours of daylight under the circumstances.

Being away from him feels good, but I'm fearful of leaving my haven.

This house will keep me safe.

Once I leave it, though, I'll have to face what we've done.

My hands hurt as they grip the steering wheel, chapped from so much washing, but I'll never wash her away. My body is rocked with tremors of guilt as my car tires grind along the gravel path. My heart thumps along with the stones.

I try to take in a deep breath, but the car heater blows in my face, and I begin to sweat as I make my way out of the woods, the world a completely different place than it was a few days ago.

I didn't sleep in the same bed as my husband last night.

I didn't run to my father's house either. I couldn't. He wouldn't agree with what we'd done, and he wouldn't let me continue on this path—one he'd know I was being forced to take.

My father is better than that.

Better than us.

He doesn't have a fortune and a family name to protect.

He has only me. Martin's ugly words about his character left me in a state of loathing, bottled with hate. I had a strong desire to see my dad, if even for a little dinner.

Martin has always been jealous of my relationship with my father. He knows when I was growing up, we were a two-person team he can't replace. No matter how hard he tries, he'll never be as close as we are. And he certainly doesn't have the same relationship with his own parents.

This incident has changed Martin, made him a crazed man, but I'm more upset by how it's changed me. Every time I comply with one of his demands, I'm chipping away at myself, who I thought I was, the foundation of our marriage, our family, becoming a kept woman—just like Mary Alice. She rules over the children, and William rules over Mary Alice, and that's just the way things go in their family. It's the way things have gone in mine too, I suppose, but I'm seeing the problem in the mechanics of how this family tree flourishes.

I wonder if Finn heard any of our argument last night. I had half a mind to call for a trial separation right then and there. I've had enough of the lies and yelling, but we share this awful secret now. What if one of us talks? We've birthed this monster as a couple, and now we have to stay together because of it. Plus, I think of Finn. He'll think it's his fault because our breakdown happened at the same time his girlfriend died.

Normally, Finn would report to the soccer field right after school on Friday, part of his weekly routine. It's late October, only a few games left in his senior season, the last year to kick the ball around with all the kids he grew up with before college swallows them whole and turns them into men. Finn is stowed away in his room instead. Martin insisted on it. We had to stay indoors, away from the press and gossip. We had to protect Finn until he isn't legally implicated in Yazmin's case anymore.

Maybe I'm just as selfish as Martin, because I'm depressed that Finn won't be able to attend soccer this evening, where I know he wants to be, in the place that will help him heal from all this, from his potential involvement in his girlfriend's death. I tremble, and the gooseflesh won't leave me, and surely Finn's indifference is a mixture of exhaustion and shock. Finn isn't super athletic like Spencer; the only two sports that he was ever into were tae kwon do and soccer. Although once he earned his black belt in martial arts, it was all about soccer.

Finn has a tall, narrow stature like Martin, the perfect build for a soccer forward. He can cut and run in between the other players in a swooping fashion that looks more like an art form than a running pattern. But as I lament over his lost soccer practice, I hate myself.

Because Yazmin will never run again.

She'll never go to a soccer practice or strum her guitar or be any of the beautiful things the world had in store for her, because she had that opportunity taken away from her. When I meet her mother today, I'm sure she'll remind me.

If Finn somehow had a part in it, is he not horrified by these same thoughts? How can he think about playing soccer?

I sigh and try to hold it together as I drive to the Sewickley Hotel—old red leather booths, brick walls, and western Pennsylvanian warmth down dusty basement stairs. It's one of my favorite restaurants in the village. I park outside by the old awning, where a green scalloped curtain hangs over the window with the name plastered on it in a nondescript font. It's the exact type of diner-esque atmosphere that spoke to my father years ago.

Most locals know the restaurant used to be a boutique hotel for the wealthy in the early 1900s, but few know about the separate bar that existed right next door. It burned down, and I know about it only because I'm invested in this community. I'm connected to this town, these people, a member of the PTA at the Academy. I'll be sad that Finn will soon graduate and my work there will be done. But it doesn't take away from the enrichment I've gained from the years I put in there. As much as I want to see justice for this poor girl, I'm scared about the threat to my own existence here too.

I don't know who I am without this place. It's the castle in the sky of my childhood, the enchanted reality of my adulthood, and parking here today, where it all started, to meet Alisha makes me feel like it's coming to an end. It's the same foreboding feeling that came with picking up the rose on the bench.

There's only so much time I can borrow here before it runs out.

Is the house trying to tell me that if I turn myself in, I'll have more time? When I woke up this morning, I noticed the rose was already beginning to wilt, and I had a scary thought that if I didn't make things right with the Veltris by the time it died, I'd die too. The dark thoughts are demanding my attention.

Maybe this is my chance to end them.

I'm early, and I glance in my side-view mirror and see one of my treasured spots a few blocks from the restaurant on the opposite side of Beaver Street. It's one of the last privately owned bookstores in the Pittsburgh area. It used to be managed by an old New York City editor.

She had short blonde hair, chic city glasses, and the best damn children's story time in the world. I know this because the story time was free, so Dad took me often. A craft store with overpriced year-round Christmas ornaments sits in a building to the left, and every year Dad would let me choose one for the tree. He hangs them every year, and I still remember how old I was when I picked out each one.

The Sewickley Hotel is extra special, though, because my father would take me there on winter days when it was too cold to play outside and the movie theater wasn't in the budget. They had the very best tomato soup, and if it wasn't too blizzardy outside, we'd take strolls downtown afterward.

The old Victorian homes shone their brightest when it snowed. They were painted in pastel colors—greens and lavenders—the white latticework like fondant, so shiny and sweet, it was almost edible. Some of the homes in the village, squashed among the shops, could be purchased for a reasonable price. I'd always dreamed one day, maybe, I could afford one.

If I colored my memories incorrectly, like Martin suggested, it started right there in the business district, on Beaver Street. Because I was a firm believer that the grass was greener on their side of the fence, the water truly sweeter.

Although I never considered that over time, the sweet water could turn sour.

That all the effort to hold those glossy blinds shut, to keep the people out, might taint the water and salt the pipes.

And that one day, when there was nothing left to squeeze from the well, no one could've warned me that the last drops of sweet water could very well turn to blood.

I shiver at the somber thought and exit the vehicle, wondering if I should seek help for my increasingly dismal thoughts.

The only person I've heard from since all this started is Camille. She tried to call me this morning, but of course Martin wouldn't let me return her call. So she texted instead. It simply read:

> I told everyone to disregard the rumors about Finn. I hope you're doing okay after what happened to his girlfriend, but in case you're not, here's my go-to gal.

When she couldn't reach me, my best friend threw me a line for her therapist with an iPhone contact share. It was so Sewickley. The things and people I used to think were solid are starting to show their cracks. *We don't have problems, but when we do, we medicate.*

I had to google Dr. Amelia Anderson before realizing it was the Amazing Amelia who had talked Camille off all her proverbial cliffs, although to me they'd seemed more like inconsequential ledges. Compared to the one I am standing on, Camille's back-ordered dental veneers don't seem so important.

I open the door to the restaurant and immediately see Alisha when I walk inside. Even though we've never been formally introduced, she's most certainly the woman with the long dark hair in the corner booth wearing black pants with a stripe down the leg, white shirt, and a man's tuxedo vest—a casino uniform.

I wave, and she nods in my direction to acknowledge me. I walk to the table a nervous wreck. *This will determine who I really am. What I'm capable of.*

"Alisha?"

She nods again, and I can't imagine what's so important that she's spending this afternoon with me instead of her grieving family. I looked in the paper for funeral arrangements for Yazmin but didn't find any. Finn was both saddened and relieved he didn't have to attend her service, but it bothered me that there wasn't one. Is she trying to investigate? Find her daughter's killer? Does she suspect us?

I'm so nervous, I can feel my teeth chattering as I approach the table. "I'm so very sorry for your loss." I can't help myself; I reach across the table and grab this woman's hands.

Tears leak from my eyes, and I start to weep.

Alisha's hands remain in a ball as my hands cup them, and she looks down, tears in her own eyes, but she's shaking her head, signaling to me that she doesn't accept my touch, and I'm left feeling rejected.

I immediately take my hands away.

"I only met Yazmin once and thought she was lovely. Very smart." My voice breaks, because she was. Smart and headstrong. I think about how she went up against William, and it shatters me even more because I think we would've gotten along under other circumstances.

Alisha doesn't say anything. She studies me with her large, nearly opaque eyes. I find myself getting lost in their sorrow until she speaks. "Sit."

I do sit—and quickly. Her text earlier was alarming.

I slide into the booth and look around, noticing the restaurant is surprisingly empty for nearly noon on a Friday. I wish for more people to walk through the door to lighten the air with their breezy laughs and superficial problems.

It's like my father used to say when I complained about our subpar life— *"If you put everyone else's problems in a pile, you'd take yours back."* This is the only time in my life I would choose someone else's.

Just not Alisha's.

"I feel so terrible about what happened. Finn doesn't remember a thing. We're hoping he will in the coming days," I say, but I'm not sure about any of that. Part of me wants him to have permanent amnesia and the other wants him to remember every detail so we can have closure on this tragedy.

"I always thought Finn was a nice boy, and I'm not sure what happened either." Alisha drops her eye contact, and her lip wavers for just a moment.

Her pain—the death of her child—how can she stand it?

"I'll do anything I can to help you." *Anything that's within my husband's warped definition of right. But maybe if you ask me just the right question, I'll do all the things he doesn't want me to do too.*

My stomach is cinched with nerves, and I think this might be the day I splinter.

"Good. There is something we're missing." She implores me with her dark eyes, the lining around the edges thick and uneven. Alisha's complexion is patchy too. I imagine it was beautiful like her daughter's before she lost her husband, beaten by the grief of his death and now her daughter's.

"We are? What're we missing?" I ask, terrified of what this might be.

Her lips undulate again, then stop. Alisha shields her face slightly beneath her hand, and I feel my own tears begin to stab again, ripping a hole in my chest where my heart used to be. We are mothers, and I try not to think about the reverse situation, Finn left for dead in those woods, but I do, and it makes my breath stop. I gasp.

"You know, with all the trouble Cash has gotten himself into, Yazmin was the only bright star in our life." She looks at me as if I'm supposed to know this already.

"I didn't realize Cash was in trouble. Yazmin was lovely. It's such a shame, Alisha." What do Cash's troubles have to do with Yazmin, or Finn for that matter? Maybe her son being in trouble will exonerate Finn somehow.

Alisha sighs. Tears trickle out of her eyes, turning her makeup into dark smears. "Yeah, well, none of us has been quite right since Jimmy died, and Cash has had the worst of it. But I think we both know what I'm after here."

I have no idea.

Whatever she's looking for must be important, and I want to give it to her if I can, but what if it's something that ties Finn to Yazmin's death? My breath rushes out in a deep exhale, and I cup my face with my hands. "I'm sorry. I can't imagine what you're going through. But I don't know what you're talking about."

I reach my hand out to cover hers again, a mark of solidarity between mothers, but she pulls it away. I'm reminded of how her daughter recoiled from me when I tried to embrace her. "I'm not here for your support. I want my daughter's journal back."

Yazmin's journal?

I look at her, confused and afraid. This could be bad. If a journal exists, it could have incriminating things about Finn inside. Bad things. "And you think we have it?" I manage.

A flash of the fingernail marks on Finn's neck fills my head. Finn isn't violent, but then again neither is Martin. But after seeing them both in the kitchen this morning, I wonder whether they're both capable of harm.

She shakes her head, and she's clearly angry now. It's my suspicion that she thought I knew both about her son's troubles and Yazmin's journal. It saddens me because maybe Yazmin spoke to Alisha about Finn, and maybe Alisha spent more time with him when he was over at their house making campaign signs for student council, but Finn rarely talked to me about Yazmin. And when he did, he called her *Yaz*, which made her sound more like a one-name enigma than an actual girl. I met her only that one time before she died. Does Alisha realize this?

"When I asked the police if I could have it back, they said they never received a journal into evidence."

My heart beats into my throat. *Where is it?* I try to remember if Finn had a backpack on him that night in the woods.

No, he didn't.

They'd just come from school. But if that were the case, where were their book bags? Do the police have them? Has Alton "cleaned" them?

Martin couldn't have the journal, could he? "Are you sure the police took the journal in the first place?"

"Yes. When they came to our house, I watched them put it in a plastic bag and mark the outside. It's all I have left of my daughter. It's her last thoughts. I just want it back." Alisha has a grouping of bangle bracelets on her wrist that keeps jangling around as she speaks. By the way they clang together, I can tell she isn't going down without a fight where this journal is concerned.

"I'm so sorry, but I don't know where it is."

"Sheriff Pembroke is your husband's cousin, no?" Her voice is laced with accusation.

There's a clawing horror stretching up my arms. I know why she can't find it.

I fumble with my answer. "Well . . . yes."

"He's the one who took it."

Alisha locks eyes with me, but I look away, my fears confirmed. "I'll ask him about it," I say, but I know she doesn't believe me. She's already decided we're covering something up, and she's right. How stupid of Alton. If he has it, he needs to give it back to Alisha. It belongs to her.

But it could also implicate Finn. These lies are like a falling stack of cards I'll never climb out of. I should fold. The weight of her words is killing me. Crushing me. Because they imply that Finn is involved and everyone knows but me.

But even worse—that Finn could've killed Yazmin. My son—a murderer. The implication lets something loose inside me, an internal gear that's been spinning too fast.

I'm overworked and out of breath.

If she asks the right question, I'll cave. I'll collapse.

Alisha looks at me, dark-cherry lipstick dried and flaky on her lips. "And I know someone else was in the woods with my daughter when she died. It had to be Finn. Just give me the journal back so we can move on from this."

A sharp squeak leaves my mouth as my head involuntarily shakes—no. How does she know this? *Does she know this?* By saying *"had to be*

Finn," she's not sure, is she? "Alisha, I don't know where the journal is, I swear. Why do you say Finn was with her?"

"Because he was the only one with her that day. She didn't have a lot of friends at that school." Alisha's words come out in a hiss, and I stare at my dry hands, still chapped from the evening I handled her daughter. I can't seem to stop washing them, hoping maybe the sensation will go away—the feel of Yazmin's lifeless flesh beneath my fingers.

"Can I get you something to drink?"

I jump. A server has appeared out of nowhere. It's a perfectly normal thing to happen in a restaurant, the preliminary drink order, but Alisha stares at the girl as if she's just encroached on our space.

"I'll take an iced tea. And for you, Alisha?" I ask, keeping my voice steady. "I assume we're not eating?"

Alisha shakes her head, and now the server is the one giving us a dirty look. "I'll take a diet soda, whatever you've got," she says. The young girl bounces away and says something snide to the bartender. Normally, I'd be worried it would get back to my circle of friends that I stiffed the staff at the Sewickley Hotel with nothing more than a non-alcoholic drink order, but today I couldn't care less. Those are problems I'd gladly take back from the pile.

"My husband said Finn was home all night." The words feel awful leaving my mouth, but if I can pretend they're true, maybe I can believe them.

"Yazmin doesn't travel alone at night," Alisha says simply, weaving her hands inside each other nervously, her bangles scraping together. This woman doesn't want our money. She wants the last piece of her daughter that exists, her final thoughts before she left this earth. I'd want that journal back too. Yet it could incriminate Finn. The tear in my moral seam is ripping further.

"I see," I say, mindful of my next remarks.

Martin knew I could easily break down today, but he let me go anyway. Maybe this is a test. If I fail, it will be proof I never belonged by

155

his side to begin with, something I've always feared. Counseling is out. Can't tell a counselor about the kind of problems we have. Martin's version of me failing him will be my inability to lie to protect our family.

I want to tell Yazmin's mother the truth, but something keeps me quiet beyond Martin's awful plea. It's the unknown. There's something we're all missing. There's a reason Finn can't remember what happened beyond the drugs, and I need to figure that out before I make any more decisions.

The waitress places the drinks down, but neither one of us acknowledges them.

"Perhaps the drugs made her less inhibited, so she ventured out for a hike to blow off steam after their fight," I suggest, and the lies are tumbling from my lips, but I'm gradually getting better at them, much to my disgust. Not only is Martin not the person I thought he was, neither am I. I'm no better than the Ellsworths, yet I can't stop. Not until I know the truth.

They were Yazmin's drugs, though. And this is a point I don't want to let go.

Yazmin would still be alive if she hadn't offered up her meth-laced pot and whatever else she'd brought with her that evening. I have to let Alisha know I'm aware of the narcotics. It doesn't justify her death. Lots of teenagers play around with substances. The only thing is, Finn had no interest in drugs before he dated Yazmin, and there has already been backlash in the community since the news broke that Finn is a *user*. Those comments cut me deeply, and they could hurt his future as well.

Martin said it would all blow over if we stayed the course, as if we're just sailing through a storm, but I'm not so sure.

"Her guitar teacher said he overheard her talking to Cash during their lesson about going for a walk and a smoke in the woods with her boyfriend. Cash confirmed it."

I inhale sharply, because there it is—the truth, like a big old lead balloon in the air that can't be retracted.

"At the Academy?" I ask. I can't imagine the kids would talk openly about drugs at school.

"No, at the local shop. In your downtown. Academy grad himself," Alisha adds with resentment.

"It's odd that they would talk so freely in front of the music teacher."

My hands pat the bottom of my oversize purse. The checkbook Martin asked me to pack has sunk to the bottom of my old Gucci bag like a rock. It's billfold leather and heavy, like everything else we own. The symbolism of what it means weighs me down even more.

I'm no better than an Ellsworth if I do this.

"Cash mentioned in front of the teacher that they were going to smoke, but he didn't say what they were going to smoke, so he wasn't giving anything away. I got the impression that the teacher knew, though. Some rocker guy from town, and he has the look too." She pulls out a pack of cigarettes and pats the bottom with her hands, her bracelets banging together. She's clearly ready to leave, ready to smoke, from all the anxiety we've caused her. "It's funny, since he's from here and all," Alisha says with contempt, and I understand her hatred. She thinks we're just another rich family taking advantage of someone like herself, hiding the evidence so we won't be caught, our hands in the police's pockets.

But there's no way the words—*"how much do you want?"*—can ever escape my lips, no matter how much Martin wants them to. It's the same thing as asking a mother how much her child's life is worth, and there's no number for that. I slowly let go of the checkbook.

I've helped more woman like Alisha—single, struggling to raise a family—than she'll ever know, but none of that matters now.

Still processing all of this, I say, "A rocker guy from town . . ." An Academy grad himself, Alisha said. Memories surface like bubbles in a baking-soda bath, and I stop myself. "What was his name again?"

It can't be. I've been thinking about him so much lately, hearing his music in my head.

Alisha slams the bottom of the pack harder. "They call him Mr. Joshua. I don't know if it's his first name or last. He asked that he not be involved. It's why he didn't tell the police about the conversation he overheard, but I think he felt guilty, so he told me when I went to see him."

I grip the table, and my vision goes sideways for a moment. My breathing does strange things. "Are you all right?" she asks.

I tell her yes, but I'm far from it.

He's back? It can't be my Joshua. It must be another.

"I wonder why he didn't disclose that to the cops. It wouldn't be involving him," I say, my voice thin.

But what I want to say is, *"Joshua Louden? My Joshua?"*

No, he lives overseas.

That's the box I've put him in for so long. It's how I've compartmentalized my life. He's gone—overseas—and there's no use thinking about him anymore.

Just a colorful character from my past.

He's not allowed to be back here again.

He can't be back—here—playing his beautiful guitar. He lived overseas doing his missionary work, but perhaps he's come home now. And perhaps the music I've been hearing wasn't a figment of my imagination.

"I'm sorry, Alisha, but I don't think I can give you what you want." My blood pressure is cooking me in the tiny wooden booth.

"I'm asking you to question your son again. And the sheriff. It will be better for him if he comes forward now."

"Okay." I'm breathing heavily.

"I want that journal," Alisha says.

She knows. She knows.

"He already said he wasn't with her. The police determined only one set of footprints in the area of the woods where Yazmin was found." *Because the cleaners have covered up the rest.*

Dear God, I deserve to burn, but why is Joshua back teaching my son's girlfriend guitar? *He can't be.*

Alisha makes a fist. "I know what he may have told you, but ask him again. And find that journal."

I flinch. *Or else.*

She doesn't say the words, but I read them in her eyes. She's lost so much already. She won't let us take this too.

"I need to go. Some of us have to work for a living." She shoots up from her seat and throws some dollar bills on the table.

I stand up, watching her leave, the checkbook inside the purse hanging heavy at my side. For the first time, I wonder if I should've used it, because if Martin finds out about Joshua, it might *really* be the end of our life as we know it.

I never told Martin about Joshua.

Not about our involvement when I was younger or the fact that we live in his old house. Or about what happened in our downstairs pool.

And certainly not about what happened when he resurfaced in my early twenties during the week Martin and I were broken up.

CHAPTER 14

December 1999

"The ring feels so heavy on my finger."

"Not a bad problem to have," Hanna says.

I'm struggling to breathe, practically choking on my own saliva. "It's obnoxious. Too large. I have small fingers."

"Try to calm down." Hanna pats my back. "Breathe." We're sitting on an area rug on our apartment floor because I think that's where I must've collapsed when I came inside.

"I just can't. I can't right now. It's too soon." Everything is hot—my itchy sweater, my wool socks, my hair pasted to my face with melted snow and sweat.

"Push out the wedding date. Give yourself time."

I fan myself. "Open a window. For fuck's sake. What is it? Ninety degrees in here?"

"This place never did heat evenly." Hanna stands, and I hear her unlatch the lock and slide open the window positioned over the heating register. A frosty breeze cools down my current hell. "How many damn karats is that anyway?" Hanna asks.

"*Hanna!* I'm totally freaking out here." I'm yanking at the ring, but it won't come off. "I said yes, but only because I couldn't say no."

I sought Martin out my freshman year after Tush died. I was the one who'd promised to keep him out of trouble, and I took that vow seriously, but I wonder now if it was too soon to make that kind of commitment.

His empathy, those chocolate-brown eyes full of pain, had sliced into me, but was I trying to put a Band-Aid over old wounds, make up for the person who wasn't there for me when I was left hurting? Martin needed me, but I needed him more. He knocked the breath out of me with his sadness, the exact kind I understood.

And now I'm hyperventilating.

"Give it to me." Hanna begins yanking on my sweaty finger. "Why didn't he check your ring size first? What kind of engineer is he?"

"How can you be cracking jokes right now?" I begin to cry. "I haven't even graduated yet." And we didn't talk about this. You're supposed to talk about these things first. But even if we didn't, it shouldn't feel this wrong.

"I'm sorry." She pets my head. "You don't have to go through with it."

Hanna runs to her room and returns with a glass jar. She begins to rub something gooey on my finger, and I try not to question why she has such a large vat of petroleum jelly in her bedroom.

It works—the ring jerks over my knuckle. Hanna falls backward onto the ground. Now we're both lying on the living room area rug, side by side. She's holding my ring up to the light. "This bitch has the cut and clarity of a paragon."

"A who?"

"A perfect diamond."

"I always forget you're going to be a chemical engineer." I guess she would know about science-y things like that, but I didn't. And this geologic fact doesn't help me at all.

"I guess it's really unreasonable that I would back out of the proposal, then." I sigh. "Seeing as how he bought me a perfect diamond and all . . ."

"You turned him down?" Hanna sits up, and her bleached hair is stuck to her forehead.

I place my hands over my face. "Well, not at first. I couldn't say no before he put the ring on my finger. I had to wait until after because he had a string quartet playing for me, Hanna!"

All Martin's gestures are big, but I'm not the girl who needs big gestures. Or one who wants them. I fell in love with the simple kid on the frat house steps who wanted nothing more than a quiet dinner with the girl who'd brought him soup when he was sick.

We have a good relationship, Martin and I, but there are more discussions that need to be had before I can transition into an Ellsworth.

Hanna rolls her eyes, unamused. "Of course he did. It's Martin."

"'Everything I Do' by Bryan Adams."

"Ugh. That's an awful song. I would've backed out too." She's laughing again, and I hate her for it, but she makes me laugh-cry too.

"I know! I had to wait until they were done playing. And then I said yes. I couldn't embarrass him. In front of all those people. We were at a fancy restaurant. It would've humiliated him."

Hanna laughs. "Not in front of the quartet. Heck no."

"And then I just said I needed time to think, and he told me to keep the ring and that every time I look at it, I'll know how much he loves me. That's why I just want it off!"

But why does he love me?

Is it for the wrong reasons? Is it because I was his good girl who kept him out of trouble? Does he expect me always to be? What does that entail exactly? I met his mother and don't know if I can be like her, if that's what he's looking for.

I didn't grow up country-club-style. There's a lot more to the weight of this ring than the karat size.

"Well, I don't really get why, but I've got this." Hanna is bouncing the ring around on her palm, watching the waves of light from the window catch and reflect in the oversize prism.

I never needed a ring that big.

I never wanted a ring that big. Why didn't he ask me before he went out and bought it? He should know these things if he's to be my husband.

I'm panting. "I'm not a huge-ass-diamond kind of girl. He should go find one of those if that's what he's looking for." It reminds me of the ring the lady had on at my mother's funeral, the survivor. I had awful thoughts when her ring had grazed my skin, scratched it, really.

I wonder if she bought it in Switzerland? A victory purchase. I wonder if she scratches her kids with that ring when she hugs them like she did me.

I've always wanted to be one of the lucky ones, but now that it's thrust upon my left ring finger with no warning, I'm not sure. About anything. Martin included. If he knew me, this ring should feel like the right one, the perfect fit. But it doesn't. It's too big in some ways and too small in others, and it symbolizes parts of myself that I'm not sure are real.

"Well, I *am* that kind of girl, but you could seriously maim your firstborn with this thing."

"My thoughts exactly. What do I do?"

"You asked for a break. So take one. Come on. Let's hide this rock in your sock drawer and hit the bar."

"I promised my dad I'd help him Christmas shop." I pant some more. "I'm already late." It's our day to go into the village and pick out our yearly Christmas ornament. He had to have known Martin was going to propose tonight. Surely he asked my dad first for my hand.

Hanna makes a worried face. "Meet me later, then?"

I nod, even though I have no intention of keeping my promise. Hanna holds out her hands and yanks me off the floor. She hugs me. "Just give yourself a minute to figure it out. No engagement should come as *this* big a surprise."

"I know. Right?" I ask.

"Right," she answers. My spontaneous, free-spirited roommate is also my voice of reason. It does feel completely out of the blue. Martin and I have talked about marriage, but not recently. It seems so sudden, surprising in a bad way, not a good one. This should be something the bride could see coming from a mile away, not a sneak attack.

I walk to the front door, still dressed up in the Christmassy attire I wore earlier. I'd normally change to meet my dad, but I have too many other things to worry about.

"Are you going to be okay?" she asks.

"Sure," I say. I let the door swing shut behind me. I will definitely not be okay.

As I walk out of the apartment, snowflakes stick to the petroleum jelly on my finger, making a white ring. I cry and laugh simultaneously at the marital design strung around my bare finger. It will be long melted off by the time I get to the ornament shop, a smeared-jelly mess. I hope my engagement dissolves as quickly. I don't understand my own feelings. I love Martin, but I feel blindsided and smothered. Martin said he wanted a very short engagement, which has only heightened my anxiety.

Sometimes it feels like Martin is playing the part everyone else expects him to play—well-mannered kid from the Heights, aspiring entrepreneur, president of the fraternity—but I get glimpses of other sides of him too that leave me confused, and even though we've been together for years, the idea of spending a lifetime with him is as unsettling as it is premature.

I meet my father in front of the ornament store.

"Well, you don't look like a happy bride-to-be."

I have my hands tucked inside my gray peacoat. "Why didn't you tell me?"

His smile crumples. "I thought it was what you wanted. It's not? We've had our differences over Martin, but I'm not one to stand in the way." Even though he's not smiling, Dad's voice deceives him. He's secretly happy I'm unhappily engaged.

"You're not telling the truth," I say.

"You know my feelings on Martin and what happened with that pledge. I'd say if you don't marry him, you can find somebody better." He looks down.

"Dad, he wasn't even there." It has become an echo. Something I've said to my dad so many times, it's ineffectual.

"Are you sure? I'm not. And it doesn't mean he wasn't negligent."

I shake my head, because we've had this argument so many times, we're both too exhausted to bring it up again. It's a three-year-long debate. Three years should be long enough to date someone before getting married, but it doesn't feel right. I imagined I'd have a job and my own apartment first. I had a plan. "I wanted to establish myself first before I added someone else to the mix. The ring just feels too soon," I say.

"Come inside." Dad's large hand is warm on my arm as he escorts me into the store. "Then take your time, Sarah Bear. Engagements can last years or longer. There's more I need to tell you about that day the pledge died."

"I asked for some more time. To think about everything," I say, and I don't think I want to hear the *more* part—about that day. Everything is confusing enough.

"Good, I'm glad you asked for time," he says. And that's that. To Dad, there's not a whole lot more to say. He didn't approve of Martin from the start, and I've always gotten the sense that it felt like a betrayal to him that I started dating him in the first place because he'd told me to stay away from the SAEs.

My dad picks up a cardinal ornament. It's not in a bulb like the usual ones we've chosen in the past but a freestanding bird perched on a snowy branch.

"I like that one," I tell him.

He bites his lip. "There's been one visiting me lately, tapping at the window." He doesn't have to tell me for me to know he thinks the bird is my mother. I don't know that I'll ever love Martin as much as he still loves her, and it bothers me immensely. Their marriage was so pure, unfettered by major issues like class difference or money or life ambition. None of those things mattered as long as they had each other. That's the way it should be.

There's something missing in my relationship with Martin, and I can't pinpoint it. Or I'm just too scared to fulfill my destiny—to really become one of the lucky ones. I'm afraid I won't live up to their expectations.

"It's decided, then." Dad takes out his wallet. "Fastest ornament pick in the history of time." His raspy laugh makes me edgy.

"I have to go somewhere, Dad." Everything is wrong. I can't pick out Christmas ornaments with my father like it's any other day. *I've made a terrible decision accepting Martin's proposal—and then rejecting it. Or have I?*

"Are you okay?" Dad squints at me, vinyl shopping bag in hand. "I thought we could grab a bite." It's part of our usual routine to eat dinner after we've chosen our ornament, but nothing about today is normal. "We can talk some more about it," Dad suggests.

I don't want to talk some more about it. I'm a little bit mad at him for not talking to me about it sooner. If I'd had some warning, some idea this was happening, I wouldn't be in a complete state of shock. I might even be all right with it. "I'm okay; I just have a lot to think about."

"Okay, well, my door's always open, sweetheart. And there was more I needed to tell you."

"I know. Thanks."

He gives me a hug. "Lots can change after college, Sarah Bear. There's a big world out there."

"Right." I know what he's telling me. There's a big world with lots of people to meet. Other people who could potentially become my husband if I'm not 100 percent sure that Martin Ellsworth is the one. The thing is, I was certain I was going to marry him up until he sidelined me with a ring. I'm not sure what has changed, but all of a sudden, I feel boxed in. Trapped.

"Bye, Dad." I walk back to my car and climb inside. As I drive away, I look out at the houses in the village graced with powdered crowns, and I don't know where I'm driving to, but I need to get the hell out of here. Christmas is coming in less than a week, and what kind of awful person does this to someone right before the holidays?

Me, that's who.

I'm despicable. Unworthy of Martin. Unworthy of the life he wants to give me and the ginormous rock that looked completely ridiculous on my small finger. Martin needs a trophy wife who can naturally fall into that sort of life, one with old money and manners, the kind of woman with long limbs and appendages to sport fancy accessories like oversize diamonds.

I cry as I drive farther into Sewickley, and I want to get a little lost for a while, so I take the back roads. I'm not sure why I start down Dad's old drive-by route, past Josh's house, the place I last suffered a broken heart.

If I'd never met you, Joshua, would I have fallen so hard for Martin?

My heart was shattered back then. Martin's heart was shattered too after Tush died. And we put each other back together, but that's not how true love should be. That's not how my parents met, and it's not the how-I-met-you story I want to tell my future kids.

I'm flying down the windy, snowy back roads because it's where I used to go to escape when I was younger, and there's never been a day I needed to disappear into the woods more than this one. It's brisk outside, but my internal temperature is on fire, so I roll down my window and start along Dad's drive-by path.

It's comforting to see that the large, etched gargoyles are still guarding Gargoyle Manor and that the Castle has added a real, retracting drawbridge. The White House hasn't lost its opulent shimmer. It's nearly blinding next to the freshly fallen snow.

I've saved the best for last, and even though my body is beginning to cool, I leave my window down because it doesn't seem right rolling by Stonehenge with it up.

I almost think I'm dreaming when I hear the music. Or is it the wind?

There are definitely some strings. It's music. I stop and park.

And I listen.

Someone is playing "Scar Tissue" by Red Hot Chili Peppers, and my fingers tap to the beat along with my heart. It's gotta be *him*. Who else could it be?

My heart leaps out of my chest, his chords soaking into my body like a warm bath on a cold day. Just listening to him soothes me.

And—so not Bryan Adams. It makes me think all my life decisions over the past four years have been wrong, a way to force myself into a life that looked good on paper, joining a family from the Heights with the right kind of background but not one that felt good in my soul, like this music right now.

I leave my car parked right there on the road and run through the yard to the pergola.

Is it him? Is he home?

I run through the snow and the mud until I can see him—Joshua.

My heart stops as I watch him play his guitar. It's windy outside, and I imagine the torrent sweeping me back in time. He stops playing and looks up, his chin-length hair wet with snow, but he looks just like my Joshua. His eyes lock on to mine through the tree line, and my heart palpitates in my throat along with the rest of my body. My feet move toward him without thinking, drawn to him.

Where did you go, my love? Why did you leave me?

"Sarah." His face lights up. The pergola is strung with Christmas lights, and it's so beautiful out there in the middle of the woods, I imagine this is our enchanted kingdom and I just fell through the back of my wardrobe into my own Narnia.

It isn't real. Nothing can hurt me here.

I walk closer until I can almost touch him. "I don't know what I'm doing here. I'm having a really bad day," I say.

He smiles, just like the day he found me in the car. Like it's nothing that I just rolled up to his house. "Let me make it better. Your day." He puts his guitar down and wraps his arms around me.

I lean into him and smell his woodsy scent, and there's never been an embrace that felt so familiarly wonderful. "You give the best hugs," I tell him. The final tears leak out of my eyes, and his flannel shirt absorbs them until they disappear.

No one knew about Joshua, my little secret. That's what made him safe. I nuzzle into his chest.

I should be crying over Martin, but I'm not. I'm letting go the tears I never cried for Joshua when he left without saying goodbye. I gulp at the air to breathe, realizing this moment is one I've needed all along. His body feels right, comfort, love, what I've been missing for the last three years. All my thoughts of uncertainty over Martin are replaced by a knowing embrace, one that feels right. Pure.

I'm tortured that this is who my heart still wants. I want to be in control of it. I want to want Martin this way, to feel this way with him, but I can't, and I don't know why.

"I'm sorry you're having an awful day. You still look beautiful if it's any consolation. I've never seen you in a dress before. Wow." I look up, and he grabs my face in his rough hands, and they're so different from Martin's, and I love it, all the contrasts, because anything that's not like Martin's perfect hands or his perfect diamond is perfect to me right now. It seems a hard standard to live up to for a lifetime. I don't want to be the stressed companion to keep everything in pristine order. I want a more relaxed life, something more like . . . this.

Joshua tips my head back and kisses me so deeply, I nearly black out.

What. Is. Happening?

I let myself disappear into him, because I need to escape more than I need to think.

We're clinging together beneath the pergola. I break away from him. "You left without saying goodbye." I'm breathless and confused, but I still need to know. All the torn emotions he left me with led me straight to Martin. I craved Martin's stability at the time, but now it feels like an insecure cop-out.

He flips his hair out of his eyes. "I hate goodbyes. We were going in two different directions. It was better that way."

All my resentment washes away in an instant. Josh didn't leave me without saying goodbye because he didn't care. He left because he didn't want to feel the sadness of our departure from each other. I can feel it in his kisses. He never stopped caring for me, his want for me uncontrolled, not planned at all, genuine.

"I've missed you," I say, and I don't realize how much I actually have until I say the words. It makes me wonder if everything I've done up until this point was a way to put a bandage over the wound Joshua left behind, the feeling of abandonment I never wanted to feel again after my mother died. I didn't have to be perfect for Joshua; I just had to be me. Martin deserves someone who can live up to his standards, wear his enormous diamond with poise, share his political views. I have so many questions for Joshua. If he ever made it to the camps to help all those people shattered by war. If he ever got to chase the Brit-pop thing he idolized as a kid. Has he even gotten to try? I need to know.

"You've never been far from my thoughts." Joshua kisses me again, this time hungrier.

I don't know if his parents are home, but I let Joshua lay me down on the cement bench this time. I'm sure he would ask me if I'd be more comfortable somewhere else, but our clothes are coming off too fast, my dress already hiked up to my hips. I can't believe how hot I am with my bare back pressed against the chilled cement bench, urgency replacing any guarded desires I had the last time I was here.

When we're finished, he says, "I've missed you too. I'm just home visiting my parents for the holidays."

"You're home for the holidays?"

He nods. *And you didn't call me?* My stomach twists. Was I wrong in assuming what we had was special?

We dress quickly, because it's cold, but I still lean into Josh, absorbing his heat. Crazy thoughts enter my brain as snowflakes swirl all around us. *What drew me to Stonehenge? Is it the house or Joshua or a little of both?*

"Are you going to leave without saying goodbye this time?" I ask.

He shakes his hair out of his face again. "Probably. I hate goodbyes."

"Me too. I have to go, though. I'm sorry I'm so out of sorts. Thank you for making my day better." I get up to leave, shocked by what I've just done. It's snowing, the wintry mist casting an ethereal blanket around the world I created here. My heart is still beating fast, but things that happen here can't hurt me. I feel invincible in Joshua's presence.

Alive and free, not trapped by my decisions.

Joshua watches me curiously, and I want him to be thinking about me after I leave.

"Don't say it," he says.

"I won't," I say.

I won't say goodbye.

I run back to my car. I can't explain what just happened, and I decide I don't have to. No one knows he exists. That pergola is like my Narnia, and now I'm climbing through my closet wardrobe, back to the other side.

Although I actually consider taking off with him. I'm almost done with school, and if he'd wait for me to finish, I'd follow him anywhere if he'd let me. Joshua and I have that special connection my mother and father shared—the one Martin and I lack.

The only problem is, when I try to go back again and knock on Joshua's door a few days later, he's already gone—before Christmas. I'm shocked. Sick. But I have my answer.

Joshua was the catalyst to lead me back to my steady arrow and nothing more. He's not a stayer; he's an abandoner, a misfit, a real heartbreaker.

Just like Martin said, I lost my head for a bit, got cold feet, but all would be forgiven.

I just wish I could forgive myself for the consequences. Because as much as I like to pretend Stonehenge was a fantasy and Joshua was a ghost, the pain he left behind is very real.

CHAPTER 15

Present

The front doorbell chimes in the tiny music store at the very end of the street. It's easy to miss tucked in a tiny alcove with a flower basket hanging in front of the gold lettering on the window. I should tell the owner to move it so people can find the place, but really, it just bothers me because I can't remember if this store has always been here or if it's one of the few places in town I haven't discovered yet.

Not that it would matter. Everyone in my household lacks musical ability except for Spencer. He seems to excel at everything he does, but by middle school, football and swimming quickly became a larger priority, and he stopped playing piano altogether. However, he barely needed lessons to learn how to play in the first place. I worried what Martin might think, but Spencer's musical ability didn't really cross his radar—Martin was concerned only about his son's prowess at sports.

We have a piano in the sitting room, but only because Martin was forced to learn how to play when he was young. He passed that burden on to his children, who also have no desire to play. The baby grand is really just an ornamental decoration piece.

"Grand dust collector," we should call it. But I love that we have a symbol of music in our home. Stonehenge should have music in it. The house probably misses it since Joshua and Spencer moved away.

When Spencer used to play, the notes filled the whole house with a special energy. Of course they did. This thought only adds fuel to the fire burning within me—why is Joshua back?

I sigh, my life a walking contradiction. No one plays music anymore in the house made for acoustics, and no one prays in the home with stained-glass windows fit for a church. I can't remember the last time we went to a service.

We're no longer the happy family we pretended to be. Poor Spencer isn't really in the know about the circumstances of Yazmin's death. Although we called him to tell him about the tragedy, he knows only the watered-down version—that Finn and Yazmin went for a walk, argued, and that she'd had an accident in the woods and died. But soon he'll come home for fall break and be a part of the real mess too. The whole morning sags with a grief that can never be lifted, a young dead girl weighing at the center of it.

But the mention of Joshua's name tinges the day with a sliver of light. He always made me feel so attuned to myself, my senses. *Could it be my Joshua?*

I'd die for just a hit of that lucidity today.

I search the music store for Joshua like he can fix all my problems.

He did when I was younger, my largest issue loneliness. I found a boy who was just like me in so many ways—an only child with an absent mother. Mine was dead, but I had to believe the fact that his being still alive and away traveling by choice was almost as painful. Josh cared about the world, people. He wanted to make it a better place even if he didn't become rich in the process. He hated that our troops were dying over something like oil, something we have plenty of ourselves, an opinion we shared.

All my feelings of inadequacy were resolved in the confines of his arms. How have I strayed so far from myself now?

My father always said that when you look at people, you either see a door or a window—a reflection of yourself or a dead end—and I've never seen a more honest reflection of myself than I did in Joshua. He was earnest and genuine, not there just to put on a show. He was down to brass tacks from the moment you met him, no fluff.

I'd give anything to see even a piece of my old self again, because after this afternoon, talking to that bereaved mother, I don't know who I am anymore. I'm horrified the checkbook in my purse even exists. That's not me. Maybe Josh can remind me of who I am.

Maybe he can also reveal clues about Yazmin, since he was her teacher. If I can figure out what happened to her, know in my heart of hearts that Finn did nothing wrong, maybe there's still a chance for my family to heal from this.

I sneeze at the dust in the store and hear a rustling in the back room. My nerves are like popcorn kernels in a sizzling pan of oil, ready to go off at any moment. I don't know what I hope to accomplish here, but part of me just wants to see Josh again.

I pretend to take interest in a violin I'm not even sure how to hold when a man appears from the back storeroom. I almost drop the damn thing, probably the most expensive instrument in the store.

It's *him*.

He's carrying a whole bunch of metal music holders. "Just a minute," he says over his shoulder as he wrestles with the stands. His voice has gotten deeper, and I wonder what it's done to his singing voice, if puberty is something that affects rocker boys who turn into rocker men. When he's finished setting the stands down, he walks toward me, then freezes midway across the store. I grip the violin with both hands and offer a tight-lipped smile, the sweep of electricity that rips through me when I see him just as strong now as it was back then.

I can't believe he can still do this to me. I hear a thumping in my throat, and I'm sure it's my heart.

"Sarah?" he says, and when I get a good look at him, I see that his voice is the only thing that's changed, really. He's still tall with shaggy hair and broad shoulders, thin frame, torn-up jeans hanging just right. He's even wearing a damn concert tee that shows off some interesting arm ink he didn't have before, and I have to blink twice to make sure it's not 1996 again. Joshua has a slight stubble on his chin too, but it all works for him.

"Hi, Joshua," I say.

"Hey, I thought you'd be in someday," he says.

Then why haven't you contacted me? The combination of anticipation and sorrow that always happens when I see him races up and down my body, my pulse quickening. I'm so happy to see him but still in shock from when he left.

Joshua grabs the side of his neck, revealing a small scar, and I wonder how it got there. I want to ask him about the scar and so many other things. I want to know if he ever made it to Europe and what he saw on his mission trips, if he ever married or had children, but of course this isn't an appropriate time to ask those things. I tried to cyber stalk him in my early years of marriage, after I had Spencer, but my searches turned up empty. I was more disappointed for him than myself, because it meant he hadn't made it in the music world, domestic or abroad.

"How long have you been back?" I ask.

He takes a deep breath, then exhales, blowing the hair off his cheek. "Almost two years."

Two years?

Disappointment settles onto my chest like a jagged rock. It was just teenage love, but he never apologized for how he'd left things. We knew it was over once I started school. He had plans to venture overseas as a missionary through his church and work on his music in between.

His parents hadn't agreed with his plans.

I know this only because when I showed up at his house after work one day in my red polo shirt, weeks before he was supposed to leave, his parents were actually home for once. When they answered the door, they looked at me and said, *"We didn't order takeout."*

I explained I was Josh's friend. The few times his parents had been home when I was there, he hadn't introduced me. The house was so large, he'd always usher me to a part where they weren't, saying things like, *"You're better off—trust me."*

I thought it was because Josh was afraid they might catch on to what we were doing, but a bigger part of me thought it was because he was embarrassed of me, where I came from. His father just shrugged and told me in a matter of a few sentences that Josh had sold his Jeep for cash and taken off for Europe early because they'd frozen his bank account in an attempt to stop him.

"Let me know if you see the spoiled brat," he said before slamming the door in my face.

I don't like to think about the second time he came back, my senior year at CMU when we'd reconnected and I couldn't believe he left home before Christmas. A different era of bad decisions.

"I never left," I tell Josh. I sound pathetic, but I can't believe he's been back that long and hasn't contacted me.

"I know," he says gently, and he's only making me more aware of the fact that he knew exactly where I was and chose not to get in touch. "Is one of your children taking up violin?" he asks, and I'm confused by the question.

He points to the instrument in my hand.

"Oh, no." I hand it back to him, embarrassed. "I was actually looking for the music teacher who taught guitar here . . . to Yazmin Veltri."

Josh breaks eye contact and takes the violin from me.

"I never expected it to be you," I lie. I'm not sure he deserves my honesty yet.

"I already talked to the cops, and I'm not at liberty to say much to anyone else. She was a nice girl. Why're you interested?" He turns his back on me and puts the violin in its place. The muscles of his shoulders pull at his snug T-shirt. It wasn't just a childhood infatuation; he's still beautiful. I fight the blush threatening to take over my face. When I jumped from Joshua to Martin, it was a monumental leap away from heartbreak and into something steady.

It might've been because Joshua was more of a phantom than a real person. I don't even think Martin owns a concert T-shirt. In fact, we don't go to concerts, and I love music.

I made the leap because I needed the stability.

I made the leap because Joshua took off, and I was looking for a steady arrow to guide me.

"She was my son's girlfriend," I say.

He stiffens and cocks his neck to the side. "That seems about right."

"What's that supposed to mean?" I ask.

Josh turns to me, and his pretty green eyes glint in the sunlight. "You know I went to school with your husband at the Academy, right? He was a grade above me, and we didn't exactly run in the same circles."

"What?" This fact, which should've been as blatantly obvious to me as a splatter of mud on a white horse, never occurred to me before. I always placed the two men in such separate buckets, compartmentalized them in a way that made sense, that I hadn't realized their connection. The Academy is small, though, so of course they knew each other. My mouth is still hanging open.

"You didn't." He frowns.

I'm wondering if he's displeased because I didn't make the connection or if he's disappointed that I haven't mentioned him to Martin. He has to understand I had my reasons. Especially after the last time he came home. I wonder if he ever thought about the consequences of his actions.

"I just never put two and two together."

"Just like his fraternity scandal. You ever put those two halves together, or did you know about the whole of it and marry him anyway?" Joshua sounds offended, and I'm not sure why.

What did Tush's death have to do with anything?

"Josh, Martin wasn't found accountable for what happened at his fraternity. Neither was the fraternity, for that matter."

"Exactly." Josh crosses his arms.

My head is spinning. "You're out of line. You didn't even live here then. You were gone for years."

And then I think about the sum of all the parts. The ones Josh is mentioning and the strange happenings in my own home.

The way Martin's been acting since Yazmin's death, like a subhuman who will stop at nothing to cover up Finn's tracks when we don't even know what it is we're covering. Suddenly it all feels tainted with a strange familiarity to what we went through in college. Martin turned overnight from a carefree kid to an adult who would convince anyone who was standing right next to him how unfortunate the accident was, as if it were a presidential address—how he had nothing to do with it. William had trained him early. I'm realizing that now.

But Josh has his facts wrong. Doesn't he?

Josh makes a face I can describe only as painfully sympathetic. "Wow, how could you not know? You were there, weren't you? At the same college? Do you know what I'm talking about? The kid who was hazed and died of alcohol poisoning?"

"Yeah, I remember. It was my first semester freshman year. I was . . . I was focused on other things."

"You were too busy to notice a student's death at your school at your boyfriend's fraternity? That seems pretty attention grabbing." Josh is absentmindedly straightening out items in the store that don't seem to need straightened.

"The headlines read differently from what you're suggesting." I cough, but his words are slicing right through me, and I can't figure out why. I was there when it all went down; Josh wasn't. I was at the party the night Tush died, and Martin wasn't even there. Josh has it all wrong.

The dust in the store is making my sinuses itch, and a familiar sensation in my lower abdomen pains me, along with the burning in my eyes. I shift my weight from one suede boot to the other.

"The bathroom is around back." Joshua points to the corner of the store.

"What?" I ask.

"I know that look. You have to use the loo, no?" *The loo?* At least I know he made it to London and tried out the Brit-pop-rock thing he'd idolized as a kid, too cool to jump on the alternative-rock bandwagon.

"Yeah." I sigh, frustrated that I've proven to be so predictable and boring compared to the girl who made love in every dark corner of his house.

Of Stonehenge. My house. His house.

Ugh. I wonder if he knows. My bladder continues to nag at me. "Thank you, excuse me." I practically run to the back of the store.

I was so anxious to see Joshua, and now I'm eager to run away from him. Ironic, since he's always been the one good at leaving.

As I wash my hands, I think of Yazmin and the sweet water that ran beside her, and the wave hits me. It's so sudden, the tremor of horror and grief that rocks my body out of nowhere. She's never far from my mind. "I'm sorry," I whisper. I take in a deep breath to quiet my nerves, and there's a scent in here that's so familiar, if I close my eyes, I can picture myself smoking it in the backyard—marijuana.

Joshua still smokes. Big shocker. And he wants to come down on me for my life choices? If he teaches his students high, I'm sure the community will have something to say about that.

I rub my hands on the threadbare white hand towel and glance in the mirror. I look like . . . "Shit."

I open the mirrored cabinet on instinct and find it—Josh's vaping pen—but I'm positive there's more than nicotine in there. I quickly shut the cabinet.

There's a bulletin board up in the bathroom, which is odd, but this place is so small, I doubt it has an office. I see a thumbtacked paper with FOR M. JANE—JAY and a phone number scrawled on it. M. Jane sounds like a person's name, but I know it's Josh's code for pot—*Mary Jane*.

Instinctively, I take a picture of it with my phone and then realize I'm doing this because marijuana is what connects Yazmin's case to this bathroom and Josh's vaping pen.

Lots of people smoke weed, and they even use it for medicinal purposes, but there's a tiny niggle in the back of my brain that won't let up. Josh knows something about what happened to Yazmin, and he doesn't want to tell me. He was tense when I asked about her, turning his back on me. And he relayed information to Alisha that he hadn't told the police—why?

Maybe he doesn't feel comfortable telling me because I married Martin Ellsworth and he thinks my husband is a scandalous bastard. But maybe if I can convince him I'm on his side, he'll help me.

I exit the bathroom and find Josh busying himself with the odds and ends of the store.

I walk up to him. "Josh, I want to help find out what happened to Yazmin. I'm not here on Finn's behalf or Martin's. To be honest, I'm not really on Martin's side at all on this one."

Josh stops what he's doing and lifts his chin up at me. "I'm not stupid. You'd never sell out your own son."

"Of course not, but I do want to do what's right. Alisha told me what you didn't reveal to the cops."

Josh looks up at the ceiling, then back at me again. "I don't know why she'd do that."

I walk over and place my hand on his arm. Touching him again feels good, a zip of warmth up my arm, the kind I haven't felt in weeks—the sort of tingles I haven't felt in years. "It's just me, you know." He looks down and searches my eyes. I hope he can find me in there somewhere. "Why didn't you tell the police that you heard Yazmin tell her brother that she intended to go for a walk with Finn after your lesson and that Alisha thought he was with her when she died?"

Josh's arm stiffens, and there's something there. Something more he doesn't want me to know.

"Did you know your son's girlfriend at all, Sarah?" he asks.

"I tried to get to know her, but she didn't like me. Refused to talk to me, really."

"Yeah, well, she was very troubled. Her family spiraled after her dad passed away. Yaz was trapped in the car with her father for hours before someone called in the accident."

I put my hand over my mouth. "I heard."

"He didn't die right away either. Yaz said people always assumed that he did. That it was easier for them that way, but it wasn't true. The car had been flipped on its side; Yaz was on the bottom. She said his blood dripped on her face all night long. It might not have been all night, but that's how she remembered it."

"I—I can't imagine." I close my eyes, and I can see it, but I don't want to.

"It was bad. The car rolled down an embankment but stopped at the river. A tree branch went through the window and punctured his stomach. She could hear him gasping for air for a good fifteen minutes. She heard him take his last breath."

I imagine myself in the same predicament with my own father, and my eyes instantly fill with tears.

"Kid was dealing with some really tough stuff. They'd been looking for Cash. She and her father. He'd run away."

I open my eyes as if a light bulb has just come on, but I don't know why. Josh glances away.

"Oh, wow. When was this?" I ask, feeling pieces inside me come apart.

"Almost two years ago," Josh says. "Around Christmas."

I can't help but think how fortunate we were two Christmases ago. I received record donations for the Heart-to-Heart Gala. The boys both made honor roll, and Martin had a boon at work, which led him to consider opening the new office he was working on now. William and Mary Alice actually had us over for a special dinner to celebrate all our achievements. William entertained the boys by showing off the brand-new Bentley he'd bought after his old one had suffered rodent infestation while in storage. Something about the ugly contrasts—this little girl half freezing in a car accident with her dying daddy while my kids spent their evening in a showroom full of fancy cars no one even drove—makes me so sick. I'm dizzy.

I swallow hard. "I didn't know any of that." No wonder Alisha said Cash had it the worst. He probably had survivor's guilt.

He nods. "Yazmin had nightmares too. Her therapist encouraged her to focus on school. She did, but she preferred pot to escape the nightmares."

"That's awful. About her dad," I say. "I wish Finn would've told me."

"It seems you didn't know many things."

I swallow hard again.

"I help young women at my shelter, Josh. I've practically dedicated my life to helping people like Yazmin. If she would've told me, I would've . . . I would've . . ."

"You would've . . . what? Not judged her so harshly?"

I look at him sideways. "I never *judged* her. Them."

"It doesn't matter. I don't care. You are who you marry, and you married into a family who take what they want and cover up what they don't."

"What're you talking about? That's not fair." He thinks I'm just like Martin, but I'm not. I always correct my husband when he makes remarks that verge on snobby. I didn't grow up with money, so why would I look down on someone who grew up the same way I did? If I did that, I needed to check myself in the mirror, find that lost reflection.

There's no use trying to explain this to Josh; he already has his mind made up about me.

"What's not fair is what happened to Yazmin. She was a good girl, very gifted musician too. Creative."

I inhale sharply. "I wish I could've gotten to know her better. Creative, you said? Did you ever see her writing in a journal?"

Josh's eyes catch mine, and he looks worried. "Yeah. I think she sometimes wrote music in one. Why?"

"It's missing now."

"What do you mean?" Josh asks, and I find it odd that he's so concerned.

"Her mother believes the cops took it, and now they can't find it." I think about Josh's words regarding the Ellsworths. They probably didn't want that journal found, so they made it disappear, just like our footprints in the woods. Martin told me as much. They went out there with plastic bags taped around their feet and rakes. They moved around the large rocks and placed them on the dragged tracks, any remnants of footprints other than Yazmin's mashed beneath them. The lengths they went to were both astonishing and unending.

"If her mother mentioned her journal, find it. If you want to help Yazmin's family, prevent her brother from being yanked out of school and thrown in jail—find the journal. Cash was into some stuff."

"Tell me what kind of stuff, because I keep hearing this phrase."

"I think he moves things. Designer bags. Electronics."

"So he's a thief."

"Yeah, petty crimes, quick-buck scams. The kid isn't motivated to go to school like Yazmin was." Josh looks up, and I'm amazed at how much he's learned about them from teaching guitar.

"Oh boy." Well, at least this plants a seed of doubt about Finn.

"If Yazmin wrote about him in her journal, the police could be using it to build a case against Cash right now. Or don't help. Be like your husband and stick your head in the sand and hope it all goes away."

I take in a deep breath and cover my mouth, the smell of cheap hand soap gagging me. "I don't know where this is coming from," I manage. I place one of my hands on his arm because I want him to look at me—see me.

"Look, he's your son, I get it, but if there's something not being said here, Sarah, it will come out. This isn't 1990; forensics have gotten better. Whether it's in that journal or not, it's time for the Ellsworths to pay, and I'm so sorry you're one of them."

My hand slips from his arm. I get it now. Josh was protecting me by withholding information about Finn from the cops, and he's bitter about compromising his own values to do so. Then he buckled and told Alisha all he knew, because he couldn't live with himself.

I'm not mad at him for it.

"Why did you act like you didn't know, then?" I ask, because I want to hear him say it.

"I wasn't sure what you were after. If you want to know about Yazmin, ask your son."

"Thank you," I say and run out of the store. I feel him watching me through the gold-lettered windows, but he won't be able to see my tears through the vines.

My father tried to warn me about them. About all of this. And I chose not to listen.

CHAPTER 16

1996—Freshman Year

We're sitting in Martin's Saab, top down, staring at the stars. He says the words effortlessly, like they're already set in stone. "I'm going to be CEO of my own company someday. Here's how I'm going to do it . . ." I don't know how he can think so far ahead, but I can't help but be turned on by his confidence. I've never met anyone with that kind of ambition, and I love to hear the passion escape his lips like a private time capsule made just for him and me—fragile and confidential.

"Once I get backers for the software . . ." He prattles on, and I half listen because I don't understand computer lingo, but I love the way he sounds when he says it.

It's not like he blurts these things out to the world. Just to me.

Five, ten, fifteen years—how long will it take my steady arrow to fly and fulfill his dreams?

"You're hitting the world guns blazing, and I'm just trying to pass midterms," I joke.

"Yeah, well . . . I need to buckle down and focus. What happened at the house . . . I can't shake it."

I can tell Martin's been struggling with Tush's death, and even though he hasn't said a word about it directly, it's managed to pop into every single one of our conversations. Martin might not have been at the house when Tush died, but he was still the one in charge of those boys when Tush drank three times the legal limit for blood alcohol level and never woke up the next day. I would feel guilty too.

"Tush would want you to keep on keeping on." I squeeze his hand.

He nods. Tush was so hard-core about being a brother. He wouldn't want the guys wallowing around, all sad. "I feel like I have a second chance now. I want to get it right." He squeezes my hand back, and I know that when he says *"get it right,"* he's thinking I'm part of the equation.

Martin + Sarah = getting it right.

I don't know how he's decided I'm the one to make him whole, but I'm not arguing with him over the fact. *"You make me better,"* he's said on more than one occasion, and it's the sweetest thing anyone has ever said to me, but sometimes it feels like he's trying to convince himself too. It's remarkable that Martin thinks so highly of me, that I bring him up a notch, this polished kid from the Heights.

It makes me wonder why he thinks he needs to be bettered.

"You will. You'll get it all. But right now I need to study or I won't get a damn thing right on my midterm tomorrow."

"I'm sorry. I'm keeping you. Go."

I kiss him.

"Go." He practically pushes me out of his car, and I go this time.

I'm giggling up the walk, and the only thing that doesn't seem right about Martin is that my father still doesn't know anything about him. That's all going to change, because my dad is standing in the doorway of my dorm room, waiting for me. I knew it was only a matter of time before he found out.

"What's up, Dad?" I ask him. I breeze past him, lie in bed, and crack open my Business Communications book. "I have a ton of studying to do." Maybe he'll take the hint and I can cut this conversation short.

"Hi there. Anything you want to tell me?" Dad's arms are crossed at his chest and tucked under his armpits. I almost laugh because he looks exactly like the caricature on the page of my book.

According to the picture, Dad's placing a barrier between us, closed off for argument. "Um . . ." I try to think of something clever to say and fail. "Nope."

"Were you out with Marty Ellsworth last night?" he asks.

I close my textbook and rest my hands on my chin. "Yes." *And today.*

"You realize he was the boy mixed up with that horrible accident at the fraternity house, right? The one where the boy died."

"I do. But he wasn't even there when it happened, and he feels really bad about it. He hasn't drunk a single drop of alcohol since."

"Wow, what a sacrifice he's made. Not drinking." Dad's arms are not only still crossed, they're squeezing his chest, and his face is red. There's no sample picture for this gesture in my book, but I know it's bad.

"And what do you think of this Marty?" My father directs his attention at Hanna, who immediately shrinks beneath her comforter.

"The SAEs are a nice group of guys. It's a shame what happened," she says.

"That's it? You still want to party with guys who leave their brother for dead?"

Hanna swallows hard and looks like she might throw up.

"Dad. Stop." It's one thing for him to throw his strong opinions at me, but Hanna's not used to how aggressive he becomes when a matter of moral high ground is tested, especially when he thinks someone's been hurt because of it.

"They settled out of court, Sarah."

I'm not sure what that means, but *settled* sounds like a good thing. "Then they came to an agreement."

Dad shifts his weight. "No. That doesn't make them good people. It just makes them resourceful."

"Dad, he wasn't there. Hanna and I were at the party that night, and I actually asked Tush . . ." I get a little choked up at the memory, his flirty brown eyes searching mine when I asked where Martin was. "I asked Tush where Martin was, and he said he wasn't feeling well."

"Is that right?" Dad asks, but I can tell that doesn't matter to him.

"Yes, I swear. And if Martin's family gave Tush's family money as compensation, then they were being charitable," I say.

My father lets out a mirthless laugh. He tells me to sit up, and I do, because he rarely gives me orders. He takes Hanna's desk chair and swings it around and sits down in front of me.

"Sarah, they were not being charitable. Martin's father was a member of the same fraternity, and he wanted to make sure the parents of the dead boy and the school didn't sue him. He also wanted to make sure those boys got to keep their damn letters."

His words are like static in my ears, because I know Martin is innocent in all of this. "If his brothers made a mistake, Martin wasn't part of it."

"Well, somebody should be held accountable for that boy. If not the pledge master and if not the president of the fraternity, then who?"

I think of Martin, pledge master, and Meat, the president of the fraternity. They're very tight, and I'm sure they went to bat for each other, but the fact that neither one was willing to take the fall only meant that neither one of them was likely responsible either.

"Who's going to turn themselves in if they don't believe they've done anything wrong?"

My dad puffs out his cheeks and looks positively frustrated. "Sarah, you're very gracious, and I've always respected your decisions, but dating this boy is the wrong one. Those SAEs are bad news, and I'd like you to stay away from them, and especially Marty Ellsworth."

Wow. Our father-daughter relationship has always been one of open communication and limited restriction. My father hasn't told me to stay away from anyone before, preferring I make my own decisions and my own mistakes.

I'm not sure why he's so adamant about this one. He doesn't know Martin like I do. He doesn't realize who he really is, all the wonderful things he aspires to do, the pain he's suffered from the accident, the lessons he's learned because of it.

"You're wrong about him, Dad." All he can see is the boy connected to the university scandal, and that isn't fair. Martin is so much more than that. He's grown up in a day since Tush's passing. He's really cleaned up, even cut his hair.

"There're lots of boys here, Sarah. I realize you didn't date a lot in high school, and maybe that was my fault, but it's not a great idea to cozy up to the first boy you meet. Big campus out there."

I roll my eyes. He's not the first. Not that Dad needs to know about that. He'll do anything to keep me away from Martin. Even if it means suggesting I sleep with other boys.

"Just ask your roommate; she knows."

Hanna gasps, and I don't know what his deal is today. "Not funny, Dad."

"I'll tell you what's not funny. I spent a week cleaning up the SAEs' mess when they closed the house, and I don't want to tell you what I found."

Uh-oh. I hold my breath, suddenly fearful.

"Please tell us," Hanna begs.

Dad sighs, and Hanna straightens up in bed as if the insult my father just threw at her has disappeared at the mere mention of potential gossip.

"For one, the floors were so sticky, I had to bleach the bottom of my boots when I left. They live like animals. The bathrooms were filthy.

And there was enough porn shoved beneath the mattresses to open an adult store."

"Dad! Stop." I cover my face, trying not to imagine Martin looking at racy magazines. *Please don't let it be his room.*

"No, don't stop—this is fantastic." Hanna has her hands clasped together like it's Christmas morning and it's her turn to open a present.

"It's true. And those magazines were sticky too."

"Eww!" I want to die right now.

"Okay, you can stop," Hanna concedes, but she's still laughing.

"Those were the minor offenses, girls. I sugarcoated it for you."

Hanna puts the palms of her hands up in a questioning posture. "Sugarcoated, huh . . ."

I make a *yuck* face. "Oh God, please stop. Both of you." I never had a brother, and I do not need to know the things boys do to survive when women aren't around.

My father defends himself. "I didn't say that one—"

"You're both at fault." I groan, disgusted. "Hanna, do you want to go for that run now?" Hanna has been complaining that the freshman ten is starting to attack her midsection.

She rolls on her back. "No, but I need to. I'm going to be a size four by Christmas if I don't," she says, as if this is life-ending.

My father gets up and rights the chair in front of Hanna's desk. "Remember what I said about those boys." He looks at me sternly, earnestly, and I know he means well—he always has—but he's wrong about this one.

"Sticky magazines. We got it." Hanna laughs.

Dad points his finger at me once and walks out the door.

When the door shuts, Hanna shrugs off her cargo pants and Henley top. I can't see an ounce of fat on her, but she manages to bunch up some skin on the side of her waist as she slips on jogging pants and a GAP sweatshirt.

"Pretty nice sweatshirt to run in." I have one GAP sweatshirt, and I use it for class.

"Well, if we're running on campus, we'll be 'seen.'" Hanna makes air quotes.

I throw my Christmas-green sweater that I've worn ten times already at her. "I thought we were doing this for exercise."

"We are . . . but while you, Miss Sarah, are here to get your degree, I have other intentions."

I'm afraid to ask. "What's that?"

"I'm here to husband shop as well."

"Oh Lord." I turn around and put on my sports bra and the rest of my exercise outfit, because I only have one, and it's not nearly as cute as Hanna's.

"My mother landed my dad in college. This is a unique time when you can figure out a prospective partner's potential net worth simply by asking their major."

"Wow. Don't you think that's a bit shallow?"

"No. If I can land a premed student I really like or a brilliant chemist or something like that, why wouldn't I? You can fall in love with a rich one as easily as you can fall in love with a poor one. Why not go for the gold?" Hanna pulls her long blonde hair up into a tight ponytail. She makes dating sound like an Olympic sport.

"I guess I don't see it the same way."

We close the door and lock it, and Hanna pulls a face at me. She looks like the front of a department store ad for athletic gear, and I'm embarrassed to jog next to her.

"What?" I ask.

"Really? You're dating Martin Ellsworth and you don't care about money. The boy drives a Saab."

We take the steps two at a time down to the front of the building.

"It was his mother's," I say.

"Right . . . and it doesn't matter to you at all that he comes from money? Tons of it. And that he's majoring in robotics engineering, one of the hardest programs to get into?"

We begin to jog down the city sidewalk.

"The money, no. The program, yes. I want someone who's motivated, but whether he's going to be crazy rich because of it shouldn't matter. Not if you really love him." The truth is that I want both—love and money—but I'd never sacrifice love for money.

"Well, his money should matter to you, because I don't think he would still be here if he didn't have it. There were a lot of lawyers in the dean's office after Tush passed . . ." Hanna stops speaking, but I don't like the sound of what she had to say. Our pitiful jog turns into a trot. We're both still feeling the pain of his loss, and I want to believe the best of Martin, because I've seen how hard he's trying in class and on campus to prove his worth since Tush died. Maybe Dad is right and Martin is just *"one of the lucky ones"*—and Dad doesn't like that.

"Is work still tense?" I ask.

Hanna works in the dean's office. She doesn't need the money—must be freaking nice—but she thinks it will look good on her résumé. She also thinks being a female engineer will give her a good shot at landing a great job when she graduates, because there are so few of them. Hanna is always looking for an opportunistic angle, and I have to envy her there.

"Things have gone back to norm since the university settled. The battle over the charter is still up in the air, though."

"I don't think they should lose their charter. It was an accident. My dad has a different opinion. He thinks there should be justice for Tush."

Our jog slows at the mention of Tush's name, and I don't know if it's because Hanna's too winded or because she agrees with my father.

"Let's turn here." Hanna points toward Schenley Park, and we make a right. We start jogging up a hill I know we shouldn't attempt, but I'm never one to duck out of a challenge.

"I think Martin is very lucky he has good lawyers. Meat too."

We start to descend, but the burning has already started in my ears and has traveled down my neck.

"So you agree with my dad?"

"That you should cozy up to more than one boy? Hell yes!"

"No, and I hate that he said that, by the way."

We get to the bottom of the hill, and I think we both realize we've reached our limit, because we stop in front of Phipps Conservatory, the largest indoor botanical garden in Pittsburgh, and just stare at the beautiful glass structure.

"What is this place?" Hanna asks.

"It's a building dedicated entirely to plants. It's named after Henry Phipps, a philanthropist who wanted to gift the city of Pittsburgh with the most beautiful green space full of gorgeous flowers because he loved them so much." *"It was my mother's favorite place,"* I want to add but don't.

"How flipping romantic," Hanna says, and I'm slightly satisfied she's breathing heavier than I am.

"It is. People even have wedding receptions here because it's so pretty." It's hard to sum up a place I loved so much as a child and actually do it justice. My father has unlimited passes to the conservatory.

"They built on over the years, adding art exhibits and a play area for kids," I add, remembering the scavenger hunt worksheets they used to hand out at the front desk. There were always one or two strange plants that were hard to find, and I felt like the master of the universe when I discovered them all. Dad would sip his coffee, sit back, and watch me explore like he was having the time of his life, even though we'd been there a hundred times before. We rarely visited my mother's grave, because it was too hard for both of us, but this place was just as good. Sometimes I even caught Dad whispering, and I swore he talked to her there.

"You Pittsburgh people have some weird hobbies." Hanna is from Bethesda, Maryland, just outside Washington, DC. She said it sucked going to school there because half the town was employed by Lockheed Martin and everyone was in your business. I'd take repetitive plant scavenger hunts over that type of cattiness any day. It's probably why Hanna is superficial sometimes, growing up under a social microscope like that.

Dad and I were in a world all our own, but right now we've never been so far apart.

"What's wrong?" Hanna asks.

"My dad really doesn't want me to see Martin."

Done with our jog, we're walking back to the dorm, officially on campus grounds again.

"Do you want to date Martin?" she asks.

"Yes . . . but—"

"Look, it sucks that your dad works here. I mean, I know that's how you pay for tuition, which is awesome, but it's not fair that he knows so much. You should be able to date the hot, rich, troublemaking frat boy and have the right not to tell your father."

"But he knows, and—"

"And you're over eighteen and can make your own decisions. And I haven't gotten a date with Meat yet, and if you break things off with Martin, I never will."

"He's a senior and the fraternity president, Hanna."

"What, you think I can't pull the prez?" Hanna stops walking and puts her hand on her waist, popping her hip. She's a little sweaty, and her ponytail is propped nicely on her head, which is wrapped in a thick headband.

A boy who's blowing by us on his bicycle gives her a whistle.

"No, I totally think you could." And she could. She's gorgeous. And smart.

"Listen, you need to do what's in your heart. And I need to find out why they really call him Meat."

"Gross." I make a face.

We're getting closer to our dorm, but Hanna stops and stretches her leg on a tree trunk, which I find laughable because we haven't even been running for a half hour.

"What, you don't wonder?" Hanna asks.

"About why they call him that? Sure. But not enough to do my own private investigation."

"Oh, come on." She giggles and finishes stretching her other leg.

"Let's speed walk," I suggest. "I have a test to study for."

"Okay, okay." We begin to walk at a quick pace. "So that's all that's got you bugging? Your dad doesn't approve of your boyfriend?" Hanna asks.

I'm thoughtful of her question. There're other things that bother me. The rumors that have been floating around have been troubling me greatly, but only because they're hurting Martin, not me.

We're rounding the corner to Morewood, and every time I pass the SAE house I'm filled with sorrow after all that's happened there. I wonder if it will always feel this way.

We're climbing the stairs to our dorm. It's not just that he doesn't approve; it's the way he doesn't approve. He's so angry about my dating Martin, and he won't tell me exactly why. It's probably because Martin is rich, not our kind of people, but it's almost like he's holding out on me, and that's a rare thing for my tell-all father. He's also planted a seed of doubt that maybe I don't know everything there is to know about what happened to Tush that night.

"Well, that, but . . ." I almost tell her this, but I'm too tired to talk and walk anymore. And I still have that Business Communications test to study for. Not only is Dad interrupting my dating life, he's messing with my academic life too. We're back on the sidewalk in front of our dorm now, and I can't wait to tear off these ugly black jogging pants so I don't have to stand next to young Jane Fonda anymore.

"But what?" she asks. Hanna opens the front door and closes it behind us.

"Do you think those magazines were Martin's?" I ask.

"Bah-ha-ha!" She explodes into a fit of laughter, and so do I.

And I think everything will be okay as long as I take Hanna's advice and just do what's in my heart.

CHAPTER 17

Present

Hanna is probably either working in the office at her part-time consultant gig or at the nail salon getting a gel fill before she has to pick up one of her gorgeous children and shuttle them to an activity. Her versatile personality has always amazed me—part brainiac, part diva, even as a mother of three. Our bond hasn't loosened either, even though we're way too busy to see each other, meeting once or twice a year. We'll squeeze in an occasional phone call if things aren't too crazy.

She picks up on the first ring. "I've been thinking about you. What do you think of a couples' trip? Xander and me, Martin and you, Cabo. Spring!"

I smile, because this is a new idea, and then frown when I wonder what my marriage will look like by spring. "Um . . ."

"Come on. The kids are almost out of the house. I still have Sienna, but she'd die for a week off from me."

Hanna's youngest is giving her a run for her money, a mini-Hanna. When I hear stories about Sienna, it makes me grateful I have boys.

"Hanna, Cabo's going to have to wait. Things aren't good between Martin and me, and I hate to be short, but I don't really have a lot of time to talk."

"Oh no. I'm sorry. What's up?"

"This is going to sound weird, but I have to ask you about something that happened in college." I wince, hoping she doesn't ask me a ton of questions.

"Okay, shoot."

"When Tush died, you mentioned Martin's dad was in the dean's office."

"Yeah, they were old frat brothers."

"They were? I didn't know that. Hanna, do you think Martin had anything to do with Tush's death?" I take in a sharp breath. I know the answer is no. We were at that party together, but I just need to hear her say it.

"Wow, rewind to 1996." She giggles uncomfortably.

"Hanna?"

She sighs. "Okay. I think something was shady about it, but I don't know what. I told you that. I said Martin wouldn't still be there if it wasn't for his money. I think the boys should've gotten their charter taken away and didn't because of his dad and his money and the dean."

"Was that it? Just the charter?" I ask. *I don't want the answer, but I need the answer.*

"I thought so at first, and I told you as much . . ."

She did, although my eighteen-year-old brain didn't translate it that way. I chose to hear the details I wanted to. "And then what?"

"And then . . . rumors started spreading that Tush was part of a hazing exercise. That he didn't just drink the alcohol on his own and pass out on the couch like they said. And that the pledges didn't lead it. Someone had to have led it."

"But Martin wasn't there! We were at that party, and he wasn't."

"You're yelling into the phone, in case you needed to check your stress level."

"Sorry."

"It's okay, but I get you. I know. That's why it's shady."

"Why didn't you tell me about the rumors?"

"Seriously? Everyone was talking about what happened to Tush back then. You were just in your I'm-going-to-save-Martin-Ellsworth-from-himself bubble back then. You were a smitten kitten. The news was out there; I didn't keep it from you."

I feel like I've just been kicked in the gut. It's like what Martin said, how I only see the memories I choose to see.

"Sarah, why in the world does any of this matter now?" Hanna asks.

"Things have . . . been hard here, and I'm just questioning everything."

"How is Finn anyway? I'm so sorry about his girlfriend. When I saw her death on the news and heard through the grapevine that Finn was involved with her, I seriously cried. I thought about texting you about funeral arrangements."

"I apologize about that. There wasn't a funeral."

"Oh . . . Is her death bringing up bad memories of when Tush died?" she asks, and she's way too smart not to know our conversation is somehow related to what happened in college. I have to get off the phone before I spill the beans. I don't need to make Hanna an accessory too.

"Exactly. I was around the same age as Finn, ya know? He's holding up. We all are. By a thread."

"Shit, I'm sorry."

"Thanks. I do have to go, though, Hanna."

"Sure, but call me tomorrow, okay? I want to talk."

"Okay, bye, girl."

"Bye, love you."

I hang up the phone. "Shit, shit, shit." William had frat-pack connections with the dean. Tush died of a hazing ritual with an unknown ringleader. None of it bodes well. I've been living a lie for the last twenty years.

The sunlight is blinding as I barrel down Route 65, heading south toward the city. I don't know why Dad would've withheld information from me about Martin when we were at CMU, but my run-in with Josh has me thinking he found a lot more in Martin's room than dirty magazines.

My hand searches the bowels of my endlessly large designer bag for my oversize sunglasses. There are too many compartments in it to find anything, and the stiff leather is unforgiving on my dry hands.

I don't know why I thought I needed such extravagances in the first place. I'd trade a mint for a happy family and some sanity right now, for my son to be in good mental health, his focus on finishing his senior year and going to college, not his dead girlfriend and his messed-up parents who left her body in the woods.

I travel farther south on the highway and remember precisely why. To my right, the Ohio River runs brown, gleaming sludge sliding down sodden riverbanks. It flows adjacent to rusty train tracks, the remnants of a once-powerful steel mill port city still recovering after business went overseas.

Once I drive beneath the overpass, I know I'm on the other side of the proverbial tracks, where I could never afford designer bags and sunglasses.

I went through a brief spending spree in my early twenties, after I'd had my children and struggled to lose the weight (by Sewickley standards). I buried my insecurities in designer goods to lift my self-esteem, and then when I regained my wits and waistline and ditched my minor case of the baby blues, I realized those purchases were just filler items for what I was missing inside from my lower-middle-class upbringing.

When the cancer survivor attended my mother's funeral with her freshly grown, silky hair, she was dripping with expensive things—a leather bag with symbols on it I didn't recognize, large diamonds that scratched when she hugged me, and nicely threaded clothing that hung just right.

She became my pace horse, my symbol for what I should strive for.

But then, when I got there, to that same place, at a very early age, I realized that wasn't how you won the race. None of that stuff really matters. Just because I have it doesn't mean I need it.

As I pull up to my childhood home, where Dad still lives, a three-bedroom, all-brick bungalow built in the 1950s, I'm saddened by how I regarded it growing up. It's a walk-up in the Avalon community with crisp green shutters, a one-car garage, and one maple tree of notable mention out front.

There was nothing dazzling enough about it to make me eager to invite over friends when I was younger, but today it looks just perfect, quaint. I think I resented it growing up because no matter how hard Dad had worked, he still seemed to struggle to pay the mortgage every month.

Over the years, I stopped bringing the boys over, even though the house has a nice concrete patio out back, which was fine for me to play on when I was a kid but seemed insufficient beneath the raucous feet of my two active sons.

Dad only comes to my house for visits these days. We have a dining room table large enough to seat an army and a hallway bathroom with extras in it, like a bidet, which Dad doesn't care for. He seems strangely uncomfortable when he comes over, most likely because he and Martin have never really gotten along, even after all these years. Dad would say off-color things like, *"Well, la-dee-da, not only do you have robot gadgets to clean your floors, you also have toilets to clean your—"*

"Dad!" I always pray he doesn't use the bathroom when he comes over so he won't comment on the bidet. Josh's parents installed it, and even though we don't use it, Martin isn't handy like Dad, so he certainly isn't going to uninstall it. Dad made it a focal point of discussion several times when the family conversation had run dry.

The boys found it especially amusing, especially when they were younger, a time when poop and fart jokes were all the rage. But unfortunately for all parties involved, Dad didn't realize the joke had peaked with his grandchildren's introduction into young adulthood.

Today, I'd love to be amused and aghast by my father's off-color jokes, but these are different times. I am here for one reason only—to find out what Dad found in Martin's room that day that'd made him so upset. What was he trying to tell me in the ornament shop? Surely Josh was way off base with his assumptions of Martin's guilt. I just need Dad to prove it to me.

Thinking back to my conversation with Hanna and the happenings in the dean's office shortly after Tush had died, her response sticks out more now than it did before. *"I think Martin is very lucky he has good lawyers."*

She mentioned Meat too. They'd both been in deep trouble, but they were also both cleared of the charges.

I think of the more recent headlines from a Penn State hazing incident that went sideways and resulted in a student's death. The frat brothers had serious charges thrown at them like manslaughter and aggravated assault.

Pictures on students' phones captured bits and pieces of the night and were used as evidence. What if someone had pictures of Yazmin and Finn? There are cameras in the sky everywhere nowadays. There's no way we're going to get away with this. Maybe Martin is comparing this to Livvy's case, but that was in the early 2000s, and things weren't nearly as high-tech as they are now.

Anxiety hits me hard as I see Dad's truck in the driveway and realize it's been a very long time since I visited him. There are also a few things I notice that are amiss as I walk to the front door. Dad is usually particular about weeding and not letting the plant life sprawl through the limestone walkway, but I see some noticeable patches of green that would've driven him straight to the shed for his special gardening shears years ago. I wonder why he hasn't taken care of them.

I climb the three corrugated slabs of gray cement that serve as the front steps and ring the doorbell. I didn't let Dad know I was coming, but he's always told me it isn't necessary to announce my visits.

Mary Alice prefers a day's notice. Not surprising.

It's taking longer than usual for Dad to come to the door, so I peek in the window, but I don't see anyone there.

I'm contemplating whether I should use the spare key in the planter on the porch to open it myself when the handle jiggles. The door swings open, and Dad is wearing his striped pajama bottoms and a Steelers T-shirt. His eyes are half-shut, and he looks as though he's been sleeping even though it's after one o'clock in the afternoon. Dad's retired, but he's always been an early riser, and this is concerning. "Rough night?" I ask.

"Sarah?" he says, as if he's not sure it's me.

"Jeez, it hasn't been that long, has it?" I joke.

He gives me a tight smile, and I realize that maybe it has. It's true—I've been busy pushing my agenda with the city on funding for the single-parent project, and before Yazmin's death, Finn's college applications took precedence in our lives, and then there is the Children's Heart-to-Heart Gala tomorrow night. I've done a piss-poor job of fundraising for it and haven't even bought a dress yet. This gala used to be one of the most important community events of the year for me, but I realize, much like the designer sunglasses and purse, it's all for show. Most of the people who attend don't really care about the cause. This shift I'm feeling to get away from Martin isn't just about him but the entire life we've built here.

"What's going on, Dad? Can I come in?"

He shimmies to the left a bit. "Threw my back out. On muscle relaxers. Don't mind the mess."

He holds his side while he scooches over to let me in, which seems to take a tremendous effort.

"Oh my."

There are empty Chinese food containers and pizza boxes piled up on the coffee table like a homeless college kid has been squatting in the living room for months. As I walk farther into the kitchen, I see the sink is overflowing with dirty dishes. Flies buzz around two bags of ripe garbage, and when I pick one up, the foul odor almost knocks me over. This isn't like Dad, always one to take care of his possessions and home with pride, and now I'm scared.

I open a window. "Jesus, Dad!"

"The bags were too heavy for me to carry with my back." He sounds defeated, and I don't like it. My big, strong dad, unable to lift a couple of measly bags of garbage.

"Ever hear of calling us for help?" As I haul the bag outside, it leaks something acrid and yellow on the kitchen floor.

When I come back in, he's balancing his body between the kitchen island and the counter. "I think you need to see a doctor," I tell him. "I'm worried about you."

"Already been. Just tweaked it lifting lumber with Sal."

I take out the other bag and then wipe up the mess on the floor. I begin to do the dishes, uncertain of how to broach the subject of the past when he's suffering so much in the present. I should've checked in with him sooner.

"Are you ever going to take your retirement seriously?" I ask. Dad still works odd jobs to stay busy, but I thought it was because he never knew how to relax in the first place.

"Staying active is important for my health as I become a senior," Dad proclaims. I hear his sarcastic tone tingling in there. There he is. He just needed to wake up a little.

"Become a senior?" I begin to remove some dirty dishes so I can fill the sink up with soapy water. The dishwasher is already full and hasn't been run.

"That's right. Got my official Medicare card yesterday," Dad says.

I take a plate crusted with marinara sauce and let it soak in the suds. My thoughts muddle as the clean water slowly turns pink. I take a quick side glance at my father, and my heart dips in my chest, then rises again. His hair looks different—grayer, thinner. And his eyes are withdrawn with dark circles beneath them. I can tell he's struggling to stand up by the way he's leaning to the side, and I wonder how he's aged without my even noticing. My emotions are on a Tilt-A-Whirl today between Alisha and Joshua and now Dad. I sniffle up the tears.

"What's the matter, Sarah?" My dad may be injured, but he's not blind. "Put those dishes down; they can wait. One more day of meds and I should be right as rain."

"I'll feel better if you let me clean while I tell you what I need to say." My voice is short and clipped. My father's physical condition is tripping up my moment of reckoning if my suspicions are true. Did he know something about Martin and not tell me?

"Yeah, fine. Okay, shoot, darling daughter." Dad coughs, and I wonder if his condition stems from his back alone or if there's something else going on. Paranoia shakes more tears out of my eyes. I don't need this right now.

"Sarah, what is it? Kids okay?" He starts to shuffle toward me.

"The kids are fine. Stay right where you are. You aren't moving so well."

"Well, you're crying, baby girl—what's happened?" He goes back to the stool at the counter and balances there.

"The girl they found dead, on the news . . ." I pause, wiping my nose on my sleeve.

"Oh yeah, I think I heard that. An Academy kid. That's awful. She looked like a real beauty. I meant to call you about that. I've just been . . . banged up. Did you know her?"

I dip a beer stein in the water and try not to think about what happens when you mix alcohol with muscle relaxers. Dad probably never thought to look at the label, and why in the world hasn't he found a woman to take care of him yet? "Yeah, she was Finn's girlfriend."

"Oh my God, I'm sorry, Sarah Bear. How is Finn? He hasn't been by in a long time. I didn't even know he had a girlfriend." Dad sounds sad. I've tried to get the kids to visit him, but they're so busy, they never want to spare the minutes to drive the few miles to the other side of the overpass.

However, they always seem to make time for their Sewickley grandparents, who let them drive their fancy cars and treat them to hot toddies at the country club in the wintertime. It always seemed okay, but maybe it isn't. Maybe I've taught them it's acceptable to spend more time with those who can serve them.

Two Christmases ago, William promised Spencer he'd let him drive his Bentley, weather permitting. It was a car Spencer had been practically drooling over since he was a small boy. Finn had never been overly wowed by his grandparents' wealth—or his grandparents for that matter—but he liked their toys.

But when William went into the auto garage to get his Bentley out, he discovered a rodent infestation had made a full assault on his leather interior. Spencer was so disappointed to hear the news over the phone, but two days later, the kids had come over to find a brand-new Bentley right in its place.

"*It was necessary,*" Martin joked, but he was completely serious when he said it.

And now I hate myself for tolerating their behavior because I wanted the boys to have the kinds of memories that involved rides in fancy cars instead of the ones I grew up with.

"He's not well, Dad." I've gotten ahold of myself and take a paper towel and blow my nose. The plate with the marinara sauce has softened up, and I begin to scrub it with a hard sponge. It makes me realize how scattered I am, because the water is filthy now. If I'd done the dishes the right way, I would've soaked the plate last. When I dip my hand in the water, it turns red, and I let out a little shriek as I think of the last time I touched Yazmin, leaving my hands wet with her blood. I look away and inhale sharply. The wave of emotion that follows is enough to take me down.

"What is it? What can I do to help?" Dad grips the counter again, and despite the fact he's eaten nothing but MSG and carbohydrates for God knows how many days, he's skinny as a rail.

"Nothing, Dad." And it's the truth. There's nothing he can do, because he doesn't know what I've done and he doesn't know his grandchildren. Part of that is my fault, but part of it is his. He's never accepted the life I stepped into, the same life where Spencer and Finn have thrived.

"You sound angry. Are you mad at me, Sarah?"

I drain the dirty water, try to wash it away, spray the remnants on the bottom of the sink, and refill it with a fresh batch of hot, soapy water.

"Maybe." I submerge a few more dirty dishes in the sink. Were all his reservations about the Ellsworths tied to something bigger?

"Would you please stop doing that and talk to me? Why in the world would you be pissed at me? I didn't kill her." He chuckles.

His joke is not funny. Fear grips my vocals. "It was an accident! No one killed her."

Do people think she was murdered? Is that what the papers are saying? I haven't been keeping track.

"Easy, baby girl." He tries to take a step forward.

"Please don't move. Please just sit." I can't handle my father being sick on top of everything else.

"Gosh, I think you're under a lot of stress. You always hated to be hugged when you were upset. Remember when you peed your pants at softball? Whew, that was a doozy. Not that I wanted to hug you then because you were soaked through, but I still tried." He laughs, but that memory is one of my worst, and it's not helpful right now. "Nothing your daddy wouldn't do for ya."

I turn to face him. "Are people saying she was killed?" I can't shake the thought.

"No, Sarah. Not that I know of, although I haven't read up much on it; I've been down for the count." Dad holds his side again, and I don't doubt that he's telling the truth.

"Okay." I sigh, relief hitting me so hard, the hairs tingle on the back of my scalp. I want to ask more questions about why my dad can't hold himself up, but right now, I need someone to hold me up.

"Are you going to tell me what your beef is with me? We've barely spoken; you've been so busy being a hoity-toity socialite." He snickers, annoyed at who I've become, and it's time we talk about it. Maybe he'd open up more if I admitted that I'm not happy with who I've become either.

"If you didn't want me to be a Sewickley socialite, why didn't you tell me everything you knew back in college when I started dating Martin? That day you cleaned the house." I knew there was more to the story back then, and I'm sure of it now.

My father almost falls off his stool but catches himself. "Martin's come clean after all these years. Was he waiting until I retired? Bastard."

Is he suggesting somehow that his job would have been in jeopardy if he spoke up about what he knew? What he found? I inhale sharply. "No, not exactly. I've come here so someone can tell me the truth."

"Now you want the truth, Sarah?" He looks at me as if I've been standing at the wrong bus stop for the last century. "I started to tell you twenty years ago, and you wouldn't listen."

"That's not true." I'm digging the sponge into a near-spotless plate. I will hate-scrub the fuck out of these dishes until they shine.

My dad cackles and then coughs again, and my concern for his health returns, but not enough to stop me from letting him explain himself. "It is true. The sun rose and set on Martin Ellsworth in your eyes. There wasn't a person in the world who could tell you a bad thing about him. You wouldn't hear of it."

I've filled up the dish rack, and now I start drying them and putting them away, too harshly. I bang and clatter my stress away. My father's shitty china with the blue flowers is paying dearly for my past mistakes.

"I'm listening now." My back is turned away from him.

"I'll tell ya all about it, but you have to stop hitting those dishes. They're old; they're going to break, and your mother picked them out."

Oh shit. I sigh. "I'm sorry." I never knew that.

I start gently massaging the plate in my hand. Dad has never moved on from my mother, and when I made my life ten miles up the street on the other side of the overpass, part of it, I realize now, was to escape the old life he refused to leave. The one where he never replaced Mother's dated drapes and still used her old dishes.

"So it's a short story, really. Your dear husband hazed the hell out of his pledges. Made them drink to excess. The smallest one didn't make it. Too much alcohol, too little body mass. And then your husband's daddy swooped down in his big black limousine and made it all disappear with a few lump sums. One to the school, marked as a donation, and one to the parents of the deceased in India, for condolences. But attached to that payment was a contract that neither party could ever file a civil suit."

"What?" I'm numb.

"Apparently, your husband wanted him to drink just as much as the other pledges. Earn his keep. Even though he knew very well he couldn't handle the alcohol. Then they all left him on a couch at the end of the night. Unattended."

"Earn your keep." It's a phrase Martin used with the boys in regard to college admittance. *"Enroll in honors classes, gifted programs. Earn your keep in the Ivy League schools among all the other kids fighting to get a spot."*

My tingly scalp is burning, and my eyes are failing. I've put every dish away and drained the sink, but I still need to busy my fingers. I grip the dish towel and yank at the stray strings.

"No, he wasn't there. He was sick that night. He wasn't . . ." My voice cracks.

When my father doesn't speak, I glance up and find him giving me a wide-eyed look of surprise. "You really did believe that, didn't you?"

I hold on to the counter for dear life. I'm going to be sick. "The nurse had records . . ."

"Sure she did. Martin had a little cold that week and went to the nurse and got some medicine. There's proof of that, a record they submitted to the cops, but he didn't have anything bad enough to put him down for days or even a full evening, like he claimed."

No. No. No.

"You think he was there, the night that Tush died?" I ask. "I was there that night—"

"I know he was there. They made up the cover story that he wasn't to save his ass. The president really wasn't there, supposedly, and there was no one else to hold accountable, because it was just Martin and the pledges, so all those good ol' boys got off scot-free."

"But, Dad, how do you know for certain Martin was there?"

"Because, Sarah, I had to clean that pigsty of a frat house, and your husband, being the super-nerdy, organized, engineer-type that he is, kept a log of everything he did. He logged what time his pledges arrived, when they completed their duties, who was shining his shoes that day. Everything."

"That sounds like him," I say absentmindedly. I tie a string around my finger and pull, but I can't feel a thing.

"I stumbled upon the log and saw that he made copious notes that evening when he claimed not to be there. Same handwriting as the ones he'd made on previous entries."

Martin has distinct handwriting. He took some sort of calligraphy class at the Academy and still leaves curlicues at the tops of his *T*s and *R*s, the serifs on his *E*s emphasized to resemble the annoyingly lavish one on the family crest.

"Maybe he came and left—"

"The newspapers said he went home for an extended period of time because he was too sick to care for himself." My dad shakes his head.

"He could've written in the wrong date."

"If he wrote in the wrong date and it didn't happen, then why did all the pledges get a lump sum of money from Mr. Ellsworth too?"

"What?"

"Well, what else would be their incentive for keeping their mouths shut, Sarah? They'd lost their friend. And they could've all been expelled for lying to the dean, but the dean was in on it too. There were seven pledges, plus the dean makes eight. He paid them each a hundred grand in cash envelopes."

"No!" I put my hand over my mouth.

"Guess where they kept their cash so their parents wouldn't find it?"

"In the house," I mutter.

Dad nods. "Campus security didn't tell the boys that the maintenance man would be in to disinfect everything the police had missed once they reinstated the house for occupancy."

"Shit."

"Guess who found the large sums of money, which I did not confiscate, in the house? All seven of the envelopes were addressed to freshmen. Tush was the only sophomore pledge, but of course he didn't receive an envelope. It didn't take me long to piece together that they were the seven pledges mentioned in the paper."

"Meat!" I scream. "He was blamed too. How do you know his parents weren't the ones to pay them off?" I ask, but even as I say the words, I know I'm reaching for the moon.

"Meat was raised by a single mother, a flight attendant who was employed by US Airways before the hub pulled out of town. She didn't make a hundred thousand a year, let alone enough to pay a hundred thousand per student," Dad says.

"But Hanna said Meat had a good lawyer," I try.

"Sure. One Mr. Ellsworth paid for."

"That's so sick." Meat was in our wedding. He stood right next to Martin's brother in the groomsmen lineup, partnered with Hanna, who'd already lost interest in him after she'd learned his nickname was just short for Demetrius. Martin and he had always been so close, even though they were two classes apart. This is probably why. They were bonded by blood.

I wipe my tears. "The nurse. The nurse . . ." I keep thinking back to her statement on Martin's behalf and how it was so pivotal to the case.

"The nurse? You mean the nice lady who took another job six months after Tushar Patel died?"

I wobble a little. *You're kidding me.* "Her too?"

"Sure. I bet she got a nice envelope. They probably asked her to stay on for a bit so no one would suspect anything."

"Why would the university allow this to happen? The dean?"

"Because it didn't look good for the university when it happened, and they wanted it to go away as quickly and cleanly as possible. And they wanted to keep one of their oldest and most notable Greek organizations on campus. A lot of the SAEs were legacy. They didn't want to uproot the precious family tree."

"That's disgusting."

"Money does bad things to good people, Sarah."

"Then where do you have yours hidden, Dad? Because not telling me about this was the worst thing you could have ever done to me!" I know he's right, but I'm just so mad that he didn't try hard enough to tell me. So angry at myself for being naive.

He loses his smile quickly, clears his throat. "Sarah, you hid the fact that you were dating Martin from me for almost a whole semester. By the time I'd gotten word, you were already lost to him."

"You were punishing me for not telling you I was dating Martin? I can't believe you'd do that!" I'm so upset, I'm dizzy. After Dad found out about Martin, things were never the same between us. It was because Dad rarely told me I couldn't do something, but when he did, I listened. He'd made it clear he didn't want me to date Martin, and I did it anyway.

"No, I wasn't punishing you. Everything I've done has been for you." His voice goes low. Emotional but angry.

"Then why didn't you turn those boys in when you found that money?" I ask. I can't fathom Dad letting this go.

"I did. I went to the dean, told him what I found in your husband's room, and you know what he said?"

"What?" I'm so terrified for the answer, I'm shaking.

"He said I shouldn't have been snooping in that frat house and he could fire me for it. I needed to forget what I saw or my job there was done."

"No." That's why he didn't speak up. It all makes sense now, why he couldn't tell me.

"That's so . . . that's so . . ." Woozy, I sit down at the island with him. "You could've gotten another job! Why didn't you at least tell me?"

My father looks so tired, and I wish he felt better so I could deliver these blows like I fully intend. "Because, my dear, the very next thing he said was that I had a daughter enrolled there, and it would be a pity to have her scholarship money yanked away for no good reason. If I'd told you, you would've blown the whistle, and your scholarship would've been damned. There was nothing I could do to stop what had already happened. It didn't seem like a good decision for me to tell you."

"How could you *not* tell me?" I'm still in shock.

"Sal tried to tell me these college relationships have a habit of falling apart on their own, but I never believed it." It sounds like something Sal would say. Dad's best friend is on his third wife. "He didn't know my daughter. She doesn't go into things with half a heart. Then I tried to tell you, if you remember, in the ornament shop, the day you were having second thoughts about the engagement."

I close my eyes, and I do remember. That day, I couldn't handle any more surprises, and I didn't let him tell me, and then I never circled back to ask him what it was. But he should've circled back to me.

"Things could've been so different," I blubber.

"And then the baby came swiftly, and once that happened . . ."

He trails off, but he doesn't need to fill in the blanks. Dad would never break up a family.

He leans into the table and grabs my hands. "Your tuition was all I had to give you, baby girl. I didn't have the money to buy you a fancy car or pay for an expensive wedding, but I could give you a free education. The best. I couldn't let *them* take that away from us."

"So that's why you hate them?" I ask.

"Yes. That's why I hate them. Not because they have money but because of what they choose to do with their money."

For the first time, I agree. It's the exact reason I hate them too, I realize—even my own husband.

"Oh my God, Dad. How . . ." I grip the edge of the counter, and Dad doesn't say anything. My belly rumbles, and the back of my throat burns. I run back over to the sink.

"Sarah . . . ," he tries.

"Don't!"

I open my mouth and lean over, but I can't throw up, and a string of spit escapes my mouth and falls into the sink. I rinse it down with the suds. I take a deep breath to calm the sick.

So sick.

Jesus Christ. To think Martin's brothers could just stash the cash under their mattresses and move on. Who are these people? Who is my husband, really?

I wipe my mouth and realize it's what Martin is trying to do now—with the journal. I need to find that damn journal before history repeats itself. I've been part of the Ellsworth reign of terror long enough.

"I'm sorry I yelled. I may need to come home for a bit to sort this out. Looks like you could use the help around the house and with your back too."

Dad shifts uneasily at the breakfast island, but he looks relieved to hear this. "Of course. You know you never need to ask."

And I do know that. It's just good hearing it, considering I spent all my time nurturing the wrong relationships and ignoring the right ones. It's a hard reality. One I'll make up to Dad.

Now, to deal with the other men in my life and their half-truths.

CHAPTER 18

The Sewickley Heights police station is located on the same property as the country club. In order to become a member of the club, an application is required, as well as a sponsor and cosponsor and four supporting members, all of whom are closely associated to the applicant. When I was knighted with my membership, I remember feeling esteemed yet unworthy. The country club sits on a plot of the golf course so verdant and landscaped in the summertime, I dare not tap my toe on it with the wrong shoes.

It's too bad the moral high ground of the members doesn't match the course. Since we found Yazmin in the woods, it's my presumption that when a member makes a mistake, they walk directly across the street to find the right person at the police station to compensate for their error.

Sewickley Heights has a population of only a thousand. Sewickley Borough is an entirely different district. The park falls under the jurisdiction of the Heights, where Alton is in charge. I imagine he doesn't have much to do other than monitor the park.

He probably knows every square inch of it, exactly where the kids had been hiking, the fastest way to cover up their tracks. My stomach knots as I think that if Finn committed a crime and can't remember it, he did it in the perfect place.

I stop walking at the thought, steadying myself on the police station railing. It's a real possibility now, isn't it? Finn could be involved in this girl's death just as Martin was involved in Tush's. I was naive to this kind of behavior once before.

Martin gave Tush the order to take his last drink.

He drove that boy to his death, yet he was able to wake up the next day, brush it off, learn the script his father had taught him to keep him out of jail, repeat it—believe it. Did Finn do the same? Have we taught him to do the same damn thing?

I blink my eyes back into focus. My throat burns again, and I swallow the stress.

Yazmin's death couldn't have been on purpose, because that would mean it was premeditated, and as much as I believe Finn might not be telling the whole truth, I don't believe he's a murderer.

At least not that kind. He'd be more like the kind Martin was.

"Oh God." I heave and then fight to keep everything in my stomach, steadying my breath. This can't be real.

Breathe. I stop and concentrate on nothing else except my own breath. Slowing it. Savoring it. Knowing that these moments of freedom with my family could be my last if I don't figure this out. But not truly wanting to, because if I do, I might discover truths about my son that will kill me.

Alton Pembroke knows where that journal is, and I'm fairly certain the answers to my questions are inside. Why would he hide it if they weren't? Alton's Range Rover is parked outside the station, and it must annoy the other officers that he can afford one, although his immediate family well runs low on sweet water.

Aunt Olivia is ten years younger than William. He doesn't often refer to her as his sister—just Livvy. She was the forgotten Ellsworth sibling who went to art school and got tangled up with an English professor who specialized in lyrical poetry, only reintroduced into the family after she had a baby boy around the same age as Martin and Bill. That's when the misadventures of Billy, Marty, and Al began.

And they're still going. Alton has probably seen a few white envelopes in his day, pleased to win over the favor of the uncles who'd likely treated him as lesser because of his wayward mother. Livvy had it right all along, though, defying her family, skipping town, and living overseas, away from all the corruption. Mary Alice likely took over as primary caregiver, hence Alton's strange servitude to her.

I swing open the door to the station, and my first thoughts are that it's far too clean and pretty to be a police station. There are no people in the waiting room, and I have to ring a bell to get anyone to come to the front desk.

A young blonde who looks more suited to work at a makeup counter strolls in from a side door. Her lipstick is a little smeared, and she futzes with her wildly patterned blouse before asking me who I'm looking for.

"I'm here to see the sheriff," I tell her.

She raises her eyebrows, which are much darker than her hair. "Is he expecting you?"

"Yes," I lie. "Tell him it's Sarah; he'll know who I am." In a town this small, I'm fairly certain I'm the only one.

She shrugs and knocks on a door behind her, the same one she just came out of.

Alton emerges, his lips pinker than they should be. Maybe the girl *did* work at a makeup counter in the past and thought she'd found the perfect brand that wouldn't wear off, and it just backfired.

I shake my head at him, and he grins as I'm escorted to his office. Alton has never brought a girl to a family dinner. At first, we thought he might be gay, but Mary Alice was more than pleased to find out he's just a womanizer instead.

"Not the staying type," as he so plainly put it, much like his father, who left Livvy when he became uninspired by the industrial grit of

Pittsburgh and decided to venture to Japan to teach. There was no pressure for Alton to procreate, since he didn't bear the right last name, so this family flop wasn't as big a deal as it would've been if one of the Ellsworth boys' wives had left them.

Like I am strongly contemplating. The thought floors me, and I grip the corner of Alton's desk and close my eyes for a minute, blindsided. Yazmin's death has destroyed us, but it wouldn't have if we were strong enough as a couple to begin with.

"Hello, Sarah, what brings you in?"

"Busy day, Alton? I wasn't interrupting you, was I?" I can't help myself from harassing him a little. These boys get away with everything in this town, and no one ever says a thing.

"No, it's fine." He clears his throat. "What did you need? Martin didn't mention you'd be stopping by. We could've had dinner at Aunt Mary Alice's if you needed to talk." He runs his hand over his shaved head. There's a clear intent in his sentence that I should be going through Martin if I want to speak to him. That these visits to discuss such private family matters shouldn't go unannounced or occur at his place of work.

"How old is she, Al?"

He sits back in his chair, and it creaks, and at least something is old in this station like it should be. We pay more property tax than some people pay in mortgage. "Old enough. What's going on, Sarah?"

"You tell me. Alisha Veltri believes you took Yazmin's journal into evidence and then didn't give it back. She's very angry, threatening to go to the media. She wants it back. I'd like to give it to her if you're done with it. And I'll volunteer to make copies of the pages if you're not."

Alton's fingers stop drumming. He turns and grabs a box with a rubber band fastened to the top labeled VELTRI.

"Did you find it?" I ask hopefully. Maybe it was just a work mistake, like hiring the woman at the front desk who clearly wasn't qualified to be employed at a police station.

"No, I don't have it," Alton says.

My heart sinks in my chest, both because I so badly want to know if there's anything in the journal that ties Finn to the crime and because I want to give it back to Alisha.

The first part is still hard to think about.

I feel guilty for doubting my child. I'm his mother. I'm supposed to support him, believe in him. My hand trembles on my purse, checkbook still inside.

There are lengths I'd go to protect him, but I need to know what he's done first.

What did you do, Finn?

Alton removes the rubber band from the top of the box and lets me look inside. "Don't touch anything, but see for yourself—it's not here."

I feel invasive looking in it, but I do, and there's very little to inspect—car keys, pictures, school notebooks. My eyes fill up with tears that this young girl's life is condensed into one cardboard box with not enough items to fill it to the top.

"Shouldn't this be in an evidence room?" I ask.

Alton has a shitty grin on his face. "You're looking at it. This is my only open case."

"Where is the journal, Alton?"

He shrugs, reminding me of the blonde. She probably picked up his body language from hanging around him, the way couples adopt each other's idiosyncrasies. "She's going to go to the media. Did you hear me say that?"

"She's not. She would've already. If she decides to now, the case will be closed by then, and the media will no longer be interested. I'm just waiting on the coroner report."

"Alton, I've gone along with everything, but I want that journal."

"I don't have it. And if I did, you wouldn't want it, because I'm sure there're things about Finn in there you don't want to read."

I close my eyes for a brief moment again and see those nail marks on my son's neck. I've been trying not to think about them. They were superficial, likely healed by now. They may have disappeared, but I can't let them go. Just like Yazmin might not have been able to let Finn go as he was attacking her.

Trying to pry her way out of his grasp, her long nails digging in.

My skin crawls at the mental image, Yazmin's pale skin flashing forward, her dark hair that'd fallen over her head in a struggle. What other explanation could there be?

No. Not my son. My gentle son who takes the ladder. No.

I can't breathe again.

I take a large gulp of air. "What do you mean, Alton?"

Alton sighs. "I mean Finn did not smoke pot once or twice; he smoked it regularly. That's how he met Yazmin."

"What?" I ask.

"Finn was smoking it with those two brothers he mentioned . . ." Alton is flipping through notes.

What? Finn, into drugs? It doesn't make sense. When did this happen? How did I not notice? I am trained for this. I didn't turn a *"blind eye,"* as my father suggested before, not to Finn. I just didn't see it.

"The Coulsons." And I'm annoyed he doesn't know their names. This town is small, and Alton is lazy.

"Right, and I guess she got into their little group, took a liking to Finn."

I look out the window as the sun streams inside, and I can't believe my son not only does drugs but that he bonded with his girlfriend while doing them. And then I think I'm the biggest hypocrite in the world, because I did almost the exact same thing.

I bolt up from the desk. If the journal isn't here and it was here, then somebody else in the family has it or it's been destroyed. But they wouldn't destroy it, because they had to have known that Yazmin's mother would come looking for it and that she'd make a stink, maybe even go to the press. They couldn't be so heartless that they wouldn't think a mother would search to the high heavens and back for her child's last words.

I would.

That means they have it in safekeeping until it's no longer a threat—incriminating pages ripped out. I bet it will magically reappear once the case is shut.

It has to be either at Martin's or William Sr.'s. Bill wouldn't take it so close to an election, and Alton lives in an apartment. There aren't a lot of places to hide it there, but being a cop, he probably wouldn't want it on his person.

Martin.

Or Finn. *Not Finn.*

But maybe, because Finn lied about doing drugs, and this changes everything. He could be lying about this too. And everything else, for that matter. Where do the lies start and end?

The nail marks? How did they get there? I need to know.

Alton shakes his head and grabs his phone off the desk. "Sarah, let it go. The girl is dead. We're doing our best to close out the case the *right* way."

Anger rises in my belly. "Because you've done the rest of it the wrong way! It doesn't make up for it, you know?"

He looks at me, dumbfounded. I charge out of the office and look back to see him furiously typing on his phone.

The blonde is tapping on the computer, pretending to work, when I stride past her. She glances up to give me a dirty look.

"You know he sleeps with all his secretaries, right?"

Her mouth drops open in shock, and I don't care. I'm done with this town.

And if I find that journal, I'm done with Martin. I could let him explain, but why? His explanation will just be more lies.

I also realize I've made a mistake. The person Alton was likely texting is Martin. He's letting him know I'm onto him where the journal is concerned, and now it's a race to the house to find it. Martin's office is in the city, in a new-age open-concept building in the strip, no cubicles, just a whole lot of space. There's nowhere to hide anything; it's the whole point of the design.

There are plenty of spots to hide it in Stonehenge.

And I know every single one of them.

CHAPTER 19

Stonehenge is a forgotten ruin when I return home. I leave the door open to bring in the crisp autumn breeze. We've all been closed in, and it's time to air everything out—family secrets included.

My mind is still racing to catch up on all the information I never knew.

Life-altering information.

Finn lied to the cops, and he lied to us about using drugs. Sure, he may not have wanted to tell me about the drugs, but he put his welfare before Yazmin's by not telling the cops, and now he can't be trusted. He may really have had a part in Yazmin's death.

I place my hand over my heart. It actually physically hurts to learn the people you love the most aren't who you think they are. It doesn't matter if the rest of the world is full of shit as long as they are real, and they're not. They're damn liars.

Martin obviously found something in that journal, and he's done everything he can to hide it from me, and now I need to find it. It has to be Martin. And there has to be something in there implicating Finn. Tears burn my eyes.

What did you do, Finny?

I can't stick my head in the sand anymore. There'll be no more living in the dark.

Light is where the truth lives.

I suck in a deep breath.

The journal has to be here somewhere; I can almost smell it.

"Where is it?" I ask the house, and I'm not whispering like I usually do so people won't think I'm crazy. I don't worry about that anymore. I know now I'm not the crazy one in this fucked-up town.

The wind howls, and our family pictures rattle up the stairwell along with it.

Up the stairs?

I run upstairs. *Where do mischievous boys who grow up to become evil men hide their buried treasure?*

Perhaps it's in the same place Martin hid what he didn't want the authorities to find the last time. Under the mattress. It's where the boys hid the money in the frat house.

I run to our master bedroom and lift the bedding and then use all my strength to lift up the king mattress. It's dense with coiled springs, encased in 800-thread-count sheets, heavy, like everything else in this house, weighing me down.

All the weight I need to shed.

It's weight I put there, though, isn't it? All the things I refused to see that were right in front of me coming back to bury me.

I drop it. "Oof." There's nothing under there.

I check the other side and slide my hand under the mattress again.

"Mom?"

I drop the mattress on my hand. *"Shit."* There's nothing under that side either.

"What're you doing?" Finn asks me.

My hand is throbbing, and I let it fall to my side. "Changing the sheets, honey. You startled me." I want to yell at him. Ask him why he didn't tell me the truth. Ask him if he knows where the journal is. Ask him if he killed his girlfriend. The anger is stifling, bottling, and I must

226

not tip my hand. Not yet. He could be hiding it, and I'll never find it if he is. My heart shatters a little more.

Finn studies our bedroom with a perplexed look on his face, and it doesn't take a genius to figure out that I wasn't stripping the sheets. The comforter is still on top of the bed, and there's no laundry basket in the room.

The garage door rumbles. *I've run out of time.*

"I need to talk to Dad and then you," I say. Finn doesn't answer, just stares, and his despondency hasn't gotten any better. I see it now as stunned guilt. I love him, but it makes me sick to look at him now. He doesn't carry his guilt as well as Martin, cursed because he's part me, and I wasn't built to hold secrets either. Carrying the burden of what happened with this dead girl will torture Finn like it's tortured me, and I need to set him free.

I need to free us both.

We robbed Finn of his chance for truth telling by making him lie, and now I need to make it better.

I race down the steps. "Where is it?" I ask the house again, desperately.

The door to the office slams shut from the wind.

The office?

I close Stonehenge's front door and then walk inside the office and close those doors too. I have maybe thirty seconds before Martin finds me.

I know he's looking for me.

When I close the french doors and swing around, I notice that Martin's office is a mess, very uncharacteristic for him. There're Post-it notes and copier papers spread all over his desk, an unusual sight for a man who organizes everything in our house, including the sock drawer. "Jesus, Martin."

The key is hanging out of the middle drawer in the desk, also rare. Usually it's locked, because that's where he keeps the checkbook, key stowed away so the cleaners can't get to it.

Although maybe it's so I can't get to it.

I sit down in his leather chair and open the drawer to snoop, but there's nothing inside but pencils, pens, and blank checks. I don't know where he has the journal stashed, but when you discover you're married to a liar, you look for deceptions everywhere.

I need to get Finn away from him, this family, this life, if he's to have a chance at being a decent human being. They've already rubbed off on him, and I realize I'm to blame too. I'm 100 percent complicit in this mess, but I'm also the only one who sees a problem with it.

So much of my life choices have been based on lies, and the only way to move forward now is to scrap my mistakes and start over fresh.

It all seems scripted now—my botched engagement—a means to something else. I agreed to all of it because after my bout of cold feet and my brief moment in Narnia, I didn't care to acknowledge my separation from Martin, willing to do whatever I could to make it up to him. Josh had up and left me without saying goodbye—again. We'd shared a tender moment, and at the time, I thought there might've been a real chance for a reconciliation, but he did what he did best—he left me.

And Martin was there.

He was still there after I'd tried to give him his ring back. That had to count for something.

It had to mean he really loved me and that our union was right.

Or . . . it meant that he'd found a girl he could keep under his thumb, nice and tight.

One who would sit next to him in his kingdom of lies, because I'd done so when Tush had passed away, and then I proved myself worthy again with Livvy and now Yazmin.

Well, no longer. I'm done.

I thought Martin was in a hurry to get married because he was afraid I was a flight risk, because no one really wants a February wedding in Pittsburgh. The Ellsworths were happy to push things along because a jilted groom would look bad for the family. It was about that too. Their appearance. The embarrassment of it all. They never really wanted me; they just didn't want the public scorn of what it would look like if I broke off the engagement, especially after the big display Martin had made at the restaurant. His engagement had made the newspaper.

I stare at the *E* engraved into the stained-glass windows—the letter—it has always been about preserving their name.

We found out after the ceremony that I was pregnant, so I always blamed the big rush on that, but he hadn't known it on the day of the ceremony, so that was poor logic. I still remember the way that dress squeezed my belly like a vise the day Martin surprised me with Stonehenge. The over-the-top gesture of purchasing that house never sat right with me, but I chose to ignore it, because it looked more than right—it was my dream home.

The door cracks open. I jump. "Sarah, what're you doing in here?" Martin pockets his phone, fresh from another call, probably with Alton. It bought me a few more minutes. Martin's breath is labored, and I'm certain he's sprinted from the basement steps to the foyer.

"I was just putting the checkbook back. I took care of it."

"Is that so?" He stares at me, and I'm staring right back at him. He knows I'm not a good liar. "What did she want? Did you offer her a certain amount, because people don't feel comfortable taking it until they see the zeros. I should've told you that before you left, to have a preset amount." Martin shifts his weight, and I want to kick him square in the testicles. *Is that how blackmail works? Thanks, Martin!*

I fight to remain controlled. "I gave her enough to cover burial expenses to compensate for Finn not being sure what happened. I made a point to let her know they were Yazmin's drugs."

I don't want to tip my hand and tell Martin it's the journal Alisha is after. If it isn't already destroyed, he'll burn it in the backyard right now if I tell him. Although Alton has probably already gotten ahold of him. I have a very limited time to get it back. There's obviously something important in there. My stomach shudders at the thought of what it could be.

He blows out a hard breath, making his sticky hair fly off his forehead. "Good job."

I *hate* him. But this is the test, and to him, I've passed. I can stay. Be an Ellsworth, sit next to him on his throne of lies, his queen. I need out of here.

"Alisha is angry, Martin. She's threatening to go to the media because she's not happy with how the investigation has been handled." I decide to give him a chance to tell me about the missing journal, and his gaze flits away to the corner of the room. "She thinks there's more that could've been done. Maybe she suspects we've tampered with things."

Martin's eyes blaze open behind his lenses. "Did she say that?"

"Not exactly, but I suspected it."

"Alton says that it will blow over once the toxicology report comes back, and then he can close the case."

"Martin, did Alton tell you Finn lied about using drugs? That he's used them frequently in the past and that is how he and Yazmin met?" My throat chokes on this impossibility. My honor student, my quiet kid. He's no stoner.

"Yeah, I've already talked to Finn about it." Martin dismisses me, and this is worse than I thought. Finn and Martin are conspiring against me, lying in tandem.

"That's just perfect," I say.

"He's going to straighten out now. He promised, and I believe him. Excuse me." Martin darts away into the kitchen. I hear his feet plod down the steps to the basement, no doubt to make a private call.

To cover up what I've unearthed. Or bury it some more.

He'll go for Finn next, poison his mind with more lies. I can't let it happen.

I'll return later to inspect the corner of his office, the one he eyed with interest. There's a safe there, and I don't want to think the horrible thoughts, but they're there: my husband's crimes have increased over the years, so he's had to escalate his efforts from hiding stolen property and bribes under his mattress to our home safe. I can't let him get away with it this time, and I can't turn a blind eye either. I left that girl in the woods to save my son, and I'm just not sure I have the courage to turn Finn in to the police if there's damning evidence in that journal.

No better than an Ellsworth.

CHAPTER 20

I pause in front of Finn's bedroom door and take a deep breath. I knock, then creak it the rest of the way open. "Honey . . ." Finn looks up at me from his desk and shoves a leather-bound notebook, like the corporate kind Martin's company gives to all his employees, back in the bookcase. He fumbles with a book as it falls onto his desk, a Neal Shusterman fantasy novel with a red-cloaked grim reaper on the cover. I can't help but take a sharp breath at the image.

One of those books is about two teens who learn the art of killing, and I can't help but grip my hands together, dried and cracked from washing and drying them. The book makes me think of the word I tried so hard to push away at the police station—*premeditated*.

Finn looks ashy and unwell. "I'm sorry—I didn't mean to scare you," I say.

His shoulders are hiked, uncomfortable. And I realize these last two days have been more about our struggle to cover up what he's done than about Finn himself.

I feel nauseous, loathsome.

My pulse races just looking at him, what we've done to him.

He's quiet and struggling because we haven't talked to him about the grieving process or how he feels about his girlfriend's death. He looks ragged, barely functioning, but it's amazing he's able to function at all, and maybe that should be my bigger worry.

Maybe my concern should be Finn's ability to thrive, like Martin, even though he potentially played a part in this girl's death. "I'm sorry we've been so busy. What have you been doing all day?"

"Reading." It's a Friday night, and Finn is shut away in his room by himself. I used to read a lot too, but most of the time it was stories about uppity families like the Ellsworths. Not how-to books on the art of killing. I swallow the bile in my throat.

I sit down on Finn's bed with him. "Do you remember anything else about the other night?" I ask, afraid to breathe, afraid to hear.

"No. I wish I did." He looks away and shakes his head. *He's lying.* "You went to see Yaz's mom today." His voice trips on his dead girl-friend's name, and I wonder if he'll ever get over this. Will he ever be able to have a normal relationship with a female again? My heart bottoms out in my chest. This is what we should've been focused on the last two days. "How is she?"

"She's holding up. Strong lady," I say, but all I can see when I think of Alisha are the awful pleas that trembled from her lips. *"It will be better for him if he comes forward now." "I want my daughter's journal back."*

I stare at my son, and he's thin and pale and dangerously depressed by his girlfriend's death—the one we forced him to cover up. He's carrying this burden because of decisions Martin and I made, and because of that I should carry the burden with him.

But I cannot carry it for him.

I can only try my hardest to find out if he made a mistake with this girl and decide how to move forward. If we'd given him the choice that night, would he have decided differently? Should we still give him a choice now or is it too late?

I decide to try honesty with Finn. I have more hope with him than Martin, although not nearly as much since I found out about the drug use. "Finn, Alisha was looking for Yazmin's journal. Do you know where it is?" I recognize the Neal Shusterman book. Finn owns the whole Scythe series. But I didn't recognize the brown leather book he'd shoved into the bookshelf. Like Martin, I want to give him the opportunity to tell me the truth.

Come on, baby, tell me what happened.

Finn shakes his head and looks away again uncomfortably. "I don't."

I suck in a sharp breath, punched in the stomach. At least he had the courtesy to look away from me before he lied.

"She used to write in it all the time. Do you think there's anything bad in there?"

"What would there be, Finn?" My heart patters in my chest. My instinct is to turn away too, plug my ears. I don't want to know if he hurt her. But the last twenty years have been about all the things I didn't want to hear. Didn't want to see. It's time to open my eyes. "You can tell me."

Finn shakes his head and squints. His hair falls into his eyes, reminding me a lot of Martin when he was younger, and I can't imagine what must be going on in Finn's head after the last two days. It must be crowded in there with all the lies we've told him and the ones he's told us.

"Alton told me you'd been doing more drugs than you let on," I disclose, my words rattling a bit. I hate how this truth about my son sounds coming off my lips, and I know I'll hate to hear the other ones that are sure to come next. But maybe if I can get him to admit it, it will set us on a path to truth.

He nods. "I thought it would look bad if I told Monroe that."

I clasp my dry hands together, firm. "Finn, it looks much worse that you lied."

"I get it, Mom," he says, but he doesn't. I didn't when I was his age either.

I rise from the bed, shaking my head. My son is a drug user and a liar and possibly a murderer. I press my hands against the dresser and stare eye level with the leather book.

It knocks the air out of me, and I rock back and forth, tears in my eyes.

"Mom?" he asks.

"Are you sure you don't know where the journal is, Finn?" I ask him, and I'm practically crying.

He looks away. "No, I told you."

You told me. But you lied!

And Martin keeps protecting his lies, enabling him to keep going. This is a failure on my part. I can't fail him again.

I need him to own this, to want to be better.

To try to be better, for Christ's sake.

"I found out tonight about something that happened when I was around your age, a mistake where I made a bad decision." My throat closes up at the memory of what Dad told me. At the thought that my son might be more like his father than I ever imagined. "They follow you, Finn. The guilt follows you too." I think of Tush and his large brown eyes and how I wish I could've saved him. "It's made me change my mind about what happened with Yazmin. This should be your decision, not your father's or mine," I tell him. This is it.

I'm handing the ball back to him. I'm giving him the chance to tell his own truth. We decided for him and we shouldn't have, and this is my best offer at making it better. I sway a bit as I turn to face him, palms pressed on the top of the dresser, creasing my sweaty palms.

"What do you mean . . . decision?" Finn hugs a square pillow, and he looks so much younger than he is that I can't imagine him going to the state penitentiary.

My son, my gentle ladder climber, a murderer.

The blood leaves my face and drains to my toes, and I think I might pass out, but I need to hear it.

"I think we did the wrong thing not going straight to the police when we found Yazmin. Your father and I disagreed on the matter, and you were too incapacitated to make your own decisions. I went along with your dad because at the time, I wasn't sure what was best. But after today, I think we're going to get found out." I'm breathless, pushing him to tell me the words I so desperately need to hear but don't want to hear at the same time.

Confess, Finn!

"Why?" he asks. He sounds terrified.

"Alisha knows you were with Yazmin in the woods when she died. It might not make a difference in the outcome of what happened to her, but maybe if Yaz's mom knows the truth, it will give them peace, and they deserve that after all they've been through." *What have you put them through, Finn? They've already lost a father and a husband; what other turmoil have you brought them?*

I remember how easy it was to take the path of least resistance when I was his age. I know what it's like to believe in what hurts the least. I'd given myself a pass of sorts because of all the pain I'd endured after my mother died, but Finn has everything—the world. He *is* one of the lucky ones. Dad warned me about this. When you give them everything, you poison them into believing they deserve it.

Entitlement. Does Finn believe he's above this girl and her family? Does he think it's okay to lie as long as he doesn't get caught?

And did he do it? Did he kill Yazmin?

"What? How do they know I was there when she died?" Finn's hugging the pillow in terror.

I was hoping the prospect of telling the truth might be a source of relief and that Finn was harboring so much guilt that he could barely live with himself, but it doesn't look like that's the case.

He just doesn't want to get caught.

The blood that left my head in a rush has left me dizzy, and I'm so chilled, I feel like I need to lie down. I sit on the edge of Finn's bed again and try to stay upright.

"Yaz had been confiding in her guitar teacher, apparently." I clear my throat because I still can't believe her teacher is Josh. "She was talking with her brother about going for a walk later with you in the woods at her last lesson."

Finn makes a complete teenage face of disgust.

"What is it?" I ask. Is he mad there's one more person who's been let in on his relationship with Yazmin? A mandated reporter who might be able to confirm his bad behavior?

Exhaustion and fear turn to anger.

This is not the boy I raised.

"I didn't like that guy. Her teacher. He thought he was some kind of hipster or something." Finn takes a huge exhale. "You scared me. That's not proof."

I place my hand over my mouth so I don't vomit. *I scared you because you thought the teacher would give you up?*

Finn straightens, and I brace for more. "We did go for a walk. I've admitted to that. And no one's going to believe the town drug dealer anyway."

"What? He's a dealer?" Or is Finn just deflecting to detract from his own involvement? Like Martin. I hate that he's so much like him, and I hate that I doubt him so much now because of it.

"No." Finn closes his mouth tightly and then bites on his lower lip as if he's made a mistake. He just revealed that he also lied to the police about knowing where Yazmin got her drugs. It seems to all go together, though. If Finn was smoking pot, he had to be getting it from somewhere. He's guilty of something here. I'm just not sure what. I grasp for something I can handle.

"What do you mean, Finn? Did the town music teacher get you the drugs?"

"No. He knows a guy, that's all." He won't make eye contact.

"So Yazmin got her drugs from her guitar teacher's drug dealer? That's fantastic." I'm ready to rip out Josh's throat. He admitted to knowing Finn was my son, yet he thought it was okay to give him and his girlfriend drugs?

"If it wasn't him, it would've been someone else, Mom. Yazmin was going through a lot. She'd seen some things she couldn't forget."

"I'm not shaming her for using the drugs. I'm just trying to understand what happened. Just tell me what happened!" I yell finally. I can't take it anymore.

Finn looks at me, shocked. "I told you I don't know." He looks away again.

"You also told me you didn't do drugs and that you didn't know where Yazmin got hers, so sorry if I'm having trouble believing you."

Finn slams the bedside table. "You started this. You made me lie, Mom, so explain to me how I'm supposed to tell the good ones from the bad ones."

I place my hand over my belly and lean forward. "I know, and I'm sorry, but we have to do better now." I'm rocking and wiping the tears from my face. "We messed up. But you need to tell me what happened, Finn, so I can help make it better. Help me understand why Yazmin was struggling, what happened to her."

He takes a few deep breaths, and we need to have this talk, but I'm about three days too late. "Her brother is worse off than she is, really. He's gotten himself into one mess after another. Yazmin said it's because he blames himself for their father's death. He keeps trying to do things to bring them up, but each one drags them down. And he wouldn't let me help. Always hated me for some reason." Finn stares at his hands balled into fists. "She'd only really open up to me after a few hits. It wasn't like she was addicted; she just needed something to take the edge off."

Cash's name keeps coming up, and Finn wouldn't mention him if he didn't have something to do with this. Maybe Cash is involved somehow. I need something more substantial from Finn, because the I-don't-remember shit isn't working for me anymore.

"I get it. I do. By *'bring them up,'* you mean Cash was trying to help out financially? Were they having trouble supporting themselves after their father passed away?" I ask.

"Yeah. Her father was a self-insured truck driver with no life insurance policy. They were left with nothing. They sold his truck, but it didn't go far."

"That's too bad." I think of my father and how screwed we would've been if something had happened to him.

"At least Alisha is employed."

"She had to go back to work after staying at home for years. Yazmin says she hates working at the casino. She gets propositioned by men a lot."

I clear my throat. "That's awful." I close my eyes and shake my head. "And it's too bad what happened with Yazmin's dad. And Cash." Alisha brought up Cash's troubles as well. Poor family, but I'm beginning to wonder about the brother.

"Finn, why do you think the drugs were laced?"

He shakes his head, still angry. "I don't get that part. I think she got a bad batch or something."

"That you know of . . ." I look at Finn because he has to realize he may not have known everything about his girlfriend. If she smoked one thing to escape her PTSD, she might've tried others, whatever was available to quiet the demons. That's what the women at the shelter with similar circumstances have told me.

"The journal, Finn. What are you worried about that might be in there?" He's never directly answered the question.

"I don't know what she wrote, Mom. Writing things down helped her cope. She called it her purge book." He grins at the memory, and then his smile breaks apart. It kills me to see the sweet smile of my little boy—shreds me more to wonder if I've raised a son cold-blooded enough to smile about getting away with murder. "She'd write lyrics in music class too."

"Well, they can't find the journal now. There seems to have been a mix-up in evidence."

239

"A mix-up with Alton?" he says. Finn's a smart kid; he understands how things work in this family. Is he in on it? Is that what I'm missing? Martin and Alton and Finn scheming behind my back?

"He's looking for it," I lie, and I can almost feel the heat of my words. I can't do it anymore. Even the small lies, the white ones, are burning me. I'm done with it all. Done with being an Ellsworth.

Martin bursts in the room, banging the door against the wall even though it's already wide open. His skin is oily, sweaty. His glasses slide down his nose, and he pushes them back up. I watch as he clutches his cell phone in one hand. "Sarah, Yazmin did not have a joint laced with meth and Rohypnol. Only Finn did. Who else did you tell about what was in his blood that night?" His panic turns to rage, the blue vein on his forehead taking on its own pulse.

What he means to say is—did I tell my father yet? I almost did. The sick feeling returns because I could've blown our cover. "No one," I say.

"Great! This is all going to go away very soon. Everything is going to be okay."

I'm horrified by his words. "What is wrong with you?" I whisper-scream. The tears I've been holding in trickle down my cheeks, but I'm so tired, I can't really cry. Not with the steam I need to express my true terror.

"It's going to be okay—didn't you hear me?" Martin says.

Nothing will ever be okay again.

I'm shaking my head, feeling faint. I need to run, but I can't move.

It's grotesque that he thinks we can all go back to being a happy family. And it's disturbing that he thinks the closing of this case will close the issues that go with it. But that's the way it's always worked in this family. When the law was no longer looking their way, they were excused.

"Why is this good news, Martin?" I ask.

Martin is elated at this grim fact. But I realize that this is really about covering up his own tracks. I see it now, why Martin was acting so strangely and why the Ellsworths were so motivated to help. If Martin could succeed in helping Finn get away with his involvement in Yaz's death, in a weird way it would be like absolving his own part in Tush's death. It's a sick circle. I can't be a part of it any longer and neither can my children. I need to know exactly what part Finn had in her death. If he was involved, I'll have to let him pay the consequences . . . but then I have to get him away from them. It's the only hope of saving him.

"Because Finn had different drugs in his joint than Yazmin did. This is a message from Alton." He waves his phone in our faces. "The toxicology report is in. It takes a couple of days for toxicology to get the results back because we don't have the same ins at the morgue—"

"What a shame." I cut him off, not the slightest bit amused by his unlawful legal connections or what he can do with them. "It's too bad you don't have money in the pockets of the coroner too."

Finn stares at me fearfully. "Why would mine be different?"

He's scared of being doped up, and I'm scared for him.

"Finn, did you tell anyone what we found in your tox screen?" Martin asks.

Finn shakes his head *no*.

"Remember, Grandma did that blood draw, not the cops. They never asked you for your blood sample because you'd already admitted to smoking marijuana. And thank goodness for that. By now, I'm assuming the drugs have passed through your system."

How long does meth stay in your system? Shouldn't that be Martin's bigger fucking worry—the effects to his son's body from the drugs he was slipped rather than the cops finding out he smoked them? And might those effects cause him to have a violent episode where he killed this girl? Does Martin even care if his son is a murderer? Or is it okay as long as he doesn't get caught? I'm having that awful moment in my marriage that divorced people talk about when they look at their spouse and ask the definitive question—*what did I ever see in you?*

"Yeah, I remember. I haven't talked to anyone, Dad, because you haven't let me. You took away my phone and unhooked the internet."

Martin took Finn's phone and unplugged the router? WTF. Prisoners. We're all prisoners, and I need to break us out.

"Right. Well, good." Martin looks disgustingly satisfied, breathing deeply, smoothing his sweaty hands on his jeans, but I'm failing to find the positive in this.

"Martin, why is this good? Why was Finn drugged, and how did Yaz die? What did the report say?"

He flips through a Xeroxed paper in his hand, and I'm disgusted that he likely hasn't even checked her cause of death. "Blunt-force trauma to the head," he says, as if he's reading a tax return.

I stare at him, shocked.

"She was drugging our son, Sarah, and she apparently didn't want him to remember why, because she gave him roofies."

I gasp.

"That can't be true," Finn protests.

"Who rolled the joints, Finn? Who handed them out?" Martin asks, fingers in his gelled hair.

"She did," he says.

"She knew what she was giving you, Finn. I don't know what she planned to do with you in those woods. Hell, maybe she did do something to you and no one knows, but I'm not sure we should be so eager to find out how she died, because she had bad intentions. It's time we move past this. It was a terrible thing that happened to you. You made a bad decision dating her, got wrapped up with the wrong girl. We'll learn from it."

"Ha! That's it?" I fan out my fingers and swoosh my hands over one another as if to say, *"Wipe our hands clean of it."* As if it makes Finn's involvement in her death go away because they were her drugs. "What about what happened after they took the drugs?"

"Sarah, this girl was not who Finn thought she was. We are good people. We were all good people before this girl waltzed in and drugged our son and tore everything apart."

"Well, sometimes you have to tear up the garden to find the weeds!"

"What's that supposed to mean?" he asks.

"It means I'm going to stay with my father until you decide what matters more to you—your precious secrets or your family. This family." I make a circle with my hands. "Because by keeping secrets, we ruin the family, Martin. It's time to come clean. For all of us. You too, Finn." I point at him, and he shrinks away.

"Oh, that's rich! Your dad has secrets too, Sarah." His smile is self-righteous, and if Finn wasn't standing there, I'd knock it right off his face. I know all my dad's secrets now.

"Not as many as you, Martin."

I might as well have slapped him, because he loses his haughty grin fast and doesn't stop me when I walk straight across the hall to our master bedroom and pack my suitcase. My dad said I was welcome anytime, but he's expecting me tonight. I pack my bag with as much shit as it can hold and slam our wedding photo down on the dresser.

Martin opens his mouth to say something, but words fail to form. I know he wants to know one thing—*how much do I know?*

"I always liked Nurse Patty. You know, the nurse at Health Services at CMU who your dad paid off. Her replacement was mean, and I dreaded when I got sick because she was stingy with the cough drops. Too bad you had to take her out too."

Finn is looking down at his feet, the same way he did when I asked him to stay for a snack when Yazmin had wanted to leave. It's clear his allegiance is no longer with me, and I fear I've lost him to the Ellsworths forever.

"Don't leave, Sarah. Your family needs you right now. You can't walk out on us!" Martin yells.

"Then make us whole again, Martin. Turn us in. Do the right thing this time!"

Finn won't make eye contact, and I can't believe he wants to stay here, surrounded by all these lies.

"You know your family will try to stop me if I go to the cops, Martin." *And I could end up no better than Yazmin—dead.* I'm scared of the lengths the Ellsworths will go to keep their secrets.

I grab my suitcase and struggle down the stairs with it. They both follow me.

"Come on, Mom. Stay," Finn pleads, and it breaks my heart. My son is begging me not to leave him.

"I can't," I tell him, and it pains me. I swing open the front door, and Martin tries to grab my arm. "Don't you dare." I pull it away from him. They continue to follow me. All the way to my car. I chuck the suitcase into the trunk.

"Sarah, *please*," Martin says.

I stumble before getting into my car. "I have to run back in and get my charger."

"Just stay," Martin says, but it sounds like a whisper in the wind as I run back into Stonehenge. Finn is beside him. It's as if he ran as far as the car to stop me and then changed his mind. He wants to come, but Martin made him feel as though he's tethered there.

Maybe Martin's so distressed, he'll think my phone charger is what I'm really after.

I jet up to Finn's room and run over to his bookcase. I grab the brown leather-bound book off the shelf and flip it over—no title. *I knew it.* And I feel sicker than before.

Finn didn't come with me because he's just like his father. He's taking his stance. I've let him become contaminated with the Ellsworths' ways, and I need to find my way back to him.

I swallow the bile in my throat. I need out of the house.

I run down the stairs, and the steps make awful groaning noises. Groans of disapproval for sure.

"Sorry I have to leave you, old girl," I say through a mask of tears. The journal wasn't in the safe after all.

I crack it open just to make sure, and I see the owner's name printed on the title page—*Name: Yazmin Veltri.*

I shove it in my oversize purse, not wanting it to be true.

Not wanting to believe that I asked Finn the question time and time again, and that each time he so freely lied to my face that he didn't know where the journal was. It had been right in the same room we were both standing in. He'd been reading it.

What is he so afraid of?

The door has never felt so heavy as it slams behind me. It echoes in my chest, my ears, my soul. Stonehenge is angry, yelling at me.

I don't know if she's shouting at me to leave or stay, but I need a break from this place and these people.

I walk to my car, where both Martin and Finn are standing. I kiss my son on the cheek. "I love you."

And I do. I love him. I just can no longer hide his guilt or his lies.

CHAPTER 21

As I lie curled up in my childhood bed, I'm sadly nostalgic for the girl I used to be. When I was Yazmin's age, I used to lie here and dream of helping the world.

Yazmin's thoughts are very different from mine.

At one quick glance, there are pages and pages of hurt in her journal. And if I had all the time in the world to read them, I would, but I have to find out if there's anything in there that could possibly link Finn to Yazmin's death before it's too late. Once Martin realizes I have the journal, he'll sic Alton on me and I'll be hunted down, journal confiscated and likely destroyed. But if I don't get it back to Alisha, she'll go to the media and expose us and whatever ties Finn has to her daughter's death.

Terror fills every cavity of my body. My ears and mouth burn with dread. I heard Alisha's warning loud and clear.

"Return my daughter's journal—or else."

She didn't say the last part, but I felt it. And as a mother, I understood it, but I need to read the pages first and determine Finn's involvement and decide what punishment fits the crime before I return it. It's what any mother would do, I try to tell myself, looking at this situation with the lights on instead of just through the filtered ones I've chosen to keep on.

I'm skimming for any mention of my son or his school or conflicts that might lead to discovering how Yazmin died and how it could connect to Finn.

I start at the back of the journal, but not the very back. I need to ease myself into what I might find. The very back has a page ripped out anyway, and I dare not think what that means or who tore it out. I don't need Yazmin's whole story; I just need to discover how it ended.

I wipe away tears, a wave rocking my body, like the ones that do when I think about how we left Yazmin, the end of her story cut way too short. The waves that hit after I wash my hands or after my fingers touch any water, for that matter—*I'll never wash her away*. It's when I can feel the grime of leaving this girl, a child, really, all alone—dead in the woods.

When the thoughts unfurl in my mind, they're like angry stabs at my soul. I feel the fresh wound each time, and I don't know how the Ellsworths don't feel them too.

They must be soulless. My husband and son included, if Finn did hurt her. Martin is lost to their ways, but surely there's still time to save Finn. I just need to figure out what happened to his girlfriend.

Who were you, Yazmin? What happened to you?
10-7

Things haven't been the same since Cash hit Finn—at home or in school.

Finn told me not to worry about it, no big deal. He let me cry on his shoulder, and it felt good that he cared. He's so sweet. Almost too good for me.

That's what Cash said. He said to watch myself. He told me not to trust Finn. He said Finn can never really love me because of where I came from, and he's only after one thing, but that's not Finn.

Cash doesn't know him.

But maybe I'm not good enough.

It's probably why I tested the limits tonight.

He played his music so well, trying to show me how. He's sexy, rough, so much older, but he gets me. He just lets me be. We smoke together too when Cash doesn't come along, and this time when he leaned in, I got closer and we almost kissed!

I'm glad now that we didn't. He told me to chill.

Why didn't I know that Cash hit Finn? Could that be the reason for the bruises and the scratch marks? Relief hits me, and I allow my arms and legs to relax a little beneath my threadbare covers. It's one of the things I'll have to get used to when downgrading my life, but shitty sheets are a welcome exchange for a shitty life.

9-18

I met Finn's mother today, and it didn't go well. I'm sorry I tried.

Finn's so sweet, and I thought maybe she would be too, but I was triggered in so many ways, I can never go back there.

HER house. I cringe thinking about it.

She laughed at me because I took off my shoes before coming inside. Well, I didn't want to trash her nice digs, and that's what I've been taught to do, but she made me feel more ridiculous in my knee socks than the first day I tried them on.

"You look like an ad for private school for rejects!" Cash laughed at me.

Loser. Totes. He's probably right.

But the house gave me the creeps too, so freakishly medieval, and those stained-glass windows . . . GOD.

I didn't want to see what I saw, and just like the man that night, I still can't be sure, but I recognized that symbol in the window, that letter, the way the sun shone through just like the flashlight flicked over it that day.

I hadn't remembered it till right then.

The therapists couldn't tell me I was imagining it anymore.

And it isn't Finn's fault who he's related to, but it's hard to believe this is all a coincidence. Cash says it was meant to be. It's Dad's divine intervention. We're meant to get ours.

We only want a million. Cash said it needed to be an amount that could fit in a suitcase. I think it's the amount Cash needs to move on. It will help us all move on.

That amount of money is probably nothing to these people. Maybe if I get Cash what he wants, he'll compromise and let me have what I want too— Finn. The money doesn't matter to me.

Money might help Mom out, but it will never bring Dad back.

They were after our money? Cash was after our money? Why? Because we're rich? Yazmin stared at my windows oddly, but why? She mentioned a symbol. Did she mean our crest?

Chills prick my arms even though I'm bundled up in my comforter. Where did Yazmin see the family crest before? And how did it connect to her therapy? I'm skipping around, grabbing on to words, grabbing on to myself. Why didn't she like me? I couldn't find a good reason, but I hadn't had a great reason for resenting the cancer survivor at the funeral either, other than she was there and my mother was gone and—she was rich. I hated her because she was so different from me, everything I wanted to be. Was Cash latching on to our family, making us the enemy to cope with his own father's death?

Keep reading. I flip back to an older entry.

9-3

The nightmare was bad tonight. It's three a.m., and I have school tomorrow, and I'm sweating and shaking, and I need to go back to sleep.

FUCK, I'm going to blow this scholarship. I don't even know how I got it, and that's part of the reason I trip so hard over it. I wrote about Dad in the entrance essay, and that got me in. It makes me sick. They tell me at least something good came out of the accident.

LIE.

Dr. Cjaskowski says to write down my thoughts, get them out, purge them, but that's shit advice. My father was punctured through the stomach by a tree branch.

His blood seeped all over my face.

The car flipped; it pinned me on the bottom, Dad suspended above. I can feel it sometimes, the car sliding down the embankment, stopping at the river. Thank God it stopped, but then—the freezing-cold water entering the window, mixed with the warm blood dripping above, washing over me.

Dad's life rushing out of him, all over me.

I felt it tonight. I scratched myself across the cheek, trying to get the blood off. The scratch is going to leave a mark, and I'm pissed.

My tears are burning the scratch. MAKE IT STOP. I can't let these kids see me crushed.

It's not the Yaz I want to create.

Sometimes in my dream, I see someone at the accident. Dr. C says it's some kind of psycho mirage created by a combo of my concussion and my desperation to live.

BR—that's him, a part of him anyway. I saw his initials pressed into the snow, but then they disappeared.

It was a "him," though. The killer. The driver. The one who used the access road by the river to drive down and check us out. He left us behind to die. Someone was there that night. Headlights. A hand on the window, then pressing into the snow to investigate, leaving the BR. A light shining right at me, blinding me. I'm on the bottom of the car, but looking up, I can make out something shiny—metal.

Another car? I was sure I was being rescued.

Dr. C said it could have been a semi passing by, the headlights. I'm not sure.

Dad was still gasping for breath when I saw the lights, and I knew someone was there and called for help. No one came. For hours.

No more sound from Dad. Just silence. He bled out. I nearly drowned even though we were on land, the bloody water seeping in from the riverbank cresting to my chin.

And then my screams. And the cold. Just cold. No more warmth.

After the dreams, the quiet kills me. I'd die for a hit. Cash wants me to stop smoking, and I haven't heard of any kids who smoke pot at this school. I'll get kicked out if I do, and I need to learn how to deal without it, but if I had it right now, I'd smoke it.

Why couldn't it have been me? I prayed for them to take me too. I still pray for it on nights like this.

The kids here don't know what happened to us, and that's the best part about being awarded this scholarship. I can reinvent myself here. I'm not the girl who was trapped in the car with her dead dad. The creepy girl.

I'll be the cool city kid here on scholarship. The one with the sunglasses on fleek, even though Cash had to steal them for me. I can use them tomorrow to cover my scratch.

The kids here all have nice accessories, like sunglasses and bags, their statement pieces in a world of uniforms. I didn't ask Cash to lift the ones he bought me, but I think he's always trying to compensate for Dad.

He's practically waged war on the upper class.

I'm tired, but I can't sleep. I'll play my guitar instead.

Oh, sweet Jesus. I had no idea it was that bad, the grim details. Another wave hits me as I imagine being stuck in a car like that with my father, unable to help him, listening to him take his last breath. It would ruin me now, forget about when I was Yazmin's age. Why didn't I do more to help her? If Finn would've let me in, I could've helped this girl.

9-11

Week three and Cash is already plotting. I want to be better here, I told him. I'm getting good grades, studying to quiet the images. It helps to concentrate on something real.

A math problem I can solve, a literature assignment I can digest and pick apart.

I decided to run for school treasurer, throwing myself into new things so I can forget the old ones. I smile at everyone I can here, and I write stellar words in the student paper to announce my reasons for wanting to run for student council. I don't know if they can tell I'm faking it, but several girls complimented me on my sunglasses today and told me they'd vote for me.

Cash said if I wanted a designer bag to let him know, and I can see how this could become habit-forming, but I tell him no. I need to make it the right way, even though it's hard; it's what Dad would've wanted.

Most of these kids have been with each other since grade school, and that's hard too, but I'm also the new kid, instantly intriguing. Different.

Not in the way I was different at my last school—the depressed kid.

I wear less makeup here, because everyone else does. I use less hair spray too and embrace my flat iron. I'm quickly learning their ways, and the boys all smile back at me. Cash says I can have my pick, but he wants me to choose "right," and everyone here seems so proper. Except for the three kids I found who smoked after the football game.

Matty and Joel are brothers and shared their weed with me once I caught them. They didn't really have a choice. Their friend Finn was there too. Matty and Joel flirted with me hard, but I liked Finn because he barely said a word, and usually I don't go for shy guys, but he seems like someone I want to get to know.

Yesterday he held the door open for me in fourth period. I almost laughed, but then I realized maybe guys really do hold doors open for girls here, and I like that. And today he told me I looked like Ariana Grande! I'll take it.

My disguise is working. They can't see the real me. I'm going to be okay here.

I page through again furiously.

10-2

Cash yelled at Finn tonight, and it's all my fault. I invited Finn over thinking no one else would be home and we could be by ourselves. Cash and Mom were working. Cash must've gotten done with his shift at the pizzeria early and snuck inside the house without me hearing him.

Finn and I were in my room. Cash walked in while we were kissing. Even though he's the younger one, he's always acted like my father when it comes to boys, especially after Dad died.

Cash wanted me to start dating an Academy kid for his money, but I'm starting to love Finn for his heart. He has a good one. Cash said I didn't have to get physical with these guys, that they were total losers and we could pull one over on them without that. He didn't want me to put myself out there like that, but this wasn't something I was doing for a score.

I wasn't Mom, dealing cards and taking side bets for other things. I think that's what he thought, but I really like Finn. What now?

There are tears streaming down my face, and my heart is beating a mile a minute.

That poor, poor girl. If she'd only let me in, I could've helped.

Like the true avoider I am, I haven't read the last page yet, and now, after reading the rest, I'm so fearful of it, I can barely breathe. I've read the part where she met Finn. There can be nothing before that page that's relevant, so really this is all of it, and it's worse than I could've imagined, the things this girl has been through.

These ugly truths are payments for all the ugly ones I've ignored.

And now for the last page—before the one that's ripped out, that is.

10-13

OMG, I can't even fucking live right now. DEAD.

I went to meet Finn's grandparents today, and I don't know why I even try with these people, but I really should've stopped at his mother if I ever wanted this thing to work.

Finn showed me his grandparents' car garage, which is bigger than my house, thinking I'd be impressed.

I wasn't. Then his actual grandparents were the worst.

Their son has zoning initiatives on his political docket to turn Green House into an apartment complex. It's one of the only state-funded mental facilities left in the county. They've been trying to shut it down for years, an eyesore on their sweet riverbank. Finn doesn't know what Green House is. I do. I spent some time there. They helped me when we didn't have insurance after Dad died.

When I saw Finn's uncle's political agenda to shut it down sitting on their dining room table, I lost it. I might not be here if it wasn't for that center. I have the scars on my wrists to prove it. Green House made me want to try again. Now other kids like me won't have a chance if this guy wins the election.

His grandmother is a witch, nothing like my gram, and I can't ever imagine her baking them cookies.

When they'd had enough of my protests, the grandfather threw his arms up in the air, and I saw it. OMFG.

His watch said Bell & Ross, and the label stuck out just like his Bentley car. Wait until I tell Cash.

My fingers run along the jagged edge of the torn-out page, the same one I let my fingers graze earlier. I wonder who tore it out.

Possibly Martin, because it incriminated Finn?

Or Finn because it incriminated Finn? The watch meant something to Yazmin, and she seemed to hate the Bentley something fierce too, but it all seems a rant of sorts against her main issue—the fact that Bill Jr.

was proposing to have Green House, a publicly funded juvenile mental health facility, shut down. This makes me angry because a great number of the women at the shelter who I've worked with were helped by Green House. Martin knew this would upset me, too, and he kept it from me.

It definitely isn't below Martin to have torn the page out, but it could have also been Alton. Obviously that page has all the answers, and getting all the way to the end of this and not knowing what really happened is like suffering through surgery and not being sewn back up. The offender, the page ripper, is leaving my guts hanging open here, just like I left Yazmin split apart in those damn woods.

Serves me right.

CHAPTER 22

The door to the music store chimes brightly, and I wave the dust bunnies out of my face, but all I can see are the imagined faces of Yazmin's dead father and her powerless beside him, waiting for someone to save them.

I try to blink them away and fail.

I take a step forward, and Joshua is standing at the register. It feels like the longest walk across the smallest room to meet him, the carpet gray and dingy, like the rest of the store. Joshua Louden is indeed the owner of the music store, and yes, he's always been a no-frills kinda guy, but people in Sewickley expect more from their downtown storefronts. Maybe that's why his is always empty.

The journal has filled in a few blanks but left more questions too.

Why did Yazmin vehemently hate the Ellsworths' windows and watches and cars? It seems like it was something more than just a preoccupation with their ostentatious lifestyle.

It was as if she'd seen the family crest before.

I still need to know what's written on the last page of that journal.

Just like I need to know why my son had laced drugs and Yazmin did not.

It's hard not asking Finn what was on that page, but I haven't seen him since I left home. I could've called and made Martin put him on the phone so I could ask him. But then Martin would know I have the journal and force me to give it back. The next logical step is to try to find out more about the drugs. Were they Yazmin's or Cash's? What didn't they want Finn to remember? It's the key to how Yazmin died, I'm certain of it, and Josh is the key to the drugs.

Josh is frowning at my arrival, and I'm upset with myself for being so disappointed he's not happier to see me, especially after what I just read about him.

He's the source for helping teenage kids acquire narcotics, and that makes him a bad human. Finding the source is half the battle when you're a kid. Why doesn't he look like a bad human, then, all snug up against the register in his three-button T-shirt, tattoos for sleeves, and ripped jeans? As I get closer, I realize he's wearing a thin black rubber necklace, and I want to know what charm is attached at the bottom because it's tucked beneath his shirt, but of course I don't ask.

"Hi, Sarah," he says.

"You know, you used to be a lot happier to see me." I try to keep it friendly, even though I'm angry.

But something Martin said to me last night trumps anything that Josh could possibly do or say.

"Hell, maybe she did do something to you and no one knows . . ."

If there are any words to keep a mother up at night, those are the ones. I'm not okay with not knowing what happened to Finn during his time in the dark. I'm afraid he got wigged out on whatever he took and hurt that girl. The journal didn't clarify it. In fact, it only worsened my suspicions that he was somehow involved.

"Those were much different times," Josh says. I notice his fingers are white-knuckled on the countertop.

"Yes. Yes, they were."

Josh raises his eyebrows. "So what brings you in?"

"Finn told me you know the guy who sold Yazmin the drugs."

Josh nods as if he expected this. "I do. You know I smoke. I don't know why this is important. I'm not the dealer."

I laugh in his face. "Way to pass the buck, Josh."

"Sarah, Yazmin was walking the streets of the north side to get her stuff from some very bad people. She could've been killed. I was doing her a solid." He leans forward, flexing his palms on the counter.

"Doing her a solid? You're so fucking cool, Josh. These are just kids," I say, but I do swish his logic around in my head, the same explanation Finn used last night. If Yazmin hadn't gotten the drugs from Josh's guy, she would've gotten them from somebody else. If Josh's guy was the safer choice, and if Yazmin was going to do drugs regardless, then maybe it did make a little sense.

But Josh's guy hadn't been the safer choice in this case.

"My guy would never harm a kid."

"Then why did he sell her laced drugs?" I reveal. There was always the chance that Yazmin laced Finn's joint herself, since her tox report was clean and Finn's was not, but after reading her journal, I can't see her doing this. Why would she *dope him up with some bad stuff,*" as Monroe said, if she really cared about Finn? Maybe Finn is innocent and he's just protecting Yazmin for some reason. The boy I raised would've willingly given the money to another kid in need, and Yazmin had to have known that about him, so what was all this plotting about with Cash?

Josh shakes his head. "I don't think he sells anything but straight-up bud. He didn't poison those kids, Sarah. They poisoned themselves."

I'm leaning on the counter. "That's bullshit! Who is he? I want his name. I want to talk to him."

"Wait a second." Josh takes a sudden step back from the register, his eyes traveling up my body, head to toe. He comes around from behind the countertop to where I'm standing and grabs me by the arm.

"Ow, what the hell are you doing?" He doesn't answer me.

His green eyes are angry and lucid. He's definitely not high right now, but I can't pinpoint a reason for his reaction. I'm not used to serious, adult Josh, and I don't like him.

"Come with me." He drags me to the back, to the storeroom.

"Stop it—what're you doing?" I'm a little scared.

When we make it into the storeroom, he flips on a light. My sinuses are overcome with dust. There are boxes everywhere, and a disorganized mound of twisted metal occupies the center of the room.

Music cases hang open on shelves like caskets waiting to be filled, and death is all around me—on my hands every time I wash them, ingrained in everything I see. I stumble over a trombone as Josh closes the door. I untangle it from my boot and hold it up, the mouthpiece caked in dirt. "Ugh. What a mess."

He takes the trombone from me and lightly tosses it.

"What's wrong?" I ask.

"Lift up your shirt, Sarah."

I almost laugh in his face. "I think you're having a wicked flashback. You no longer have rights to that property."

He crosses his arms in front of him. I notice he has a scar on his wrist too. "I just want to make sure you're not wearing a wire. Did you find Yazmin's journal? Is that what this is about?"

"What? No, Josh, I'm not wearing a wire. I'm just trying to find out what happened to that poor girl." I don't want to tell him about the journal just yet, because I'm not sure whose side he's on here. I need to protect Finn until I figure this out.

"Then show me," he says. "You're an Ellsworth, and I don't trust you. I didn't come back to this town to get caught up in this shit, okay?"

"Then why did you come back?"

"My mom got sick." He pauses, and I try to remember the last time I saw Catherine Louden in church. She always sat in the back—by herself. "I had to take care of her. There was no one else." He looks down at his Vans shoes, and I think his answer is odd, because he hated his parents. He takes a step forward and makes a gesture with his finger for me to lift up my shirt.

I'm wearing a long tunic sweater and skinny jeans. It would be an easy up-down for me and nothing he hasn't seen before, ground he's traveled well. He takes another step toward me. "I swear to God, if you're trying to get me into trouble after everything I've done for you, Sarah."

"Everything you've done for me . . ." I'm speechless. *Like what—supply my kid with drugs? Get his girlfriend killed? Lie to me about your involvement?* The thoughts are like fireworks on my lips I can't properly launch.

He crosses his arms again. "You like your house, Sarah? I used to like it too."

I close my eyes, the pain that rests behind them like a migraine that's been brewing for two decades. He's talking about Stonehenge. Of course he is. He thinks I've taken it out from under him, the place promised to him in his parents' will before they sold. And maybe he's right, but it wasn't my doing. It was Martin's. He'll never know how hard it was for me to raise my kids there knowing he ran those same halls as a child, especially after I had my first son. By the time Finn came along, it'd settled in a little better, but Joshua's ghost was always present.

"I know your dear husband bought it for you. When it wasn't even for sale."

Fuck. The last part is the worst. His parents weren't intending to sell. They were intending to leave it for him. And Martin bought them out.

"I swear he didn't know about you." What I mean to say is—*"He doesn't know that one of the reasons that house is so special to me is because you lived there and because of the memories we shared there together."*

"You never told him?" He inches closer. "About me?" My mind is going fuzzy, and my nose is tickling with allergies. This all feels like some kind of test, but it's hard to remain present when all my senses are gravitating to the past.

"No," I whisper.

A slow, satisfied smile spreads across his lips, because I'm sure he hasn't told anyone about me either. Those dog days of summer were ours and ours alone, but the temperature is escalating in this storeroom too. I feel my cheeks flush and my body respond. He's standing so close. His belt buckle brushes the waist of my pants, making a familiar yearning creep down the front of them.

A song comes on the store radio. There's always music playing when we're together. It's our song. Of course it is. The universe hates me. The universe wants me to do bad things when I'm with him.

That first night. Those lyrics. Was I with Martin because I couldn't find a better man? Or was it because I lost the one I thought I'd found?

Josh smiles at the opening beat. "Now lift up your shirt, Sarah," he whispers.

I take a deep breath, and it's all Josh's scent—a crisp, woodsy, soapy scent with a hint of patchouli. No cologne for this guy.

"Okay." I lift up my sweater. He looks at my body, and his face softens. He's *remembering* me.

"Turn around, Sarah," he whispers again.

And nothing is as intimate as it is with Joshua. The pool. The storeroom. The pergola. How many rooms of my life can he fill?

He whisks into my life to fill one space and then disappears again, lifting a burden as he goes, leaving another in its place.

I turn around, shaking a bit as I do, but there's something stimulating about him ordering me to turn—for him. No wire: he must see that now. I'm an Ellsworth, but not that kind. Or at least I'm taking a step in the right direction—away from them.

Have I passed his test?

"Turn to face me again," he says, and I do, still holding my shirt up over my lacy pink bra. He takes a step forward, and now we're a nose apart.

He takes his hands and strokes my exposed sides, and I let him. His hands are roaming the entire underside of my shirt. I close my eyes and grip his neck and pull his mouth to mine, his kiss the most wonderful feeling in the world, so nice to feel needed for being me and not the perfect wife I've been pretending to be for someone else.

He backs me up into an old bookcase, our bodies synching like a perfect melody. It feels good to be held, desired, but I can't let it happen this time. I can't escape.

The weight of a dead girl's life is not a burden Josh can lift.

It's not a burden anyone can lift.

My fingers dig into the flesh of Josh's back, and all I can think about are the half-moons on Finn's neck. Was it from a struggle with Cash or Yazmin? These are answers I need to find out. Pictures I can't unsee.

Like my dirty fingernails the day after I found Yazmin's body. Dirt and decay and pieces of her.

I can never wash her away. My body quakes with an awful wave of deceit.

"Stop," I gasp.

Josh doesn't seem to hear me, and I have to give him a little shove at his shoulders for my resistance to register, especially since my body is disagreeing with my head.

"Josh, stop," I say.

His eyes flicker open, and I know what's happened. He was lost too, and it would've been easy to stay in that place of lost comfort, our bodies entwined, but that's not our place anymore.

"I'm sorry," he says. He blinks again and backs away from me. "I just wanted to make sure you weren't trying to get me in trouble."

"I think you're the one trying to get me in trouble," I say breathlessly.

"I shouldn't have done that . . . I know you're married. I didn't even want to come back when I heard. You married him so early . . ."

"What?" It never dawned on me that Josh had even thought about me after he took off—twice—but obviously he had. "I'm taking some space to figure things out because of all this, Josh. I'm staying at my father's. Martin wanted to handle things a lot differently than I did."

"Right." He's pulling the door open and waving me out.

"Are you going to give me the name of your guy? I promise I won't turn him in; I just want to talk to him." It's not that I think Josh's dealer has all the answers, but if he can give me even an iota of a clue as to whether Yazmin laced those drugs or if she bought them that way, it will determine whether she and Cash did something to Finn to try to get money. It sounded like it from the journal, but Yazmin also mentioned letting him in on it, so then why drug him?

I need that last page.

"J—" He stops. "My guy won't be able to tell you anything. He received an order; he filled it."

"Like a good pharmacist." I wipe my mouth where we kissed, but there's no shame attached to it. And if I questioned it before, this brief betrayal only confirms my lost feelings for Martin.

Our marriage is over. My time here in this twisted fairy tale is up.

"He doesn't generally like to handle high school kids, but I told him they were okay."

"Why would you do that?" I ask.

We're at the front of the store now, both still unsettled from our encounter, but I think we've bridged a gap too. Josh can see now that I care about this girl. He likely suspects Martin wanted to cover it up just like the scandal in college, but I hope he understands that I don't agree with Martin's decision to do the same thing here.

Maybe we can find common ground. I promised myself I wouldn't fall into Josh again, but I needed him to know it's still *me*. Josh is the only one who really knows me, all my secrets, especially the unspoken one we share. Our ideals were one and the same, our hearts melded together years ago, the kind of joining that's never matched once you leave adolescence.

Whereas Martin and I were always opposed on the basic ideologies that are fundamental to a relationship. It hadn't mattered because we were strong enough without them, but it sure matters now.

"That girl was really suffering." Josh grabs the side of his neck again to expose his scars. "I know you think you understand her world because of your work at the shelter, but you can't. Especially tucked away, safe at night in my pretty mansion in the woods."

He said *"my pretty mansion in the woods,"* and he doesn't even realize it, and I sort of love and hate it at the same time.

"Josh, I know she's been through a lot. It sounds awful, being trapped in a car with her dad like that." I shake the image away—blood dripping on her head, Yazmin crying. It's all I can see when I close my eyes. Her journal entry will haunt me until I make this right. I open my eyes. "But I need to know why she tried to hurt Finn, because if those drugs were laced, Martin thinks she had bad intentions."

"Martin thinks . . ." Josh looks at me like I've just let him down. "What is it you really want?"

I suck in a deep breath. "I want to know how she died and if Finn had anything to do with it." The last part is the hardest to say, but I need Josh's help. Maybe if I tell him about the journal but preface it with saying I'm afraid the Ellsworths will botch the investigation again, I'll regain his trust.

Josh narrows his eyes. "Just let the police do their jobs."

I sigh. He doesn't know all the special measures we've put into place to make sure that the police can't do their jobs, and I certainly can't tell him now, not when I think he's beginning to trust me again. I'm the only one who can bring justice to Yazmin now, but if I try to step above or around Alton, he'll squash my efforts.

Or—I shudder at the thought—he'll squash me. As in, have me killed.

If I'm the one who could potentially bring them all down, I wouldn't be taking a pot from William's well; I'd be draining the whole damn thing. I bet they have cleaners to handle those kinds of problems too. I need concrete proof if I'm going to turn us in, not just a hunch. The journal isn't enough. It doesn't have any tangible evidence in it.

"How did you get those?" I point to his scars, still a little dazed as I stare at his lips, swollen from our kisses.

"We all have scars, Sarah. Some of us are just better at hiding them."

I cock my head to the side. "Right." I wonder if Josh is talking about him and me, and then I think of the odd marks on Finn's body too, the nail marks, their origin still unresolved.

Nothing about life or humanity makes sense lately. Josh never did talk in direct sentences, though. None of the men in my life did, it seems, with Martin and my father lying to me about life-altering events.

"Did you find the journal?" Josh asks. It's the second time he's mentioned it, and I know why. He doesn't want me to find out he smoked with the kids. I wipe my mouth on my sleeve again, this time swiping away his kisses.

"No," I lie. I want to trust him, but no one can know I have it, not until I figure everything out. "I'd like to find it for Alisha, but it would be interesting to see how Finn and she . . . came to be." I try to say it tactfully, that beyond my son's interest in politics and her running for student government, he and Yazmin seemed to have nothing in common.

Except for the drugs, of course.

Every time I think of my conversation with Alton, I lose my train of thought and try to think of any past clues that Finn was a user. He'd been an anxious kid and had mellowed out after his sixteenth birthday. I thought he'd just outgrown it, but I was wrong. Could that anxiety lead to violence?

"Maybe she saw something in him that she found safe." When Josh says this to me, I feel like it's one of our old conversations again, where he's trying to say more than he lets on, our secret language. He's trying to say that's what I did with Martin. He was rich and stable—the safe choice but not the better man.

He's probably right about that.

"He's a kindhearted kid," I say.

"She wouldn't have picked him if he wasn't," Josh says, and I'm confused again by how well he seems to have known Yazmin. It's clear he bonded with her beyond the student-teacher relationship. The journal entry about the near kiss makes me queasy, and I wonder if they ever got close like that again.

We keep edging toward the door. Customers outside are reading the sign, deciding whether they should come in or not.

"How's your other son? And how is he taking all this?" he asks, and I let out a shaky breath, panicked. Why is he asking about Spencer?

"He's doing great. Spencer is at school right now, premed." Josh smiles slightly, and it hurts. All of this hurts so much. "He called to offer his condolences to Finn, but he doesn't know all the details." I shake my head.

"I see."

"He'll be home for fall break soon," I say, and Josh looks hopeful that everything will turn out okay. But this won't. It can't.

The new customers decide to enter, and the front door chimes.

"Be well, Sarah," he says.

But in his language, it means *"Farewell, Sarah."* And it's for the best.

"Goodbye, Josh."

CHAPTER 23

I don't feel like I gained much more than I arrived with, except for an extra dose of self-loathing for letting Josh seduce me—again. There's no more room for weakness.

I need to pull it together for Finn. For Yazmin.

Martin isn't worried right now about Alisha going to the media with the missing journal, but that's only because he thinks I paid her off. I'm very worried now after reading it.

She probably knows what's in there, and she's desperate to get it back for fear it will hurt Cash. It sounds like he's been in enough trouble with the law.

Does Alisha know more about his involvement in Yazmin's death than she's telling?

I told her I'd look for it, and my silence is most likely perceived as an admittance of guilt, but I can't give it back yet. Not until I figure out what really happened.

So now I call Jay.

I'm not sure how I'm going to pull off a believable act to buy drugs, but Josh made his dealer out to be a nonthreatening character.

Finn told the cops that he didn't know where Yazmin got the drugs, and they believed him. Now the case is closed—girl from the Rocks smokes pot in the woods, gets super high, falls, and dies. Everything in the coroner report confirms the facts above. There's no need for them to investigate any further.

It fits Yazmin's profile. Monroe's report said the few friends Yaz had at school confirmed that she smoked pot. The thing the cops don't know is what was in Finn's joint. Only Alton knows.

I have evidence that suggests other elements were at play, given the Ellsworths' interference and Yaz's journal, but there's nothing concrete. The journal doesn't have anything in it to tie anyone to a crime. I need solid proof.

I wonder if Monroe's been to our house and if he knows I'm not living there anymore.

I texted Martin this morning to see if the detective had come to the house to further question Finn. He texted back:

Negative. I told you it's done. Come home.

If he'd only acknowledge this isn't a quick fix, I might feel obligated to text him back and tell him I'll be staying at my father's a lot longer. Dad thinks I'm still just angry about what happened with Tush, and it's safer to let him believe that for now. The last thing I want to do is drag anybody else I love into this mess. One person at a time. I'm still confused as to why Alisha hasn't made good on her threat to go to the press.

I'm guessing she doesn't have any real proof either, with the journal gone. I also wonder if Finn told Martin that I questioned him about the journal and if Martin is trying to get me home so he can get it back. Finn lied about the drugs, and he lied about the journal. I can't help but think he lied about his involvement in Yazmin's death too.

"Oh no, Finny," I say out loud to myself, because I have no one to talk to about this.

I think of the nail marks again and try to discern what Alton was trying to cover up by hanging on to the journal—that last page. I wonder what Martin's reaction might've been to Finn disclosing that I've been looking for Yazmin's journal. Did he feel deceived that I didn't give him all the information?

What's it like, Martin?

I pull up the picture I took of Josh's corkboard with Jay's number. What am I supposed to say to solicit a dealer?

I need to talk to you about getting some reefer.

Nah, people don't call it that anymore, do they? Hell, they didn't call it that when I was young. Josh called it *"bud,"* so is that what I'm to say?

"Crap." I'm no good at this. I'm shaking in my knee-high suede boots because I'm much better at being the good girl than the bad girl. I've never bought drugs before. It was the way I legitimized doing them the few times I had in high school and college. As long as I didn't buy them, I didn't have a problem. It wasn't a smart way to think then, and it isn't a smart way to think now. Just because I didn't lead the charge for the evil doesn't mean I'm not a part of it.

After Martin got into trouble at his fraternity, he didn't want to do them at all, and I was okay with that. I was supposed to be the good girl who kept him out of trouble, and I loved that responsibility, but it's freshly horrific now that I know the real reason he stopped using them. The few times we did smoke were at concerts, usually Dave Matthews when the saxophone player would go nuts, and someone would pass one around. It was akin to pouring out a little liquor for our lost friend Tush, and I didn't realize we were exonerating Martin a little more each time we did it, acting as if his death were just an average passing.

My hands shake on Jay's contact name.

Then I receive another text from Martin:

Spencer is home. He's wondering where you're at. Family dinner at six. I'm cooking.

Oh shit. Spencer isn't due home from fall break until tomorrow. He must've come home early because of Yazmin's death. He was torn up for

Finn when we told him about it over the phone. He's going to catch on right away that something is very wrong with our family.

I text:

Okay.

Martin texts back:

Thank you.

He should be thanking me for every last minute I grant him under the circumstances.

I remember the Sewickley Children's Heart-to-Heart Gala is also tonight, and I'm not sure how to handle it. We bought tickets to support the cause this year, serving children's organizations across western Pennsylvania—back when I thought we were good and decent and did wonderful things in our community. Will I still go? And will Martin be by my side if I do?

The women tend to clock the entranceway with their eagle-eye glances, surveying the other guests' dresses and jewels, new partners and old. Questions would be asked and answered by mere sideways looks. Which couple would be the highest bidder at the auction, and who would donate the most expensive item? Who sponsored it this year, and did they pull in more money than the sponsors from the year before?

They will suspect something is wrong if I don't show up with Martin, and as much as I don't care what they think of me anymore, it's my business how I want what happened with Finn circulated through the community. And Yazmin for that matter. There would be no one there to defend her.

William and Mary Alice will be there too. What if Martin is complacent and victim blames like he's been doing, saying they were Yazmin's drugs and she got Finn into trouble? I could see him mentioning where

Yazmin came from with cynicism and William tacking on how Yazmin was apparently rude to them when she visited, and it niggles at me that there's more to the story there too. The whole scene at the gala plays out in my head like a twisted Ellsworth diatribe against Yazmin, and I can't let that happen. We left that girl's dead body, and I won't let Martin drag it through the mud too.

I need to go.

But I don't know if I can do it.

I could barely look at Martin last night, so damn happy to discover Finn had been pumped with methamphetamine and Rohypnol that I'd wanted to throttle him.

Look, she tried to drug him!

Look, she deserved to die; we did the right thing!

What about Tush? What has Martin been telling himself all these years to alleviate his guilt for what happened to him? Probably the same thing I've been telling myself with Finn. Martin might use the excuse that William influenced him, and I might say the same thing about Martin, but the truth is we are all creatures of our own free will, and I've been no better than them. But I can be better in the future.

I climb back into my car and drive to my father's house.

My father. That's who I could ask about the weed.

Dad rolls his eyes to the top of his head, thinking. "You'd ask for it in grams. Teenagers would probably ask for two or three grams or a baggie, whatever they've got. Why? You that stressed? I've got a bottle of Glenlivet in the cabinet. I was saving it for a special occasion, but you can have it if you're that hard up."

"Thanks, but no thanks. Investigating a little into what Finn took," I say.

He nods. "It seems like the ones with more money than they know what to do with always get mixed up with drugs."

"Yep." I don't argue, because I realize he's been right all along and that I've been chasing the wrong dream ever since I left my mother's funeral.

He looks at me, surprised, but doesn't say anything more about it. "It'll be great to see the boys." He hasn't said anything to me about Martin either, and I'm guessing he's just giving me time to let everything sink in after hearing the whole story about Tush.

"Yeah, I'm sorry if everyone isn't in the best of moods tonight," I say. Martin didn't ask me to invite my dad to dinner, but I sort of had to, because I'm living with him now. It saddens me to think that I probably wouldn't have invited him otherwise. Spencer is in town, and it's not like Dad gets to see him often, but before all this happened, I'm not sure I would've made the call to ask him to join us.

It makes me realize how mixed-up my priorities were before, and I'm sorry it took Yazmin's death to fully grasp it. Dad's back seems to be feeling better today. He's still on muscle relaxers, but at least he's sitting in my front seat comfortably, his gray wool cabbie hat covering his head. He looks like a cute old man.

A senior with a Medicare card.

Sure, Dad made some mistakes, but he's done the best he could. It's my turn to take care of him now.

He fiddles with the heat in the car. "So . . . you don't think this will be an awkward dinner, do you? Seeing as how you took all your shit and left last night." He sucks on his teeth, waiting for me to answer.

"Probably. Spencer knows Finn's girlfriend died, but not that the kids were doing drugs beforehand. At least, I don't think. Or that I moved out. Martin probably told him I was just visiting with you."

"So you two are still not speaking?"

"No . . ." I debate mentioning more. That this is not about something that happened over twenty years ago at CMU. It doesn't feel like the right time. There's not enough time, actually, because that would prompt Dad to ask about a hundred questions to follow, and dinner is in five minutes.

"I wouldn't bother Spencer with your marital problems." He shakes his head. "Even though I think your husband is rotten, he's been good to your boys. Not my choice of role models, though."

I think of Josh and what transpired in the music store storeroom, and what a poor role model he would make too.

"So I don't mind having you around, but are you thinking about a real separation here?"

"Maybe." *Yes.* I just don't want to talk about it right now.

"Well, you know I'm behind you one hundred percent. Your bedroom is always yours to come home to."

Tears prick my eyes.

"I don't even know him anymore, Dad. He's not the person I thought he was. I don't feel the same way about him. I just don't know how he can look himself in the mirror."

"I'm surprised you're just coming to this conclusion now. He hasn't changed, Sarah."

Dad would never know the weight of his words. Martin hasn't changed. But I have.

Maybe things would've worked out differently between Josh and me if I hadn't married Martin so early and stolen his house away from him. Life is so twisted up right now, I can't tell the front from the back anymore. "I get that Martin made a mistake, but it's more than that, Dad. Window. Door."

Dad's old saying resurfaces, and I don't have to explain it to him. He knows what I mean.

"And where I used to see a window, now I see a door."

Dad nods. "I get it. I always saw a huge brick wall when I looked at that knucklehead, if it's any consolation."

I laugh a little despite myself.

"Although I will say, life doesn't get any easier when you're living alone, baby girl." He's giving me an out if I want to stay with Martin, because no parent wants to see their kid divorced, their family split up.

"Okay, Dad. Let's not talk about any of this over dinner."

My dad sucks on his teeth again. "This shouldn't be awkward at all."

God, I miss my dad. How did I let such an enormous rift grow between us? I claimed busyness, but it was also selfishness, placing my priorities in front of spending quality time with the one person who's always had my back. "I'm sorry I haven't been around much."

"I'm glad you're here now," he says, and it's the perfect answer. He's not mad at me; he's just glad I found my way back.

When we pull up to my driveway, Stonehenge greets me with a sad wink. One of the spotlights is burned out, and the house is trying to get my attention. It misses me and so does everyone inside. Wheeling my suitcase away last night was brutal, but seeing everyone tonight together around the dining room table will be even harder.

We'll all be there as a family. My dad, Martin, and the boys, in our warm house with a meal my husband prepared himself, which will no doubt be wonderful, because among Martin's dazzling talents, cooking is one.

He'd easily find another wife to woo with his expensive tastes and debonair behavior. She'd be fooled into believing that his kindness passed for honesty, which it doesn't, and that his morals were as shiny as his polished silverware, which they aren't.

I walk up my stony walk and pull at my puffy vest. I wish I had my quilted jacket, but it was burned when the cleaners seized everything incriminating from our house and torched it. I gulp at the morbid thought, all my sins going up in flames with it. How freeing it will feel not to be under the control of the Ellsworths any longer.

If they'll let me go.

Spencer opens the door and gives me the college try at a bear hug. His light eyes and confident smile make me melt. I let him hold me tightly, my strong, boisterous boy who I worried about so much when he was younger. He's channeled all his untamed energy into helping others by pursuing his medical degree. I don't want to think about how he'd side in this situation if he knew all the facts; I'm only happy that he's not affected by them—yet.

Spencer greets his grandfather next with a large smile. "Hey, Grandpa, I didn't know you were coming!"

"Neither did I." Martin is standing in the foyer with a white apron strung around his neck, clearly uncomfortable. "Hi, Vic." He gives my dad a little wave, and I can tell Martin's looking for clues as to what I've told him. I haven't told him anything about that night in the woods, but Martin can sit there all night and wonder.

"Hey there, Martin." Dad is unusually kind, and I'm sorry that he's trying to behave himself on my behalf, because it won't make a difference where my marriage is concerned.

Finn is finishing setting the table but stops when he sees us. He drops the silverware and gives me a fearful look. Wild emotions crash into me, and I freeze in place. I settle my breathing and wonder if it will always be this way. Will I ever be able to look my son in the eyes again without feeling this way?

Finn walks over and gives his grandfather an extra-tight hug. "Hi, Mom," he whispers in my ear, and he has to know by now that I've taken that journal, but he's pretending he doesn't. I just don't know what to do with this kid. I can see his gentle, battered soul when I look in his eyes, but he won't tell me anything. He's so much like his father, but I feel the dark side of his human prism might be even darker.

Martin disappears into the kitchen, and everyone is being a little too friendly with one another. Dad takes his seat, and Spencer pours him a bourbon.

"Would you like any wine, Mom?" Finn asks.

"Sure, Finny." I guess he's grown up a lot in the last week.

"Red or white?" he asks.

"White is fine." I choke on the words. Everyone looks up at me. The tension is palpable in the room.

Finn removes the wine from the chiller and pours it in a crystal glass, a hand-me-down from Mary Alice.

Martin reappears with a baked chicken speckled with green and black seasonings, resting on a silver serving platter of juices. He scurries right back into the kitchen and returns with a baked dish of brussels sprouts, crisp and drizzled with oil. There's a side of horseradish sauce reduced with balsamic vinegar that I taught him to make. He goes back into the kitchen for a plate of cheesy potatoes to top off the meal.

"Yum," Spencer says, and even though we bought him the best meal plan there is at Northwestern, I'm sure nothing compares to a home-cooked meal. Although he has to feel the tension in the air, know something is off.

"Well, this looks delicious," my dad says.

Martin raises his eyebrows, and I can't help but notice my father's unusual attempt at passing the olive branch. Martin must assume by now that I haven't told him about what happened with Yazmin by the way he's acting, and Dad is trying to ease the pain in the room, but his uncharacteristic gestures are only making it feel more awkward.

I try to swallow, my throat feeling thick. I'm starving, but I don't think I can eat.

"Thank you," Martin says, and I'm not sure who he's thanking exactly or why my father's being polite.

Maybe it's because my father doesn't want to see me get divorced or be alone, but I think it has more to do with the fact that he feels guilty. He believes the downfall of my marriage is because of something he withheld from me years ago, and it makes me feel terrible because it's about so much more than that. Once the divorce is finalized, I'll tell him everything and ease his mind, but this is not the right time.

We spoon food onto our plates, and Spencer oohs and ahhs in between bites. He either hasn't caught on that there's anything wrong yet or he thinks we're acting strangely because of Yazmin's death.

Martin looks at me expectantly, the lenses of his glasses dirty with the fruits of his labor. Oil, I think.

"It's very good," I offer.

He smiles.

"So sorry about your girl, Finny," Spencer says. There it is. Spencer's too smart not to know something is up.

We all tense around the table, but I'm glad he's bringing it up. Martin can't expect us to forget Finn's dead girlfriend instantaneously just because the police have.

"Thanks. It's been a rough few days." Finn looks down at his plate.

"I would've come home for the funeral, but Mom said there wasn't one," Spencer says.

Finn shrugs. "Yeah, there wasn't."

"I don't know why. Sometimes in these circumstances there isn't one," I say. "Too hard for families to bury their children, maybe," I whisper.

Martin gives me a questioning look, and I know it's because he thought I gave Alisha a check to pay for the burial expenses. Again, let him wonder. He should know what it feels like.

Spencer sits up straight in his chair and places his silverware down. "You know, my freshman year there was a girl, a student, who drank too much and passed out outside of our dorm on a brutally cold Chicago night. There are many."

"I bet." Martin laughs, but I want to kick him under the table, because I'm guessing this story doesn't end well.

"Thank goodness I got to her in time before she froze to death. Everyone has to watch out for one another." Spencer's green eyes glint when he says this, heartfelt. He'll make a great doctor someday. At least he inherited the right genes.

"I only knew her in passing, so of course it's not the same thing, but it could happen to any of us. Accidents happen, and I'm sorry it happened to her." My family agrees with Spencer's statement, and I appreciate his sentiment, but it's all wrong.

Martin is nodding, eating it up, as well as Dad, but this is not a simple case of a teenager partying too hard, and the nagging feeling makes my skin itch.

Something else is coming because of what we've done; I can feel it.

I've felt it all along. I ignored these warning signs years ago before I married Martin, and I need to listen to my inner voice now.

After dinner, Spencer is already on his cell phone talking to his old friends, making plans, and Finn is doing the same. It sounds like they're conspiring to hang out together, and I think of what a great kid Spencer is to include his younger brother in his plans. Spencer likely realizes that Finn needs him right now. It makes me feel like I've done at least something right raising them. Although if they really bond tonight, I worry that Finn will tell him the truth.

Then I remember that he's been alone with Martin and that this potential issue has most likely already been addressed.

Don't tell Spencer a thing about what happened in those woods or kiss your Brown application goodbye!

It makes my belly tense and curdle. I place my silverware on my plate, unable to take another bite.

Everyone is clearly ready to move on from this tragedy except me. No one, including Martin, has said one more word about Yazmin's journal, but decoding it is important. It's more than just blind yearning for truth and justice; it's the warning festering inside me that we should not move on without finding out why this happened. It started last night, when we discovered the difference in the drug screens, and it has only grown, this feeling I can't shake that something much worse is on its way.

"Sarah, can you help me clean up in the kitchen?" Martin asks.

My dad gives me a stern look, as if to say, *"Go on."*

I follow Martin into the kitchen, more for my father than for him.

"Thanks for coming." He's clearing the plates, his formality of thanking me reminding me of how he speaks to his parents, and if I wasn't completely turned off by him before, we're there now.

I take Martin's glasses off his face and clean them on my sweater, because they're driving me nuts.

"Oh, thanks, dear." He's squinting now.

"Don't call me that," I say.

Martin sighs and then slides behind me and places his hands over mine. "What's the matter, Sarah? Did you lose your glass slipper?" *Is he kidding me?* "We're okay now," he adds for good measure.

"We are far from okay, Martin." I drop the dishrag in the sink, not because his words are disgusting but because he has absolutely no remorse for what he's done. I wipe my hands on my jeans to get the water off, but I can never get them clean.

I'll never wash her off.

She's always with me. He doesn't feel that way. He washed himself clean of them both—Tush and Yazmin—as soon as the police closed their files.

"Look, I can't tell you how sorry I am about not telling you about Tush. We were barely dating when it happened, and I knew it would drive you away if you found out. My father orchestrated the whole thing. I was just a kid, Sarah."

"What about the part where your father collaborated with the dean to threaten my father's job and my tuition?" I'm still not facing him, and I haven't really been able to look him square in the eye all night. He's damaged. We're all so damaged. And it's not the kind of damage that can be fixed. It's the first time I'm seeing the true extent of it, feeling it, the way his touch truly revolts me, and it's beyond repair at this point.

"That wasn't my doing," Martin defends.

"Innocent bystander, huh?" *Just like me.* I can see it now, how it could happen. The tragedy wasn't that it happened when he was a teenager and he said nothing. It was that it happened again when he was an adult—and he said nothing.

"Look, so much has happened in a few days. I want to work on it. Don't let one bad week end a twenty-year marriage." His words make me pause, but what does it mean when a wife can't physically stand to look at her husband? Can't stomach his touch? Fled into the arms of another man just to escape his?

"I don't think you understand the problem, Martin. We can't just pretend this didn't happen," I whisper.

"Don't give up on us, Sarah. We're your family."

I clench my eyes shut, because now he's using the kids, and yes, tonight was nice sitting around the table eating dinner with them, and I wish to coparent in a way that it could happen again in the future, but I know that dream is a stretch at best.

"I'll do anything to make it better," Martin says, his voice growing needy at my silence.

"Okay. Then go to the police station and tell them what really happened with Finn's girlfriend, Martin. Because we can't just leave it like this. And I can't do it myself. Alton will bury me or your parents will destroy me, somehow, for giving us up, but you *can* do it."

"They'll book him because we didn't offer the information sooner. The case is closed, and if we go down there now, they'll assume Finn had something to do with it. He can't even defend himself because he doesn't remember. Do you know why he doesn't remember, Sarah?"

I know what's coming, so I just place the last dish away and don't answer.

"Because she was trying to hurt Finn. Going to the police is not the right move for our family," he says definitively.

"You don't know that for certain; you just want it to be the truth. There's what happened and there's what you think happened."

"Then instead of turning away from me, let's figure this out. Let's be a team."

"There's a novel concept, three days too late. How can I be your teammate when you've been ordering me around like an indentured servant? Telling me where I can go, who I can talk to, what to say to them, taking my phone? Taking Finn's phone. I don't even know who you are anymore."

I give him a shove to the chest. He's too close to me. The expression on his face is the saddest I've ever seen, and I think he might cry.

"Give us a chance to find our way back. Come to the gala with me tonight," he pleads. "We need a night out together, to talk, alone," he whispers, and I realize our voices travel in this old house and that maybe they can hear us in the dining room.

Martin is asking me to give him another chance, and he actually looks like himself again. His beady dark eyes have regained their warm glow. The grim lines that flank both sides of his face have transformed back into the half smile I remember. It's all trickery, I know, but I wonder if this cover-up madness has possessed him and if the Martin I knew, the good Martin, is really in there somewhere.

I don't want to go with him, but I have a strong desire to protect Yazmin's memory.

"Okay, I'll go to the stupid gala, but I make no promises about the rest."

CHAPTER 24

The gala is tonight, but the mystery of the laced drugs is still eating at me, as are the missing pieces to the clues in the journal. My gut is telling me the two are connected, although I'm not sure how. I may just be searching for answers where there are none, but my body won't rest until I figure this out.

I finally gather up the nerve to call Jay.

Shit. What do I say? I give him an order in grams, just like Dad said.

"Meet at the GetGo off Ben Avon Heights Road, fifteen minutes," he tells me.

"Okay," I squeak, and the line goes dead.

Jay meets me in a white van parked outside of a little grocery store just north of the city, and this is not what I had in mind for our discreet rendezvous point. It's hard to have an investigative conversation with a man who wants to drop his shit and run, but I get it; it's hard to catch a criminal who works out of a mobile office.

Jay rolls down his tinted window and nods at me, and I nod back to signal I'm the woman who called him. He looks over his shoulders both ways, baggie in hand.

I flash a $100 bill in his face. "I was hoping we could talk first."

He snags the bill, then asks, "You want the stuff or not, lady?"

Jay looks to be a twentysomething guy with a beard about a foot long. It's tied off in multiple ponytails with different-colored rubber bands.

"I do," I say and hold out two more twenties for the actual drugs, which he slides out of my palm in exchange for the baggie. It feels dirty, and I don't like it at all.

"What was it that you needed?" he asks, but he's already switched the gear in his van from "Park" to "Drive." Jay looks over his shoulder again.

I cough up the words I practiced on the way there, and they come out pitchy.

"I'm a friend of Cash's. I want some of the stuff you gave him that had a little extra in it."

He makes a face like he doesn't trust me at all, and I do suck at this, so I don't blame him. "You 5-0? Because that's a little less than two grams you've got, not even worth an overnight in the cell. And I got nothing else in this van."

"But I paid for two grams," I say. Not that I care, but if he's to believe I'm a real customer, I need to sound angry about the deficit in my drug order. People become enraged when the dealer doesn't deliver as promised. I've watched enough Netflix shows to know.

"Well, once I trust you, you don't get shorted anymore, and right now, I don't." Jay waves his arm full of tattoos goodbye.

"Look, I'm not 5-0. Just looking for the same stuff."

He shakes his head. "No way. You're no friend of Cash's. Turn your cop mic up real loud. If Cash had different stuff from what you have in your hand, he put it in himself. It's not from me."

Jay pulls away without saying another word, and I realize a few very important details from our exchange.

Yazmin didn't buy the drugs that eventually led to her death. Nor did she lace them with anything to harm Finn. It was her brother, Cash.

An awful avalanche of terror floods my body, and I can't quite process what this all means, but I know it's bad.

So Cash escorted Yazmin to the guitar lessons. Cash had conversations with his sister in the presence of Josh, who pretended not to listen to them speak but heard every word.

And Josh covered for Cash.

He must know it was Cash who purchased the drugs, not Yazmin. Josh said Jay didn't sell to kids, but he'd made an exception for Cash. So it had to be Cash, not Yazmin, who'd bought the weed. He'd had some sort of plan all along where Finn was concerned, but not one he'd shared with his sister. And now she was dead.

What does it mean?

Before I can try to figure it out, I have to suffer through this children's gala with Martin tonight. I'm curious what Martin is going to tell people when they ask him about Finn. The Ellsworths probably have their trained responses drawn up. Well, I hate to tell him I might go off script tonight if they say anything negative about Yazmin, especially after what I just learned.

Yazmin wasn't trying to hurt Finn after all.

I stuff the drugs in my glove box and drive back to my father's house to get ready. Martin told Spencer I'm not staying there, and the only reason I know is because Martin sent me a cryptic text that said, Spencer wants to know when you're coming home.

I never replied, and Martin wins no points by using our son to push his agenda.

The dress I choose from the limited ones I've packed is so black and plain, it screams *drab* and *depressing*, but I have no care for appearances right now. The panic that started when Martin read the results of Yazmin's coroner report has turned into full-blown anxiety after my conversation with Jay.

Certainly, Cash didn't mean to put his sister in harm's way. So what happened, then? And why has the curiosity for closure turned into stark terror, the feeling that if I don't figure it out soon, something else horrible is going to happen?

My head gets caught in the lining as I throw the flimsy floor-length dress over my head. I hate dresses, but I hate them even more tonight. I apply minimal makeup because I don't want to doll myself up for these people. I also throw on a pair of diamond studs for a tiny bit of flash, so I don't appear like I'm in a state of emotional collapse because of my son's involvement with Yazmin's death. They'll all be looking for that.

They look at everything in Sewickley.

Martin drives up to my father's house and rings the doorbell right on time with a bouquet of flowers in his hands. It should be sweet, but my father scowls and rolls his eyes, and I just toss them on the end table.

I kiss Dad on the cheek and leave.

Martin is dressed in his black-tie garb and looks very nice, but I'm so distracted from my afternoon drug deal, I can't comment.

Martin opens the car door for me. "You look lovely."

"Thanks." I slide into the passenger side and feel like a stranger sitting on the cool leather seat. I'm already dissociating myself from Martin. Our marriage is disintegrating at an uncontrollable rate, but the kids are older now, and they've had a wonderful upbringing—a nice, tight family of four. Their childhood memories will be of us together. That's the most important thing, I tell myself.

"Have you thought about what we talked about in the kitchen? I have a wonderful therapist in mind who—"

"Martin, let's just get through tonight," I beg. It's annoying how he already has a plan. Martin always has a plan.

"Okay, okay," he says, drawing in a deep breath.

Even if I would give him a second chance, which I won't, it's way too soon to try.

We make it to the gala and find our seats just in time for the host to give the same speech he gives every year about the importance of the Children's Heart-to-Heart Foundation and the generous patrons of the community who've donated items to be auctioned off to support the cause. The curtains on the stage glitter red. The townspeople perch on their chairs attentively, their jewelry sparkling as brightly as their effervescent smiles. I usually feel special pride for my community and look forward to this event every year, but right now, I cannot wait to get out of here.

My skin crawls with unanswered questions and unknown fears.

If Yazmin didn't aim to hurt Finn, then it had to be Cash. If he's the one who handed Yazmin her weed, then he's the one who gave Finn the bad joint, who slipped Rohypnol in it to make him forget.

Why would he do that? What didn't he want Finn to remember? Could those nail marks possibly be Cash's?

No, I saw her long, jeweled nails.

Wouldn't I know if Finn had a major beef with his girlfriend's brother? He never mentioned a word. Although that's the boy he's become. The one who tells his mother *nothing*.

All Finn said was that he barely knew Cash, that he wasn't friendly with him when he came over, and that he went to a different school. I read the parts in the journal about the arguments and the fight over the kissing, but that seemed pretty minor, teenage quarrels.

"Sarah?" Martin whispers. I look at his face. It's close to mine, and his spicy cologne scent that usually makes me curl into him is making me turn away. His eyes plead for attention, my eager dachshund. "Where have you gone?" he asks.

I shake my head. I cannot answer him. If he wants to know where I've gone, where I've been, he should have joined me on this journey to figure out what happened to Yazmin. But he would have to care about what happened to her in the first place in order to do that.

The speech is completed, and cocktail hour begins.

Camille and her husband, Dallas, waltz over to our table. I stand up to greet Camille and give her a tight hug while Dallas accosts Martin with his loud Southern accent and a pat on the back. "I heard you're fighting for property on the riverfront." Dallas is a lawyer who specializes in real estate.

Martin chortles. "Yes, news travels fast. I've been thinking for some time that we need to get together."

"How're you holding up?" Camille asks me. "Haven't seen you at the club."

"Hanging in there," I tell her.

"It's too bad about that girl. Is Finn doing okay?" she asks, and I see some other women lean in as they walk by, sharp smiles and gentle waves to disguise their desire to scoop up yummy gossip.

"He's coping, but it's hard, you know? She was a nice girl," I say, tilting my head and feeling my crappy updo begin to unravel. The honey brown of my hair has turned syrupy because I haven't had time to get to the salon to highlight it, and after seeing how nicely Camille's hair is done, I'm ready to take myself out of the game completely. I'm tired of trying to keep up with these people.

"Have you called Amazing Amelia yet? I don't know a good child therapist, but I can ask her for a referral." Camille smiles, but for the first time, it looks plastic—fake—like everything else in this paper town. If Hanna lived here, she would've been at my door with precooked meals and wine and tissues after Yazmin was found dead. Nothing is real here, not even my so-called friends.

"Not yet. Thanks, we'll get him help if he needs it." The continual mention of Finn creates a burning sensation in my body, and it might be because it's the first night he's gone out since Yazmin died. I'm worried about him. Nothing feels right.

Camille fluffs her blonde mane over the pointed shoulders of her floor-length red ballgown, cinched in the middle for extra accentuation of her curvy figure. "I heard the girl was into drugs," she whispers. "I told everyone I knew your boy wasn't like that. Love me some Finn," she says with a wink.

"Thank you," I manage, even though I want to tell her Finn's not perfect and neither are her children. Finn does do drugs and so does Camille. Just because hers are prescribed doesn't make them better, but she's trying to be kind, so I shut it.

"It's a shame, after William pushed for her to get that scholarship and all." Camille bats her eyelash extensions at me.

What did she just say? Camille is on the board for the scholarship program. The burning sensation heightens. *William knew who Yazmin was before this happened?* Something is wrong here.

I take her by the shoulders. "What do you mean?"

"He didn't tell you? William is one of the alumni who fund the scholarship program."

"I knew that . . ."

"Well, he reads the essays of all the kids applying to get in. All the sponsors take part in choosing the student. He pushed for her to get it. There were more qualified candidates, but he was really moved by her essay." She shakes her head sadly, but I've stopped listening.

The Ellsworths don't do charitable things out of the goodness of their hearts. All their actions have self-serving motives. I look around the ballroom for them.

Why the hell did they want Yazmin to get the scholarship? Something's definitely not right. How do their dirty hands connect to Yaz's death?

"Thanks for your kind thoughts, Camille." I tell her goodbye and walk back to my table, briefly mourning the losses as I glance around the room, because you can't keep your married friends when you're divorced here. That's not the way it works in Sewickley. Everyone is connected like a fat thatched rug. When you remove one piece, the whole thing comes apart.

There's an announcement made at the front of the room that the auction is about to begin, whereby all the local stores and collectors will present their pieces and put up for bid anything from haircuts to jewelry.

Martin squeezes my hand when the Sugarmans walk away. "They're great, aren't they? Would you like to have them over for dinner? We don't do enough couple things." He seems so earnest in his suggestion, but he's also trying to mix business with pleasure, acting like he wants to entertain the Sugarmans, but it's so he can discuss his property deal with Dallas.

"Martin . . ." I shake my head, and he looks like he might cry.

"It's just me," he says, and he wants me to look at him, but I really can't. "Hi, Sarah . . ."

Memories of our first night together and his little phrase float back, and it's not cute and sweet this time, and it doesn't make me feel adored; it just makes me angry. He can't use old romantic overtures to fix new problems.

The first auction item is a stunning set of emerald earrings from a local jewelry store. They're teardrop shaped, a karat or so, lined in diamonds, and embedded in fourteen-karat gold.

"Would you like those, love?" he asks, squeezing my hand again.

I pull it away. "Absolutely not. Those emeralds could feed a village," I snap.

He leans back in his chair, defeated. I won't give him an inch. He can't buy his way back with fancy dinners and expensive earrings. But it's not just the auction items making me nip at him. Everything feels off since I learned about William's involvement in Yaz's scholarship.

The auctioneer is prattling on about stupid items, and I want to break away and check on Finn, but Martin is squeezing my hand so tightly, I'm afraid I won't be able to break free.

We don't bid on anything, and the haircuts go for over $1,000.

Martin laughs, but I think it's gross. Even his little mannerisms I used to think were endearing are bothering me, and I don't know how I'm going to make it through the evening with this man, let alone the rest of my life.

Afterward, we run into the Ellsworths, who've arrived fashionably late—after the auction. They're seated with their country club friends, as always, and it's all I can do not to throw William's martini in his face. Bill Jr., city commissioner elect, is there with Greta, who's been left out of the web of lies, and I can only assume it's because her vocation as a dietitian doesn't benefit the circle.

It's always irked me how I am the one who gave Mary Alice grandchildren, yet Greta is still somehow the favorite because she grew up on the right side of the overpass. Then again, Mary Alice doesn't exactly love children—they talk back.

I offer Greta a small smile, and she greets me with one of her Queen of England half waves.

Get me out of this family.

"Hello, lovely daughter-in-law of mine." William's face hangs flat and long, reminding me of a full-grown dachshund, an aged version of Martin. William and Mary Alice both rise from the table and usher us out of earshot.

Mary Alice pulls me aside. "Hello, dear, hopefully you feel better about everything after the coroner's report." Her voice is persnickety, as if I should be thanking her for her amazing foresight at drawing Finn's blood on the spot.

"It doesn't tell me everything I need to know," I say.

She places her arm on my shoulder, cold to the touch. She doesn't often handle me. We're about the same height, and I turn my head to meet her eyes. They're so blue, they're almost clear, and I imagine I can see to the back of her warped brain, rotten and dulled from years of life with people just like her. "You have to be careful about who you let into your circle, Sarah. Best to give Finn the same advice. That girl wasn't one of us," she says.

I don't want to be in her damn circle anymore, but I have to tread carefully. These people are dangerous.

"I'm not sure I know what you mean," I say.

She sips her fluted glass of something sparkling. "You're having trouble catching on tonight, dear."

"Oh, I think I understand perfectly. You're only content to let people in your circle who can benefit you. They either serve you in the courtroom or they serve you tea."

Mary Alice sucks in a breath as if I've just slapped her, and William grips his drink like it might run away from him.

The band starts playing, thankfully, and people are dancing all around me. The Sugarmans have taken to the floor, slow and steady, and you can't dance like that if your marriage is going along poorly. They are in love and living the dream, the same one I lived just last year. It's funny how fast things can change.

Dallas spins Camille around, and she rolls back to him, practically nuzzling him on reentry. They look so happy, it makes my heart split like firewood beneath the sharpest of axes.

I was much happier when I was naive—when we were Martin and Sarah Ellsworth of Blackburn Road.

"There's a new ballroom dance studio in town. We should take lessons," Martin says.

"Shut up, Martin," I say. Martin shrinks away from me and sighs.

Mary Alice makes an awful sound in the back of her throat. It's likely tight back there, just like her ass.

William looks to his front and his side, Mary Alice standing on the other, a nice buffer to my rebuke. "That's no way to talk to your husband," William says, but I have a feeling he's more embarrassed that others might have heard me.

I'm the only one who actually ever cared about Martin's feelings, and I want to believe he's a good person, but all the years of poor nurturing by these people have poisoned him at the core.

"I'm only responding to the way he's been talking to me for the last few days, William, and the way you've been talking to me my whole life. I'm done. With him and with you."

I try to walk away, but William slyly grabs my arm and manages to wheedle me back his way. We're in a dark corner of the room, closer to the band, and not even those walking in and out of the nearby restroom can possibly overhear us.

We're all facing each other, Martin and Mary Alice pressed to one wall, the gaudy pink-and-white wallpaper making them appear like two horrible dollhouse figurines.

William's face smells of aftershave and liquor. He leans in and says, "Now, listen here—we've given you everything, despite the fact that you were the janitor's daughter. You're not a special snowflake, Sarah, and you will not upend this family."

Martin's mouth drops open to speak, but I beat him to it.

"Is that right? Well, if you never thought I was good enough for your family to begin with, then why did you approve of the wedding?" I ask, flustered but wanting answers to the question I've held on to my whole life.

"Because, dear, it was the only way to make sure your father would keep quiet, even after you graduated, about the little accident Martin had in college. As long as we had you in our pocket, we had the best collateral there was. Don't you see?"

Martin's face drains of all color, and he tries to reach out to me, but I've unstuck myself from the wall.

"It was all a lie?" I ask. "You never loved me?" I ask Martin, but it's not a question; it's a realization.

"Yes . . . I mean no! I did," he tries. "I do."

"No. Stay away from me," I say, my legs taking flight.

William's laugh is low and contemptuous, and Mary Alice smiles for the first time in forever. All the flowers on the gaudy wallpaper shift and whirl, pink and white and black and gray, the world's most mottled candy cane. There will be no Christmas brunch at the country club this year with the Ellsworths.

Martin is reaching out to me, but I've already started running.

Running through the dance floor, past every person in town watching me as I do, champagne flutes tipped on trays. One glass lands all over me, but I keep running for my purse at the table, because Martin slipped his keys in there. Either he didn't have room in his dress pants for them, or he had hopes he'd be going home with me tonight. I'm running out the door to his vehicle, still partially registered in my name.

And then I'm driving—to find Cash Veltri and figure out why he drugged my son.

Because no good can live in a house of lies. I realize I finally have to give back this borrowed life that was never mine. I also realize why I've been so sick to my stomach with worry ever since Yazmin Veltri's toxicology screen came back different from Finn's. Martin was so sure it meant that *she* drugged him, never figuring in a third party.

It isn't promising news at all, and no, Finn is not in the clear. If Cash bought the drugs and laced them, it's possible that neither Finn nor Yazmin knew about it.

It could just mean that Cash wanted to hurt Finn, which makes sense from the journal entry.

Cash could still want to hurt Finn.

My stomach flops, and my mind goes to dark places. Cash Veltri drugged Finn with the hope of doing something very bad to him while Martin rested in his selfish comfort of not knowing the whole story. I have a startling realization that just because Cash's sister is no longer alive, that does not mean his hatred for Finn died with her.

Cash wanted to hurt Finn. He could still want to hurt Finn.

He could be hurting Finn right now.

I call Finn's cell, and it goes straight to voice mail. I call Spencer's cell, and it rings and rings and goes to voice mail too. I leave them both urgent messages to call me, and texts as well. I know they're together, out with friends.

I call my dad, and he picks up on the first ring. "Hey, baby girl, how's your date going?" he asks.

"Awful. Listen, I need you to go to my house and key in and wait for the boys. I'm afraid Finn is in danger."

"Okay, but what's going on, Sarah?"

"I'll explain later."

He doesn't ask any more questions, as expected, and tells me he's leaving right now. I hang up. There's an urgency building, a retribution coming that needs to be paid. I've felt it all along, but I've done nothing about it, caught up in their world. But I'm so afraid that now Martin and I will pay for Tush's death, and we will pay for Yazmin's as well.

Or Finn will.

CHAPTER 25

I dial Josh. "Hi, Josh. Listen, it's urgent that I speak with Yazmin's mother. Do you have their address in your office files?" I ask.

"I don't require an address to give lessons, but I've been to their house. I know the one."

"I hate to ask you, but can I pick you up and can you show me where they live? I don't have time for . . ." I trail off, because I don't know what I don't have time for, only that time is short.

"Umm . . . give me five minutes to close up shop, and meet me outside of the store."

"Okay, see ya." I hang up the phone.

I send Martin a quick text—Have you heard from the boys?

Martin: No. Call me. Or come to Mother's. We can work this out.

No time to call. No time for arguments. My foot taps on the accelerator as I drive through the business district of Sewickley to pick up Josh. The only reason I'm involving him is because I need to know where Yazmin's mother lives, and I don't have time to figure it out myself.

They're safe in the presence of friends, I keep telling myself when I think of the boys.

Then I think about all the acts of violence that have occurred in public places—churches and movie theaters and nightclubs—and my chest heaves and swells with panic. Would Cash want to make a large display of Finn's demise, set an example of sorts? Did Cash blame Finn for Yazmin's death and wish him harm?

We've kept Finn indoors every day and night since Yazmin's death, and now he is roaming free somewhere, an open target.

I dial Finn's phone again, and it goes straight to voice mail. *"Shit."* *Has he shut it off?*

Maybe all my fears are unwarranted, but if Cash drugged my son, I need to know why. And if Josh helped Cash get the drugs, I need to know that too. These are not stones that I can leave unturned. These are stones that will roll into boulders and crush us, I'm sure.

When I round the corner of Beaver Street, Josh is standing at the end by the stop sign, smoking a cigarette with a backpack slung over his shoulder. He puts his hands up, motioning for me to slow down. I brake in front of the stop sign, and the car lurches forward.

Josh opens the passenger side door and gets in, placing his backpack on the floor. "Holy shit, speed limit is twenty-five. Slow down!"

Then he takes a good look at me, and his whole demeanor changes. He shuts the door and cracks the window, probably so he can still smoke. "Did they serve bad punch at the ball again?" He pushes the passenger seat back to fit his long legs.

I must look a fright in my black evening gown, soiled from the champagne I spilled down the front. My eyes are most certainly rimmed in red, my updo undone from my tirade through the country club, my race to claim Martin's keys to the Lexus. "We have to talk," I tell him. "Tell me where I'm going first."

He nods and stares out the window, smoking his cig. "Oh . . . kay. But are you sure you want to go there?"

"I have to, Josh. I think Finn's in danger. Spencer too."

He stares at me and then exhales deeply. "Let's go, then. McKees Rocks. I know where it is once we get across the bridge."

I plug McKees Rocks into my GPS even though I know how to get there. I don't know if Alisha will tell me where Cash is, but she can at least call him and find out.

Time feels short for no explainable reason at all. If I stop for even a brief second, I feel like I'll run out of minutes. My mother's intuition is pinging hard, and I hope I'm wrong about Cash, but if I'm right, I need to move quickly.

It's unfortunate that I don't know much about where Yazmin lived, only that it was somewhere in McKees Rocks, and I only learned that after Monroe asked Finn about it. I didn't care to ask Finn myself because he said she wasn't from Sewickley, a city kid on scholarship, so therefore I wasn't interested enough to ask more.

If she'd been from Sewickley, I would've wanted to know exactly where she lived, which house was hers, and then I'd compare it with mine and decide all the ways Stonehenge was better. I'd want to know if the Veltris resided in the Heights like we did, the most luxe and secluded wooded home sites with no less than five acres of green space, and then I'd want to know where in the Heights, because those who lived there knew every single property.

Or were they in Sewickley Village, in one of the pre–Civil War charmers, walking distance to the business district and the shops? Sewickley Hills could also be an option, a more suburban conglomerate of new prefab homes, a real draw for Pittsburgh transplants, often snubbed by the locals for lacking old-world love. I did maintain a vanity about my own home, because you can't live in the Heights and not, and now I hate myself for becoming that person.

I asked nothing about Yazmin's residence because she lived in the not-so-nice area of Pittsburgh. It's the same way my in-laws treated me when they'd heard where I was from, even though it's far nicer than where Yazmin's family lives, and as much as I chastised them tonight for their behavior, I've been turning into someone who is no better. I see it now.

This whole situation makes me like nothing about myself or the reflection of the person I've become, but if God grants me my sons' lives, I promise I'll do better.

I can do so much better.

As we turn on Route 65, Josh asks me, "Sarah, why are we going to their house, this wrecked family still suffering from Yaz's death?"

"I don't know, Josh. Maybe I'll answer your question when you explain to me why you never told me it was Cash who purchased the drugs from your buddy Jay and not Yazmin?"

Josh opens his mouth, but no sound leaves his lips. I can almost hear his internal gears grinding—*how does she know about Jay? Who else knows about Jay?* He flicks his cigarette out the window and rolls it up.

"And those things are going to kill you, Josh," I say more quietly.

"I hate when people use that phrase. Anything can kill you. My mother ate perfectly, rarely drank, ran three full marathons, and still died of a rare neurological disease, so please stop with the lecture."

"I'm sorry," I say. Josh told me the last time we were together that he'd come back to care for his mother, and I was too self-absorbed with my own problems to ask about the outcome.

Josh sighs. "It's okay. I'm sorry. I know the smoke stinks. Your husband will probably bitch about the smell."

"We're done," I state plainly. "Martin and I. Turns out we were never really together." I laugh, but it's pitiful.

Josh looks at me sympathetically. Those green eyes of a martyr, too cool for school, have some serious tenderness behind them. "You're just hitting a rough patch. Dealing with death can be hard," he says, and I don't doubt he's had a very difficult time of his own dealing with his mother's passing.

"It's not just a rough patch. I found out tonight that marrying me was Martin's collateral for making sure my father never turned him in back in college when he hazed that kid to death. And it was kind of hard for my dad to say anything to me after we married, especially seven months later when I had his first grandchild."

"Damn," Josh says, eyes ablaze. "I'm sorry." He starts humming "Better Man," and I don't know if he's trying to be funny, but it pisses me off.

"No, you're really not the better man. Why did you leave without saying goodbye, Josh? And when you came back, and I was on a break from Martin, why didn't you fight for me?"

He stops humming and stares out the window. "Because . . . I wanted to give you what you wanted, Sarah. This is the life I grew up with, not the one I wanted for myself."

I inhale sharply, and he sounds just like my father, and it makes me think he really is the better man.

"You could've said goodbye."

"You know how I feel about goodbyes. Besides, when I saw you that last time, you didn't tell me it was the same night you'd gotten engaged."

I start to cry. *How does he know that?*

"It was the talk of the town the next day, how Martin Ellsworth was officially off the market. My parents were talking about it. Why do you think I split before Christmas?"

That's why he left early? "I assumed you'd gotten into another argument with your parents," I say. I blamed Josh all these years for hurting me, continually deserting me, but this changes everything. He left me because he thought I already belonged to someone else.

"And . . . when you got pregnant . . . right away . . ."

I cough and fight to keep my eyes on the road.

"I thought you were exactly where you wanted to be. Married to him. In my house."

I choke and cough and cry. How could I fucking blame Josh for not fighting for me? "Right," I manage.

I place my hand over my mouth. "You must hate me."

299

He looks at me. "I could never. But there are limits . . ." And I get what he's saying. He cares for me, but he's already sacrificed a lot for my happiness. His silence about what happened between us, for one.

We pull up to a slim row house smashed next to twenty others. The porch railing is black, the paint chipping. There's likely no time for a single mother to paint it, and Cash doesn't sound like the type to pitch in on home repairs.

I knock on the front door without thinking twice. Alisha opens it slightly, sees me, and then tries to shut it fast. I stick my foot in the door to stop her. Her dark eyes light up with anger. "What do you want?"

"I need to speak to Cash," I say.

She uses all her body weight in an attempt to push the door shut, but I won't let it close. She's told me all I need to know with her response.

Finn is in danger.

I push my way inside, a feral mix of fear and determination. The force throws Alisha on the ground. Josh is still standing on the stoop, stunned.

"Cash is not here. What do you want?" Alisha quickly gets up and steps back when she sees Josh standing behind me. She's wearing her casino attire again. We're lucky we caught her before she left for work.

"We're not leaving until you tell us where Cash is," I say. Josh nods. "I know Cash gave the kids those drugs, and I need to speak to him."

Alisha's lips twist into an ugly scowl. "I don't know where he is. It doesn't change anything. Yazmin is dead. Your child is alive. What more do you want from us? You've taken enough."

I have no idea what she means, and then I remember the journal.

"Finn's drugs were laced. Yazmin's were not. That means Cash gave Finn something extra." I point in her face. "I need to know why he drugged my son."

"He's at work," she says, not seeming to hear the rest of my sentence.

"Where does he work?" I ask.

Alisha grabs her purse and starts riffling through it, then holds up her keys, satisfied. "That's where I need to go. Work. Now get out of my house."

She takes a step toward the door but doesn't answer my question.

The rest of the house is a total train wreck. A near-empty bowl of cereal sits on the coffee table, unfolded clothes are strewn near end tables, flowing out of laundry baskets. I imagine Alisha probably sitting down with the intention of folding them but too exhausted to finish the task.

Josh crosses his arms over his chest in the doorway. "Not until you call him and find out where he is." His complexion has turned the color of alabaster. I don't think it's because he's scared; I think it's because of the new mention of the laced drugs and that Cash was behind them. He knows the boys are in peril.

"You've destroyed my family," Alisha hisses. "You can't take him too. Now get out or I'll call the city police. Your cousin can't help you here. It's out of his jurisdiction."

She's still upset about the journal, and she'll sic the wolves on us in a second if it gets us out of her way.

"Alisha, I just want to know why Cash tried to hurt Finn," I blurt, desperate.

"He didn't," she says, but she looks at Josh when she says this.

"Why didn't you follow through on your threat to call the media? You were so sure Finn was there in the woods with Yazmin when she died. Tell me what you know," I plead.

Alisha's eyes are venomous beneath her eyelashes. "I can understand why you didn't tell them Finn was there, but how could you leave her to rot?" she seethes, and I'm so taken aback, I don't know what to say. "All night, the bugs ate at her face, the animals picked at her skin, my gorgeous daughter. When they found her, there wasn't much left, but I knew it was her, because of her hair, and this . . . ," she cries.

Alisha pulls a necklace from beneath her collar and dangles it in my face, a chain with a gold horn strung at the bottom. I recognize the charm, the lucky Italian pendant worn to ward off the evil eye. "It was my mother's," she says.

"She was already dead when we got there," I say shakily. *But how does she know we were there?*

One thing is for certain, though—she does know.

The blood drains from my face, a pins-and-needles sensation filling my arms and legs. I'm sick that she knew the truth about her daughter.

But now she knows the truth about us too.

Woozy, I reach for Josh, but he takes a step away from me, and I can feel a coldness settle between us at my terrible confession. He's probably wondering what kind of monster leaves a dead child in the woods, and I've been wondering the same thing for days.

How could we do this?

"We never wanted your fancy schools or your fancy clothes." Alisha wrinkles her nose at my outfit, and I think she might slap me. "I just wanted her journal back, her final thoughts. To protect her memory. To protect her brother, so no one could take anything else away from us. But you had to take that too."

I did take the journal. I deserve this. "Alisha, where is Cash and where is Finn?" *What did he do with him?*

"Whatever happens to your son now is your own fault."

My heart seizes in my chest. "What do you mean, whatever happens now?" I grab her and shake her by the shoulders, but she won't say another word. Josh drags me out the front door.

I'm right. Finn is in danger.

CHAPTER 26

"Let me drive." Josh takes the keys, and I don't argue.

When we're back in the car, Josh says, "Cash works at a pizza shop, but I don't know which one."

"Why couldn't she just tell us where he works?" My voice quakes.

"Maybe your son's welfare isn't her primary concern right now." There's something colder than ice in Josh's voice, and I understand why he's saying this. I didn't care enough about Yazmin's life to respect her dead body. Why should Alisha do me any favors? I get it. But this is about her son too.

Josh is revving the engine of Martin's car, and I take out Yazmin's journal, which was jammed in my extra-long clutch, trying to find anything in it that can possibly help me here. I can't believe all the things I never knew, especially about myself. My intention was to get to know Yazmin, welcome her into my home, but instead she thought I'd mocked her.

"What is that? What're you reading?" Josh asks.

"It's Yazmin's journal," I admit.

Josh grits his teeth. "You have it? How could you?"

It's far from possible, but I need to get Josh back on my side. It's not like he's perfect. "I know you kissed her, Josh. How could *you*?" I ask, but I don't stop reading or beat him up too badly. Our offense is much greater here.

"*Shit.* I knew it. She tried to kiss me, Sarah, but it didn't happen. I yelled at her. Told her to never do that again, but I felt bad. She was such a messed-up kid. The journal . . ." Josh is visibly sweating.

"She didn't mention you by name."

He exhales.

"And it's only one entry that I can find so far."

"Because it only happened once." The needle on the car keeps climbing, and I want to tell him to calm down, but we need to get to Finn as fast as we can, so I don't.

"Right," I say, but I'm not sure that I believe him about the kiss. "I didn't tell Alisha I had it because there are clues in here that might help me figure out what Cash was intending to do to Finn and where he might be now."

"I thought Yaz's mom said the police have it," Josh says.

"Well, they don't."

"Where was it?" Josh asks.

If I tell him, he might not help me find Finn.

Josh pounds his fist on the steering wheel. "I can't help you if you don't tell me what's going on."

"Okay. I went to Finn's bedroom to talk to him and kind of crept in. I saw him push a brown leather book I'd never seen before into his bookcase and grab another one real fast. I knew right away."

"Christ, Sarah."

"I know. Believe me, I know. There must be evidence in here, and if Martin had it and knew that, he'd just burn the journal or bury it in a place no one would ever find it, but maybe Finn wouldn't let him or stole it. Finn still keeps the birthday cards I give him. He probably didn't want to ditch his girlfriend's last words."

"Or he was covering something up."

I'm not sure yet—how will I ever be sure? So I say nothing.

I reread the part about her meeting me for the first time and sigh.

"What's wrong?" Josh asks. "You can't make sounds like that right now without an explanation." He veers onto the McKees Rocks Bridge, leading home.

I suck in a deep breath. "Yazmin thought I made fun of her for taking off her shoes before she came into my house."

"Brilliant," Josh says.

"And she seemed to think we owed her something. It sounds like they were planning to rob us."

Josh glances at me sympathetically.

I don't mention the part about how I touched her in a way she hadn't preferred. I'd misread her shyness for rudeness, and all the while, she was struggling with intimacy issues, listening to her own mother put herself in terrible situations to pay the bills.

I'm speed-reading, which seems disrespectful to her in itself. Yazmin's delicate thoughts should be carefully digested, preserved, honored, but I still can't figure out why Cash would want to hurt Finn. I'm looking for clues everywhere. I've already misunderstood so much.

"What do you make of this?" I read the part of the journal that's been grinding at me day and night, written so cryptically, I feel like I'm missing the hidden message. "We only want a million. Cash said it needed to be an amount that could fit in a suitcase. I think it's the amount Cash needs to move on. It will help us all move on. That amount of money is probably nothing to these people. Maybe if I get Cash what he wants, he'll compromise and let me have what I want too—Finn. The money doesn't matter to me. Money might help Mom out, but it will never bring Dad back."

"Jesus. And you didn't take that to the cops?" Josh asks.

"My family is the cops, in case you haven't noticed."

"Right." Josh softens for the first time since we left Alisha's, and I think he understands my dilemma. If the police had this journal and did nothing with it, then they never will. Alton is the police.

"I will take it to the detective on the case, outside of the borough, but I need more than this. This isn't proof of anything."

"Not to ask personal questions, but does your son have access to that kind of money?"

"A million dollars? No!" I laugh.

"Does he have access to any money where a crazy idea like this could've worked?"

"Just his trust. The kids can't touch it until they're eighteen." I shut the journal and then gasp.

"What now?" Josh ask.

"Finn is eighteen." He turned eighteen this past August. There isn't a million in there, but he does have six figures.

"Maybe that didn't suffice for Cash if he was stuck on the million-dollar price tag," Josh says solemnly.

Alisha mentioned that she was trying to protect Cash, and she was right to worry about the journal entries. There was the entry about the sunglasses. I remember the fight over the Instagram picture, and now I know why Yazmin was adamant about taking the post down. Her sunglasses had been stolen. And now this.

"Has Finn called you back?" Josh asks.

I check my phone, even though I'm gripping it so hard, there's not a chance I missed anything. "No. I haven't heard anything from either one of my sons. It's not unusual for them to dodge my calls when they're out with friends," I say, but I'm just creating excuses to make myself feel better. "They wanted a million dollars from us. But it's as if they think we owed it to them." I scratch my head. "Do you know anything about this, Josh?"

"They never mentioned anything like this in front of me," he says.

There are too many journal entries to read and not enough time. Clearly, I missed something in an earlier entry. "Yazmin mentioned that Cash waged war with the upper class. But why did he target us?"

Josh is biting his lip, and I think there's more he's not telling me. He stretches his arms uncomfortably, revealing the scar I noticed earlier. He never did answer my question about it directly.

"Where did that scar come from?"

He glances down at it. "There was a building that collapsed while I was playing in France. A woman was trapped; I pulled her out," he says matter-of-factly.

"Wow."

"I almost got her clean out without a scratch. A piece of glass got me."

The contrast to what my own son might have done to a woman makes me feel ill.

"You're not telling me something," I say.

"Look, I'm sorry I didn't tell you that Cash was the one who bought the drugs from Jay. I didn't think it mattered, and at the time, I didn't want to bring any more hardship to that family. I was afraid you'd pay one of your heavy hands to go in and shake him down. He seemed like a nice kid."

"Heavy hands?" I ask.

He glares at me out of his peripheral vision, and he's not letting me play innocent anymore. I think of Alton and the Ellsworths and their dirty money and *the cleaners*, and I cringe, because I do have more heavy hands than I can count, some of which I've never even met.

"The Veltris didn't have a chance even if they would've found evidence against Finn, and you know it," Josh says.

I sigh too, because it's true. "But what does that have to do with Finn? Did he make them promises he couldn't keep to please Yazmin?"

Josh shrugs. I think about how young we were when we got together. Finn still seems so young to me, but he's about the same age we were. Josh is flying down Route 65 toward home, even though we have no real destination. If we don't get pegged for breaking and entering, we might get nailed for speeding, but I don't care because I still have a foreboding feeling that time is short.

Finn's time.

"What about your husband? Did the kids text him? I know you're mad at him, but maybe you can just—"

"I texted him asking if he's heard from the boys, and he said that he hasn't. He also begged me to go to my mother-in-law's, but I can't . . ." I grapple with the words. As if I'd ever step a foot in Mary Alice's home again. She probably viewed me as someone she'd had to endure all these years for the sake of her family—her little pawn girl who kept her pampered son and privileged husband from seeing the wrong side of a jail cell.

Well, she's free and clear now.

Josh seems flustered, continually checking his rearview.

"What is it?" I ask.

"Did you really leave Yazmin in the woods? Please tell me Alisha was mistaken. I heard wrong, please," he whispers. He wants to believe better of me, but I can't lie anymore. I open my mouth to tell him, and my words break apart at the unspeakable.

"Finn called us the night Yazmin died. He was there, in the woods with her, and we followed his iPhone pin because he couldn't walk."

"Why?" Josh asks.

"We both thought maybe he drank too much, because he sounded out of it. Then he said he couldn't find Yazmin, didn't know what happened to her, so we drove straight there to investigate."

"And?" he asks, but he sounds like he doesn't really want to hear the rest. That if he could turn back time and not get in the car with me when I picked him up in front of the music store, he would.

"And . . ." I'm crying now and fighting to get it out. It's so hard to say it out loud, what we've done. "When we got there Yazmin was lying on a rock with a head wound, and when I examined her, she had no pulse. We found Finn some distance away, and he was in a bad state, a little beaten up and half–passed out, drugged. Martin said we had to leave Yazmin and take him home. That they would blame Finn immediately and he wouldn't have a chance to explain himself, but if the police couldn't place Finn at the scene of the crime, he'd be okay."

"And history repeats itself." Josh sighs, so disappointed in me that I know any connection we'd recovered is now lost.

"She was already dead, Josh."

He's shaking his head. He can't look at me. I don't blame him. It's been hard to look at myself in the mirror for days.

"Martin was so sure it would ruin Finn's life if we called the cops. He said they might let him out on bail or that they'd put him on house arrest, but that his life, as a whole, would be marred because of the drugs and the scandal surrounding the girl's death."

"Sarah, you can't be that blind." Josh's voice is angry.

"He also didn't believe Finn had done anything wrong. He said the colleges would refuse to accept him if they caught wind of what happened, and he'd worked so hard and hadn't had any problems—"

"Stop!" Josh is furious now. "All these excuses he told you, Sarah. Don't you see now this was never about Finn?"

"What do you mean?"

"What did he do to you when he had you locked up in that ivory tower?"

"I don't understand," I say. My arms have grown a slow chill, pushing up goose bumps, but I can't wrap my arms around myself to quiet the cold. Everything that used to be good is gone. It's not the idea of not having Martin or the Ellsworths anymore; it's the loss of everything I've believed in.

"Sarah, Martin was protecting his estate, his reputation, and his business. He has enough money to pay the masses to make sure Finn never saw a day in prison, and surely he could pad the right pockets at the universities to make the scandal surrounding Yazmin's death disappear too."

"No . . . you're not right about that . . . Then why . . ." My mind whirls in disbelief. It can't be true. We left Yazmin because we had to protect Finn. "Martin said . . . Martin said—"

"Let's see, the girl from the wrong side of the tracks on scholarship at the Academy is found dead with the townie rich kid. What could that mean for Martin Ellsworth and his family? He was worried he'd be sued. He was worried he'd lose his money and be defamed at work as the man who was connected to the death of a poor girl from the Rocks, and most of all, he was worried it would affect his brother's seat as city commissioner. Everyone in town knows Martin's been looking at that riverfront property—"

"No." I'm shaking my head now, my vision blurred with tears. This cannot be politically motivated. It cannot. My stomach is gyrating like Dad's old washer.

"I thought you wanted to help kids. Use your degree to do good," Josh says.

"I did," I say. "I've dedicated my life to helping young women. Their children too."

He's been here two years. If he knew I was stuck in this ivory tower, why didn't he try to break me out?

Josh sighs. "Funny. I passed my old house one day and considered stopping by, because I knew you lived there, and I had mixed feelings about it, but I tried to be happy for you, because I knew how much you loved that house. Then I saw the political signs in your yard, and I drove right on by."

"That's not fair." Those damn signs. They'd become a game in our house. I would take them out and throw them away, and Martin would manage to find more and restake them the very next day. It was a prank to us—the staking and un-staking of the signs. But to Josh, it was a statement of who I'd become. One that kept him away.

As Josh talks, I can't take my eyes off the journal. I thumb back through Yazmin's pages that detail her struggles with sleeping, closing her eyes, reinventing herself, loving my son despite the fact that her brother was trying to use him for his own devices to make up for her father's death—something no one had any control over. Cash was trying to regain control by misdirecting his anger, and for some reason, he chose us.

"Josh, she was dead when we got there," I reiterate. "I don't see how we could've changed the outcome."

"And did you think it ended there? With her death."

My throat constricts. I know what he's going to say next. Alisha was more upset with the condition of Yazmin's body than the fact that we hadn't reported her death. Her hissing mentions of animal life and insects eating away at her daughter's face resurface, along with images of Yazmin's face frozen with her eyes wide-open, her mouth stuck in a screaming position. I never actually saw it, but this is the picture I see in my head when I lie down at night. Only now it will have worms and animal bites to go along with it.

"How would you feel if another parent did that to your child?" He pauses, his voice strained. "To her and her family, you did much more than just leave the woods."

"I know." I wrap my arms around myself, my goose-pocked flesh feeling dirty and soiled with shame. "Yazmin was in the car accident . . . her father died . . . she was stuck in the car for hours, almost died. Why didn't they come after us if they knew we left her? She was left to die once. You would think they wouldn't stand for it again."

"She tried, right, to get you to make Finn come forward? Maybe she thought Finn left the girl and came home and that you did nothing to find her daughter. Or it's possible she was afraid that if it was found out that Cash gave the kids the drugs, he would be charged? She likely feared her last child would be taken away from her and that people like Martin could make it happen if it threatened the family's wealth."

"He would never . . ." I let my words trail because I know they're falling on deaf ears, and because Josh is right. Martin would put Cash away if it meant preserving his wealth, his business status. He's that kind of man, and I am just as guilty for marrying him. I can no longer pretend I'm the innocent half in this partnership.

But we aren't the only parents at fault here.

Alisha had to have known we were there, but how? Cash. Cash had to have been there too? He told his mother. But that would mean he was there and saw us and left his sister too, and I just don't believe it. Not after what I read about him in the journal, being so overprotective.

The car is quiet again, and this is the longest, shortest car ride of my life. It's only when I look over at Josh that I see he's practicing a deep-breathing exercise—in through his nose, out through his mouth. It's like I'm a toddler he's grown impatient with because I've acted so poorly, and he has no other way to cope.

"You must think I'm terrible."

"I've never thought that, Sarah, but I do think you only see the things you want to see. It's amazing that you see the good in everyone, but you also fail to see the bad. It's dangerous."

I wince at his last words.

"I never knew . . ." I think about Hanna running with me that afternoon around Phipps Conservatory, insinuating Martin's criminal wrongdoing by saying he and Meat had some really good lawyers to get them out of trouble. I judged her for scouting for men according to their majors, but in a way, she was living a more honest life than I was. Hanna scored a doctor, and they are deliriously happy with their three children, but she'd been transparent about her intentions from the beginning. Meanwhile, I had my head in the clouds, believing what I wanted to believe, and it *is* dangerous. To myself and everyone around me. I traded everything to become one of the lucky ones.

"But you knew something wasn't right," Josh says.

I don't argue the point. Looking back now, I remember a phrase I hadn't heard before it was thrown out that day, one my ears had grabbed on to—*"settled out of court."* It had sounded so friendly to my eighteen-year-old ears, but as I got older, I had to have known it wasn't friendly at all.

"Yeah, I think I did." I chose not to think of it or acknowledge it, because everything else about Martin had seemed so perfect. He said he'd learned his lesson, and I believed him.

Well, he may have learned his lesson about not hazing freshmen, but he didn't learn his lesson about taking responsibility for his actions, or that human life can't be bought with money, or that using political agendas to cover those same lives was wrong. I've stood by Martin, which is the same as approving of his actions, and now we've passed those same tragically hazardous lessons on to Finn.

"I knew it was wrong this time too." I sniffle. "Martin used Finn to . . ." I can't finish the sentence because I can't blame Martin anymore. I was a part of the decision to leave Yazmin, and I can't deny it any longer, a sick truth.

"It shows he knew just what to say to you. He's been manipulating you for years." Josh shakes his head.

I remember what Martin said to me. *Did you lose your glass slipper?* Did he brainwash me?

"I'm sorry, Josh, but I've known you again for all of two minutes. How do you know so much about my marriage?"

Josh clears his throat. "Because, when I went back to visit my old house, I did it more than once . . ."

He trails off, and I say nothing. It's a little strange, but I used to drive by to visit that house too. It's like a magnet for those who've been bewitched by it. Or was there another reason?

"Why?" I'm scared to know the truth.

"Because that's where I learned how to play guitar. That pergola was my stage." He sounds almost dreamy. "I hated it and loved it at the same time. It was too large, but it was mine. The backyard spotlights gave me my first taste of what it would be like to perform, and something about how the sound seemed to beat off the stone columns instead of escaping into the sky was special. Can't explain it."

He's right. That's exactly what it sounded like when he played back there. And then the gravity of Josh's words hits me, and I shut the journal.

"Wait a second. Have you been sneaking off and playing back there? Floyd and Petty?" My heart is beating furiously. I wasn't imagining it. Martin and the boys slept soundly, but I've always been a light sleeper.

"Wow, those are supposed to be leaded windows. I always played after two a.m., when you good folk are nice and sated in your REM stage. No amp."

"Holy shit. Thank you for confirming I'm not completely nuts. It always made me smile the next day when I thought I'd heard you play. For a long time, I thought it was your ghost. And what about the rose?"

He nods. "My mother loved that trellis. Those roses."

Mine too, I think.

"Why did you rip them out?" he asks sadly.

My body wilts into the passenger seat. "That was an accident."

"Like the signs," he says.

"What is your problem, really? You left me. This isn't about signs or roses," I say, because I'm tired of this. He's mad at me about something else, and he needs to come out with it.

"Okay, I'll tell you. My mother loved those roses. And she loved that house. Then your greedy husband offered my equally greedy father twice its estimated value. Over two million in 2000. My father couldn't say no."

I drop my mouth open and let it hang there. "I had no idea." I saw the receipt for the house but hadn't known Martin had paid way over market value for it to seal the deal.

"Seems to be a running theme with you. What must you have thought when he surprised you with *that* house?" he asks, but it's his subliminal secret message, and what he's really asking is, *"What must you have thought when he surprised you with my house?"*

Sick, I want to tell him. *I felt sick.* "It was a moment of mixed emotions," I answer and look out the window.

I cried in the bathroom and thought of you.

I fought flashes of our naked bodies tangled in the downstairs pool and every outside area of the house.

I thought of you playing your guitar out back and couldn't even sit there without hearing your tortured melody in my head, growing melancholy as I did, even in the middle of a summer party.

I couldn't tell him any of that because then he'd wonder why I accepted the gift.

Josh says, "I'm sure. It was a moment of mixed emotions for me too when I found out who the new owner was. My parents' marriage didn't survive the sale of that house, Sarah."

"What?" I ask, but I think I understand. The house has its own pulse, spellbinding those who reside in it, or, in Yazmin's case, the pulse was strong enough for her to despise it like a mortal enemy.

"My dad made the decision to sell the house without her, wowed by the money. He bought her a new, beautiful house in the Heights, but she never liked it as much. She talked about the old one all the time, and it was the beginning of the end for them."

"That's terrible. I'm sorry."

"He eventually left her for someone else, someone younger, because that's what greedy men do, and then she got sick, and I was the only one to take care of her. We grew a lot closer toward the end."

He sounds so solemn, and I'll be forever upset I didn't do more to reach out to him.

The clock flashes on the dash like a warning bell—9:11. I may have given myself the briefest reprieve from my horrid situation, and maybe Josh granted it to me because I basically begged, but the urgency to find my boys is back.

"Josh, what does all this mean for Finn? Yazmin and the journal and the drugs? I know he's in trouble."

"I don't know. Hopefully, Cash made that joint for himself and screwed up the distribution . . . but . . ."

"You don't think so, do you?" I ask. I'm clenching the journal in my hand. It's so hard to read it, because every word slices me deeper, this girl and all she's suffered. How she was manipulated by her own brother to do things she thought would ultimately help her family but lose the only boy she'd ever really cared about in the process.

"No, I have a really bad feeling," Josh admits.

Just then, a text comes in from my father:

Sarah, I called the cops. Someone's in your house. It's just a kid but not one of yours. He ran from me and is hiding upstairs and I don't think he's alone. Stay away until you hear from me.

CHAPTER 27

Cash is at the house. That's where he has my boys. I imagine them bound and gagged. *Death is all around me.*

"Josh, drive to the house!" I don't need to tell him which one. "Please drive fast—Cash is there."

We're almost home.

Martin picks up on the first ring. "Sarah, where're you? We've been waiting at my mother's. My father would like to—"

"Shut up, Martin. There is an intruder at our house. My dad is there. He's called the cops. Where're the boys?"

"What? Are you sure? I don't know. I'll call Mr. Coulson and see if he knows." Chances are good that if the boys are out together, they're with Matty and Joel, but I never did ask them where they were going tonight or when they were coming home.

"Good idea. Dad told me to stay away, but I'm going home. Meet me there."

"Do not go there alone, Sarah!" I hear the terror in Martin's voice, the car keys jangling from his fingers as he hurries out of his parents' house.

He does love me.

He just doesn't love me the right way.

I didn't know there was such a thing until this week. I always thought as long as we loved each other, that would be enough. But it's not.

"I'm not alone, Martin."

Josh is pulling onto Blackburn Road.

"Who's with you?" he asks.

There's no time to explain that right now. "See you there, Martin. Please text if you hear from the boys." I hit the "End" button on my phone.

When we pull farther down the road, I see the streak of orange before I see anything else.

A frisson of horror floods my body. It can't be. No. God, no.

Then I see the billow of smoke, and I know what it means. I drop Yazmin's journal on the floor of the car. My heart cracks open along with it.

Stonehenge is on fire.

Before Josh can shift the car into "Park," I've tossed off my heels, opened the door, and am sprinting up the driveway.

Josh is running after me, his phone in hand. *"Blackburn . . ."* He's screaming my address to someone on his cell as he runs, probably 911.

"Stop, Sarah!" he orders, but I'm already to the front door.

"My dad is inside!" I yell. I grab the brass door handle, and it's so hot, it scalds my hand.

Josh grabs me, pulling me away. "Wait for the fire department!"

"They won't be able to make it up the road!" I wail.

Josh's face crumples, because he knows it's true. Even the real estate agent warned us that one of the pitfalls of living here was the restricted gravel roadway.

My judgment time has arrived. The ticking clock has finally run out.

I'm fighting Josh to get back to the door handle, all the while thinking this is my punishment for all of this—wanting, pining over a house set way back in the woods, so private, so exclusive that it's nearly inaccessible.

A road that's too narrow to properly host large vehicles—like fire trucks.

This is my penance for turning a blind eye to Tush's death and letting Martin snake the house out from under Josh's family. And most of all, this is what I get for leaving Yazmin in those woods.

For allowing her body to be desecrated by the wild.

And now my house is burning to the ground.

And my father with it.

I'm in a coughing fit from the smoke as I fight off Josh.

"Stop, Sarah!"

I've taken hold of the door handle again by wrapping a piece of my long dress around it and yanking it open.

Heat and smoke rush out of the front, almost knocking us over. I hold my breath and wave the smoke out of my eyes. We step inside, and the fire is raging up the wood paneling in surreal licks of bright caramel and orange that would be almost pretty if they weren't practically melting off our skin.

"Dad!" I scream, but the fire and the smoke fill my lungs, and I cough the word back up. My eyes are stung shut. I can hear the crackling of wood just above me. Josh grabs me and swings me out of the way. A ceiling beam splits and falls, black ashes burning my bare feet.

I swing myself down, step on the floor. Pure pain, but I have to, because—*my father.*

Navigating around the beam, I hold my hand over my eyes, looking for any sign of him.

"Sarah, we have to get out of here!" Josh says.

The great room looks like an inferno, the gateway to Hell as the flames rise up and up, all the way to the high ceilings. Straggles of wood hang from the raised pulpit, the maple-paneled ceiling fully engulfed in the room made for acoustics in the house where no one plays music—and no one ever will.

Shrieking sounds escape the walls as the fire splits apart the wood. Stonehenge is screaming: *This is all your fault. I tried to warn you.*

"I'm sorry!" I shout back. *All these years you've protected me; I'm so sorry I couldn't do the same.*

"Dad!" I try to move farther into the house, but Josh holds me back. We're squinting, and neither one of us should still be standing there, but I think we're both paying a brief homage to our lost home. I have the slightest inclination to sit down in the middle of the floor and let the flames take me too.

It's then that I notice there's broken glass everywhere, and I look up and see billows of black smoke streaming out of the places in the great room where the stained-glass windows used to be. Someone has knocked them out. I'm sure of it, because the other windows are intact. The narrow channels of oxygen seem to only feed the flames.

I know in an instant, as I'm dragged back on the porch, who knocked out those windows.

Cash was here.

Josh is carrying me onto the lawn now, but all I can see are my broken windows.

Cash knocked them out. Cash set my house on fire. I just know it. Yazmin journaled about how much I love this house and how much she despised those windows. She likely told him about them, and he knocked them out for her, in her honor. No one needs to tell me this; I already know.

And Cash killed my father—that's why he's not downstairs—and he may have killed my sons too. I know it.

I'm desperately hoping my father has already made it out, but I know in my heart that he hasn't.

The Veltris lost someone and so should I.

This could've all been so different. The Veltris wouldn't hold so much hate in their hearts if I'd done the right thing and not left their daughter behind. They couldn't report us because they have no proof and they knew we'd win the fight, so they took back from us the only way they knew how.

By burning our riches to the ground and taking our family with them.

And where're my boys? Are they in there too? Burning to death?

Josh is carrying me away from the house as I'm having these awful thoughts, no longer able to fight him. The smoke has overcome my lungs, and I'm fighting to remain conscious. There're sirens in the distance, but they're too far away, and they'll never get here in time to save my father—or my house.

"Oh my God, my dad," I choke out. "Not my dad."

Dad doesn't belong at Stonehenge; I do. Dad shouldn't die in Stonehenge; I should.

"Sarah, he wasn't downstairs. Is the trellis that goes up the side of the house to the front bedroom still there? I used to climb on it when I was a kid to sneak out," Josh says.

"I think so," I say, because I don't remember ripping it out, but I'd forgotten all about it, because the vines grow over it.

Shielding the executives' homes with their leafy veils and climbing green vines.

"Do you think the boys could be inside?"

I know why he's asking.

"Yes," I say.

"Sarah, is he mine?" Josh asks.

And I can't be sure, but I am sure. I've always known. It's a memory I colored differently because it was the shade I wanted to see. "Yes," I say.

Josh gently rests me on the ground and dashes to the side of the house. "No, Josh," I try, but I'm too weak to protest or stop him from saving his own son.

I would have told Josh about Spencer, but when the doctor gave me my due date after I was already married, I dismissed our brief encounter. It's probably the moment in my life when not having a mother hurt me the most.

I would've given my ring back, had the marriage annulled if I'd figured it out sooner. If someone had made public notice of the fact that pregnant women are actually with child for about ten months instead of nine. I would've had a serious talk with Martin about what had transpired during our brief time apart and let him decide if he still thought this marriage was a good idea.

Now it's a memory I mark in black, so dark I can't see it—until someone comments on Spencer's green eyes, not blue like mine or brown like Martin's. Mary Alice pointed out that brown is usually the dominant trait, and it's amazing how the light color pulled through.

But the fact is, it didn't. Finn's eyes are brown because they are a true by-product of mine and Martin's. But Spencer's are green—just like his biological father's.

I was also reminded of Josh when Spencer played that piano effortlessly with little to no instruction. No one else in the family had a lick of musical talent, and Spencer just happened to be able to sit down and play. Spencer looks like Josh too. Taller than both Martin and Finn, wider shoulders.

My beautiful boys! Are you in there? Burning?

I roll on my side and try to watch Josh, smelling the scorched skin on my feet, the excruciating physical pain of my wounds secondary to everything else I'm feeling. There's no way Josh has a chance of entering the second floor and living to tell about it, but I'm still hopeful that maybe he can and will find my father. I can't even stomach thinking that the boys are in there too, a loss I couldn't manage.

I can barely focus, but out of my peripheral vision, I can tell Josh is climbing up the side of my house as it burns down. I'm fighting not to pass out, my breaths shallow, my lungs burning with lack of oxygen and fear.

Am I to lose Josh too? Will the boy with the guitar return to his home for good?

I hear the fire trucks struggling on the road, their gears grinding on the gravel, their sirens loud and urgent, but they must be stuck. There's a tight turn in the path where the trees seem to droop over and make a tunnel, and sometimes the hood of Dad's pickup would get scratched if the trees weren't trimmed, and I can't remember the last time Martin had them trimmed. Someone might have to cut them down for the trucks to pass, but it will be over by then.

All over.

This is what I'd always wanted—a house so tucked away, a world all my own, my personal fairy tale. The only problem is that I was so tucked away, no one could reach me in a hurry, and now my fairy tale has turned into my personal Hell as my family burns, trapped inside.

I open my eyes briefly, and I see the stars, and they are bright tonight. "Mother, *please*? If you're up there, don't take them," I whisper. "Don't take them from me. Don't take my boys."

The most important men I've ever met are in that house because of me, and I'll never forgive myself if they don't make it out.

I feel the oxygen mask first, and my eyes snap open second. I see three of them as I'm hoisted into a vehicle with blinking red lights.

Somewhere in between my thoughts of life and death, Martin has arrived. I'm on a stretcher, and my sons are on each side.

My sons. Thank you, God. They're alive.

I'm overcome with emotion and reach out, but they all tell me to lie down. Martin climbs inside, and the medic closes the doors, and I try to talk, but everything goes black.

CHAPTER 28

The oxygen mask is still on my face, but Martin is gone. My lungs ache, and my throat is so dry, I want to cry. I immediately push the nurse button for water. Both my feet are wrapped in white bandages, and I can't remember exactly what happened to them, but I kind of do.

I went barefoot into a burning building.

That's right.

Luckily, I can't feel the pain from my injuries yet. My feet are completely numb from whatever painkiller they've given me, and my brain is fuzzy.

The nurse arrives, and she seems happy I'm awake and calls more medical staff into the room to check on me, but none of them are the people I want to see. A man in scrubs grabs my arm and fastens a black cuff around it to check my blood pressure, but that's not important to me right now either.

Is my dad alive? I need to know.

Did my boys make it? I need to make sure I didn't imagine them before I passed out in the back of the ambulance. I need to ensure that they weren't in that blaze, because I blacked out on my lawn insisting that they weren't.

And what about Josh? Did he ever make it inside the house to look for Dad? If so, did he make it out?

Cara Reinard

The mask is pulled off. "I want to—"

I try to speak, but someone is shoving a straw in my mouth and asking me to *drink*. My throat feels tight, but the water goes down. I cough, and my head is woozy, the smell of smoke everywhere, no matter which way I turn my head.

It's in my hair, and the smell is so pungent, I think it might be soaked into my bones.

My worries are endless, but no one will listen to me.

Have they caught Cash, and what have they done with him?

And . . . the house. I finally put it last on the list, where it belongs.

Did Stonehenge's exterior withstand the elements thrust upon it like the historic landmark it was named for, or is it beyond repair? Will I be able to renovate the damages or is it lost forever?

The aching in my chest deepens.

Martin rushes into the room. He's one of the people I don't care to see, but he's the one who has the answers to all my questions. I haven't figured out how to break it to him yet that we're getting a divorce, but this isn't the right time. I don't have my voice back yet to argue with him.

"Sarah?" he says. "Thank God." He has this stupid, hopeful look on his face that this near-death experience of mine will put us back together.

"The kids?" I manage.

"They're fine. They were actually together, at the same bonfire in the country, no cell phone coverage. They didn't get your messages until after they'd driven away, and they rushed right home once they did." His grin turns dismal at the mention of our home.

"My dad?" I close my eyes, and all I can do is listen to Martin's voice, because if his face betrays him, I will lose it.

"Your dad is in critical condition, but he's alive."

Thank God! Relief sweeps through me. Martin grips my hand, and I allow it. Then I let out a huge exhale, and my lungs burn from the effort. The cough that follows next rattles even worse, and I let out a yelp because it hurts so much. "How bad is he?"

"Oh, you poor thing." Martin's voice makes me sick. "He's suffered severe smoke inhalation; he's unconscious but breathing on his own, so that's good, but he's got some third-degree burns on his legs. The rest of him was spared."

"Oh no."

"The fire chief said it could've been so much worse. The fire started upstairs. You must have gotten there shortly after."

I think about the towering flames of Hell engulfing the inside of the house, and I can't fathom that the fire had just begun. If so, and we'd gotten there moments later, my father would be dead. I didn't imagine the internal ticking time bomb sensation, the extreme sense of urgency building in my chest. I knew after leaving Alisha's house—*"whatever happens to your son now is your own fault"*—that we were on a stopwatch to figure out what'd happened to Yazmin or someone else was going to die, but I didn't anticipate it would be my father.

"And Cash?" I ask. Does Martin even know he's the one who set the fire? Do the police?

"He's been detained. And don't you worry. He's going to go away for a very long—"

"The house was retaliation for us doing what we did."

"We didn't do anything, Sarah—"

"Yes. We. Did. Martin. None of this would've ever happened if we would've made different choices that night."

Martin makes a clicking sound with his mouth and stares up at the fluorescent lights as if choosing his words carefully. He didn't read the journal. If he'd read it, he would know I'm right, but he still doesn't believe he's done anything wrong. If the burning down of our home didn't teach him that, there's no redemption for him. Martin was ruined by the Ellsworths long ago, and there's nothing I can do to change the person they've created.

"You can't blame us for—" Martin tries.

"Yes, I can, actually, but we'll save that for a different time. I don't have the strength to argue right now." My words are coming out in dry patches.

I try not to focus on the fact that I withheld the journal from Alisha. I'll be eternally remorseful for not turning it in to her sooner. It's all Alisha really wanted. Although I feel bad that I left it in the car. Now the real police (not Alton) will see it and have proof of all Cash's wrongdoing. And possibly Josh's. I still don't know what Finn was trying to hide or if he was involved in her death or not. But Monroe will question him after reading the journal, and that's okay. It's time for the truth.

"Sarah, I know I've made a lot of mistakes . . ."

Bite your tongue. There's no amount of marital counseling that can fix this problem, but I still have a chance with Finn.

Martin hasn't stopped talking. "And, Sarah, part of me always thought you kind of knew about Tush, but it was something we just never talked about." Martin's searching my eyes for some acknowledgment. I nod, but it's all I can give him for right now. Acknowledging doesn't make it right on either of our parts; it just makes it exist.

As to whether I colored my memory the way I'd wanted to, as Josh suggested, I wasn't sure anymore.

Josh. What happened to him?

"And what my father said was completely out of turn. He apologizes," Martin adds.

Fuck your father.

"Martin, what about the man who dragged my dad out of the house? Is he okay?" My vocal cords are aching, and I wonder if they've been permanently damaged from the smoke.

"Oh, the music teacher?" Martin lets out a snarky laugh. "Yeah, he's in stable condition, a few minor burns. He did save your dad's life.

Your dad was attacked, knocked unconscious, and Vic is a great deal bigger than the kid . . ."

Ew. I hate how he says that—*"the kid."* Like he's nameless. Like he doesn't matter, just like Yazmin never mattered. I treated Yazmin the same way—insignificant. Martin and I made for an awful pairing that needs to split.

"Cash," I correct.

"That's right. I guess your dad was on muscle relaxers for his back, and he'd had a few beers, and the combo diminished his reflexes."

"Ugh." I close my eyes and mentally punch myself for not telling Dad about the warning label on the muscle relaxers. I'll never forgive myself if he doesn't survive his hospital stay. I realize now more than ever that sometimes our greatest offenses are not in what we say but in what we don't say.

"And the house?" I ask. *Dare I ask?*

Martin moves from the chair beside my gurney to the window, probably unable to look at my face.

He doesn't need to say the words.

"Stonehenge . . . is . . . gone?" And my heart is broken. But the punishment seems to fit the crime. The Ellsworths' symbol of wealth burned to the ground because of the secrets we'd kept to protect it. The windows were smashed out. The ones with the family crest.

I remember the way Yazmin's face filled with horror when the light filtered through them, grabbing her attention. It wasn't because she found them remarkable; it was because they scared her to death.

That symbol meant something to her. And it meant something to Cash. Something ugly. That's why he bashed those particular windows out. William had everything emblazoned with that damn symbol. Cuff links. The hubcaps to his Bentley. The bathroom hand towels.

Where did Yazmin see the symbol? What did the Ellsworths do to her family? Whatever it was, William thought he could make it up to Yazmin with a measly scholarship. Just like them to try to smooth things over with money.

"When I went to move the car, the seat was pushed all the way back. Was the music teacher driving my car? That was some heroic move of him climbing into a burning building to save your dad. We'll have to invite him over for dinner and thank him," Martin says.

"Invite him over *where?*" I ask.

Martin's shoulders slump. "We'll rebuild."

No, we won't, Martin. There is no rebuilding Stonehenge. Or anything else between us.

I close my eyes, hoping he'll just leave me alone. I don't have the energy to explain the whole story to him. What leaving Yazmin's body in the woods truly meant to the family who had already lost so much, but maybe someday, long after we're no longer together, he'll take the time to figure it out himself. The Veltris probably didn't have the funds to have a proper burial, being so strapped for cash. That's why there was no notice in the paper. If I'd known, I would've paid for the funeral myself.

But one thing is for certain: If we'd reported Yazmin's death, none of the other horrible things to follow would've happened. There'd be no cover-up. No secrets. No journals stealthily stowed away in bookshelves.

A house to go home to.

I still don't even know the whole story—the why—behind Cash's actions. I have a feeling there's more bad news coming, but Martin doesn't seem to care about Cash's motives for burning down our house. Just like he never cared about the consequences of leaving Yazmin's body behind—he was too eager to cover it up. But we're not done here.

Two police officers enter the room. "Mr. Ellsworth, we're investigating the fire at your home. May we have a word?" The one with the spiky hair is too young to be under Alton's regime. Monroe is with him, and even I'm smart enough to know that Monroe is part of the homicide division, which does not generally investigate fires.

"Sorry, gentlemen, but I won't be speaking to you without my lawyer."

I glare at Martin, his statement so smug.

"I will talk to you," I say. I'm going to tell them everything. It's time for the truth. If they want to wheel me from the hospital room to a jail cell, I'll gladly go.

Enough of this.

Martin shoots me his mercurial look that goes from a tight smile to a dark grin. *There he is*—the real Martin who hides deep down below the surface until someone gets their fingers in his money. He knows I'm about to give him up.

"My wife's on painkillers and is in no condition to speak to you, and I won't allow it without a lawyer present."

He won't allow it.

When those words can no longer be spoken will be the greatest day of my life. The day the divorce papers are signed.

When the cops leave our room, Martin runs out without saying another word to make a phone call. I'm sure it's to one of his lawyers or his daddy. I really don't care which anymore.

But the cops aren't done here.

I expect my sons to rush into my room at any moment, and I can't wait to see them. But when I see Finn floating by my hospital room, he's not there to visit me.

He's in handcuffs.

CHAPTER 29

There are many things I learn in the next few days as I'm stuck in the hospital room with nothing but my smartphone to keep me company—because one of my sons is in jail.

And my husband is absent, fighting with an army of lawyers to get him out.

Spencer has gone back to school early at the advice of the Ellsworths, but not before telling me he loves me no matter what happens. Someday I'll tell him Josh is his father, but we have a lot of healing to do as a family before we can open any fresh wounds.

As I seek to understand, I'm overcome with so much grief that I lie to the nurse about my pain level to get more morphine, anything to numb myself after all my wrongdoings. I think about all the things I've pushed aside so I didn't have to see them—Tush's death, my first pregnancy, how we handled Yazmin's tragedy. I went on a blind pursuit to become one of the lucky ones, using my mother's death as a crutch, a way to assuage my part in it all, my ugly truths. And now I understand what it's like to have demons roaring so loudly in your head, only medication can quiet them.

Stuck in my hospital room, in purgatory, I begin to research who the Veltris were.

Jimmy Veltri died on a snowy December evening on a windy stretch of Route 51 that was commonly traveled, but not that evening, because motorists were warned to stay off the road. When another car hit Jimmy's sedan, it spun around, flipped, and skidded to the shore of the river, which couldn't be seen in plain sight from the road. Yazmin was in the passenger seat, helping her father look for her little brother. He had run away from home.

There's a drastic difference between the social media posts before the accident and after.

Before: Jimmy, an avid fisherman, reeling in trout with Cash.

Camping trips. October—hunting season. Cash with a buck. Jimmy empty-handed but obviously thrilled for his son. Rite of passage. Becoming a hunter like his old man.

Winter—Yazmin and Jimmy at a Penguins game. #LetsGoPens #DaddyDaughterDate

Another post—Yazmin made honor roll again. Jimmy is so proud, he posts a picture of her award. She's smiling, but everything about her is softer than the Yazmin I knew. Alisha too. Her smile is bright, her skin less worn.

After the accident is posted, there is a funeral announcement with a little quote from Alisha that says: "When I worried about Jimmy on the road for all those days driving a truck, he told me not to, because anything that came up against his tractor trailer would likely lose. We never factored in what could happen on his day off, just a few miles from home."

There was a GoFundMe page set up by a friend to help cover funeral costs. The goal had been $5,000 and they'd reached only $3,000. This makes me sadder than all the other posts.

The Veltris had very little support. No family or friends who could help with the funeral expenses. I think about how much the haircut went for at the gala and how much I wish it could've gone toward Yazmin's funeral costs instead.

Why didn't I question more why Yazmin didn't have a father?

The punishing thoughts are endless. Martin feels none of this suffering, and there's no way back to him, to the old us.

We are no longer Martin and Sarah Ellsworth of Blackburn Road. There is no house on Blackburn Road.

Martin would have to do the full research on Yazmin's family and read her journal to understand why I'm leaving him. But he'll do neither of those things. He'd rather stay in the dark, slap a Band-Aid on it, move forward. We almost lost my father because of it, and I can never forgive him for that.

Telling the cops the truth was freeing. Detective Monroe fought surprise at my admission. I still don't know why I'm not handcuffed to my hospital bed by now like they do in the movies.

My only guess is, Martin hasn't wavered from his stance that I wasn't in my right mind with all the medication I was on. Additionally, there is no evidence that we left a dead body. If I said I did and Martin said we didn't, his version wins out, because there's no proof.

Detective Monroe alerted me that he is also going to look into the hit-and-run that killed Yazmin's father and almost killed her. It's then that I know the piece of the puzzle that I've been missing. The reason that Yazmin was staring so crazily at our windows with the family crest.

It was all in the entrance essay to the Academy that Yazmin vividly described in her journal. Yazmin wrote about the accident—she'd said so in the journal—and William was on the board for the scholarship program, one of the largest contributors. Of course he recognized the last name of the daughter of the man he'd killed. And the girl he'd almost killed.

William was the one driving the car that killed Jimmy Veltri. He granted Yazmin the scholarship because he felt guilty about killing her father.

Yazmin said in her journal entry that she saw something at the scene of the accident, a reflection in the window. It could've been on anything William had that night—a cuff link, a hubcap, who knows.

The only thing I do know is that when Yazmin walked into my house and saw that symbol on my windows—she recognized it. And then she told Cash, and he walked into our house and he smashed those windows out, the ones with the family crest.

What else did she say in her journal?

The initials—BR.

Those aren't William's initials.

My eyes are shut, but even with the drugs, I can't sleep.

I think I'm dreaming when the next thing I hear is Josh's voice humming.

My eyes flicker open, and I see Josh's jade eyes squinting back at me. "Hey, sunshine." A ray of light streams through the hospital blinds, specks of dust floating around like tiny atoms in a gravity storm. Morphine thoughts.

"I thought I'd check in on you before I check out," he says. Josh graces me with a little smile, and I smile back at him, so happy he's here. It's hard to stay mad at him. We're all guilty of making mistakes to protect the ones we love.

"Thank you for saving my dad. So much. I can never repay you." My voice is still dry. It cracks with the strain of speaking.

"You're welcome." His left arm is bandaged from his wrist to his elbow, and it's hanging in a sling. His head is swathed with gauze on the same side as the scar on his neck.

Josh's scars.

From pulling injured women out of rubble and running into burning buildings to save old men. I'm not worthy of him and all his well-earned scars. I've caused so much more pain than I've endured.

"I still don't know how you made it in and out of there . . ." When my mind isn't imagining Yazmin's riddled face, it's remembering flickering images of my home engulfed in flames.

"I was lucky he was in the room leading to the trellis. If it would've been any other room . . ." He shakes his head, and I take a deep breath. It doesn't need to be spoken. "Also, my lungs operate better filled with smoke. It's like my superpower."

I have to laugh, even though it hurts. "Don't think you're off the hook there."

"Right, right. I heard you confessed. Good girl. What about you? Are you off the hook?" he asks nonchalantly, but there's nothing casual about going to prison.

"I don't know. They haven't locked me up yet, but I'd understand if they did. You must think I'm just terrible."

Josh leans in, his sudsy scent filling me with comfort. "I don't think you're terrible. I think you're a good person who made a terrible mistake."

My breath does a fluttery thing that would produce tears if I wasn't so dehydrated and looped on opioids. "Thank you for that; it's more than I deserve."

Josh places his palms on the side of my bed and rests his head down on the top of his hands. He must still be tired from scaling a stone wall. "No, it's not. I feel bad I didn't tell you about Jay and Cash sooner. It's just hard to give up your drug dealer."

I laugh again despite myself. "Cash would've gotten them from somewhere else if not him. Don't feel guilty. You're not the one at fault here. There're so many variables."

"Right." Josh doesn't sound so sure.

"I'm sorry I didn't tell you about Spencer." Since we're apologizing here, I might as well just put the big one out there. There's always been a part of me that wished Josh had asked to meet Spencer, because it sounded like he had a hunch he existed, both in the music store and definitely outside of Stonehenge. But I'm okay with him not asking too.

"I understand why you didn't. You had your nice little life all hemmed up, and I've never been good at staying in one place." It's nice to hear him confirm the story I've been telling myself for years, but part of me wonders if he's only saying it to make me feel better.

"Thank you for being kind." I close my eyes, weaving my hands gently through his light-brown hair streaked with blond. I've always loved the color. Not quite brunet, not quite blond, all mixed up somewhere in between—that's Josh's story.

"I'm sorry about our house," I say.

"Me too," he says sadly.

A nostalgic part of my brain takes over, and I've been wondering—if Josh had never caught wind that I'd married Martin and stolen his house away from him, would he have come home earlier from Europe to reclaim my love? Would we have ended up living together in our house like he promised we would as kids? With our son?

"At least the pergola was saved," he says.

I exhale, so unbelievably relieved by this. "I'm happy to hear that too."

"Yes, it was far enough away from the blaze that it was left untouched."

"Your stage." I smile. "That's good."

"Who knows if the new owners will keep it, though," he says.

"They'd be fools to tear it down." The insurance company deemed the house unrecoverable, and I refused to rebuild with Martin, so he put the property up for sale. He said he didn't want to live there without me.

Josh's breathing quiets and syncs with mine. "I grabbed something from your car for you. Don't worry—I'll give it back once things settle a bit."

"Uh-huh," I say, my eyes still closed. We're held together in a serene silence, lost to a past, a place that doesn't exist anymore. Just as I'm about to drift into my first peaceful sleep in days, my heart thrums in my chest like a chain saw.

I'm not sure what Josh has taken from Martin's car. I drift off, and when I wake up, Josh is gone. I'm left wondering if I've dreamed him until I see it—a single red rose left on top of the windowsill. He'll wait to give me the rest.

CHAPTER 30

Statement of Mr. Cassius (Cash) Veltri [October 24 interviewed by Detective Harvey Monroe]

Detective Monroe: Mr. Veltri, you've been charged with first-degree arson of the residence of 846 Blackburn Road, which you've already confessed to. Do you understand the charges?

Cash: Yes, sir.

Detective Monroe: Why did you commit this crime?

Cash: The house fire was an accident. I broke into the home because the Ellsworths stole my dead sister's journal, and my mother wanted it back.

Detective Monroe: Please describe in as much detail as you can why you believe they stole her journal. How did you know the journal was in the house?

Cash: I didn't, but I was sure they at least knew where it was. I was going to wait for them to get home and threaten them until they returned it. No more lies. No more cops covering for them.

Detective Monroe: Why burn down the house then?

Cash: That was an accident. They had candles everywhere. I must've knocked one over when I broke in. I don't know who leaves a house with that many candles burning. Once the fire started, it wouldn't stop. I ran out. I knew it was over for me then, so I bashed out the windows first, the ones my sister hated.

Detective Monroe: So this was motivated by revenge?

Cash: It wasn't. I never would've went in there if it hadn't been for the journal. I was just trying to get back what was ours.

Detective Monroe: Cash, why do you think the Ellsworths wanted Yazmin's journal?

Cash: Because it had the truth in it. About what happened to my sister. And my father.

Detective Monroe: What happened to your sister?

Cash: Finn Ellsworth killed her.

Detective Monroe: Please explain why you think Finn Ellsworth killed Yazmin.

Cash: [Sighs.] The Ellsworths owed my family some money they were never going to repay. Times were hard. I was staging Finn's kidnapping. Never intended to hurt him. I laced Finn's joint so it would be easier to take him.

Detective Monroe: With meth and Rohypnol.

Cash: I guess. I honestly wasn't sure what I bought. I didn't tell Yaz I laced Finn's joint; I thought she'd back out. I wanted to still be able to take him if she didn't agree with how I changed our plan. I wrapped Yazmin's in pink paper like I always do so they wouldn't get mixed up. She was in on hitting Finn for two hundred and fifty Gs. But not kidnapping him for more. I never believed her that he'd hand over the money, but she said to give her some time. He was going to screw us, though. That's what his family does. And we deserved more. I wasn't letting them get off that easy.

Detective Monroe: Okay, so what happened next?

Cash: They smoked their joints.

Detective Monroe: Then what happened?

Cash: [Crying.] No one was supposed to get hurt.

Detective Monroe: I'm sorry. This part must be hard. I know that you were only trying to protect your sister. I have three of them. I can tell by the way you speak of her that you loved her very much. Cash, I need to understand everything that happened. Especially in tying the right person to the crime.

Cash: Okay . . . Finn was shouting about an Instagram post and so was Yazmin, yelling to take it down. Finn was wobbling already from the drugs, and all I had to do was knock him out, zip-tie him, throw him in the truck.

Detective Monroe: What happened?

Cash: He was angry and drugged. Yaz was probably confused because I hadn't told her I'd slipped him anything different. She didn't see me hiding in the woods.

Detective Monroe: And?

Cash: I popped out of the bushes and scared them. I tried to tackle Finn, but he turned into some kind of martial arts . . . soldier. I hadn't anticipated the rich kid having street smarts. His eyes were closed, and he could barely stand. He didn't know it was me. I wore a ski mask. He immediately reacted by kicking my knee backward until it almost snapped.

Detective Monroe: And then what happened?

Cash: Yazmin was screaming, "No, don't. Stop!" She was trying to grab Finn and tell him to run. On his back, grabbing his neck. She didn't know who I was at first. They'd been hiking on these rocks, and Finn was swaying unevenly on one of them.

Cash: [Crying uncontrollably. Barely able to speak.] When I tried to grab Finn, my sister jumped on my back, realizing who I was. Finn suddenly seemed to find his balance again, standing on one foot, and then he gave me a hard, front kick. Yazmin and me, we flew backward. [Crying.] She cracked her skull and broke her neck. I knew she was dead, instantly.

Detective Monroe: [Pauses.] I'm so sorry, Cash. What happened next?

Cash: Finn crawled into the woods in the other direction with his cell phone. He was calling the cops, so I got out of there. I mean, I checked Yazmin first. [Crying.] Yazmin was . . . gone. I couldn't go home.

Detective Monroe: Where did you go instead?

Cash: I couldn't go back to the pizza shop, but I was done with my shift, so I went to a school friend's house and slept on their couch. I waited for the call from my mom, after the police got to Yazmin, but it didn't come.

Detective Monroe: I see. And then what?

Cash: And then when I got home, I found out that no one had ever called in Yazmin's death. Her body lay there all night. The Ellsworths had taken the life of another one of my family members, and no one would ever pay the price.

Detective Monroe: What do you mean, another life?

Cash: We were trying to get the money they owed us because we could never file a lawsuit because it was a hit-and-run.

Detective Monroe: A lawsuit for what?

Cash: The one that should've been filed after my father died in his car accident.

Detective Monroe: Why would a suit have been filed?

Cash: Because . . . William Ellsworth was the one driving the car that hit my father.

It's good that Martin and I are able to read Cash's police report together. It makes it a lot easier to say "I want a divorce" when we get to the very last line.

Finn didn't kill Yazmin when he defended himself with martial arts skills as innate to him as walking. And Cash didn't kill Yazmin when he set up a kidnapping scam to try to earn enough money so that his family could get retribution for his dead father. William killed Yazmin when he left her in that car all night immersed in freezing-cold water mixed with her daddy's blood. The chain of events that followed that accident was on him, as far as I'm concerned.

I remember William Ellsworth's Bentley gone one day, replaced the next. Most people go to a repair shop when their car is damaged, but William had his scrapped, the whole car, and then got a new one—sans the crest on the wheel center caps.

"Vermin," he claimed. The only rat here is him.

Martin had said it was *"necessary."*

Necessary to destroy the evidence. Martin knew what his father had done. Still, he covered for his father, just like William had covered for him in college—one big, ugly circle. I relayed all the information to Monroe to try to break the chain.

"I'm sorry," Martin whispers, but he'll never be sorry enough.

I snatch the police report away from him. My hands brush against his watch, and I see something.

I grab his wrist and turn it in my direction. "Oh my God."

"What? Are you late for a meeting with the lawyer?" I don't answer Martin. He's still trying to plot and scheme.

But all of a sudden, I know who BR is.

I know what the symbol was in the snow in big letters—BR—Bell & Ross, the family watch brand. When William knelt by the car to make sure the passengers were dead, he left the logo pressed into the snow. But it disappeared. Of course it did.

CHAPTER 31

When the Ellsworths' involvement in covering up Yazmin's death broke, a full investigation was conducted on William's scrapped car, and the junkyard confirmed that his Bentley had been wrecked before he turned it in. There was no rodent infestation as he'd claimed. There'd been pictures taken beforehand, and a close analysis of the pictures showed dents consistent with a collision with another vehicle.

The car was also taken to the scrapper the day after Jimmy Veltri's accident. With the evidence stacked against him, William's lawyer recommended he confess and try for a plea deal—and of course that weasel took it. But the judge still gave him the maximum sentence for vehicular manslaughter, given the circumstances surrounding it and the fact that he'd left the scene of an accident in which two people were injured, one of whom died. William Ellsworth was sentenced to ten years.

William may die in prison.

His reasoning for leaving the scene of the accident—he thought Yazmin was already dead. How convenient. But when he read her essay, William claimed that he was so overcome with guilt after all the pain he'd unknowingly caused her, he'd granted Yazmin the scholarship, never anticipating she'd end up with his grandson.

That made for a nice story. But I know the Ellsworths. And I am sure that when Yazmin died, it gave William even more incentive to cover up the car accident that killed her father by taking extra measures to make sure no one ever found out about what happened with Finn in those woods.

But he failed, and the Ellsworth name is finally showing the true rot beneath the shine they tried so hard to preserve. Mary Alice, from what I've heard, has become a shut-in, ordering her groceries online, not going out for church or to the club, living in shame, as she should—a fate worse than death for someone of her social standing.

Bill Ellsworth Jr. lost the election for city commissioner, so Martin's sure vote for his riverfront property flew right out the window.

An internal investigation was opened at the Sewickley Heights Police Department, and Sheriff Alton Pembroke was suspended indefinitely without pay until the investigation is complete. After I confessed our part to the cops, I asked for leniency for Cash. The Ellsworths were the ones who started this, after all. My request was somewhat granted; Cash was sentenced to a year in juvenile detention and then house arrest after that, but it still didn't make anything right.

Alisha was thankful for my plea and didn't push the issue any further when Martin and I weren't charged with jail time. We were charged with a misdemeanor for leaving the scene of the crime and had to pay a nominal fine. Again, it hardly seems justified, but at least Martin finally has a criminal record . . . and so do I.

I'm living with my father in my old house now, and it does seem so small, but we've never been closer. Much to my pleasant surprise, Finn has decided to live with us until he leaves for Brown. He was accepted into their computer science program. I didn't fight with Martin when he'd asked to get the best lawyer that money could buy to defend him. Yes, Finn had accidentally killed Yazmin, but it was deemed self-defense.

His saving grace was that nothing on his person had touched anything on hers. There'd been a body between them—Cash's.

It was a legal point that I didn't understand, but Finn hadn't hit Yazmin with anything that had caused her death. He'd been defending himself against an unprovoked threat after being drugged, and she'd fallen when she was forced backward. It was a sticky situation, and the community wasn't thrilled with the verdict, and I wasn't entirely sure how I felt about it either.

I'd agreed to the lawyer Martin wanted only if he arranged to pay for counseling for Finn, because he still hadn't come back to us. At least not the boy I knew. I understand traumatic events can change a person, but I still catch Finn staring absently out the window sometimes, and it worries me.

Cash revealed in his statement that Yazmin had hung on Finn's back to stop him at one point once she figured out the attacker was her brother, but Finn was so startled by the masked man and the drugs, it hadn't registered. At least that explains the nail marks.

I've never been happier to be wrong about something in my life. Finn didn't assault Yazmin.

I still worry about the drugs, even though Finn promises he won't do them anymore. The fact that he's chosen to stay with me for the rest of the school year and not his father tells me that he's taking a step in the right direction.

It's also promising that Finn confided in me that he'd hidden Yaz's journal from Martin because he knew he would destroy it. I can never really know for sure—is Finn more Denning or Ellsworth? Only time will tell. Right now, I'm just focused on getting him well, improving his mental health enough so that he might go off to college a semi-normal kid.

Alton was the one to give the journal to Finn, but only after he'd begged and promised to keep it hidden. Alton probably thought no one would press him for it. That he was above the law.

Doesn't surprise me. He's a dirty cop.

Dad is still healing. We had to attach a handicap ramp to get him into the house, but I'm happy I'm here to help.

"You don't think a little house fire could take Vic Denning down," he said the first time I was able to visit his hospital room. When I told him the heinous details of Yazmin's death, he didn't seem surprised. *"I told you long ago—rich people keep the best secrets."*

Boy, was he ever right.

He's been a tough bird to care for since, but he seems to really like the visiting nurse—Elena—so there's something. I've invited her over for dinner next weekend.

I still struggle with what happened to Yazmin and our part in it, but at the same time, peace falls over me now at the end of each day because the Ellsworths' time of terror is over.

I walk outside of my father's house to the little bench that sits by the babbling brook where I used to play as a child, the same body of water that streamed past Stonehenge.

Turns out I've always lived by the sweet water; I just never knew it.

A touch of red grabs my eye, and my breath catches in my throat as I realize what it is.

Yazmin's journal with a rose sitting on top.

I drove by the music store just yesterday to thank Josh again for saving my father, fully conscious and off all my meds this time. I parked out front, but I could already see the FOR SALE sign strung up where the flower boxes used to hang.

He'd sold the store and left without saying goodbye. *Of course he did.*

But he left me this.

He told me in one way or another in the hospital room, but I wasn't sure if I'd dreamed it. I thought maybe Alton had the journal in his possession or it had been lost in the blaze.

But here it is.

I palm the brown leather book in my hand. Josh obviously took it from Martin's Lexus before the police could confiscate it. Maybe it was to protect Finn. Maybe it was to protect himself. It doesn't really matter to me why he did it, only that he did.

My eyes fill up with tears as I open the book—backward—because Yazmin's journal is nondescript and leather, and you can't tell the front from the back.

I rotate the book.

A cool breeze touches the back of my neck.

I hear Dad's walker crunching on the ground. I turn around, and he and Finn are walking toward me. Dad is holding matches. "Are we having another bonfire?" he asks.

"Maybe," I say breathlessly. I hold up the journal.

Finn stops walking. "Where did you . . . ?" His face goes ashen, like the remains from the fire ring.

Like the remains from our house.

I'm tired of that look of shock. It needs to end here.

The fire ring brims with leftover charcoaled debris from the bonfire Dad made last night. It reminds me of Stonehenge.

Returning to my home after the fire was one of the worst days of my life.

"A kingdom fallen," I said aloud, staring at the mess of stone, charred wood, and broken glass. Stonehenge was shattered. It could no longer keep me safe. *It never really did. It was all an illusion.*

But my boys are real.

My love for them is real.

My house can burn to the ground, but nobody can take them away from me.

Dad settles in beside me with a little growl. "What's that?"

"Yazmin's journal. We're giving this back to Yazmin's mother," I inform Finn.

Finn exhales and nods, and there's an unspoken truth exchanged between us.

He knows that I know he had it, but he watches me to see what I'm going to do next.

Finn's breath escapes his throat in a huff, a tailwind of mistakes he was too afraid to tell me about.

"I'm sorry, Mom." He stares at his hiking boots.

"I know. You want to tell me how this story ends?" I open the book and run my finger over the jagged edge of the missing page.

He shakes his head and slips his wallet out of his back pocket. He pulls out a piece of computer paper. "Dad wanted me to destroy the whole thing, but I convinced him it was just the last page that tied me to anything. So he made me rip out the page and burn it. He said he'd keep the journal in his safe."

"But you made a copy of the page first?"

He nods, tears in his eyes.

"And took the journal out of the safe without asking your father?" I ask, putting it together. Martin probably hadn't noticed it was gone until Alton tipped him off.

"He grilled me for it after you took it, but I told him it was gone, and he was so mad at me."

I frown, and I'm so happy my marriage is over. "Can I see it?"

He hands me the paper, and Dad doesn't say anything, only watches.

I run my finger along the edge. Yazmin's final words.

My stomach sinks, and I collapse on the bench.

10-20

The day after tomorrow is the big day, but tonight I have a horrible feeling.

My head is spinning, my stomach a mess.

Finn is going to go along with Cash's demands. Cash wants a million.

I was shocked when Finn agreed to help, but he said he can only get us $250,000 for now. In exchange, he doesn't want us to turn in his family, but that's all he has in his trust. He'll get us the rest later. He hates his grandfather for what he did to us, but he's afraid they'll take his parents too. And even though he doesn't like Cash, he wants to make it better. He's going to take the money his grandfather put in his trust for him and give it to us.

He LOVES me. He told me so tonight. I'M SO HAPPY.

We'll ditch school, go to the bank tomorrow, make the withdrawal.

Finn will do ANYTHING to help me, whether Cash likes it or not. Cash has to let me have my treasure once I give him his.

Everything will be fine now.

My heart churns in my ears. "No," I whisper.

The realization of what this means is unfathomable.

"You knew," I whisper. My vision goes sideways, and I squint through the sun, clutching the journal. Finn knew they were extorting us for money. He just wanted to help. He hated William for what he'd done to them. I couldn't blame him. His lies were to protect her. And us.

He was in on the whole thing. Well, part of it anyway. He could've prevented her death if he'd just told me. I would've given them the money. Is this criminal? Attempted extortion that resulted in death? It could be. The press would turn it into something malicious, something that could overturn the court ruling, new evidence.

My house can burn to the ground, but nobody can take them away from me.

But this will. This could. This could take Finn away.

Finn knew that William killed Yazmin's father, and he chose to say nothing. He withheld information about a murder. And then he offered Yazmin $250,000 so that the Veltris wouldn't say anything about it. The word—*exchange*—is right there in Yazmin's journal entry. Finn was paying Yazmin and Cash for retribution for their father, but he was also paying them for their silence. The journal entry is evidence of a bribe to cover a murder. I want to be angry at Finn's poor judgment, but he was trying to do the right thing here. He just didn't want to lose his whole family while doing it. Finn didn't want to implicate his father, who he could only assume was aware of the accident, in the mess. Finn probably blamed himself because he's the one who took Yazmin to William's house, which must've been the day she was triggered by the family crest and figured out who the driver of the car was who hit her father.

An old threat takes over, and a sweat breaks on my forehead. I close my eyes and wish the page away.

It explains so many things.

Why the kids didn't have their book bags that night in the woods even though they'd come straight from class. They were planning a little trip. They didn't need schoolbooks where they were going—to ditch school the next day and withdraw money from Finn's trust. The missing backpacks were something I'd thought about in the Sewickley Hotel when I met with Alisha, but it didn't seem like a major detail then.

My belly churns. What does this mean? What do we do now?

"And you never withdrew the money?" I ask.

He won't look at me, tears collecting in his eyes. "No. We were going the next day, but what I had in my trust wasn't enough for Cash. He wanted a million, so he surprised us in the woods and tried to kidnap me."

"So he was going to use you for ransom?"

"Yes." Finn sniffles. Finn is not the villain here. He was put in a terrible spot. He was trying to pay his grandfather's debts and protect his parents. "I should have let them take me. They wouldn't have hurt me, but Cash was masked. I didn't know who he was until it was too late."

I try to see in my head how this played out. Finn high on something he'd never taken before, ambushed by a random man in the woods. Yazmin screaming. Her hanging on Finn's back to stop him once she realized it was her brother, then switching to her brother's back once she realized Finn was no use. Cash was smaller than Finn, and when he kicked Cash, he fell backward, falling on Yazmin—accidentally killing her.

"I'm sorry," he says again.

"I'm so sorry that happened. I know you were trying to help, but now you know to come to me if anyone asks you for that kind of money, right?"

Finn nods and wipes his face. "I knew Grandpa got away with the accident, and I was just trying to help them."

I understand why he did it. He *is* more Denning than Ellsworth.

He knows he messed up.

He won't do it again.

How can I preach to Finn about living an honest life if I let this go, though? But what good will it do to reveal it now?

We can't bring Yazmin back by this truth. It can only hurt Finn. No money was exchanged between the parties, but there was a promise of an exchange.

It reminds me of something Martin said to me on the car ride home from his parents' house the night Yazmin died. *"We do what we have to do to protect our family."*

I hate that his words resonate with me now. I thought Martin was a monster for saying them, but now his words echo in my head and squeeze my heart.

"I'm sorry. I love you," he says, and it breaks me.

"I know. I love you too," I say, and I do feel the right parties have paid. William and Cash are in jail, Alton is fired, Finn is on probation, Martin and I have criminal records. None of these things can bring back Yazmin, but this isn't about bringing her back. It's about remembering her as she should be remembered, her truth, and not the one we created for her. It's also about learning from our mistakes so we don't repeat them. And so future generations don't repeat them either.

"I don't need to know." Dad looks at me with a half-cocked smile and throws some kindling onto the firepit. "Shall we?"

I nod and toss the last copied journal page on top of it. The one that incriminates Finn. The one that will help no one if the information is revealed. Dad hands me the matches.

I strike one and let it go. The dry page catches fast, one last memory I'll color in black.

And all the sweet water in the world can't put it out.

ACKNOWLEDGMENTS

When I wrote this book, I wanted to create a setting that felt like a character and characters who felt like real people, with music that was symbolic of a time period that meant something to me. Thank you, book genies, for granting all my wishes, and thanks to the bands that I mentioned in this book for existing; I cherish you all.

To Ella Marie Shupe, my agent and my extra pair of eyes, thanks for keeping me in check (we did it!). To my editor, Liz Pearsons, who loved this story and gave me a shot, I'm forever grateful.

To my developmental editor, Tiffany Yates Martin, who took this book to the next level with her editorial magic, I can't thank you enough. And to Sarah Shaw in marketing and the whole crew at Amazon Publishing, working with you on this project has been a wonderful experience.

In my own neighborhood, I'd like to thank Megan Bombick for helping to oversee the legal things on this project and Natalie Schirato, who read a messy first draft of this book. It's a pleasure living next to you ladies. Thanks for helping with my book—and my children.

Other first readers include: Lisa Coulson, Virginia DiAlesandro, Vickie Reinard, Janice Sniezek, and the North Pittsburgh Critique Group: Dana Faletti, Nancy Hammer, Carolyn Menke, and Kim Pierson, your support means everything, and my words are better because you read them first.

A very special thanks to Robyn Carson Jones, longtime Sewickley resident and real estate agent. You live in a special place; thank you for sharing it with me and answering all my research questions, much appreciated.

And last, but certainly not least, thanks to my family and friends who've encouraged me along the way, and special props to my husband, Justin, for always supporting my writing endeavors and thoughtfully considering all my crazy plot questions. You're better at fiction than you think, babe. And to my children, Jackson and Charlotte, who inspire me to be creative every single day—everything I do is for you.

ABOUT THE AUTHOR

Photo © Lisa Park, Moments Kept Photography

Cara Reinard grew up north of Sewickley, Pennsylvania, in a steel mill town, raised by a single mother. Sewickley, with its grand houses in the Heights and boutique shops on Main, was a magical place, out of reach. Cara then attended a private college, Gannon University, becoming the features editor for the college paper and receiving a scholarship. The residence in *Sweet Water* was inspired by the party home of steel mogul B. F. Jones—the property still exists, including the pool and pergola. Cara is an author of women's fiction and domestic suspense. She currently lives outside Pittsburgh with her husband, two children, and Bernese mountain dog. For more information, visit www.carareinard.com.